PRAISE FOR PETER ROBINSON'S
INTERNATIONALLY BESTSELLING
INSPECTOR BANKS BOOKS

"Taut, clean writing and subtle psychology."   —Ian Rankin

"Top-notch police procedure."   —Jeffery Deaver

"Among the best detective fiction in the world."
—*Edmonton Journal*

"Robinson is not just a master storyteller, he's a literary magician."   —Montreal *Gazette*

"One of the grand masters of the genre."   —*Literary Review*

"Robinson brings to bear his considerable knowledge of police procedure."   —*Booklist*

"Robinson also has a way of undercutting the genre's familiarity. With a deceptively unspectacular language, he sets about the process of unsettling the reader."   —*Independent*

"A mighty force to be reckoned with in crime fiction."
—*Publishers Weekly*

"A slow-burning intensity that deepens from beginning to end."
—*Kirkus Reviews*

PETER ROBINSON

NOT DARK YET

McCLELLAND & STEWART

Library and Archives Canada Cataloguing in Publication

Title: Not dark yet / Peter Robinson.
Names: Robinson, Peter, 1950- author.
Description: Previously published: Toronto: McClelland & Stewart, 2021.
Identifiers: Canadiana 20200391720 | ISBN 9780771029493 (softcover)
Classification: LCC PS8585.O35176 N68 2022 | DDC C813/.54—dc23

Cover design: Kelly Hill
Cover images: (texture) Wylius; (sunset) Southern Lightscapes-Australia,
both from Getty Images

Printed in the United States of America

McClelland & Stewart,
a division of Penguin Random House Canada Limited,
a Penguin Random House Company

www.penguinrandomhouse.ca

2 3 4 5   26 25 24 23 22

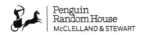

Penguin
Random House
McCLELLAND & STEWART

To Sheila

I

Zelda hadn't visited Chișinău since she had been abducted outside the orphanage at the age of seventeen. And now she was back. She wasn't sure how she was going to find the man she wanted – she had no contacts in the city – but she did have one or two vague ideas about where to begin.

As she walked down Stefan cel Mare Boulevard, she noticed that while many of the shops and their colourful facades were new, the wide pavements and road surface were still cracked and pitted with potholes, and the old ladies in peasant skirts and headscarves still sat under the trees gossiping and selling their belongings to make ends meet. Spread out at their feet lay everything from articles of clothing to children's toys and pink plastic hairbrushes.

The heat was oppressive, dry and dusty. Zelda felt it burn in her chest as she walked. And the smell of the sewer was never far away. She looked behind, not because she seriously believed someone might be following her, but because such caution had become a habit. All in all, she knew that she was much safer here in Chișinău than she was back in Yorkshire, or London. She had been worried that Petar Tadić would work out that she had been responsible for the death of his brother Goran, and that he would come to find her. But how could he, she asked herself in more rational moments? Even if he discovered that a woman had killed Goran, there was no reason why he should assume that was Zelda. Goran had abused a lot of women. Why would his brother think for even a moment of that young, frightened Moldovan girl they had raped and abused on a long drive across Romania over thirteen years ago?

The underpass Zelda took to get across the broad road was dark and scrawled with graffiti, mostly swastikas and erect penises. The concrete steps going down were cracked and missing huge chunks, making them awkward to negotiate. The passage was dark and smelled of urine. Zelda picked up her pace, and when she emerged, it was into an altogether different part of Chișinău, an urban wasteland of neglected grey Soviet tower blocks and swathes of sparse grass and spindly trees. A couple of children were kicking a football around, and a scrawny dog lifted its leg against a dead tree.

There were signs of construction – huge piles of dirt, concrete blocks, wooden rafters, metal bars – but the sites were deserted and the mechanical diggers idle. In the midst of all this stood a brand new shopping centre opposite the crumbling blank-eyed stare of the National Hotel. A luxury Intourist hotel in the Soviet era, and once the hottest party spot in town, the National had been built in the late seventies and had stood empty for as long as Zelda could remember. Its decayed grandeur was a cynical reminder of the faded glory of the old days. In front of the hotel stretched a sunken area of dried up and litter-strewn fountains, now overgrown with weeds and home to empty beer cans, broken bottles, used condoms, McDonald's wrappers, needles and whatever other rubbish people tossed into it.

Past the Beer House and a row of travel agents and car rental outlets, Zelda wandered into the backstreets off Constantin Negruzzi Boulevard, and before she knew it, she was standing on the very corner from which she had been snatched.

It was a narrow street by Chişinău standards, tree-lined, with a mix of older, more elegant Russian-style buildings and modern uniform Soviet blocks, what Zelda called Stalinist architecture. Everything was grey and pockmarked, chipped and pitted. Very few cars passed by as she stood fixed to the spot. The old bar on the corner was gone, turned into a brand new *farmacie*, complete with green neon cross, but the rest of the street was much the same.

There, all those years ago, with the dazzling promise of a great future, Zelda's life as she knew it had come to an end. She remembered seeing the small scuffed suitcase break open on the cracked road surface, spilling what few possessions and memories of her dead parents she had – her mother's music box, her father's scuffed leather wallet, the book Zelda was reading – *Bleak House* – her clothes and the scrapbook and diaries she had diligently kept over her years in the orphanage, and her father's chipped shaving mug, which broke into fragments when it hit the concrete.

And the photographs. It had hurt most of all to lose the photographs. While there were plenty taken with friends during her years at the orphanage, there were only three that showed her parents. It was too long ago to remember the details, but she did remember the day the suitcase arrived at the orphanage, only a few months after her parents' deaths in 1992. The contents of the case were the only remnants left of her life from those days.

One photograph showed her father, young and handsome with a shy smile, and another her mother wearing a bikini on holiday in Odessa, with the Black Sea in the background, pretending to strike a sexy pose and putting her hand over her mouth to stifle the laughter. The third showed a stiff and formal family group in a studio portrait taken when Zelda was about three. She sat on her mother's knee, wearing what must have been her very best dress, hair tumbling in ringlets over her shoulders, and her father stood, straight and serious, in his suit, one hand on her mother's shoulder and the other on Zelda's. None of them smiled. All stared directly at the camera.

Zelda had expected that she would feel angry or sad when she returned to the spot where she had lost everything, but all she felt was numbness. Whenever she had looked back on the life that had been stolen, she had simmered with hatred, but now, at the very spot where it had all begun, she felt nothing at all. She thought of all the cars that had driven by since then, all the people who had walked there oblivious, none of them knowing what momentous event had occurred there. Somehow, her own experience was lost in the ceaseless flow of quotidian life, as if she were Icarus falling into the sea, while all around him everyone went on ploughing their fields and tending their sheep.

Now it was just a place, a street corner like any other. Sometimes she wondered who had picked up the music box, her book, the diaries, the wallet, and what they had made of it all. Had anyone actually *seen* her get taken?

It wasn't until she approached the orphanage building itself that the full horror of the past hit her right between the eyes, and she began to tremble at the power of the memory. The building was still there, an early twentieth-century Russian construction in the classical style, of dark stone with rococo touches. With its broad steps, small arched portico and chipped columns, it formed a contrast to the monstrous towers surrounding it. The windows on the lower floor had been boarded up, but the upper ones remained uncovered, jagged frames of broken glass.

Zelda couldn't stop trembling, and the breath seemed to solidify in her chest. This had been her home between the ages of four and seventeen. This was the place that had made her what she was, or what she *could* have been. Now, though, it was a ruin, and so was she, and the irony didn't escape her. What the hell was she doing here, running away from the good life she had found, despite all the odds, and from a good man, who was more than she deserved, seeking God only knew what? Revenge? Atonement? Reconciliation?

There were very few people about, and those who were went about their business, heads down, not paying any attention to Zelda or to anyone else. Trying to push the knot of troubling thoughts aside and to control her shakes and breathing, she walked up the steps and, with a quick glance around her, shoved at the door. It didn't budge. She turned the heavy metal handle and pushed harder with her shoulder, and this time it made a screeching sound, like fingernails on a blackboard, as it dragged across the tiled floor. Again, Zelda glanced around to make sure no one had seen her, then she gave another shove and found herself standing in the hall.

She pushed the door shut behind her.

When the day of Tracy's wedding dawned, Detective Superintendent Alan Banks awoke early to the sounds of birdsong and the glare of bright sunshine through a chink in his curtains. Another perfect midsummer day in an unbroken run of nearly two weeks. He ate a leisurely breakfast of toast and marmalade in the conservatory, listening to the Brahms clarinet quintet on Radio 3 as he glanced over the *Guardian* review section, then took his second cup of coffee out to the garden to contemplate the day ahead.

He had offered to pick up his parents from their sheltered housing on the Northumberland coast but, fiercely independent as ever, his father had insisted that they would make their own way down. Banks knew better than to argue.

When the time came to get ready, he dusted off his dark grey suit – thank God it wasn't a morning-suit affair – and dressed. It was to be an old-fashioned C of E wedding at St Mary's church, at the far end of Market Street, not far from where the Banks family had lived when they first arrived in Eastvale. Old-fashioned apart from the 'obey' bit, Tracy had assured him, though he was to 'give away' the bride. He was nervous, as any father would be, but proud, too. His son Brian would be there, as would his ex-wife Sandra – Tracy's mother – with her husband Sean.

Finally, he was ready, and he went out to the car.

He drove the familiar road with a light heart listening to Mendelssohn's *Octet*, which lifted his spirits even higher. He arrived in good time for a quick glass of red at the Blue Monk before the bridal party was scheduled to meet at the church, just around the corner.

Outside the church, Banks met up with his parents and his son Brian. His mother fixed him a buttonhole, then Tracy's car arrived, and they decided they shouldn't keep poor Mark waiting too much longer. Everyone went inside except for Banks, Tracy and the two bridesmaids.

Needless to say, Tracy looked gorgeous, and Banks felt a lump in his throat as he walked down the aisle beside her and she smiled at him. Tracy had been the sort of child you always wanted to be happy, to keep her innocence. Of course, that was impossible, and though she had been a carefree child, she had lost her way for a while after university and veered towards the dark side, but she had made it back. Now, when Banks looked at her, he saw a grown-up woman, but he felt the same way as he had when she was a child. He could no more protect her from the world now than he had done before – he knew he had been far from a perfect father – but that was what he wished for her in his heart.

As he walked down the aisle beside Tracy, Banks felt as if he were floating through the moment, with faces drifting in and out of vision as guests turned in their pews to catch a glimpse of the bride. Everything seemed somehow unreal, in slow motion; even the swishing of Tracy's wedding dress sounded like soft waves against the shore. He saw Sandra from the corner of his eye, sitting with Sean on the front row. She flashed him a quick smile. Then he saw his parents, his mother already with her hanky out. Tracy gave his hand a squeeze when they got to the front and everyone took their places. Tracy turned to Mark and smiled. He looked scared as hell, Banks thought.

Everything went smoothly, everyone got their lines right and it seemed that in no time they were all walking back down the aisle.

After the photographs and confetti, the crowd dispersed. The reception was to be held over an hour later in the banquet room of the Burgundy Hotel, where most of the out-of-town guests were staying for the night.

Banks found himself walking close to Brian, Sandra and Sean down Market Street, past the end of the street where they used to live, and he was lost for words. To him, Sandra appeared hardly any different than when she had left him. She had kept her figure, and though her hair colour might have been bolstered with a few drops of one of Boots's concoctions, there was nothing false about its lustre. Her face seemed still relatively unlined, her dark eyebrows nicely plucked. She wore a powder blue skirt and jacket over a plain, silk white blouse. A St Christopher on a silver chain around her neck was the only jewellery she wore.

Sandra and Sean edged away to talk to Mark's mother and father, and Banks and Brian slipped away to the Queen's Arms for a quick drink before the reception.

*   *   *

The silence inside the ruined orphanage rang in Zelda's ears, interrupted only by the distant motor of a car, shout of a child, or bark of a dog. The place smelled musty with rotten wood, mould, dead leaves and stagnant water. For a while, Zelda just stood there as her eyes adjusted. Dust motes floated in the pale light that came in through the broken windows on the upper level.

Ahead of her, a broad staircase led to the first and second floors, mostly dormitories and classrooms. Down here, on the ground floor, had been the administrative offices, staffrooms, cafeteria and communal areas where the children could sit and chat, watch TV, play chess or table tennis. There was also an assembly hall, where they gathered every morning for hymns and prayers.

When Zelda could see clearly, she noticed that the plaster was crumbling from the walls, and in places was completely gone. The thick pile carpets that had once graced the stairs had rotted away to stained tatters, and their patterns had faded. There had been paintings on the walls – nothing special, just landscapes and portraits easy on the eyes – but they were all either gone now or lying torn and broken on the floor. Even in here there was graffiti, the usual sort of crudities, and the floors were strewn with rubbish. Somewhere in the distance she could hear water dripping. Then she heard something skittering down one of the corridors. It wasn't loud enough to be another person. Probably just a rat.

When Zelda moved, she realised she had been holding her breath so long she was beginning to feel dizzy. She grabbed a banister and took a few deep breaths. The wood felt as smooth under her palm as it had years ago, when she and her friends had slid down, strictly against the rules. Olga. Vika. Axenia. Where were they all now? She knew that the beautiful Iuliana had been sold, the same way she had, for they had met a couple of years later in a brothel in Užice, in Serbia. Iuliana, her body and spirit broken, had told Zelda about seeing Lupescu, the orphanage director, watching as she was taken in the street, and drawing back inside as soon as he realised she had spotted him. Nothing was ever said or done about it, and that was one reason Zelda thought he was to blame. Iuliana had killed herself soon after their talk. She was why Zelda was here today.

Zelda carried on up the stairs, wondering what she would find there. But it was just another scene of vandalism. More sunlight poured in through the broken windows and illuminated the clouds of dust Zelda kicked up as she walked. By instinct, she went first to her old dormitory, beds for twelve girls arranged into opposite rows of six, each with a cupboard and bedside table. She thought of the conversations they had had there after lights out, secrets shared, hopes and dreams, grief at the loss of their parents, plans for the future, crushes and loathings, mostly for the boys, who teased them mercilessly. But Zelda had experienced her first feelings for a boy there, she remembered. Radu Prodan. She had buried the memory for years, but now she remembered he had been beautiful, shy, quiet, intelligent, with an untamed shock of blond hair and a habit of trying to smooth it down. Perhaps she had loved him, as well as any girl could love a boy at the age of nine. She had no idea what had become of Radu. Had boys been sold, too?

The old beds had all been stripped down to their metal frames, the tables upturned and the cupboards smashed. There was more graffiti. Zelda wondered whether the vandals who had done all this had any idea what the place had been, what lives had been nurtured here – nurtured and then stolen, in some cases. It didn't matter.

She wandered the rooms and corridors in a daze until she came to an old storage room, which was still full of boxes and packing crates. It was in one of these that she discovered a damp, misshapen cardboard box full of old books, mostly water-damaged, mouldy and warped, with curled pages and stained covers. But they were the books she remembered, the English books: *Jane Eyre, David Copperfield, Five Go to Mystery Moor, 4.50 From Paddington, The Sign of Four, The Lion, the Witch and the Wardrobe.* As she handled them, she felt tears burn in her eyes, and soon the sobbing wracked her body. She let herself slump on the filthy floor to cry. These were the kind of books that had filled her teenage hours with joy, romance and adventure.

When the whirlwind of emotion passed, leaving Zelda feeling numb and tired again, she put back the soggy book she had been holding – *The Wind in the Willows* – and made to close the box. As she did so, she caught sight of a label affixed to the corner of one of the flaps. It was faded and almost completely peeled off, but when she got closer, she was able to make out a name and address: Vasile Lupescu, the name of the orphanage director, and the address of the place she was in. But there was a second name, unknown to her. It was an English name, William Buckley, and the address was in Suruceni, a village on the shores of Lake Danceni, about twenty kilometres west of Chişinău.

Was this, then, the address of her mysterious benefactor? She had always wondered who it was, where the books had come from. Was he still alive? Still in Suruceni? She hadn't made any kind of plan beyond visiting the orphanage, hoping she might find some clue to Vasile Lupescu's whereabouts. Everything had depended on what she discovered here. And now she had something concrete to go on. The first person she would go to for information was William Buckley.

All the outside tables were occupied, but Banks didn't mind being relegated to the inside of the pub. They found a quiet corner and Banks fetched a pint of Theakston's bitter for each of them. Brian was moderately famous, as a member of the Blue Lamps, and one or two of the drinkers stared as if they thought they recognised him but weren't quite sure.

Cyril had recently installed some air-conditioning on the cheap, and it managed to send a blast of chill air across the room every two or three minutes. And then there was the background music, one of Cyril's never-ending sixties playlists, always full of surprises. There was something about that era of early sixties pop, before it became 'rock' and started taking itself seriously, that smacked of innocence and the sheer joy of being young and alive. It was epitomised especially by the song playing at the moment: The Crystals singing 'Then He Kissed Me'. It sounded just like that first kiss tasted.

'You all right, Dad?' Brian asked.

'Why? Don't I look it?'

'You seem a bit . . . I don't know. Distracted.'

'I suppose it was all the excitement of the wedding,' he said. 'The emotion. My little girl getting married. And seeing your mother again. It's been quite a while. I suppose I'm feeling just a little bit sad. And old.'

'Yeah, it was weird walking past where we used to live. Are you sure you're OK, though?'

Banks swigged some beer. 'Me? Course I am. Tough as old nails. It just feels like a momentous occasion. That's all.'

'It is for Tracy. What do you think of Mark?'

'He's all right, I suppose. Could be a bit more . . . you know . . . exciting. Adventurous.'

'He's an accountant, for crying out loud. What do you expect?'

Banks laughed. 'I know. I know. And he does like Richard Thompson. That's definitely a point in his favour. She could have done a lot worse.'

'She almost did, as I remember.'

'Yes.' Banks remembered the time when Tracy had taken up with the archetypal 'bad boy' and almost got herself killed as a result.

'So maybe a little dull isn't too bad?' Brian went on. 'What about you, though? Still living the exciting copper's life?'

'It's rarely exciting. But what else would I do?'

'Same as everyone else your age, Dad. Putter about in the garden. Get an allotment. Ogle young women. Drink too much. Watch TV.'

Banks laughed. 'I already do all those things. Except the allotment. Maybe I should write my memoirs?'

'You always said you hated writing reports.'

'Well . . . yes . . . but that's different. Enough about me. What about you? The farewell tour? How's it going?'

'Great so far. Mum and Sean came to the London show. Are you coming to see us?'

'Of course. Wouldn't miss it for the world. The Sage. I've already got the tickets. Ray and Zelda are coming, too.'

'No date for you?'

'Not these days, it seems. I think my allure must have deserted me.' The music had changed again. Neil Sedaka was singing 'Breaking Up is Hard to Do'. He managed to make even such a sad song sound almost joyful. At that moment, Banks's mobile played its blues riff. The number was withheld, but that happened often enough not to be a problem. He excused himself for a moment and went outside.

'Yes?'

'Banksy?'

It could only be Dirty Dick Burgess; no one else ever called him that. 'Yes?'

'Where are you? You sound funny.'

'I'm standing in the market square outside the Queen's Arms on my way to my daughter's wedding reception. So make it fast.'

'Sorry,' said Burgess. 'Give her my . . . you know . . .'

'Right.'

'Keeping busy?'

'Oh, you know. The usual.'

'Getting anywhere with the Blaydon murders yet?'

'It's still early days,' said Banks. 'As I said, I'm on my way to a rather important wedding reception. I'm guessing you've called for some other reason than to yank my chain?'

'Oh, you're no fun. But as a matter of fact, I have. You're not the only one working on a dead-end murder investigation.'

'Where do I come in?'

'I don't want to say too much over the phone, but I think we should meet and compare notes. Are you seriously busy?'

'No. Well, yes, but . . . we're trying to make a case against Leka Gashi and the Albanians for Blaydon's murder. Trouble is, we don't even know where they are.'

'Leka Gashi and the Albanians,' repeated Burgess. 'Sounds like a rock band. Anyway, the Albanians can wait. They'll be back. Don't worry. You'll nail them. Do you think your boss will let you come out to play?'

'You want me to come down to London?'

'I honestly can't get away at the moment. Not for longer than an hour or two, and that won't even cover the train ride. Meetings up to the eyeballs. Otherwise, as you know, nothing would please me more than a trip up north.'

Banks couldn't always figure out when, or if, Burgess was being ironic.

'I promise you it'll be worthwhile,' Burgess went on. 'And if you can get here by lunch tomorrow, I'll even buy. How's that?'

'An offer I can't refuse.'

'Excellent. Whenever you can make it. Pret on—'

'Hang on a minute. I'm not going all that way to be fobbed off with Pret A Manger.'

'Zizzi's, then?'

'You must be joking. Next thing you'll be telling me it's the NCA canteen.'

'Do we have one? Well, it's not going to be Gordon bloody Ramsay's or Michel Roux's, either, I can assure you.'

'I'm sure you'll find somewhere suitable. Text me in the morning.'

2

Zelda called at one of the car rental agencies she had passed earlier and managed to rent an old grey Skoda with a starfish crack on the windscreen and so many dents and scratches the young man at the counter didn't even make her sign off on them.

It was an easy drive to Suruceni, and after the outskirts of Chişinău – more ruined buildings and half-built tower blocks – she drove through pleasant, rolling countryside on E581, encountering very little traffic.

It was early evening when she pulled up in front of William Buckley's house in the southwest of the village, not too far from the lake. It was a small, detached bungalow of beige stucco with a matching pantile roof and white mouldings around the arched windows. The house was slightly raised, and there were four steps up to the side porch and door. The small garden was untended, with not much but stones, dirt and a few blades of parched grass. Even the weeds were struggling against the heat. Two fat crows sat on the pantiles. They didn't move as Zelda walked up the steps and knocked on the door.

At first, she thought there was no one home. The silence was resounding. But she knocked again and heard a slow shuffling sound from behind the door. Eventually, it opened, and a white-haired old man with what could only be called a 'lived-in' face peered out at her in some surprise. A book-jacket photo she had seen of W.H. Auden came to mind. His face was a road map of a life hard lived, but his eyes were a startling childlike blue, and by far his liveliest feature. They could have been the eyes of someone her own age, Zelda found herself thinking.

'Yes?' he said, speaking Moldovan. 'Can I help you?'

Zelda spoke English. 'Perhaps. Are you William Buckley?'

'Ah, a compatriot,' Buckley said. 'Yes. I am he. And call me Bill. Please, charming lady, do come in. Don't be afraid. I'm a harmless, toothless old man.'

Zelda smiled and followed him inside, taking in the framed Japanese-style paintings and drawings on the wall and the sunlight through the arched windows. Buckley shuffled ahead of her, a hunched figure, walking stick in his right hand. The bungalow was small inside, just a living room, one bedroom and kitchen/dining area, Zelda guessed, but it was cosy. Bookcases lined two of the living-room walls, and each was so stuffed with books they lay on their sides on top of other books. All in English.

'To what do I owe the pleasure?' Buckley asked, indicating that she should sit in a damask armchair at right angles to the matching sofa which, judging by the little table holding a tea mug and a copy of *Phineas Finn*, was his spot. 'May I fetch you a cup of tea?'

'I don't want to trouble you.'

'It's no trouble. As a matter of fact, I just made some. It should still be hot. Milk and sugar?'

'Just a little milk, please, then.'

Buckley shuffled off and Zelda glanced around at the books. They covered all subjects – fiction, history, poetry, music, art, literary criticism, theatre, architecture – and were of all shapes and sizes, from dog-eared paperbacks that looked as if they had been bought in used bookshops, to recent hardcovers in shiny dust jackets and oversized coffee table volumes.

She was still reading titles, her head slightly tilted, when Buckley came back with the tea. 'A keen reader, are you?' he asked.

'Yes,' said Zelda.

Buckley nodded slowly and handed her the tea, his wrinkled hand shaking slightly.

Zelda smiled. The room was stifling, and there was a slightly unpleasant smell of neglected hygiene and spoiled food, but she could put up with it. If Buckley lived here alone, it would be hard for him to deal with the myriad daily matters of simply keeping things ticking over.

As if reading her thoughts, he said, 'I do have a local lady who comes in once a week and cleans for me, but I'm afraid she's not due next until tomorrow. I do apologise for the air of neglect.'

'It's nothing,' said Zelda.

Buckley half reclined on the sofa and grimaced, as if the movement caused him pain. 'You wanted to see me for some specific reason? Do I know you?'

Now that she was here facing him, Zelda wasn't sure how to get things started. 'Yes,' she said. 'I mean, no, you don't know me, but I do want to see you. It's about the orphanage.'

'St George's?'

'That's the one.'

Buckley narrowed his eyes. 'Don't tell me you were there.'

'I was.'

'You poor thing.'

'Oh, no!' Zelda cried. 'Don't think that. I had a wonderful life there. Everyone was so kind. The books and . . .' She found herself on the verge of tears. Was this man truly her benefactor? Or could he have been her destroyer?

'I meant to lose your parents at such an early age. But I'm glad St George's was good to you. That was certainly the idea behind it. Yes, I do believe it was a place where much good was done in a time when such things were the exception rather than the rule. But how did you find out about me? I did my best to remain an anonymous donor.'

'I've been back there,' Zelda said. 'Just now. It's in ruins, but there was a box of books in a storeroom, and your name and address were on them.'

'Yes. I'm afraid St George's closed its doors in 2009. A real tragedy. In Moldova, as I'm sure you know, everything no longer used is simply left to decay at its own rate.' A mischievous smile crossed his features, giving Zelda a glimpse of what he might have been like as a young man. And while he wasn't exactly toothless, he wasn't far off. 'Even many things which are still in use are falling apart. We are great believers in entropy. We have a very cavalier attitude towards progress and development.'

'You say "we",' Zelda said, 'but you're English, aren't you?'

'If you want to be accurate, I'm Welsh, but as I've been here nearly thirty years now, the matter of my origins is quite academic. I have certainly retained my interest in British culture, if that's of any interest to you.'

'Thirty years? B-but, how? I mean . . . what . . .?'

'What have I been doing all that time? Why am I here?'

'Yes. All that.'

'It's a very dull story. I was what's called a cultural attaché to the Romanian embassy in Bucharest. A diplomat and cheerleader for the British Council. I moved here to Moldova during the civil war, after the Soviets left in the early nineties. I suppose the long and the short of it is, I fell in love.'

'With?'

'With the country, and with a woman. *Cherchez la femme*. It was a second chance for me, you see. My first wife had died some years earlier, and I had never expected to fall in love again. I was fifty four years old. She became my wife. Sadly, she, too, died five years ago.'

'I'm sorry.'

He waved his hand. 'Not for you to be sorry, my dear. Though I know what you mean, and I thank you for the sentiment. I'm surprised you don't ask me why I fell in love with the most undesirable country in Europe.'

Zelda laughed. 'Love is blind?'

Buckley smiled his approval. 'Yes. That would be the easiest response, and perhaps the most accurate. But there's a simplicity to the place, to life here, once you know the ins and outs. I'm happy to end my days here in Suruceni. There's still corruption everywhere, I know, but the people have a spirit and a strong sense of stoicism. We always managed to get by. We lived in Chișinău then, my wife and I, and our house was always full of artists, writers, musicians. I taught English whenever I was allowed to do so. I also supplemented my income by writing books and reviews.'

'Would I know your work?'

Buckley laughed. 'I hope not. No. I wrote under many pseudonyms. Potboilers in every genre you could imagine. Novelisations of movies or TV series, romance, crime, horror, science-fiction. You name it. I seem to have a talent for ventriloquism but no real voice of my own. But you're not here to talk about me.'

'I am in a way,' said Zelda. 'Besides, it's an interesting story.'

'Probably not half as interesting as yours.'

Zelda looked away. 'You wouldn't . . .' she said. 'You don't want to . . .'

'I've upset you, my dear. I apologise. It was a flippant remark. I can see there has been much grief in your life.'

Zelda shook her head. 'It's not . . . Oh, never mind. It's about the orphanage.'

'What about it?'

'The books, for a start. Did you send them?'

'I did. For many years. I suppose I was trying to spread my culture to a heathen land. No, that's not strictly true. Forgive me, I was arrogant. Moldova has her own poets. I wanted people – I wanted the charges at St George's in particular – to experience the same pleasures I myself experienced when I read those books as a child.'

'Were you an orphan, may I ask?'

'You may. And, yes, I was. Am. My parents were both killed during the Blitz, in London. I have no brothers or sisters or any other living relatives as far as I know. It gave me more freedom than I knew what to do with. I don't mean to belittle the grief and terrible sense of loss and aloneness, but did you have that experience yourself, a kind of odd relief that there was no one else to satisfy, to please, no one to make demands on you, to tell you what to do or in which direction to push?'

'I'm afraid I never got to experience the positive side of being an orphan. At least, not in that way. Kind as they were, the nuns were always all too willing to make demands and tell us what to do!'

Buckley smiled. 'Of course. I meant later.'

'There was no later.' Zelda leaned forward and clasped her hands on her knees. 'But the books. I must . . . I have to thank you. Without them, I don't know what I would have done.'

'I'm happy my gifts didn't fall on stony ground.'

'Oh, not at all! Those were some of the happiest times of my life, curled up in bed reading Enid Blyton or Charlotte Brontë. I felt as if I had always known English, as if it were my first language. I don't remember working hard to learn it. Even later, in my darkest times, when I couldn't make time to read, I always tried to summon up those memories. Peggotty. Jane. Julian, Dick, Anne and George. And Timmy, of course. And

Modesty Blaise. I loved Modesty Blaise. She became my benchmark if ever I was in trouble. Sometimes it worked. Sometimes they made me feel safe again, but . . .'

'It's a hard, cruel world out there, my dear. I know,' said Buckley. 'And there's rarely a Willie Garvin to charge in and rescue you.'

Zelda stared down at her clasped hands. She felt the tears struggling for release again. Held them back. This man could not have been her destroyer; she was certain of it.

'So you were born here?' Buckley asked.

'Dubăsari.'

'I don't know it.'

'There's nothing to know. It's a small place. In Transnistria. Near the Ukraine border. There's an amusement park.'

'And your parents?'

'Both killed in the civil war. They weren't participating, you understand. Just civilian casualties.'

'Indeed. There was plenty of "collateral damage". You must have been very young.'

'I was four.'

'And so you arrived at St George's.'

'Yes. It was very new at the time. Only in its second year, I think.' Zelda laughed. 'You could still smell the fresh paint.'

'For all that you have to thank a man called Klaus Bremner.'

Zelda frowned. 'Klaus Bremner. I've never heard the name.'

'You wouldn't,' said Buckley. 'Besides, he's long dead now. But for a while, in the uncertain days of the late 80s, when the Russian Empire was collapsing and a new Eastern Europe was struggling to be born, we were the best of friends. It was Klaus who put up the money for the orphanage and established the St George's Trust to keep it running even after his death. For a while, at any rate.'

'But why? Was he an orphan, too?'

'Klaus? No. And he was much older than me. He was a German soldier during World War Two. He fought in the Jassy-Kishinev Offensive.'

'I remember learning about that in history class.'

'It was an important battle. 1944. The Russians defeated the occupying German army and drove them out of Moldova. It was what Klaus witnessed in Kishinev, as it was known then – especially the number of orphaned children wandering the streets – that stayed with him. The guilt. He had never been a fully-fledged Nazi. Like many Germans, he was just doing his duty to save himself from being shot. He didn't do it with as much relish as some.'

'But what has that to do with St George's?'

'After the war, Klaus went to America, where he made his fortune in the engineering industry. I don't know all the details, but he was a very clever man, an industrial engineer before the war, and he came up with a few new ideas that were embraced by the new West Germany. I imagine he took a few of those secrets with him to share with the Americans. That way they could easily overlook his having been on the other side during the war. By the end of the Soviet era, when the Wall came down, Klaus, now called Claude, was a very rich man. He travelled to Moldova and Romania often and he even owned a winery here, near Cricova, but less famous.'

'When you were the cultural attaché?'

'Towards the end of my time in Bucharest. But that was where we first met, yes. Klaus was a very cultured man. We shared a passion for opera and symphony concerts. He and I travelled from Bucharest to Kishinev together on several occasions. He told me about the devastation he had witnessed, the scale of human suffering, the misery of the war. You won't remember, but there were also terrible stories about Romanian orphanages then, too. Abuse and neglect. I suppose you could say he had an epiphany. And he hatched a plan.'

'For an orphanage?'

'Yes. St George's.'

'Whose idea was the books?'

'Both of us. Believe it or not, Klaus was an anglophile. Teaching English was to be a priority. Other languages, too, of course, but particularly English. Your English is excellent, by the way, my dear. He saw it as the future, and none of us knew what lay ahead for Moldova or Romania. We both loved the English classics, and I was still able to get my hands on as many books as I wanted through my connection with the British Council and the newspapers I reviewed for. Also, I don't know if you're aware, but this village is famous for its monastery, the Monastery of St George. It's been here since 1785 and is home to a group of Orthodox nuns. Even the Soviets tolerated them. They still farm the land on the edges of the village. I had been coming here for years to get away from city life in Bucharest, for peace and quiet to write, and I had got to know some of them.'

'The nuns?'

'You remember, of course. Yes. These nuns helped with the orphanage. They taught lessons, cooked the food, did the cleaning, took care of you children.'

'I never knew,' Zelda said. 'Where they came from, I mean. Why they did what they did.'

'They did it because it was in their nature to do good.'

'They were kind. Distant, but kind.'

'So I heard. Not always the case with nuns, as I understand. Ask the Irish. So that was your lucky childhood.'

'Your books and Klaus Bremner's epiphany. Yes.'

'And the nuns.'

'And the nuns.'

Zelda swallowed. She felt overwhelmed by the information and the emotion it generated. But she knew she had to steel herself to find out what she had come for, even though the thought of doing so made her feel duplicitous. From all she had heard and observed so far, she was convinced that neither William Buckley nor Klaus Bremner had anything to do with her fate. She knew she might be wrong, of course. Often the nastiest of monsters lurk behind the most pleasing facades, and Nazis, of course, were among the nastiest. The whole orphanage, for example, could have been a scheme to raise young virgins for the sacrifice. But she didn't think so. Nor did she think they knew what went on. After all, both Buckley and Bremner had only distant connections with St George's. She had never heard of either of them the entire time she was there. They weren't involved in the day-to-day management of who was coming or going. That would have been Vasile Lupescu.

'Do you remember Vasile Lupescu?' she asked. The name almost turned to stone on her lips.

'Vasile? Of course. He was director from the beginning until the end.'

'Do you know what happened to him?'

'Nothing happened to him, my dear. It was 2009, the wake of the great financial crisis, the collapse of so many economies. The trust Claude had set up failed. Apparently, it wasn't quite as inviolable as he had intended it to be. It was all a terrible tragedy, a very sad time for us all. But there was nothing we could do. When the orphanage closed, Vasile was just about ready to retire. So that was what he did.'

'And now?'

'As far as I know he lives in Purcari. It's in the far southeast, not too far from the Ukraine border. Odessa. Good wine country. I think he has family down there.'

'I've heard of it,' said Zelda. 'Do you ever see him?'

'Not often. I rarely see anyone these days. You're probably the first person I've spoken to in ages, except for my cleaning lady, and certainly the first I've had any sort of conversation with in weeks, maybe months. And we weren't close friends, Vasile and I, even when we were both in Chișinău. The last time I saw him was when he travelled up to the city on business, and we met for lunch. But that was over a year ago. Why do you ask?'

'I just wondered, that's all. He was an important presence in our lives.'

'He certainly was. He took care of all the administrative details – admissions, transitions and everything. I'm sure he'd be very pleased if you were to tell him that. Are you planning on going to see him, too?'

'Yes, I might do. Can you give me his address? Would that be all right?'

'Of course. I don't see why not.' Buckley had a small diary on his table, and he leafed through it, then gave her an address in Purcari. Zelda glanced at her watch and realised she wouldn't be able to make it down there until well after dark. Instead, she decided to go back to the Radisson Blu in Chișinău and try to get a good night's sleep, if such a thing were possible after the conversation she had just had. She had one more day left in Moldova before her flight left at 5.35 the following evening, so she might as well spend it in Purcari.

At the door, they shook hands, and Buckley said, 'I don't know why you came here, my dear, and why you wanted to hear an old man's ramblings, but I sense some sort of mission on your part, some desire to reacquaint yourself with your roots, make peace with the past. Is that it?'

'Something like that,' said Zelda, hating herself for misleading him.

'Then let me thank you for your company and your conversation. And I wish you good luck in your quest.'

Zelda thanked William Buckley again for the books, for giving her a childhood and early adolescence, at least, then she took her leave.

Banks knew he shouldn't have done, but he drove home from the reception when the whole thing was fast becoming an endless DJ ego trip to a soundtrack of bad nineties synth-pop and electropop music.

Brian and two fellow band members who were with him had performed a brief unplugged set earlier, including 'Blackbird', one of Banks's favourite Beatles songs, even though it was McCartney and he had always regarded himself as a Lennon man.

The music had started to go downhill soon after Brian and his friends had left. Banks said farewell to his own and Mark's parents, all four still bravely soldiering on, and to Sandra and Sean, who were themselves just about to leave. Then he walked over to Tracy and Mark, embraced his daughter and shook her husband's hand. Tracy thanked him for his cheque, and he could tell by her tone that it had been enough. That was a relief.

Before leaving, he took Mark aside and said, only half joking, 'Break her heart and I'll break your neck.'

'Don't worry, sir. Mr Banks,' Mark replied nervously, his Adam's apple bobbing.

'Alan,' said Banks, patting him on the back. 'You're family now. But remember what I said, or you'll have me to answer to.'

Despite having had a couple more glasses of wine on top of the pint, enough time had elapsed that Banks felt perfectly sober as he got in the car. As a cop in the Eastvale region for many years, he knew well enough that there weren't any patrol cars out in the dale at this time of night, but he drove carefully. Not so much so that it seemed as if he were *trying* to drive carefully, but sticking to the speed limits and signalling properly. He made it back home in one piece, without incident.

There was a chill in the air, so instead of going out into the garden, he poured himself a glass of claret, sat in the conservatory and put on Dylan's *Time Out of Mind* to counteract the DJ's music that lingered like the aural equivalent of a bad smell.

Burgess's call intrigued him, and he wondered what it could be about. It was true that he didn't have a lot on his plate at the moment, but what he did have, the Blaydon case, had become much more complex and frustrating over the past few days.

A crooked property developer called Connor Clive Blaydon and his factotum Neville Roberts had been found murdered by Banks and DC Gerry Masterson in the swimming pool area of Blaydon's mansion just over a week ago. The post-mortem revealed that both had been shot and that, while Roberts had died of his wound, Blaydon had subsequently been sliced open from the groin to the breastbone and his body dumped in the pool. Technically, he had drowned to death because the bullet hadn't hit any major organs and he had been using his hands to hold his intestines inside rather than to swim to safety.

The major suspect, Leka Gashi, a member of the Shqiptare, the Albanian Mafia, was a 'business partner' of Blaydon's. The 'business' included money laundering and county lines drug dealing, two activities that could easily result in violence. The MO matched Gashi's style, too. He was suspected of being behind the murder of a Leeds dealer called Lenny G, also gutted, who had previously managed a county line.

There was no clear motive, but Gashi and Blaydon were old partners in crime. Gerry had recently discovered that the two had met in Corfu some twenty years ago, much earlier than she had originally thought. Blaydon had owned a villa there since about 2002, and he had kept his yacht, the *Nerea*, moored at a marina near Kavos for a few years before that. A falling-out among thieves was not unusual, in Banks's experience.

Because Gashi and his cronies had an alibi and were now thought to be hiding out in the Albanian countryside, the case would have been languishing in limbo until they found him, as they had no other leads. But just a couple of days ago a cache of MiniSD cards and a wad of cash amounting to £30,000 had been found hidden in a special compartment at the back of the wardrobe in the factotum's cubbyhole. Apparently, what none of the guests at Blaydon's famous parties had realised was that several of the bedrooms were fitted with minicams, which were motion- or sound-activated. This discovery, of course, raised the possibility that it was Neville Roberts, and not Blaydon, who was the intended victim. On further investigation, it turned out that Roberts used to be an audio and video technician until he was jailed for his part in the illegal surveillance of a client's business rival.

DI Annie Cabbot and DC Gerry Masterson, Banks's 'team', were patiently going through and logging the material on the cards. So far, they had found that Roberts's victims included judges, a local MP, one ex-chief constable, a pop singer, an American evangelist keen to make property investments, an award-winning film director, a bishop, a premier league foot-baller and a Scottish rugby international, among others. No royalty appeared to be involved, except a minor baronet, who didn't really count. All had enjoyed Blaydon's parties, fuelled by vast amounts of alcohol and cocaine and the loving attentions of hordes of beautiful young women, many of them probably *too* young.

But the most recent development had occurred just the previous day, when they came across what appeared to be a video recording of a rape among a number of films that Annie Cabbot called 'married-men-who-should-know-better shagging young girls'. There was something wrong with the recording, a technical fault it seemed, and the images were dark and blurred. Neither the rapist nor his victim was recognisable. A video technician Gerry knew at County HQ was working on an enhancement. And that was where things stood. Two separate cases, perhaps, but occurring in the same house and separated in time by only five weeks: Blaydon and Roberts had been killed on 22 May and the rape footage was dated 13 April.

Banks ran his hand over his hair and stopped thinking about the case for a few moments to listen to 'Cold Irons Bound', then checked his watch and headed for bed. He needed to be up bright and early in the morning to catch his train.

Before he fell asleep, snapshots of Tracy, from childhood to the present, flashed through his mind, and the last image that came was of her beaming in her wedding dress just as the ceremony ended. She was beaming at Mark. Banks had given her away, and then, as he had stood beside her, he had felt that he had lost something, though his heart was filled with happiness.

3

Zelda got up early to prepare herself for her journey to Purcari. She had never been in the far south-east of Moldova before, though she knew of its reputation for fine wines and beautiful landscapes. As she sat over her breakfast of fruit and yoghurt, she looked at the map she had bought the previous day and checked it against the Google Maps on her laptop. It wouldn't be an arduous journey. The fastest route would take her straight south-east and should take no longer than a couple of hours. Moldova wasn't a big country. She also had to check out of her hotel before she left and arrange to leave the rental car at the airport.

Her visits to the derelict orphanage and to William Buckley had thrown her askew, brought back feelings and memories she hadn't known she had, but she had enjoyed a good night's sleep – no nightmares or sweats, for once – and she felt ready to go on and bring her quest to an end. Lupescu would be the last one; she was almost certain of that.

She finished her breakfast and refilled her coffee cup. Her room was fine, but there wasn't much of a view except the car park below, so she sat cross-legged on the unmade bed and watched the BBC World News on TV. There was nothing new, and certainly nothing pleasant. She checked her email and sent Raymond a quick upbeat message.

The address she wanted was on the northern edge of Purcari, which wasn't a big place. Zelda still had no idea how

she would play the confrontation with Vasile Lupescu, and
every time she tried to imagine it, it turned out differently. She
hadn't done a great deal of forward planning, and she couldn't
do much now. Nor had she planned any sort of fail-safe
escape. If all went well, she would have no problem doing
what needed to be done and getting to the airport in Chișinău
in time to drop off the car and make her flight to London. *If
all went well.*

But the best-laid plans, in her experience, often went wrong.
She had learned from her past that murder was an unpredictable business. There were too many variables. What if he
wasn't in? What if he was surrounded by family? What if he
simply refused to see her, shut the door in her face? What if he
lived on a busy street and there were lots of people around? In
these circumstances, Zelda realised, she might well have to
abort. Or at least postpone. If things went smoothly, then she
simply had to make sure that there was no chance of discovery before she was well on the way to London. With a little
judicious cleaning up and a certain amount of care in not
appearing too conspicuous, or being seen by too many people,
that should be easy enough.

She worried a little about William Buckley. If he heard about
anything happening to Lupescu, he would no doubt remember Zelda's visit. He might tell the police if they asked him, but
why would they? And the odds were that he most likely
wouldn't hear about it anyway. Besides, there was nothing she
could do about it now. She didn't know how good the detectives were in Moldova, but she doubted they were up to the
same level as Alan Banks and his team; there was surely no
way they could trace and arrest her within a couple of hours.
They had done nothing to find or help her when she was
abducted.

Zelda showered and dressed, amazed at how calm she was

feeling. She held her hands out. No shakes. She didn't want to get caught. She wanted more than anything for it all to be over so she could get back to Raymond and get on with their life together in Yorkshire. Explore the world of painting and sculpture in more depth. Cook dinners for friends. Learn to enjoy that dreadful sixties music Raymond played. Try to persuade his daughter Annie that she wasn't such a monster. But then, she realised, she *was* a monster, wasn't she? How could she fool herself into believing otherwise? She shrugged off the thought. Lupescu would be the last one. Then she would put it all behind her. But she had to do this. Until she did, the past would keep growing, like a cancer inside her, consuming or blotting out all that was good in her life.

One thing she had to make sure she didn't forget, she thought, as she packed her bags ready for checkout, was the knife she had bought in the shopping mall yesterday after her meeting with William Buckley. She held it in her hand, saw the blade glint in the sunlight through the window, then slipped it into her handbag.

That following morning on the train, Banks relaxed in his seat, his mild hangover fading under the ministrations of two extra-strength paracetamol. He listened to Abdullah Ibrahim's *Dream Time* as he watched the summer landscape of the English heartland flash by: bright-coloured canal boats, anglers casting their lines from the grassy banks of large tree-lined ponds, farmers out working the fields, distant green woodlands, squat church towers with gold weather-vanes catching the light. It could be another age, he thought, another country, not the troubled and troubling one he was living in. He succeeded in relaxing to such an extent that he drifted off to sleep before the music ended, and the sudden arrival at King's Cross came as a shock to his system.

Banks took off his headphones as the train disgorged its passengers, and merged with the rushing river of humanity. Unintelligible messages crackled over the loudspeakers, and travellers dashed for connections, dragging enormous wheeled suitcases behind them, running over toes and bumping thighs, oblivious to everyone else. Others stood and stared at signs and noticeboards as if lost.

Banks threaded his way through the crowds and took the escalator down to the Underground, where it got hotter and more humid the deeper he went. He found the right platform and took the Victoria Line to Vauxhall, standing all the way, and walked up behind the MI6 building, famous from the James Bond movies, to The Rose on the Albert Embankment, where Burgess had arranged to meet him. It was a Victorian pub, or gastro-pub, as it was called now, with a view of the Houses of Parliament, warm gold in the early afternoon sun, over the river beyond Lambeth Bridge.

Burgess was already waiting in a booth, and Banks joined him, glancing around at the chandeliers and vintage furniture. 'Very nice,' he said. 'At least the decor beats Pret's.'

Burgess passed Banks a menu. 'The food's supposed to be good,' he said. 'And not too expensive. Let's order first. I'm having the homemade fish-finger sandwich.'

Banks scanned the menu and settled on a roast beef burger with smoky chipotle mayo.

'Drink?' Burgess asked.

'What are you drinking?'

'Krombacher Pils.'

Again, Banks glanced at the menu. 'Brixton pale ale, please.' Hair of the dog.

Burgess went up to the bar. The pub was crowded, obviously a popular lunch spot for both local office workers and tourists walking along the riverside. And what a day for it.

Banks glanced out of the window at the throng of people walking up and down the Embankment in the heat of the midday sun. Most wore sunglasses, shorts, sandals and T-shirts. Many carried cameras, pushed prams or held hands with small children. He found himself thinking how quickly things could change if a terrorist with a knife ran into the crowd and started stabbing people. Or a speeding van suddenly veered off the road on to the pavement. It was the police officer's curse, he told himself, to be so often imagining the worst. But things like that *did* happen. Had happened not so long ago, not so far away, and would certainly happen again. Relish every moment, as his poet friend Linda Palmer had told him.

Burgess returned quickly with the drinks. Banks remembered how good he was at bars; not for him any worries about who was first in line. It was all to do with who could push hardest and shout loudest. Banks sipped. It tasted good. They chatted briefly about Burgess's morning of meetings up the road at NCA headquarters and Banks's journey through the heartland. Now, though, he was back in the present in the thriving capital, just upriver from the centre of power. He tried not to think about what nefarious business might be going on in there. Backstabbing and prevarication, for the most part, he guessed. Perhaps politics had always been like that, but it seemed to him to have taken a turn for the worse over the last three or four years.

'So what is it?' he asked. 'You said you were working on something that might concern me.'

Burgess leaned back. 'Don't get your hopes up too high. But, yes, I think it might.'

'In what way?'

'In two ways. That bloke you've been after for so long. The one who tried to kill you, set fire to your house.'

'Phil Keane.'

'That's one.'

'And the other?'

'That young woman you've got a thing for. Zelda.'

'I'm intrigued,' said Banks. 'Do go on.'

'It's a bit complicated. I've been trying to put it all in order while I was waiting for you.'

'Give it a try. I'm sure I'll be able to follow.'

Burgess took a deep breath, then a few gulps of beer. 'Right,' he said. 'You know about Zelda's boss?'

'Trevor Hawkins, the one who burned to death in a chippan fire?'

'That's the one. Well, the two officers who've been investigating his death, Deborah Fletcher and Paul Danvers, haven't found any evidence of foul play, but there are one or two anomalies, and Danvers isn't quite convinced that it was an accident. It seems that your friend Zelda visited the street where Hawkins lived a couple of days after the fire.'

'I know that,' said Banks. 'You told me all about it the last time we talked.'

'Hear me out. Allow me my preamble. It's difficult enough as it is.'

'OK.'

Their food came, and they took a few bites in silence then carried on talking while they ate. 'Paul Danvers was suspicious enough to widen his inquiry a bit, ask questions around the street and so on,' Burgess went on. 'They talked to Zelda again, for example, but she was about as helpful as the first time. Mmm, this fish is good. How about your burger?'

'It's fine,' Banks said. 'Zelda couldn't be helpful because she didn't know anything.'

Burgess raised an eyebrow. 'Are you sure about that?'

'What do you mean?'

'Let's not forget how important Hawkins was. He was an agent of the NCA, running a special bureau compiling a database and facial recognition data of known sex traffickers. Your friend Zelda worked for him as a civilian consultant, using her special skills as a super-recogniser and her experience of the trafficking world to put names to faces. That way, they could track the movements of major players, keep an eye on who was climbing up the ladder, who was in, who was out, and so on. The long and the short of it is that a young bartender down the road in Hawkins's local pub, The George and Dragon, recalls a woman coming in one lunchtime shortly after the fire and asking questions about Hawkins.'

'Like what?'

'Whether he was a regular. Whether he had ever met anyone there.'

'And what did he tell her?'

'That Hawkins was a regular, but that he usually only dropped in for a quick half and the *Times* crossword after work.'

'Usually?'

Burgess took a bite of his sandwich before answering. 'He said he did once, quite recently, see Hawkins meet and talk with another man in the pub. Said it appeared as if they knew one another and the meeting was prearranged. Apparently, the woman showed Chris – that's the bartender – a photograph, and he recognised the man from it.'

'Who was he?'

'That we don't know. And Chris wasn't able to give us a clear description. You know – medium, medium, light brown hair, ordinary. He had a beard, too. One of those artsy type thingies. Van Dyke or goatee, whatever they call it. He didn't know the man's name, either.'

'Pity.'

'There was one tiny pinprick of light.'

'Yes?'

'He certainly remembered the woman, and he gave us a very detailed description of her. Sounded as if he was more than a little smitten, so Danvers told me. And I have to say, Banksy, that she sounds remarkably like your Zelda.'

'What if it *was* her?' Banks asked, spearing a fat chip. 'It doesn't necessarily mean anything.'

'I disagree. Where's your copper's instinct? Don't you think it's odd? I mean, I can just about swallow that she visited her dead boss's burned-out house because she was curious. But asking questions in his local about who he'd been meeting is going a bit too far. Don't you think so? Why? And who was it in the photograph she showed Chris the barman?'

'So you think Zelda's involved?'

'We *know* that she didn't kill Trevor Hawkins. She was out of the country at the time of the fire. And neither Danvers nor I can accept that she somehow paid for it or arranged to have it done.'

'Which leaves?'

'Danvers's theory is that she was suspicious of Hawkins's activities. For some reason, she suspected him of being in the pay of the enemy, the traffickers, or somehow in thrall to them. Does that make any sense to you?'

Banks drank some beer and thought for a moment. 'I suppose it does,' he agreed reluctantly. 'But what of it?'

'Surely it's significant if she had some reason to suspect him of being bent? She may have been watching him, observing him at work, even following him. Maybe his trafficker paymasters found out, and he started to become a liability?'

'Are you saying Zelda was responsible for Hawkins's death?'

'I'm saying that she was sticking her nose in where it wasn't wanted. The outcome was unpredictable. Though anyone with half a brain could probably have worked out it would end in tears.'

'But we don't *know* any of this. It's mere speculation on your part.'

'As is so much of our job. And you know that, too. Come on, Banksy. Are you so pussy-whipped you can't see the wood for the trees?'

Banks bristled, but he knew Burgess was right. Up to a point. There was nothing sexual between him and Zelda. She was Ray Cabbot's partner, and he respected that. Even if he believed he was in with a chance, which he didn't, he wouldn't make a move on her. He didn't do things like that to his friends. Not that she had given the slightest inclination of interest. But, yes, he liked her company, and yes, he lusted after her. What man wouldn't?

'I'm *not* pussy-whipped, as you so delicately put it.'

'Sorry, mate,' said Burgess. 'Maybe that was below the belt. But I need my Banksy back, not some mealy-mouthed apologist.'

Banks tried to think rationally. He had to get beyond his bias and see things straight. At worst, Zelda could be involved in something dodgy, and at best she could be on the side of the good guys and in danger from the same people who had hurt Hawkins. And it would always be a good thing to keep in mind that Phil Keane was a killer, and that his preferred weapon was fire. But quite where Keane came into all this, Banks still had no idea, except that Zelda had said she had spotted him in a photo with Petar Tadić, a known sex trafficker. And that also connected with Blaydon's murder. The police knew that Tadić had supplied Blaydon with girls for his parties. What did it all mean? Did Hawkins know that Zelda had seen the photo and recognised Keane? How was he connected with Keane? Was Keane the man he had met in The George and Dragon?

'As far as I can see,' Banks said, 'even if Zelda did do everything you say, she's done nothing illegal.'

Burgess sighed. 'Hardly the point. Nobody's saying she's bent.'

'Then what?

'She *is* involved, and you know it. She's up to her neck in it. Whatever *it* is. If just for her sake, try and focus that lasersharp mind of yours on all that. I'm trying to help you save her from herself, not getting you to convict her.' He finished his plate of food, pushed it aside, gulped down some lager and burped. 'Besides, that's not all. It gets even more interesting.'

The drive to Purcari was easier than Zelda had expected, and she was passing a winery on the outskirts of the village before noon. It was a journey of low hills, soft greens and yellows, opening occasionally on distant panoramas; a journey of small villages, mostly neat and tidy and colourful, and with no one about except roaming cats and the occasional barking dog. Here and there, geese and chickens wandered the roadsides, and in some places, old women in traditional garb paused and eyed her sternly as she drove slowly by. Sometimes she imagined they knew what she was going to do. It was more like travelling back in time than in distance. The sun shone all the way, and she kept the windows of the old Skoda rolled down. Off the main highway, the paved roads were of variable quality, and she saw signs on them now and then that said, 'PAID FOR BY THE AMERICAN PEOPLE.'

At last, the chateau came into view, with its tower, white walls and orange roof against a backdrop of hillsides planted with rows of vines. Beyond the hills, Zelda knew, lay the River Dniester and Ukraine. She paused at a crossroads to breathe

the sweet air, and a gentle breeze wafted through the open car windows. She could smell manure and fresh-mown grass.

Lupescu's house, at some distance from any neighbours, was a contemporary construction in the Art Deco style, all white cubes and curves, topped with a large dome, like an observatory, and shiny, as if it were made out of plastic. It was hard to find a point of entry, but Zelda thought she discerned a door somewhere in the whiteness. There was no doorbell, so she knocked. She had realised a while ago that there was no point in trying to sneak up on Lupescu as he wouldn't know her from Eve. The last time he had seen her, she had been an excited seventeen-year-old girl on the verge of making her own way in the world.

At first, she thought there was no one home. Everything was silent except for the birdsong and someone hammering far in the distance. Perhaps Lupescu was old and slow, like William Buckley. Then the door opened abruptly and she found herself looking at the man himself. He was probably about five years younger than Buckley, she guessed, and had been retired for around ten years, which made him roughly mid-seventies. His skin was sallow, and the flesh on his cheeks and throat sagged into wattles and jowls. His hooded eyes, buried deep above the bruise-coloured bags, were pale and glaucous. He had very little hair, and what he had he wore in an absurd comb-over across his liver-spotted skull. But it was Vasile Lupescu, no doubt about it.

He spoke to her in Russian. 'Yes? Can I help you? What is it you want?'

'I was just speaking with William Buckley in Suruceni,' she said, also in Russian, hoping the speech she had rehearsed on her way came out right. 'He said if I was heading down south I should say hello. So here I am.'

'And you are?'

'You knew me as Nelia Melnic. One of the beneficiaries of Claude Bremner's largesse. And your hard work, of course.'

Lupescu frowned.

'The books,' Zelda explained. 'At St George's Orphanage.'

Lupescu's thin lips twitched in a smile. 'Ah, yes. The books. Please, do come in. Forgive my bad manners. I'm an old man and not much used to visitors.'

'Not at all.' Zelda stepped inside. In contrast to its bright exterior, she found the interior dark and dull, lightened only by abstract paintings sharing the walls with knock-off old masters and surrealist sculptures in nooks adjacent to ancient religious icons. Other than that, with its sepia and grey tones, it felt more like a tomb. She also got the impression that Lupescu's cleaning lady didn't come nearly as often as William Buckley's. How could anyone live here? she found herself wondering. Then she realised that it was probably more an indication of status than aesthetic pleasure, and that made sense. *This was a man who wanted to show the world that he had made money.*

Lupescu himself was wearing red carpet slippers, baggy grey trousers and a button-up maroon cardigan over his white shirt, despite the temperature, and he looked like nothing more than an old man near the end of his time who had no idea what to do or how to go about it. The cardigan was open and Zelda noticed a reddish stain down the front. Pasta sauce, she guessed.

'Would you care to sit down?' he asked, gesturing to a leather-upholstered armchair. Zelda sat and felt immediately as if she were falling backwards down a bottomless pit. The seat sagged under her, and she was sure she felt the prick of a spring where she least wanted it. She shuffled around a bit, rested her arms on the scuffed leather and managed to acquire a modicum of comfort. Lupescu sat opposite her in a similar chair. He didn't offer refreshments.

Zelda glanced around at the paintings. Most of the abstracts were probably original works. Some of them were quite good, she thought, though she would have been the first to admit she wasn't exactly the best judge of abstract art. For the most part they looked as if someone had stood near the canvas and flicked brushes dipped in various coloured paints in random patterns, which is probably exactly what had happened.

Zelda found herself wondering whether Lupescu liked this stuff or whether it was merely another instance of fortune-signalling. They made quite a contrast to the madonnas and classical scenes hung adjacent to many of them. The sculptures were better, she thought. Smooth, round, curving objects with surprising holes and twists in them, mostly made of wood, crying out to be stroked, though a couple seemed to be cast from brass. She ran her hand over a small wooden infinity figure within reach that seem to languish over its base like Dali's watches melted over their surfaces.

'So you're a St George's girl?' Lupescu said.

'I was,' Zelda replied. 'A long time ago.'

'Yes,' Lupescu said. 'The old place has been closed for ten years or more now. A great loss. I was sorry to see it go. I was there right from the beginning, you know.'

'So I heard. Tell me, were you selling girls to sex traffickers right from the start, or did that come later?' She hadn't planned for it to come out that way, or so soon, but it did.

Lupescu seemed to freeze. He might have turned pale, but Zelda couldn't tell, as he was so ashen to start with. 'What do you mean by that?' he said, a quiver in his voice.

'Well, when I left St George's, two men were waiting for me at the street corner. They hit me and bundled me into a car and drove me across Romania, raping me all the way, until they dropped me off at a breaking house in Serbia. Do you know what a breaking house is?'

'But that's got nothing to do with me,' Lupescu spluttered. 'How can you assume I had anything to do with that?'

'It's a house where they break in the new girls. That means rape, day and night, beatings, humiliation, starvation, until you toe the line.'

'No!' said Lupescu, shaking his head so that his jowls wobbled, and half rising from his chair. 'I won't listen to this. That wasn't me. You can't blame that on me.'

'I'm not saying you're the one who did it, just that you're the one responsible. You're the one who made all the arrangements, who knew all the details, the one who spotted the pretty girls. I met others over the years, you know. In Pristina. In Zagreb. In Ljubljana. In Sarajevo. Girls who suffered the same fate in the same way as I did. Girls from the orphanage who were marked, chosen. One of them even saw you out on the street, watching as it happened. But you didn't call the police. You did nothing. That was Iuliana. Do you remember her? She killed herself. Slit her wrists. Nobody ever came looking for any of us.'

Lupescu shrank back into his chair. 'What could I do?' he said. 'These men were powerful gangsters. They had guns. You have no idea. You had a good life at the orphanage, didn't you? You were well taken care of. Taught. Fed. Coddled.'

'I suppose we were,' Zelda agreed. 'Like free-range chickens being fed and readied for the slaughter.'

'But what could I do?'

Zelda sat up and leaned towards him, half standing, her palms on the arms of the chair. 'You could have stopped it! You could have gone to the police. You . . .' She shook her fist at him. Then she made an effort and calmed herself down, subsided deep into the armchair again. 'I think it would be better if you confessed before your punishment, don't you?'

'Why? What punishment? What are you going to do to me? I'm an old man. I'm sick. I've got health problems. Heart. Diabetes.' Lupescu's eyes darted about the room, as if searching for a way out or for someone to come to his aid.

'You should have thought about your health problems back then,' said Zelda. 'Though I doubt anybody could have done anything about your heart, however hard they tried.'

Lupescu tried to get to his feet, but age had slowed him. In one smooth movement Zelda stood up, picked up the infinity sculpture from the table beside her and hit him on the side of the head. He sagged back in his chair, then slid to the floor, a trail of blood spoiling the symmetry of his comb-over.

'If there's more,' said Banks, 'I think I'll need another pint. You, too? My shout.'

'Go on, then,' said Burgess. 'You've twisted my arm. It's just a bloody boring security roster meeting this afternoon. I can easily sleep through that and nobody will notice.'

Banks went to the bar, his head still whirling with Burgess's story, connections spinning like plates on sticks. He wasn't quite as brash as Dirty Dick, but the bar wasn't too crowded, and he managed to get served quickly enough. As usual in London, he was gobsmacked at the price of two pints.

'You realise that we've probably consumed our entire weekly allowance of alcohol units this one lunchtime,' Burgess said when Banks got back. Then he contemplated the remains of the roast beef burger. 'Not to mention you being responsible for a few more icebergs melting in Antarctica.'

'It always puzzled me, that,' said Banks.

'What?'

'If cow farts are bad for the environment, how would stopping eating beef help?'

'If we didn't eat beef, we wouldn't need cows, stupid.'

'So what would we do with them to stop cow farts for ever? Kill them all and burn their bodies?'

'Well, no. Burning that many cows might cause environmental problems, too. Carbon emissions.'

'Not to mention that we'd be guilty of the genocide of a species. *Bovicide.* That can't be good, surely?'

'Talk to David Attenborough. I'm sure he'd put you right on the matter.'

'Or perhaps we should put them all in a big building where they can fart to their hearts' content, and we can use the gas to run the country.'

'We've already done that,' said Burgess. 'It's over there.' He pointed out of the window towards the Houses of Parliament.

Banks laughed.

'As I was saying,' Burgess went on, 'there's more. But first off, remember, I'm trying to do you a favour.'

'What's that?'

Burgess sighed and ran his hand over his lank hair. 'Danvers and Debs don't trust your Zelda for a number of reasons. You have to admit, she has a very shady past.'

'Shady?' said Banks. 'She was snatched off the street at the age of seventeen and forced to work as a prostitute for nearly ten years before she escaped the life.'

'I know that. But do you know *how* she escaped?'

'It's all a bit vague,' Banks admitted. 'Something happened in Paris, something big, something to do with the government, and it was hushed up. She obviously helped some very influential people with a problem. That's how she got her freedom and her French passport.'

'No details?'

'No.'

'Me, neither,' said Burgess. 'But don't you think it all sounds as fishy as that sandwich I just finished? Maybe she didn't *help* anyone; maybe she *blackmailed* them. You have to see it from the NCA's point of view. And from that of immigration. She *has* lived a nomadic life – she's never filled in any appropriate immigration or residence forms, she's filed no tax returns, her passport was not exactly official issue, and she spent most of her working life as a prostitute, which could reasonably be conceived as criminal. All in all, she's not the kind of person Britannia Unchained wants. We have plenty of prostitutes of our own without importing them from Europe, or anywhere else, thank you very much.'

'That's not *her* fault,' Banks argued. You make it sound as if it was *her* choice. She wasn't working as a prostitute, she was a sex slave, subject to rape, to violent beatings. Ever since she was abducted outside that orphanage, her life hasn't been her own. Until she came here. And now you're trying to take that life away from her.'

'*I* know all that, Banksy. And I'm not trying to take anything away from her. I'm just telling you how Danvers and Debs and their mates at the NCA and Immigration Enforcement might view things differently. She's on their radar now. I'm trying to keep her out of their hands and let you deal with it. I'm trying to do you both a favour, mate. But we need *some* answers from somewhere.'

'OK, so now I know. What am I supposed to do?'

'It's awkward,' Burgess said. 'And getting more so. They want to bring her in for questioning.'

'Danvers and Debs?'

'Yes. And someone else. There's more.'

Banks frowned. 'All right. Go on.'

'Ever heard the name Faye Butler?'

'I can't say as I have.'

'No reason why you should have. It's a case I took an interest in recently. It wasn't one of ours to start with. It was a Met case, and a Commander Barclay was in charge. I've known Ted Barclay for years, and after a few days he called me in. It's a strange one, all right. Disturbing, too. About a week ago, some young lads playing near the river down Woolwich way found a young woman's body snagged on a tree branch half out of the water. She hadn't been in there more than a day or two. At the post-mortem, it was discovered that she had died by drowning, but not in the river. The water in her lungs was tap water, not the Thames variety. It also turned out that she had been tortured. There was evidence of burn marks, as if from electrodes, of cuts, and significant bruising. Three of her teeth were missing and two fingernails. It was also clear to the pathologist that she had been sexually assaulted.'

'Bloody hell,' said Banks. 'The poor girl.'

'Indeed. Her name was Faye Butler, and she worked at Foyles on Charing Cross Road, in the art section. She was twenty-eight years old. Her body was found on 23 May. That was a Thursday.' Banks remembered. It was the same day he and Gerry Masterson had found Blaydon's body in the pool. 'Her flatmate in Camden Town had reported her missing.' Burgess paused to drink some pilsner. 'You know as well as I do, Banksy, what it's like with missing persons. You do your best to reassure the family or friends that nothing bad's happened, that it's perfectly normal for a young woman not to come home one night without phoning or anything. But it fucking isn't. We know it isn't. And from the moment you take the first call, you get that cramped feeling in your gut, and you just know that something's wrong.'

Banks knew the feeling. Missing persons were some of the hardest cases to handle if you let your imagination run away with you. Especially young girls. You could picture terrible things happening while you were reassuring the rest of the world that she would probably come walking in full of apologies at any moment, tell you that she'd stopped at her boyfriend's and just forgot to mention it to anyone. 'What happened next?' he asked.

'We made inquiries, but they didn't lead us anywhere. Naturally, the boyfriend came in for a bit of grief. Bloke called Grant Varney. They'd been together about three months. He said he hadn't arranged to see her that night and that she hadn't called around at his place. There were some of her things there – clothes, books, cosmetics, toothbrush – and apparently, she spent a fair bit of time there with him. They hadn't made any final commitment to live together or anything, but he said he was hoping she would agree to a more permanent arrangement. He knew she was still on the rebound at the moment, he said, and he was willing to wait. Varney was devastated. Ted said he thought he was a decent kid, and he was cleared pretty quickly. We did reconstructions of her route home, talked to people who took the same route, had seen her on occasion, but nobody noticed anything out of the ordinary.'

'How did she travel?'

'Faye usually walked home as long as it wasn't pissing down. She'd head up Tottenham Court Road, then Hampstead Road, and on a nice evening she'd cut through St Martin's Gardens on Camden Street. One witness thought she saw her talking with a man in the gardens, walking towards the road. She didn't get a good look at him, so we have no description except that he was stocky and was wearing a black T-shirt and ice blue jeans, but she did say that Faye seemed quite at ease, as if she knew him. You know, she didn't appear uncomfortable or scared, wasn't trying to get away. And the man wasn't in physical contact with her. He didn't grab her or anything. As far as our witness could tell she was just walking along chatting with a friend.'

'And that was the last time she was seen alive?'

'Yes. Except by her killer, of course. And he must have had transport of some kind. Her body was found some distance away from Camden. But nobody saw her getting into a car. We've had appeals out and done reconstructions, but no one's come forward with any new information and we got nothing from CCTV. It was as if she just disappeared into space.'

'He must have had a car waiting nearby,' said Banks. 'And maybe an accomplice.'

'We thought of that. I think you're probably right, but nobody remembers anything. It's also likely she got in the car willingly, if it was someone she knew.'

'I agree it's a nasty one,' said Banks, 'but where do I come in? And Zelda?'

'When we made inquiries at Faye's place of work, one of her colleagues told us that she was working the third floor about a week before the disappearance, and this woman came around asking for Faye. The colleague said she sent her to the ground floor, where we found out that she asked a lad called Lee Wong about Faye. Lee went and fetched her. The two of them chatted, then went upstairs to the cafe. Lee said he didn't know Faye well, but we talked to some more of her workmates, and they all said the usual. You know, what a fine person she was – nice girl, always cheerful, helpful and so on. Ask about the dead and you'd think we were all saints. It was the flatmate, Agnes Hall, who told us that Faye had been a bit down in the dumps for a while after splitting up with her previous boyfriend. Apparently, she found him in flagrante with another girl.'

'Any idea who he was?'

'We couldn't get any further questioning Agnes or Faye's friends at work. No one remembered the ex enough to give more than the vaguest of descriptions. As far as Agnes knew,

Faye had never invited him back to the flat. At least not while she was there. Medium height, good-looking, light brown hair, small beard, no particular accent. Rather like the barman's description from The George and Dragon, I thought. Only she added she thought the hair was maybe just a bit *too* light brown.'

'Dye job?'

'Sounds like it. He'd been in the shop a couple of times, apparently, chasing after an art book, and that's how he and Faye first met. All her workmates knew was that his first name was Hugh. A couple of them told us they thought he was too old for Faye, despite the hair. Naturally, he became a person of interest very quickly.'

'Any luck?'

'No. Not at first. But when we searched Faye's flat, we found some printed selfies of her with a bloke taken in Regent's Park, and it wasn't Grant Varney. This bloke was medium height, good-looking, light brown hair, little beard.'

'Age?'

'In his mid-forties, maybe, but well preserved. Could've been older. Fifty, even.'

'Hugh?'

'The roommate confirmed it. The dates matched, too. They'd been taken around Christmas – you could tell by the lights and decorations – a few months after she took up with him, and not too long before they split up. Her mobile went missing with her, but we found her laptop in the flat, and there were emails from a bloke called Hugh Foley. We couldn't trace him from them, though, and the email address is no longer in use. There was no entry for him in her contacts list.'

'Anything in the emails?'

'Plenty,' said Burgess. 'All along the lines of, "I can't wait to suck your throbbing—"'

'I catch the drift,' said Banks.

'That's from her, by the way. The ones from him seem to involve agricultural metaphors, mostly to do with ploughing and irrigation. No addresses, mobile numbers or arrangements to meet.'

'I assume they did all that through texts, or maybe even over the phone. Again, I'm having a bit of trouble working out how I could be involved. Unless you've got something up your sleeve. Something you're not telling me.'

'Just two things,' Burgess said. 'First, the description of the woman asking about Faye Butler in Foyles bears a remarkable similarity to Chris the barman's description of Zelda, right down to the faint accent, and secondly, well, see for yourself.' Burgess dropped a photograph on the table in front of Banks.

Banks stared at it and his jaw dropped. Despite a few minor cosmetic changes – hairline and colour, the addition of a light beard – the man in the selfies with Faye Butler, the man who went by the name of Hugh Foley, was a ringer for Phil Keane.

'Jesus Christ,' Banks muttered, pushing the photograph aside. 'And what's the link with Zelda?'

'Ted Barclay would like to have her brought in to talk to her, too, and maybe find out the answer to that. Which is where you come in. I managed to persuade Ted to let you have a go first, told him you were familiar with aspects of her background and so on. I also lied a bit. Told him you were an excellent detective, and as you already knew her, and she trusted you, you'd be far more likely to get something out of her. He didn't like it, but he agreed to give us some leeway.'

'Why did you do that? Why are you being so helpful to Zelda?'

'For fuck's sake, Banksy. I might not be as soft-hearted as you – or maybe I *am* getting soft in my old age – but I'm not the cold and calculating bastard you sometimes paint me as. I don't know this Zelda. I've never met her. But a woman like her, what she's been through, what she's suffered, it almost beggars the imagination. You've met her, and you know her. And I trust your judgement, even if I do think it's a little biased by female pulchritude. God knows, I've made enough errors in that direction myself, over the years. But can you imagine the effect that being interrogated might have on her, not to mention any detention and imprisonment that might result? Does it sound so strange that I don't particularly want her put through the ringer with Danvers and Debs and Ted Barclay? If she's as fragile as many of the women who've been through what she's been through, it could do her permanent damage. I don't think she's killed anyone. Not Hawkins. Not Faye Butler. If I thought she had, I'd have her in before her feet could touch the street. But she *knows* something. It's all connected. I'm giving you the chance to find out what that is. And now Keane's involved, too. You know he is. And don't forget that photograph of him with Petar Tadić. Petar is certainly a person of interest, along with his brother Goran. These are people from Zelda's past, and now they're starting to figure in our present. It's all tangled up in a knot, and until we manage to sort out one or two threads, your lady friend is going to be a target. You can help her, Banksy. I'm giving you the chance. Talk to her. Loosen her up a bit. Are you going to take it?'

He was right, Banks knew. Zelda affected a tough veneer, but he had seen beyond that to the seething fears, anxieties and conflicting emotions underneath; the guilt and self-loathing, shame, despair and depression that she tried to suppress and overcome. He saw something else, too, a sort of steely purpose, a sense of quest or mission, perhaps.

Banks shook his head slowly, reached for his glass and murmured, 'Of course I'm going to bloody well take it. Of course I am.'

4

By the time Lupescu came around, Zelda had him trussed up on the sofa. As soon as he realised the predicament he was in, he asked for a glass of water and a bottle of pills from the kitchen table. Zelda checked the pills. They were sublingual nitroglycerin, for angina. He drank the water first then put a pill under his tongue. She used a damp cloth to wipe the blood from the side of his head. He winced as she did so.

'What is it you want?' he said. 'Money?'

Zelda took out her knife and glanced around at the paintings. 'Seems as if you have plenty to spare,' she said. 'It must have been hard buying all this artwork on an orphanage director's salary.' Zelda touched the knife to his throat. He flinched. 'You can cut the lies and excuses. We both know what you did. You sold me to the Tadić brothers. Me and the other girls.'

'Who?'

Zelda was thrown. Was she wrong about all this? Had she jumped to the wrong conclusion? 'The Tadić brothers,' she repeated. 'Petar and Goran.'

'I don't know them.'

Of course not. 'Just the drivers,' Zelda whispered, almost to herself. Then she prodded him again and drew a bead of blood. 'You dealt with their boss, didn't you? Who was he?'

'I still don't know who you're talking about.' She could tell from his eyes that he was lying now.

'The man you sold us to. Would you rather I went to the authorities and told them my story? Then they could investigate your actions and your finances, find other girls to testify against you. Send you to jail. Confiscate everything you own.'

'Or what? Or you'll kill me? You're going to kill me, anyway, aren't you?'

'Perhaps. But whatever happens, I want to hear you admit what you did to me and the others first.'

Lupescu paused, as if weighing his chances, determining which direction to go. He licked his lips. 'All right, then. Say I did what you're accusing me of. What then?'

'Don't you think you deserve punishment?'

'You've got it all wrong,' Lupescu said. 'I'm not a monster or a pervert. They forced me to do it.'

'Forced you? How?'

'They threatened my family.'

Zelda felt as if a trickle of icy water had run down her spine. 'They did what?'

'They threatened me. My daughters. The twins. They were thirteen at the time. *Thirteen*. And the man said if I didn't do what he asked, he would take them and my wife instead and put them in brothels so bad they would be dead within a week.'

Zelda let her knife hand drop, though she held on to the handle. She had known brothels like that but survived to tell the tale. Lupescu was shaking now, with tears in his eyes. If he was lying, she thought, he was a good actor. But how could she tell? She had assumed that Buckley had nothing to do with what happened, but she could even be wrong about that. Was she judging the man who gave the books against the man who sat in the office? But no. She must stop second-guessing herself. William Buckley had nothing to do with St George's apart from donating the boxes of books. Zelda had never seen or heard of him before yesterday. But Lupescu was there all the time, handled the day-to-day running of the place, knew who was leaving, when and how, where they were going. Maybe he was forced into it, as he claimed, but he was certainly guilty of it.

'What did they ask you to do?' she went on.

'Tip them off when a pretty girl was leaving. I didn't know what they were going to do with you.'

'I'll bet you had a good idea.'

'I didn't ask. I couldn't let myself think about it. My lovely twins . . . my wife . . .' Lupescu hung his head. 'Please believe me.'

Zelda passed him the water again. 'How many girls?'

He looked up, horrified, and after a brief silence whispered, 'Twelve.'

Zelda froze. *Twelve girls.* Sold into slavery like her. How many hadn't survived? How many had killed themselves or tried to escape and been beaten to death? How many had died of disease, drugs or violence? It hardly bore thinking about. How could Lupescu live with himself? She felt the anger rise in her, and her hand tightened around the knife handle as she raised it. Lupescu shuddered and cringed like a frightened reptile, edging away as best he could. 'No!' he said. 'It wasn't my fault. I had to do it. You must understand. I had to! For my family.'

'You could have gone to the police.'

'That wouldn't have stopped them. You know that. There are always more. And they buy the police.'

'This man who came to you. What was his name?'

'I don't know. Honestly. He was Hungarian. He was in charge. I just called him The Hungarian.'

'What about the money?'

'What money?'

Zelda gestured around the house with the knife blade. 'Come on. All this. The house, the works of art. Like I said before, you couldn't afford it on your orphanage director's salary. How much did they pay you?'

Lupescu hung his head again, and when he spoke he muttered so softly that she could barely hear him. 'Five thousand dollars for each girl.'

Zelda felt her muscles tense and the breath tighten in her throat. So that was what her life had been worth. Five thousand dollars. They had made more than that out of her in the first few months. Multiply that by twelve. And the years. She couldn't stop herself from slapping him backhanded across the face, hard. He grunted and his top lip split, spilling blood on to his chin. She hit him again.

'Stop,' he pleaded. 'I told you. They threatened my family. I'm sick. You'll kill me.'

'And I had no family,' Zelda said. She didn't know why she said it; the words just seemed to come out of nowhere. It hardly mattered whether she had a family or not. But she couldn't help herself. 'Like I wasn't worth anything to anyone except men like that. You bastard. You selfish, evil bastard!' She punctuated each syllable with another slap until his skin was raw and his nose was broken and bleeding.

'Please stop,' he sobbed. 'I'm sorry. I'm sorry. My heart.'

'You took their money. Admit it.'

'Yes. But only later. When they made me.'

'What do you mean? You told me they threatened your wife and your daughters.'

'They did! This was later. They made me take their money.'

'Why would they do that if they could force you to do what they wanted for nothing?'

'To make me complicit,' Lupescu said. He licked the blood from his lips and lifted his tied hands up to wipe his nose on his forearm. His voice was hoarse. 'Don't you understand? There was always a chance I might go to the police and tell them everything in exchange for protection for me and my family. Or that they might come around to St George's asking questions. I wouldn't have told the police anything, of course, but they didn't know that. I was too scared for my daughters. If they paid me, I couldn't tell the authorities without implicating myself. Don't you see? The payments went into my bank account. It was their insurance, their way of making certain I did what they wanted, that I was no different from them. There's not a day gone by when I haven't regretted it, but what could I do?'

'Well, you bought the house, didn't you?' Zelda flopped back in her chair and looked at Lupescu, shaking her head. The money they had paid him was her insurance, too, that he wouldn't talk. She had killed Goran Tadić, one of the brothers who had abducted her in Chişinău, and she had killed Darius, her vicious French pimp, and she didn't regret either murder for a moment. But she didn't consider herself a cold-blooded murderer. And this time, she just couldn't do it. Or didn't want to. She felt dirty and cowardly for beating this pathetic tied-up old man, whether he was telling the truth about his motives or not, and the whole encounter was fast making her feel disgusted and empty, even of hatred.

Lupescu had been responsible for her abduction from the street and her subsequent years as a sex slave, but she couldn't bring herself to kill him. He wasn't the one who had abducted her and sold her; he had only tipped off The Hungarian when she would be leaving the orphanage. That was the extent of his participation. She was still angry, twisted up in knots inside, but if she believed him – that they had threatened his family – what man wouldn't have done what he did in that situation? It wasn't that she forgave him; she could never do that. Twelve girls in his charge had been sold into lives of unbelievable humiliation, pain and terror at his say-so. But would it have been better if his thirteen-year-old daughters and his wife had suffered that fate instead? What kind of a bargain was that? How could you reckon such a calculation? No matter how you played the figures, they came out wrong.

So Zelda put her knife back in her bag, glanced down in contempt at the sobbing, bleeding old man hunched on the sofa, and left. Someone would find him and free him, or he would work his own way free eventually. Or maybe he would die of a heart attack. It was all the same to her. One thing she knew was that, if he lived, he could never breathe a word to another soul about what had happened here today without implicating himself.

'So what did this cost you?' DI Annie Cabbot asked, fingering the picture Gerry had laid out on her desk.

'More than you could ever know.'

'Seriously? Oh, get away with you. You didn't, did you?'

Gerry laughed. 'No, I'm joking.'

'So, what? You don't get this kind of service for free, in my experience.'

'He asked me out to dinner, that's all.'

'And you agreed?'

'Well, I had to, really, didn't I?'

'That's coercion, Gerry. You don't have to put up with it, you know. Haven't you heard of #MeToo? You should report him.'

Gerry blushed. 'No, it's fine. He's quite nice, actually.'

'*Quite nice?*' Annie rolled her eyes. 'That sounds like the beginning of a torrid love affair.'

'I'm not after a torrid love affair, but I'll be quite happy to go out for dinner with him. He didn't coerce me. As a matter of fact, I've had my eye on him for a while, so there.'

'You and Jared Lyall from tech support? Well, I never. Who'd have guessed it.' Annie paused. 'Still, I suppose he *is* rather cute, in a Justin Bieber sort of way.'

Gerry punched her arm lightly. 'Anyway,' she said, 'he told me there wasn't a lot he could do. The tech was right, there was some fault with the minicam. Something to do with fields and pixels and so on. Like sound sampling, missing bits out, only you can't always put them back. I'm afraid I'm not very well up on the technical language, but he said what he had done was mostly guesswork, trying to imagine what might be missing and replacing it. That's why it took him so long. It's quite a work of art. There was nothing he could do with the rapist. He never showed his face, or anything else, like one of those faces on TV they have to blank out.'

'Could it have been?' Annie asked. 'Tampered with? Blanked out?'

'Jared says not. It's all to do with his position and what little light there was. Besides, it would have been difficult for someone to get just the rapist's face blanked out and his victim's visible, no matter how distorted she is. I still think he's done a pretty good job with the girl. Jared also ran this reconstruction through our facial recognition software, too, but he came up with nothing. Still, we'd hardly expect *her* to be in the system.'

'Maybe it was because of the poor image quality,' Annie said. 'Couldn't Jared just enhance it more? I've seen them do it on TV. You make a square around the bit you want enlarged and keep pressing enter.'

Gerry laughed. 'Yeah, we tried that.'

'Well, what happened?'

'The bit we marked out got bigger and bigger and in the end you couldn't tell what it was. It was just a bunch of dots with spaces between them, like a piece of abstract art. Jackson Pollock or something.'

'Ray likes Jackson Pollock. Oh, well. So much for TV. I'll never believe anything I see in future.'

'It's not a video recording,' Gerry said. 'It was recorded on to a microSD card through a high-end mini spy-cam working on a motion sensor. The problem is that the bedroom was very dark, a room without windows, or so it seems. Usually the cams compensate for that, especially the expensive ones, but this one wasn't doing a good job. It just wasn't working properly.'

'I'm surprised Roberts didn't return it to Amazon.'

Gerry rolled her eyes. 'Jared worked from the original SD card, and he did his best with what he had.'

'I'm sure he did.' Annie held the image at arm's length. 'I think we may have a possible recognisable likeness here. It wouldn't stand up in court, but . . . maybe her own mother might recognise her.'

'As I said, it's the best Jared can do. I think we have to go with it. He said we could send the card away to a tech lab in London, and they *might* be able to salvage a sharper image, but that would take weeks, for a start, and cost a fortune, with no guarantee. What we've got now is a hell of a lot better than what we had. I'm pretty sure I could recognise her from that, if I saw her. If I knew her. We need to show it around to people who might have been at that party.'

'When we find out who they are,' said Annie.

The enhanced image showed a young girl in semi-profile. It was a segment from after the rape, when the rapist had gone and she had turned over on to her side and curled up in the foetal position. Her eyes were glazed and her jaw slack, but there was just enough definition to her features to make iden-tification possible. The waifish look and the short hair were clear enough, and they had already estimated from the origi-nal footage, measuring her against the length of the bed, that she was maybe five foot seven or eight in height, or about 170 centimetres. It was impossible to tell her age beyond estimating that she was probably in her late teens.

Annie and Gerry watched the recording again, and it was even clearer that the girl was being raped, perhaps because they had a stronger idea of what she looked like. She had no chance. The man threw her down on the bed, ripped off her clothes and raped her. It didn't last long. Her struggles were weak and ineffective because she was clearly drunk or drugged, and after a while she didn't resist at all. There was no sound, so it was impossible to tell if she had screamed or called out, but when he left her half-naked among the rumpled bedsheets, she appeared to be sobbing.

And there the recording ended.

'Do you remember seeing the girl in any of the other videos?' Annie asked.

'No. Those women were all Tadić's hookers. Or at least we assume they were. None of them resembled her, at any rate, and they seemed to at least pretend they liked what they were doing.'

'It's true she doesn't look like a classy hooker.'

'Maybe she was working behind the scenes?'

'Possible,' said Annie. 'We need to find out how the parties were set up and organised. How people got invited. I know we've already recognised a few prominent figures from what we've watched, but there must have been other people there, ones we wouldn't recognise. Ones who might be more likely to talk to us. Someone must have seen something. Were any of the other films taken at the same party?'

'Only two,' said Gerry. 'I checked them out, and they were both fine as far as quality goes. Different rooms, too. So it was clearly just that one defective camera.'

'Who have we got?'

'One of them I recognise, but it's a woman.'

'Did Blaydon or Tadić supply men for fun, too?'

'Er . . . well, maybe,' said Gerry. 'But, I mean, it's not a man she's—'

'Another woman?'

'That's right.'

'Who is it?'

'Rosemary Vale.'

'No! You mean that actress? The one in that costume drama that's on at the moment?'

'That's the one,' Gerry said.

'She's gay? I don't believe it.'

'Well, you would if you watched the video.'

'OK. Who's in the other video?'

'Craig Lonegan.'

'What, that footballer with the big house out Swainshead way?'

'That's the one.'

'And what's he doing, or need I ask?'

'I'd blush if I told you,' said Gerry. 'But involves rubber sheets and cooking oil, and whatever it is, he appears to be enjoying it.'

'We need to have a crack at them,' said Annie. 'One of them might have seen something. At the very least they might be able to fill out the guest list a bit.'

'Do you think it could have been Blaydon himself?'

'I suppose it's possible,' Annie said, 'but there's no way you could even guess from what we've got, let alone prove it. It could have been any one of a number of people.'

'What it amounts to, then,' said Gerry, 'is that we don't know who the girl is or who she was with. She's definitely quite young, and she's not the same type as the others, if that's not a terribly judgemental thing to say. But that's all we know about her.'

Annie smiled. 'I wouldn't worry about being judgemental,' she said. 'I'm the last one to judge you on your woke quotient. Besides, it's our job to make judgements about certain things. No matter what "type" she is, she's somebody's daughter, and it's our job to find out who she is and get the perpetrator behind bars. If there is a connection with Blaydon's murder, then all well and good, that might come out, too. What about guest lists for the parties? They must be somewhere.'

'There's that woman who used to work as Blaydon's personal assistant,' Gerry said. 'Remember her? She's on our list. Her name's Charlotte Westlake, and she lives near Leeds.'

'Right. If she was working for Blaydon back in April, she might be able to point us in the right direction.'

'Any more ideas?'

Annie shook her head, then said, 'Except that Zelda knows the Tadić brothers. I know she's talked to Alan about them, and in the photo of Keane she saw, he was with Petar Tadić. If they supplied the women for the parties, maybe she could shed some light on things?'

'Where is the super today, by the way?'

'London,' said Annie. 'Left early this morning. And very cagey about it. Some sort of mysterious appointment.'

'What about Timmy and Tommy Kerrigan?' Gerry suggested. 'I know we've interviewed them about the murders, but remember those photos taken around the pool in the cache, too? People having fun, letting their hair down. Timmy and Tommy feature in some of them. They don't seem to be doing anything illegal, unless smoking big cigars and drinking extremely large glasses of whisky is illegal now.'

'And wearing skimpy thong swimming trunks if you look like Timmy Kerrigan,' Annie added.

Gerry laughed at the image. 'Right,' she said. 'Well, it seems there are a few directions to follow up on after the weekend.

The assistant and the Kerrigans for a start. Maybe the Kerrigans will be able to tell us something about this Charlotte Westlake? First off, though, I want to have another trip to Blaydon's house and check out the actual room.'

Banks found himself with a lot to think about as he made his way back to Vauxhall Underground station. He had originally intended to do some shopping while he was in London, check out the big Waterstones on Piccadilly, visit FOPP at Cambridge Circus, but he decided he couldn't face it. Like everyone else, he did most of his shopping online these days. London was too hot and too crowded today; he just wanted to go home.

He wondered how he had managed to become such a recluse and homebody. He had always enjoyed trips to London before, as he had also loved living there with Sandra in Kennington in his early days on the force. The disenchantment seemed to have crept up on him slowly, ever since he had first moved into Newhope Cottage alone, after their divorce. There had been women since then, of course, but nothing that lasted. Commitment had never been a strong point with him after Sandra; he was dedicated to his job, and he tended to take up with women who were similarly dedicated to something other than hanging on to a partner. This meant, inevitably, that they drifted apart before long. Now he had women friends and colleagues, but not lovers.

He caught a mid-afternoon train, which would get him home by about six o'clock, in plenty of time for a little pottering in the garden and a good read. As he listened to Bach's Sonatas and Partitas for Solo Violin, played by Rachel Podger, he drifted and gazed at the passing landscape as he had done on the journey down, this time mulling over what Burgess had told him.

It seemed as if Zelda had been busy behind his back, if the accounts were to be believed. And he saw no reason why they shouldn't be. Why was she asking the barman questions in her dead boss's local? He had no idea. Was she becoming overzealous in her search for Keane, or was there some other reason? Banks and Annie had warned her not to get too involved right from the start, told her that Keane was dangerous, but she seemed to have ignored them. Where had she come across the connection between Hawkins and Keane in the first place, and what was it? Was Keane now working with Tadić?

And how did Zelda get on to Faye Butler? That was a gigantic leap. The evidence pointed towards Faye being Keane's ex-girlfriend. Or Hugh Foley, as he called himself now. Why was she tortured and killed, and who did it? And what was Zelda's part in it all? Unanswerable questions at the moment, he knew, but they nagged away at him.

Burgess had asked Banks to talk to Zelda first and, if possible, avoid further action. He had agreed to try to find out what her meeting with Faye Butler was all about. But how was he to do that? Was he really going to bring Zelda into the station and question her, caution and all? If so, on what charge? Besides, that was one of the things Burgess had said he was trying to save Zelda from by letting Banks talk to her.

It would probably be best, he thought, to try an informal talk, but he had to be more probing and less willing to believe her than he had when they had talked before. He didn't think she had been playing him, but she *had* been holding out, and he was still worried about the possible danger to her. One only had to consider what happened to Faye Butler and Hawkins to worry about that. And he wondered about the man Faye had met in the park. Who was he? Keane? But Keane wasn't stocky. The only positive thing was that Zelda had been back up north when Faye had disappeared, as she had been in

Croatia when Hawkins had been killed in the mysterious house fire, so the police could hardly change tack and accuse her of those crimes. Her behaviour was suspicious, yes, but complicit, no.

The question of Phil Keane remained. He could be Hugh Foley. It would certainly make sense for him to change his name if he returned to England, especially to Yorkshire. Keane was fortyish when he and Banks had first crossed swords, so he would be about fifty now, definitely too old for Faye Butler, by her friends' standards. But Banks remembered that Keane was a smooth-talker and that he had been in youthful good shape. He seemed the kind of man who was attractive to women. He had taken in Annie Cabbot, after all. No doubt he still seemed younger than he was. Besides, Banks thought, the age thing was often irrelevant to the people involved in a relationship, such as Zelda and Ray, and was of concern mostly to prissy moralists who loved to pronounce judgement on other people's lives based on the view from outside. Superficial morality for superficial people.

Keane was good-looking, medium height. Ten years ago, his hair had been dark, with touches of grey, but he could easily have dyed it light brown. The beard would have been easy to grow, too, and a thinning hairline is natural for some people with the advance of years. The art book also made sense. Whatever he was up to now, ten years ago Phil Keane had been an art expert, not to mention a forger of provenances, and there was no reason to believe that his interest in art had lessened as his climb up the slippery pole of criminality had taken him higher and higher. So was Keane/Foley involved in sex trafficking now? It wouldn't surprise Banks. Even Zelda had pointed out early on that his document-forging skills would be every bit as useful in the world of people trafficking as in his previous enterprise.

The Bach finished, and Banks switched to Xuefei Yang playing music by Debussy, Satie and others arranged for guitar. How he wished he could play like that. He hadn't tackled any classical pieces yet. Truth be told, he hadn't even got beyond Bobby bloody Shafto in Bert Weedon's *Play in a Day*. That and holding down a playable G chord without breaking his little finger were pushing the limits of his patience and endurance these days. But he would get back to it.

The train rattled past the Darlington Arena and into the train station. The barriers were open, and Banks walked down the ramp and under the tunnel, then back up to the car park opposite the station exit, where he had left his car that morning. Behind the car park, a cattle auction was in progress, and he could hear the auctioneer's calls.

He was thankful, as always, to see the Porsche was undamaged. After half an hour of motorway driving, it was also a pleasure to turn off into the Dales along a winding road, lined with trees that opened every now and then on the magnificent vistas of rolling green hills dotted with bright yellow squares of rapeseed. And soon he was pulling up on the crunchy gravel in front of Newhope Cottage in Gratly. The sense of relief he felt as he turned his key in the door was only partly drowned out by the worries resulting from his conversation with Burgess, and where they might lead him.

It was the first time Gerry had visited Blaydon's house since she and Banks had found his disembowelled body floating face down in the indoor swimming pool. She felt some trepidation as she wound along the long drive towards the open area in front of the Tuscan-style grounds. When she turned off the engine and got out of the car, she felt the silence weigh down on her. The fountain out front was still turned off, the cherubim and seraphim surrounding the stone pond dry. Last time, she remembered, there had been a dead bird floating in the brackish water. That was gone now, and the water was covered in a greenish scum. The topiary was grotesquely misshapen, deprived of a gardener's ministrations, and the trellised arbours and wisteria groves overgrown with weeds, the roses in the rose garden all dead. Bindweed wrapped itself around whatever vegetation there was, strangling it, sucking the life out of it. Long shadows of trees fell over the gardens.

The bland house itself towered over her, three storeys of lime-stone, brick and stucco, with gables, shuttered windows and a low-pitched slate roof, its facade like a crudely drawn face. Gerry remembered the beginning of a film she had seen years ago with her parents, who loved old black-and-white movies, especially horror movies. She couldn't remember the plot or the title, but it was something about a house being insane, and the idea had terrified the twelve-year-old Gerry so much that she had experienced nightmares about it. Had Blaydon's mansion taken on the essence of things that had happened inside it? Was this house insane? She told herself not to be so silly.

The heavy front door was locked, and police tape warned any prospective trespassers to keep away, along with a lone constable on guard duty, having a quick smoke. Gerry knew that the house was still an official crime scene and that the CSIs and various scientific support officers came back to check on things from time to time. But there was no one else around today, except the bored constable, who checked her warrant card and had her sign his clipboard. She walked up the steps of the porch, with its stone columns, and gave a little shudder as she put her key in the lock and opened up.

Her footsteps echoed in the high-ceilinged entrance hall. She paused to gaze at the gilt-framed paintings on the wain-scotted walls – a stormy seascape, harvest time, eerily lit docks at night. She was here to find and check out the room where the rape had been filmed, so she moved on through the corridors, following the diagram she had brought. Eventually she found it.

The small bed had been stripped and even the mattress taken away for forensic examination. The lampshade where the camera had been hidden had been removed, too, leaving a bare bulb. Gerry turned it on as the room had no windows, just as she had expected. A fairly wide-angle lens would capture the whole bed from above, but only from that one perspective.

Gerry took some photos with her mobile. She was certain that the CSIs had been through the room and left nothing behind, but she looked around in any case – under the skeletal bed, in the empty wardrobe, in the drawers of the bedside table, also empty. As expected, she found nothing except traces of fingerprint powder here and there. It felt odd to be standing here, in the room where it had happened. She tried to imagine the poor girl's fear and panic, hoping only that whatever drugs the man had given her had dulled it to the extent that she hadn't suffered too much. Gerry remembered the final image of her half-naked body left among the tangled sheets, how the girl had turned on her side and curled up in a foetal position. Feeling a sudden surge of revulsion deep in her stomach, she turned and walked out of the door.

Before she knew it, she found herself standing in the doorway to the pool area. No traces remained there of Blaydon's gruesome death or Roberts's slightly less gory one, but standing there and smelling the ghost of chlorine brought it all back. Roberts had been over the other side of the pool, sprawled against the glass wall, which had been smeared with blood where he had slid down after being shot.

And Blaydon was like nothing she had ever seen before. At first, she had thought his body was some kind of sea monster from those old films she had watched with her parents. The water was tinged dark red around it, and a cloying sweet metallic smell mingled with the sharp chlorine. All she could make out was a dark tangle that looked like tentacles below the body, and his arms stretched out at the sides, like a cross. He was naked, and the whiteness of his skin stood out in contrast to the dark water. She shivered as she relived the sight.

But today, the bodies were gone, the pool empty, the sickening mix of chlorine, blood and severed bowels no longer cloying the air. Gerry hadn't expected to find anything new on this visit; she had just wanted to get a feel for the scene. But she hadn't expected it would have such an effect on her. She stood for a few moments until the waves of nausea and shock the recollection had brought on ebbed, then she went back to her car.

The drive was easy, with very little traffic, and Zelda made it to the airport with time to spare. With any luck, if her flight left on time, and if she took a taxi from Heathrow to King's Cross, she would be able to catch the last train home to Raymond. She felt nervous as she went through the immigration and security formalities. She had dumped the knife she hadn't used in a river on her way up from Purcari and was carrying nothing incriminating. She cleared all the airport hurdles without hindrance and settled back in her seat as the plane took off.

Zelda felt edgy and rattled, but she was glad she had handled Lupescu the way she had. Perhaps the guilt was enough, if he felt it as much as he had professed to do. A decent man with a wife and family didn't do what he had done and sleep easy at night. Perhaps it hadn't been so difficult at first to avoid thinking too much about what happened to the girls he picked out. They say some people lack empathy and can't imagine the suffering of others – the kind of thing that permeated Zelda's nightmares and kept her awake at night – and perhaps Lupescu was one of them. Maybe he did deserve to die, but that was out of her hands now; she would leave his fate to karma.

The plane landed and Zelda made her way through the busy terminal. If there was any air-conditioning it wasn't doing much good, because the air felt hot and sticky. When she got to the e-gate, she stepped forward when the green light came on, inserted her passport in the slot and looked up at the camera. It seemed to take for ever, and she began to feel nervous. Eventually the light turned red and her progress was barred. Her heart began to beat fast and hard. So much so that she was sure she was shaking. An immigration officer waiting on the other side let her through and led her over to a desk, where he pored over her passport and ran it through his computer.

The wait seemed interminable. Zelda did her best not to appear nervous, but there was nothing she could do about the beads of sweat on her brow. Perhaps Lupescu *had* called the police, after all, and they had informed immigration. Perhaps they were going to deport her. Or maybe it was nothing to do with Lupescu but something about her French passport, her settlement status. The hostile environment. She knew that she hadn't lived in France for long enough to gain true citizen-ship, or lived anywhere else for long since Chişinău, for that matter. But that wasn't her fault.

The real problem was her past. Danvers and Debs had certainly known that she had been a sex slave. How easy it would be for a hostile government department to translate that into the idea that she had worked as a prostitute. Definitely an undesirable alien. And much worse, she *was* a murderer.

Fortunately for Zelda, nobody knew about Goran Tadić, and the French authorities had even more reason for keeping the demise of Darius secret than she did. He had been pimp to a number of high-priced call girls, Zelda included, and had collected a great deal of compromising material on certain prominent French politicians, material that Zelda had been stealing when he had caught her, and she had killed him.

The fact remained that deep down she felt she didn't deserve to have a happy life in England with Raymond. Or anywhere. But she wanted it so badly. In her best moments she could justify what she had done – these were evil men who had done terrible things – but there were darker times, when her deeds haunted her and drove her to the brink of despair. Was the past to be her undoing? Could she ever get beyond it and remake herself into a decent, normal human being?

'What's the problem?' she asked.

'No problem, Miss. Minor glitch. The machine's sensitive.'

So am I, she was about to say, but stopped herself. These people weren't known for their sense of humour. She waited and chewed on her lower lip as the officer continued to study her passport and frown. He asked her where she'd been.

Zelda thought it should be obvious from her passport stamp, but there was no point acting the smart arse. 'Moldova,' she said. 'Chişinău.'

'What was the purpose of your visit?'

'Revisiting childhood places. I was born there.'

He gave her a sharp glance. 'How long were you away?'

Again, she thought of referring him to the stamp on her passport, but dismissed the idea. 'Three days,' she said.

'Not very long to visit childhood places.'

'It was long enough,' Zelda said. 'I had a deprived childhood.'

Oops. Nervous humour. *Big mistake.* But he simply failed to react. 'How long are you staying here *this* time?'

'For ever, I hope,' she answered, sounding as cheery and confident as possible. 'I mean, I live here.'

He didn't smile. He simply handed her passport back to her and said, 'Have a nice day.' She was going to inform him that there wasn't much of it left, but again her common sense kicked in before she opened her mouth, and she remembered that it was more sensible not to engage an immigration officer in conversation. Just get out of there. Fortunately, she had no checked luggage, so she could head straight for the taxi rank.

Not much more than an hour and a half later, she was settling into a first-class seat on a train heading north. Finally, she was on her way, though she was too tense to read. She still felt unsettled by her experience at immigration. Why had that happened? Was her passport flagged? Had Danvers and Deborah spread the word? Would the immigration police soon be knocking on her door in the small hours? Or would it be someone else, someone far more dangerous, who didn't even bother to knock?

She had got the passport quickly in Paris because her lover Emile had sway in the government, and because the powers that be had wanted both to reward her and get rid of her. So maybe it was dodgy, even though Emile had assured her it was genuine. But Emile was dead now, and she didn't think she could count on any further support from the French govern-ment. She had given them what they wanted, and they had no more use for her. She should count herself lucky that she had come out of it smelling of roses. There were times when she thought she was also lucky that they hadn't decided to have her eliminated instead. It must have been an option. And she clearly couldn't count on the British for anything, the way things were heading. But why now? She had used the

passport several times since she had been living in England
without any trouble at all.

Most of the journey she stared out of her window at the
slowly darkening summer evening and listened to one of her
three favourite symphonies. This time it was Tchaikovsky's
Pathétique, and as she listened and rocked gently to the train's
rhythm she thought about William Buckley, Vasile Lupescu
and her immigration fears. When the train arrived at York, she
felt better. It still wasn't quite dark. Midsummer evenings. The
longest day wasn't too far off. She breathed a sigh of relief as
she stepped on to the platform and walked to the taxi rank.
Home, Raymond, and peace at last, she thought, as the taxi
made its way along the A59 past Kirk Hammerton towards
the A1.

5

Over the weekend, Banks had given a great deal of thought as to how he might get Zelda to 'loosen up'. First of all, he ruled out an interview room, or even his office, as too formal. Moving on from there, he counted out the entire police station, which reeked of authority. She could never relax in such a place, and nor could he. In addition to the personal trauma Zelda had been through, Banks thought she was, like many Eastern Europeans since Stalin's days, genetically terrified of the knock on the door in the middle of the night. And of the police in general. To them all cops were the FSB, KGB or Stasi, whatever, but Banks thought he had forged a bond with Zelda and that if he approached her in the right way, she would feel more at ease.

Finally he decided on a long walk interrupted by lunch at the Relton Arms with its spectacular views of Swainsdale below its spacious beer garden, and Zelda had agreed over the phone. There was plenty of room in the beer garden to get an isolated table, and perhaps with a little strenuous walking, the heat of the sun and a cold drink, Zelda might let her guard down. As Burgess had said, if they believed she had done something illegal they would have her in like a shot and inter-rogate her as long as the PACE rules allowed. But she hadn't. She wasn't a criminal, as far as Banks knew, but a victim, and perhaps a witness – to something, at any rate.

Zelda arrived in Banks's driveway at the appointed time. He had taken that Monday off, leaving Annie and Gerry to deal with the Blaydon murder and its assorted spin-offs. He had watched the rape video once more over the weekend, still searching for the telling detail, something he might have missed, and all that had happened was that it had sickened him all over again. How on earth, he found himself wondering, could one human being do something like that to another? But he knew he was being naive; he, of all people, ought to have some idea. The thing was, he knew that men did it, but he had no idea why. Unless it was, as one serial rapist had told him: 'Because I want to. And because I can.' Could it be as simple as that?

Human beings did far worse things to one another than what he had just watched. Men routinely raped women during war, as a strategy to unman and humiliate their opponents and signal superiority. It had been going on ever since man climbed out of the primordial swamps, and it would probably go on until his presence on the planet was nothing but a vague memory lingering like an unpleasant smell with no one to smell it. But such thoughts were not for a day like today, and he tried to push them aside, knowing that they only led to that one dark and lonely place he had found himself inhabiting too often lately.

It was another glorious, sunny day, and a light, cooling breeze alleviated the heat to some extent, which was a godsend to walking in such weather. He hadn't seen Zelda in a while, so there would be plenty to catch up on. She was wearing shorts, showing off her smooth tanned and tapered thighs, and a white shirt tied at her waist, sunglasses hooked over the top fastened button. Her dark hair hung in a ponytail down her back.

'Will I do?' she asked.

Banks looked at her feet and saw she was wearing short white socks and a sturdy pair of trainers. 'You'll do,' he said. 'Stylish but road ready.'

They walked through to the back of the house, where Banks strapped on his small rucksack.

'What have you got in there?' Zelda asked.

'Just essentials. Chocolate, apples, bottled water, mobile, Ordnance Survey map, compass, Bluetooth headphones, a book, portable first aid kit.'

'Which book?'

'Flashman at the Charge.'

'We had a Flashman book at the orphanage once. Not that one. It was about the Indian mutiny. It was very funny. What's this one about?'

'The Charge of the Light Brigade.'

'"Onward, onward, rode the six hundred."'

'That's the one.'

'Is it dangerous, this walk?'

'Of course not.'

'We are not likely to get lost?'

'No. I've done it dozens of times before.'

'Are you going to ignore me and listen to music or read your book?'

Banks laughed. 'No,' he said. 'I realise it might seem odd to be carrying these things, but I usually walk alone, and I always pack the same stuff. Fresh water and chocolate, of course, but the rest is automatic. Just habit. Sometimes I listen to music, but mostly I prefer the sounds of nature when I'm walking. And sometimes I like to have a rest and sit on the grass and read for a while.'

Zelda put on her sunglasses. 'OK. Lead on.' They headed out of the gate and over the stile on to the footpath up the slope to Tetchley Fell. Single file, with Banks leading the way.

Tetchley Fell could be a daunting climb, deceptively easy at first, but soon getting tougher with every step as the incline steepened. To get to the top, beyond about twenty-five feet of almost sheer limestone, you needed a few mountaineering skills and some basic equipment. But they weren't going that far.

'What did Ray have to say when you told him we were going for a walk?' Banks asked over his shoulder.

'"Have a good time,"' said Zelda. 'He's been involved in a new painting project these past few days, and he doesn't come up often for air.'

'And you?'

'Between projects. Resting, as they say.'

They walked over a patchwork of fields, saving their breath for the ever increasing gradient. Sometimes they disturbed a group of sheep, which scattered at their approach and stood at a distance, backs turned, as if somehow that would make any danger go away. After a few more stiles, they paused briefly and sat on a drystone wall to drink some water, eat an apple and look back at the view.

Already it was stunning, the huddled limestone houses of Helmthorpe below, its squat church tower, high street shops with racks of postcards out front and tourists browsing. Beyond the town, the river Swain meandered through the flatlands of the valley bottom, lush and green, speckled with blue, yellow and purple wildflowers. Further out, the opposite valley side began its ascent, green at first, then culminating in the long grey-gold limestone edge of Crow Scar, like a skeleton's teeth bared against the clear blue sky, where only a few wisps of white cloud twisted through the air like chiffon scarves.

'It's magnificent,' Zelda said. Her cheeks were flushed with walking, and beads of sweat glistened above her upper lip and on her brow. Banks felt that he was sweating like a pig, and it took him a while to catch his breath. His ears were popping, too, though he didn't think they had climbed high enough for that.

'How's work?' he asked.

'They closed down the department. The others were all serving police officers – NCA, anyway – so they got transferred somewhere else, but I was just a civilian consultant, so my job simply ceased to exist. Made redundant. Unemployed.'

'I didn't know that,' Banks said. 'I'm sorry. I'd have thought they would want to keep a worthwhile department like that going.'

Zelda shrugged. 'Worthwhile has nothing to do with it. You should know better than anyone that it all comes down to budgets.'

'The NCA's never been short of cash, as far as I know,' said Banks. 'I doubt that's the only reason.'

'It's not,' said Zelda. 'Naturally the death of Mr Hawkins caused quite an upset, even though they say they don't suspect foul play. The temporary shutdown was the perfect excuse to cut the department completely.'

Banks passed her the water bottle. She tilted it and drank. Banks watched her throat muscles move as she swallowed. 'I don't think Danvers and Debs are convinced that there was no foul play,' he said, 'but they've got no evidence of any wrongdoing.' Zelda passed back the bottle. Banks took several swigs and a few deep breaths of fresh air, then said, 'Shall we carry on?'

Zelda slid off the wall. They were on the Roman road that ran diagonally down the hillside all the way to Fortford, which had been the main settlement in Roman times. It was a stony path, used as a drover's road now, and had low drystone walls running along both sides broken by the occasional farm gate. It was broad enough for them to walk side by side, which they did. Once they had to slow down when they got behind a farmer moving his sheep across the road from one field to another. He said hello to Banks and asked how he was.

'Do you know everyone?' Zelda asked when they had passed.

Banks laughed. 'Not quite. But it's surprising the people you get to know when you do my job.' He gestured over his shoulder. 'Take old Tibor there. He had some of his sheep rustled a while back. It was an organised gang, all over the county, so we were involved.'

'Did you get them back?'

'Not much chance of that. They were probably in Bulgaria by then. Or a butcher's shop window. Now we even have rustling gangs who butcher the sheep in the field in the dark and take only the meat.'

'How horrible,' Zelda said. 'Tibor? That's an odd name for a Yorkshireman, isn't it?'

'Tibor's family came over from Poland just before the war to escape the Nazis. We have a long history of immigration in this part of the world, quite a patchwork inheritance, a sort of international brotherhood of farmers. Working the land is a tough job.'

As they walked on, Banks noticed Zelda glance over her shoulder once or twice, as if to make sure they weren't being followed. Flies buzzed around their heads, along with the occasional wasp, but other than that, it was mostly silent save for their footsteps and a few birds singing. They saw rabbits running in the fields and, once, a hedgehog curled up among the wildflowers by the roadside. A curlew flew over their heads making its high plaintive trill, and Banks pointed it out to Zelda. Only one couple passed them, going the other way, giving the usual Yorkshire greeting: a nod and a grunt.

'Nice day,' said Banks.

The man pointed to the sky. 'Aye. Won't last, though, like as not.'

After about half an hour, Banks led the way over a stile and across a field to a winding lane. On the way, they got too close to a tewit's nest and set off a flutter of frightened and angry squeaking. They could see a cluster of low stone buildings ahead, and Banks pointed. 'Lunch,' he said.

Zelda wiped her brow with the back of her hand, smiled and said, 'In the nick of time.'

'Where did you learn your English?' Banks asked as they headed towards the Relton Arms. 'I'm not being patronising. I just mean you seem to have all the idioms and everything. Things people pick up over a lifetime.'

'I've always had a knack for languages,' Zelda said. 'I listen. Most of the nuns at the orphanage spoke English, and we had lessons from a very early age. I read a lot. When I was in London and later, at Raymond's commune in St Ives, I watched a lot of British television. Not so much now. But I write in English. I even *think* in English.'

'I had more than enough trouble learning French at school,' Banks said.

'Oh, French is easy.' Zelda put her hand to her mouth. 'Sorry. I didn't mean to boast.'

'No, it's all right. I just wish I had your language skills, that's all. I'm envious.'

They entered the tiny hamlet of Relton, halfway up the hillside, passed the small general store with its Walls ice cream board propped outside and approached the whitewashed facade of the Relton Arms.

'Ah,' said Zelda. 'Now it begins.'

'What?'

'You know. The interrogation. The grilling. The thumbscrews. The rack.'

'What are you talking about?'

'Oh, come on, Alan. You didn't bring me all this way just for the pleasure of my company. You want something. I can tell. You've been edgy and evasive all the way here.'

Banks could have complimented her on the pleasure of her company, but decided it wasn't appropriate. 'I do have a few questions for you,' he admitted. 'But that's all. No thumbscrews. No rack.'

'Promise?'

'Cross my heart.'

'And you're not going to arrest me?'

Banks laughed. 'Should I? Have you committed a crime?'

'Don't joke,' Zelda said. 'I'm serious.'

'No, I'm not going to arrest you. Now shall we go inside and order some drinks and food? I could murder a pint, myself.'

Annie made her way past the flashing screens, and the pings, screeches, bangs and screams of a video arcade in full flight at school lunchtime. Negotiating the narrow path between the machines felt like walking the gauntlet, and with so much sunlight outside, she wondered why it was always so dark in these places. Lack of windows seemed to be the answer.

'Excuse me,' she mumbled, pushing her way through a cluster of lads from Eastvale Comprehensive busy splattering aliens into millions of pieces as they stuffed themselves with Greggs sausage rolls. They shifted only grudgingly, and Annie heard one of them whisper, 'Pushy cunt, she must be on the rag,' as she passed by. The others giggled. She chose to let it go. That wasn't what she was here for. She did, however, turn around and have a quick glance at the speaker, committing his face to memory. Satisfied she would know him if she saw him again, maybe smoking a joint down Casper's Wynde, she moved on.

It was turning out not to be her lucky day. Tommy Kerrigan was the only one in the cramped office at the back. The Stan Laurel of the two. She had hoped it might be his brother Timmy, who, though much larger and thereby taking up more valuable office space, was marginally more pleasant. At least he was civil and didn't give her the creeps the way the long, lugubrious pasty-faced Tommy did, with his milky eye and all. He looked like a cross between a funeral director and a vampire, and though nothing serious had ever been proven against him, he was known to have psychopathic tendencies. He also suffered from halitosis, which was definitely a minus in such a confined space.

There was room for one small chair on the opposite side of his desk, and Annie shifted some papers and sat down.

'Well, well, look what the cat's dragged in,' Tommy said. 'Detective Sergeant Annie Cabbot. We'll have to stop meeting like this or people will talk.'

'Detective *Inspector*,' Annie corrected him. Even his voice was annoying, Annie remembered. An affected southern drawl with a nasal edge of Geordie.

'Well, *pardonnez-moi*.'

'You should do something about your clientele,' Annie said. 'They're an ignorant bunch of yobs out there, feeding their faces and insulting your visitors.'

'They're not supposed to bring food in the arcade,' said Tommy. 'There's a sign. But what can you do? I'm short-staffed.'

'How's business?'

'Fair to middling. Not that it would interest you much.'

'Club running OK?' The Kerrigans also owned The Vaults, Eastvale's only nightclub, on the opposite side of the market square.

'Like a dream. Pleased as I am to see you again, Inspector, I'm a busy man, so if you could—'

But Annie beat him to it and slid the enhanced image of the young girl across the desk. 'Recognise her?' she asked.

Kerrigan examined the photograph and passed it back to her. 'Should I? It's not very good, is it? I mean, I probably wouldn't even recognise my own daughter from that.'

'What daughter's that?'

'Figure of speech.'

'So the answer's no?'

'Sorry.'

'Only she was present at one of Connor Blaydon's parties that we know of, the one on 13 April, and we know you and your brother were also there.'

'We did business with Connor, as I've told you. It's only natural we'd socialise once in a while.'

'The party looked like fun. I saw you and your brother in some poolside snapshots. There were home movies, too, shot secretly in some of the bedrooms.'

A flicker of alarm crossed Kerrigan's features. 'What movies?'

'Oh, you didn't know? Seems your business colleague's butler, Neville Roberts, liked to film Blaydon's guests having a good time. Too good a time, in some cases, if you know what I mean. And you should tell your brother about those thong swimming trunks. Nasty. Constitute a public menace, they do.'

'I don't know what you're getting at,' Kerrigan said, 'but even if we were photographed, unbeknownst to us and against our will, we did nothing wrong.'

'*Unbeknownst*, eh? That's a long word. Don't worry, you don't feature in any of the videos, unless you've already paid Roberts off for one. But you *were* there. Did Neville Roberts ever attempt to blackmail you? Did he have any video recordings to sell to you?'

'Blackmail? About what?'

'Those trunks of your brother's, for a start. And the drugs.'

'What drugs?'

'Or maybe you were in bed with an archbishop?'

'What the fuck are you talking about?'

'Never mind. Back to the photo.'

Kerrigan glanced at the image again and passed it back. 'I still don't recognise her.'

'Never seen her in here, or the club?'

'No.'

'Are you also sure you never saw her or anyone like her at Blaydon's parties?'

'There were always plenty of girls around. But not like her.'

'So you *can* tell something about her from the photo?'

'Enough to know that if I'd seen anyone vaguely resembling her, I'd remember, and I haven't. Most of the girls were ... well, models or escort types ... if you know what I mean.' He sketched an hourglass figure in the air. 'Shapely. Curvy. Definitely enhanced, in some cases, if not naturally well-endowed. This girl looks quite natural. You can tell that much even from this photo. So if that's all ...'

'Not quite, Tommy. How young were the girls at these parties?'

'You've seen the videos, so you should know.'

'Humour me.'

'They were all over the age of consent, if that's what you're getting at. Mostly in their twenties, I'd guess.'

'Check their birth certificates, did you?'

Kerrigan gave her a look. 'Oh, come off it. It was obvious. They weren't kids. Most of the girls were strippers and tarts, like, with big tits and legs up to here.' He lifted his arm. 'All right if you like that sort of thing, I suppose.'

Annie knew that Tommy didn't; he preferred young men, rough trade, if available. 'Heard of a woman called Charlotte Westlake?'

'Course I have,' he said. 'Charlie. She's Connor's personal assistant. Or she was. Took care of pretty much everything on the business side. Ran errands, organised events, booked entertainers. "Indispensable," he used to say about her. But she hasn't been around for a while.'

'Was there anything of a romantic nature between them?'

'Not that I ever noticed. But you never knew with Connor. I wouldn't put it past him.'

'What do you mean?'

'He played his cards close to his chest. Especially when it came to his private life. I couldn't even tell you which side he played for, if you follow my drift.'

'Is she married, this Charlotte Westlake?'

'Dunno. Never saw a husband around, at any rate.'

'Was she involved in any of the action?'

'Charlie? You must be joking. A bit of posh was our Charlotte, don't you know. Cheltenham Ladies College and so on. Didn't even like you calling her Charlie to her face.'

'What about Neville Roberts?'

'What about him?'

'What did you think of him?'

'To tell the truth, I always found him a bit creepy. You know, sly, shifty.'

Pot and kettle, thought Annie. 'Go on.'

'What's to say? Connor swore by him.' Tommy scratched his nose. 'I reckon he was a bit of a snob, Connor was. Liked the idea of having a butler, you know. Someone to keep the Aga burning. Though Roberts wasn't really a butler, more of a factotum.'

'*Factotum*,' Annie repeated. 'Good one, that, Tommy. Your command of the English language is definitely improving.'

'Fuck off.'

Annie stood up. The halitosis was getting to her. 'Turns out Mr Roberts was quite the expert in audio and video surveillance. As I said, he had a nice little sideline in filming Blaydon's married or respectable guests doing the naughty. Know anything about that?'

'No. But I'll tell you something for nothing.'

'What's that?'

'One or two of these "respectable" guests, if they found out they'd been secretly filmed, well, let's just say I wouldn't give tuppence for Roberts's chances.'

'Or Blaydon's, if they thought he was behind it?'

'Goes without saying.'

'Thanks, Tommy,' Annie said. 'You've been a great help. And if you remember anything at all about the girl in the photo . . .'

Kerrigan's eyes narrowed. 'Why's she so important?'

'We'd just like to talk to her. That's all.'

'You think she was a witness? That she saw what happened to Connor?'

'Like I said, we'd just like to talk to her.'

'It's those fucking Albanians I'd be after if I was you,' Kerrigan said as Annie turned to the door. 'You ask me, that's who did for Connor. Those fucking Albanians.'

'Mr Banks,' called the landlady Sally Preece when Banks and Zelda entered the Relton Arms. 'Nice to see you again.'

'You, too, Sally,' said Banks. 'Any tables outside?'

'Take your pick. What would you like to drink? I'll bring them out to you along with the lunch menus. We've got a lovely game pie on special today.'

'Drink?' Banks glanced at Zelda.

'I don't know,' she said. 'I'll have what you're having.'

'Right you are,' said Banks. 'That'll be two pints of Black Sheep bitter, then, Sally.'

'Can I have some water, too, please?' Zelda asked.

'Coming up.'

'You seem to know her as well,' Zelda said. 'What was that, a burglary?'

'No. It's just somewhere I come for a quiet drink sometimes on my walks.'

Banks steered Zelda towards the door that led into the back garden, a broad and undulating stretch of grass. Fortunately, there was no bouncy castle; Sally Preece didn't go in for family fun. They picked a table overlooking the valley, close to the low stone wall and a field full of sheep. The lawn was uneven, but they managed to get their chairs stable enough, and Banks didn't think their glasses would slide off the wooden table.

They didn't. Sally Preece arrived soon after they had sat down with the beers, water and menus on a tray and said to come back to the bar and put in the food order when they were ready.

Banks had thought a great deal about what to say, how to approach questioning Zelda. He hadn't come to any firm conclusions – a great deal of it had to be played by ear – but he had at least a general approach in mind, and he had already brought up the Hawkins investigation when they had sat on the wall.

'Why do I feel so nervous?' Zelda said, fingering her menu.

'You don't need to,' said Banks.

'Do you think I'm lying about something?'

Banks paused. 'Let me put it this way: I don't think you've told me everything. There's something you're holding back. Or some things.'

'Like what?'

'That's what I want you to tell me.'

Zelda lit a Marlboro Gold, and Banks took a long pull on his pint. It tasted especially good after the exertions of the walk. There's nothing like a good pint when you feel you deserve it.

Zelda tapped the menu. 'What do you suggest?'

'Depends,' said Banks. 'I'm rather partial to the steak and frites, myself, but I think it's going to be game pie today. You might want a salad or something.'

'Don't mistake me for Annie.' Zelda put the menu on the table. 'I don't like game, but steak and frites is fine with me.'

Banks went and ordered. When he got back, Zelda was stubbing her half-smoked cigarette out in the green ashtray. Her beer was still untouched, but the glass of water was empty.

'You might as well know,' Banks began, 'that I already know you walked past Trevor Hawkins's burned-out house and questioned the barman at The George and Dragon about him.'

'How do you know that?'

'It doesn't matter,' Banks said. 'The point is that *you* didn't tell me.'

Zelda turned sulky. 'I don't have to report to the police every move I make or conversation I have, do I? It's not a police state yet.'

Banks smiled. 'Not yet. But I thought we were supposed to be working together. Like partners. Remember?'

'I'm not your "partner",' said Zelda. 'That's Annie.'

'You know what I mean. You said you wanted to help us find Phil Keane.'

'You told me to be careful.'

'But you weren't, were you?'

'Well, I'm still here, aren't I?'

'Is survival your only criterion of success?' Banks immediately noticed the pain in her expression. 'I'm sorry. Maybe that was insensitive of me after all you've survived, but what I mean is, partners are supposed to share. Why didn't you tell me?'

'Because it was all so vague,' Zelda said. 'I didn't really find out anything that would help you. What I found only complicated the situation I was in to start with.'

'Then why don't you tell me about that now, and we'll try to make sense of it all? Together.'

Sally Preece walked across the lawn with their meals. They already had the condiments and cutlery on the table. Banks thanked her and she left. 'Better eat before it goes cold,' he said.

He immediately felt lucky that Zelda didn't tell him he sounded just like her mother. Then he realised she probably didn't remember her mother. Zelda sawed at her steak, head down. Banks took a few mouthfuls of pie and washed them down with beer. It was good, plenty of pheasant and rabbit, and a touch of venison.

'Let's go back a while,' Banks said. 'Remember that dinner Annie and I had with you and Ray up at your cottage late last year? Remember when you told us you'd seen a photograph of Phil Keane with someone you recognised in connection with your work?'

Zelda finished chewing a piece of steak. 'I remember.'

'You were going to keep an eye out for anything else of interest, but you never came up with anything.'

'That's right. What did you want me to do, make something up? There was nothing. Just that photograph.'

'Of Keane with Petar Tadić?'

'Yes.'

'But you weren't even going to tell me about that, were you? I heard it from Superintendent Burgess.'

'Well, if he's so all-knowing, why don't you ask him?'

'Zelda, stop being petulant. It doesn't suit you. Talk to me.'

Zelda pushed her half-full plate away and studied a spider spinning its web in the drystone wall beside her. 'All right,' she said. 'All right. I didn't tell you because I thought you'd be angry with me for pursuing it when you said I shouldn't. OK?'

'I'm not sure that's the reason.'

'What, then?'

'I think there's something else you're not telling me, but I think it shocked you more than you said it did when you saw Keane and Tadić together in the photograph. It was two worlds coming together, or colliding, and one of them was yours. You didn't want to let me in on that, did you?'

Zelda fingered another cigarette out of her packet and lit up. 'What if that's so? What Petar Tadić and his brother did to me is not an experience I care to remember so often.'

'But why the sudden interest in Hawkins? I didn't ask you to spy on *him*. How was he connected with all this?'

Zelda took a deep drag on her cigarette and blew the smoke out slowly. 'All right,' she said. 'I'll tell you. Something happened. I was going to tell you before, at Christmas, but I lost my nerve.'

'Why?'

'Because I thought I was on to something, and I thought you'd take it off me and go charging in like a bull in a china shop, scattering all the pieces.'

'You don't have a very high opinion of me, do you?'

Zelda smiled and touched his hand briefly. 'I didn't mean it that way. Just that, in my experience, when the police get fully engaged, as a force, as an institution, then they have their own rules to follow and justice isn't always done. Remember, I grew up in the Soviet bloc.' She paused, then said, 'I saw Hawkins and Keane together once and had reasons of my own for wanting to know what they were doing together.'

'And did you find out?'

'Not really. I'll admit I went a lot further than you wanted me to. That's another reason I didn't tell you. I followed Mr Hawkins after work on a couple of occasions. One time he went into a restaurant in Soho, and I waited in a pub across the street, where I could see the place. After a while he came out, and he was with two other people. One was this Keane, and the other was a woman I didn't recognise. I took some photographs.'

Banks thought he might like to see these photographs, but he didn't want to interrupt the rhythm of their conversation by asking for them. 'And then when you went to The George and Dragon, you found out that Hawkins had met Keane there, too? It was him, wasn't it?'

'Yes.'

'Christ,' said Banks. 'You found out that Hawkins was meeting with Keane, who you already knew was connected with Tadić and who had once tried to kill me. For crying out loud, why didn't you tell me? Or someone. Hawkins could have been selling NCA information to Tadić's gang. Or he could have been in trouble. You knew what Keane was. Annie and I told you. A killer. A pyromaniac. And you know Tadić, too, from painful experience.'

'Yes. I was curious, that's all. They parted company, and I followed Keane and the girl.'

'Where did they go?'

'Just window-shopping on Oxford Street. Then they got a taxi on Regent Street and I never saw Keane again.'

Banks just shook his head slowly. 'Another drink?' he asked.

Zelda gave him a thin smile. 'Some more water, please.'

Banks went to the bar and got himself another pint and Zelda a large glass of tap water. His head was spinning with information. What did all this mean? What might he have done if he'd known six months ago or more? But somehow, he didn't think Zelda's story was over.

She was sitting as he had left her, gazing over the broad valley, smoking. The spider was still spinning its intricate web beside her. 'I'll miss this place,' she said softly.

'You're going somewhere?'

'Oh, I think so, don't you?' She sipped some ice water. Her beer was still untouched. 'Thank you.'

'With Ray?'

As Zelda told him about her experiences with immigration and worries about the pre-settlement form, he sensed a deep sadness in her, almost a sense of defeat, as if she felt no matter what she did, what happiness she found, it was bound to be snatched away from her before long, either by sex traffickers or immigration officials. She went on to tell him about Danvers and Debs hinting that her French passport didn't quite cut it, and that her past actions left a lot to be desired.

'It hasn't happened yet,' he said when she'd finished. 'And if it's of any comfort, I don't think you'll be going anywhere. Not if you don't want to. Ray's a wealthy man. He can take care of you. It's not as if you'd be a burden on the state. You're not poor.'

'I don't want to be a burden on Raymond, either.'

Banks laughed. 'I hardly think that's possible,' he said. 'Ray adores you.'

Zelda flushed. 'I've made money from my work, too,' she said, then paused. 'I mean my art work. The jewellery and sculptures, maybe not original paintings, but some copies I have made for people. But I haven't paid tax. I haven't filled in the proper forms. Not ever. I just came here from Paris and started living in London, doing that pavement art thing and living in a squat with a group of other immigrants. I didn't register or fill in any forms. Then Raymond came along and . . . You know the rest. They'll get me if they want me. What is it they say? I'm *undocumented*.'

'Is that another reason why you didn't tell me anything? Because you're afraid of immigration?'

'You can't understand this if you are not a stranger here. How it feels. It might have put me on their radar. As it happens, this Danvers and his woman have done that.'

'No,' said Banks. 'You did it yourself. They were only doing their jobs.'

'Ah,' she said. 'There you go. You're all the same, covering each other's bottoms.' She stubbed out her cigarette viciously. Sparks flew. 'I did nothing to draw attention to myself. I just did my job, made sculptures and jewellery and lived a quiet life with Raymond.'

Banks couldn't help but smile. 'Calm down,' he said. 'Believe it or not, I'm on your side. And it's arses, not bottoms.'

'It doesn't sound like you're on my side.' Zelda sulked for a moment then drank some water. 'There's more,' she said. 'You might as well know it all. Do you want to hear?'

'Of course. Go on.'

'The girl who was with Keane.'

'Faye Butler.'

'My God, you know about her, too!'

'I heard just the other day. Burgess again. She was Keane's girlfriend back then.'

'I'd like to meet this Burgess who knows everything.'

'I don't think so,' Banks said. 'But he's on your side, too, or we wouldn't be here having this nice friendly little chat right now.'

Zelda put her head in her hands and sighed, then took a deep breath and ran the backs of her hands over her eyes. Her fingers were long and tapered, like a musician's.

'Do you know what happened to her?' Banks asked.

'She's dead. Murdered. I read about it in the newspaper.'

'Yes.'

'The waitress in the restaurant knew where she worked. I went back there and asked about her. She was a regular customer. After that it was easy.'

'You went and talked to Faye Butler at Foyles?'

'Yes. I thought I might be able to get to Keane through her, but I hit a dead end. They had split up. She hadn't seen him for months. She didn't know where he lived. He was going by the name of Hugh Foley. I would have told you then, honest, if I had been able to find him for you.'

'And that was it?'

'That was it. I know I was going against what you told me, but I thought that if I could locate Keane for you it would be good for us all. I would find the Tadićs and others like them and just maybe you would be able to arrest them. Maybe even Annie would start to like me, too.'

'Annie doesn't dislike you,' he said. 'She's jealous, that's all, and protective of her father. Forgive the amateur psychology, but her mother died when she was very young, and she's felt responsible for Ray ever since.'

'Must have been quite a life,' Zelda said with a smile. 'Feeling responsible for Raymond.'

Banks laughed. 'I should imagine it took a lot out of her. But things will improve. Believe me. She'll accept you in time.'

'Do you really think so?'

'I do.'

Banks finished his drink and they left with a passing good-bye to Sally Preece. They walked back to Gratly mostly in silence, with heavy steps, each lost in thought, and as he gazed on the rolling hills, drystone walls, grazing sheep and flimsy white clouds snaking across a clear blue sky, Banks had the strangest fleeting feeling that they were leaving some sort of paradise behind and danger lay ahead. He shivered despite the heat of the sun.

6

It was early that Monday evening, and Banks was pottering about in his garden out back to a soundtrack of Schubert lieder sung by Anna Lucia Richter when he heard a car pull up in front. Curious, he walked through the house and opened the door to find Ray Cabbot standing there, hands on hips.

'What the fuck's going on?' were Ray's first words.

Banks gestured him inside and shut the door. 'What do you mean?' he asked.

'You know damn well what I mean,' said Ray, following him along the corridor to the back door. 'You and Zelda. I might be an old hippie, but I can still knock you into the middle of next week.' He stood in the conservatory with his fists clenched.

'Calm down, Ray. Come on outside and calm down. Tell me what's up.'

'Zelda is what's up. As if you didn't know. She's upset. Ever since she came back from her talk with you this afternoon she's been in a right state. What the fuck did you say to her?'

'I can't see how that was anything to do with me,' Banks said. 'We talked, yes, but I didn't say anything to upset her. What did she say to you?'

'She wouldn't explain. She just said you interrogated her, humiliated her, as if she was a criminal. We had a row. Then she just went off to her studio and banged around. I've got a bloody lecture to give at Leeds Art Gallery tonight, so I left her there to stew. What's it all about? You must know something.'

'Ray, sit down.'

Ray sat on one of the spindly chairs around the table on Banks's lawn. Birdsong filled the brief silence, and Banks hoped it would help to inject an atmosphere of calm. 'Drink?' he asked.

Ray shook his head, then said, 'Go on, then. Just the one won't do any harm. Got any beer?'

'I think I might have a couple of bottles of Stella in the fridge.'

'That'll have to do, then.'

Banks went and fetched Ray a bottle of Stella and a glass of iced water for himself.

'Not indulging?' Ray asked.

'Just thirsty from messing about in the garden,' Banks said, then leaned forward. 'I didn't interrogate Zelda,' he said. 'We talked about some of the things she's done to help us find Phil Keane and where it led her. And some of the things she hadn't told me. Maybe I was a bit annoyed that she hadn't shared this with me before, but I can't see why it would upset her so much. I'm sorry if it did. She was a bit quiet and jumpy when she left me, but that's all.'

'What was it all about?'

Banks sipped some ice water. 'Believe it or not, Ray, I was trying to help her out. There are some cops down in London who would dearly like to talk to her about various things, but an old mate gave me the chance to get in first. The softer option. Believe me, they wouldn't have been as easy with her about it all as I was.'

'About what?'

'I can't tell you that. But take it from me – Zelda may have made one or two foolish moves, but as far as I know she hasn't committed any crimes.'

'Well, thank the Lord for that.' Ray buried his face in his hands. 'I don't know,' he said. 'She's been having a hard time lately. I'm worried as hell about her.'

'But why? I thought things were going well for you.'

'They are. Or so it seemed. I don't know what it is. That's why I – I'm sorry, I shouldn't be blaming you. I just thought you might have an explanation for her moods.'

'What moods?'

Ray slouched in his chair and guzzled beer from the bottle. Banks listened to a blackbird singing and admired the view of Tetchley Fell while Ray collected his thoughts. He could make out a couple of tiny figures way up on the top of the fell, walking the edge. Banks had been up there on a number of occasions and remembered how pure the air was and how invigorating the exercise. Even a climb as far as the Roman wall, where he had gone that morning with Zelda, was exhilarating.

Ray took some Rizla papers from his pouch of Drum and rolled a cigarette. He glanced up at Banks as he did so and said, 'Just tobacco.'

Banks shrugged.

Ray lit the cigarette with a disposable lighter. Condensation was forming on his bottle, pooling at its base on the table. Banks hadn't seen him for a few days and thought he was looking tired. Even so, you'd never think he was in his seventies, despite the straggly grey beard, bandana and grey hair tied back in a ponytail. He resembled Willie Nelson, but with fewer wrinkles. Normally he had the drive and energy of a man twenty years younger, but not today.

'Come on, then. Give,' Banks said. 'What's up? What's the real reason you wanted to see me, apart from the pleasure of knocking me into the middle of next week.' Banks could hear faint strains of Schubert's 'Das Heimweh' coming from inside the cottage. Ray was clearly too distracted to notice or he would surely have made some comment on the choice of music.

Ray looked sheepish. 'Sorry about that,' he said. 'Bit of hyperbole. I'm a pacifist at heart.'

'Not to worry. Is it a police matter?'

'With Zelda? Maybe. I don't know.'

'Tell me, then.'

Ray took a drag on his cigarette and a pull on his beer. 'She's got something on her mind, Alan,' he said. 'This past month or so, ever since I got back from my big American trip. Since she got made redundant. She's been distracted, paranoid, jumpy, on edge. Anxious. She disappears into her studio for ages.'

'She said the same about you.'

'That's different.'

'Any idea what the cause is?'

'Not really. I've been thinking it might have something to do with Immigration Enforcement. You know she has to apply for this pre-settled status because she's been living here under five years? Can you believe it? She has to fill in some long form, and it's been giving her a lot of grief. They want stuff like P60s or P45s, utility bills, council tax receipts, passport stamps, proof of where she's been and when, bank statements and so on.'

'Well, surely that's not a problem? The NCA would be able to supply details of her employment.'

'She thinks they'll just wash their hands of her now the unit's been shut down.'

'No. They don't work like that. Besides, she should still have plenty of evidence to show how long she's been over here.'

'Everything's in my name,' Ray said. 'The payments just come out of the bank automatically. Before we met she was practically living on the streets.'

'Surely they would understand that?'

'You and I might think so. But she's been trying to live under the radar.'

'She said the same thing, but I didn't understand why.'

'Circumstances. It's partly her past, the Soviet legacy. Lists, interrogations, secret police, all that sort of thing. It's anathema to her. She's got a dodgy French passport, but she's from Moldova. I didn't know it, but Moldova isn't even a member of the EU. That means she's not technically an EU citizen. She's not sure how well her French passport would hold up to scrutiny. She assures me it's not forged or anything, it's the genuine article, but she's still not comfortable about it. I try to talk her down, you know, tell her not to worry, but it's not easy. She's convinced they're looking for a reason to chuck her out of the country, especially now she's unemployed. And not only because of all this Brexit rubbish. She thinks those two coppers who hassled her about her boss's death are behind it, took a dislike to her, dug into her past and didn't like what they found.'

'Paul Danvers and Deborah Fletcher? Yes, I got an inkling she wasn't too happy with them when we talked this morning. They've got nothing to do with Immigration Enforcement.'

'Zelda's got a bee in her bonnet about them. Thinks they're all in cahoots. Like I said, she's been acting paranoid. She thinks people are following her. She said they know things about her past, about the sex trafficking and all, and they could make it seem like she was a prostitute, an undesirable alien. She doesn't like to talk to me about the old days, so I don't push it. Oh, I know the big picture, what happened to her, and I know something big happened in Paris that changed everything, but I don't know what. Even when I can get her to talk about the past she's vague about it. Always skimpy on the details. Croatia, too, and Serbia.'

'You can't blame her, can you?' said Banks. 'The things that happened to her. She probably wants to forget, put the past behind her as best she can, the way our parents did with the war. It just sounds like she's having a bout of uncertainty and anxiety, what with Brexit and losing her job. I'm sure it will work itself out in time.'

'Easy for you to say.'

'Maybe she'll run into problems with Immigration Enforcement and maybe not,' said Banks. 'I've heard the Home Office can be pretty nasty when they want. Or even stupid. Sometimes they don't do anything when they really should. But it's not as if she's likely to be a burden on the state, is it, even if she is unemployed? And she did work for the government. They owe her something. Think about it. We're not exactly a nation without a heart.'

'I wouldn't put anything past those fascist bastards these days.'

'Ever the sixties firebrand, Ray.'

'Someone has to be.'

'I read the *Guardian*, too, Ray, but I don't take it that seriously. Maybe you should try the *Mail* or the *Telegraph* as well and get a different perspective, figure out perhaps the truth lies somewhere between.'

'Traitor. I think I'll stick with *Private Eye*.'

Banks laughed. 'There you go again.'

'She's even been talking about wanting to move to Italy or Greece.'

'And you?'

'I love Italy and Greece, but I love Britain more. It's my home. Besides, I just moved from Cornwall to Yorkshire. I don't want to move again. I'm too bloody old. And there's Annie to consider. We've had a couple of arguments over it, Zelda and me.' He paused and rolled another cigarette. 'But if they treat her badly . . . I've considered getting an Irish passport, you know, to make travel easier if we do have to move or spend more time out of the country.'

'How can you do that?'

'My mother was Irish. Annie's grandmother. Country girl from County Clare.'

'I never knew that.'

'Hell of a woman,' said Ray. 'Tough as nails. Ask Annie. They adored one another.'

'I will.' Banks drank some more water. It was already too warm. 'I really don't think Immigration Enforcement are after Zelda, though I could be wrong. They don't confide in me. More likely it's just a figment of her imagination.'

'Is there any way you can find out? Put our minds at ease.'

There was one way Banks could think of: ask Dirty Dick Burgess.

'I'll see what I can do,' he said. 'In the meantime, just try to carry on as normal. Whatever her problem is, she needs your support more than ever.'

Charlotte Westlake lived on a quiet tree-lined street of large detached houses in Adel, near Alwoodley in North Leeds. Gerry parked the car on the opposite side of the street, and she and Annie walked up the path by a well-kept lawn surrounded by colourful flower beds. It was early Monday evening. The house itself, half hidden by a fat old oak tree with a gnarled trunk, was an ordinary enough combination of stone and red brick, with a bay window on the ground floor and a dormer in the slate roof.

Annie rang the bell, and a few seconds later a woman answered. She was casually dressed in tight-fitting designer jeans and a white fuzzy top with a scalloped neckline. She was slender and tanned with expensively coiffed blonde hair tumbling in bouncy corkscrew waves over her shoulders. Sometimes Annie found herself wondering why some women paid a fortune to arrange their hair in exactly the kind of tangled mess her own naturally aspired to. This was one such moment. Annie pegged Charlotte as about forty, with smooth skin, high cheekbones and the kind of figure she would have had to work out at the gym at least three times a week to maintain. Annie felt immediately aware of her own failed determination to lose the ten pounds she had put on recently.

They showed their warrant cards, and Charlotte Westlake invited them in. Annie noticed gold embroidery around the shield-shaped back pockets of her jeans as she led them through to the back of the house. A glassed-in area like a conservatory, but still an integral part of the large open-plan living room, it overlooked a lush and rambling garden, complete with birdbath and gazebo, on to Adel Woods, a vast expanse of woodland, open meadows and heathland popular with walkers, cyclists and joggers.

'What a lovely view,' said Annie.

Charlotte inclined her head regally. 'Yes,' she said. 'One never tires of it, no matter what the season. Please, sit down.'

Annie and Gerry sat in comfortable armchairs facing the windows, and Charlotte sat opposite them.

'Can I ask you what this is about?' she said.

'Of course. It's to do with Connor Clive Blaydon.'

'Ah, yes. Poor Connor. Such a sad loss.'

Annie was surprised by the comment but held her tongue. As far as she was concerned there was nothing 'poor' about Blaydon, and he was no great loss to humankind. 'We understand you were Blaydon's personal assistant,' she said. 'What exactly was your role?'

'Just what you'd expect, really. Pretty much whatever came up. I helped him organise his busy schedule, reminded him of appointments and meetings and so on. Fielded requests I thought he wouldn't want to be bothered with. Smoothed ruffled feathers, oiled creaky wheels, calmed troubled waters.'

'Good Lord,' said Annie, 'I wish I had someone like you to organise my life for me.'

Charlotte laughed. 'Maybe you should try it?'

'On a copper's salary? You must be joking. What about Blaydon's parties?'

'Them, too. Invitations, catering, drinks, performers some-times – you know, a string quartet, DJ or a rock band, that sort of thing. I used to be an events organiser. Am again, as a matter of fact.'

'Do you have any of these old invitations?' Annie asked.

'No. I'm not speaking literally, you understand. I didn't exactly address envelopes and lick stamps. We never sent anything by post. It was all fairly casual. Connor would give us a list of names, then my secretary would either phone, text or email.'

'Pity,' Annie said. 'Do you remember the names of any of the people who attended?'

'It varied. I remember some of the more famous people, of course, and I can name you a few media people and local politicians. Tamara took care of most of it.'

'Tamara?'

'My secretary.'

'Is she still around?'

'I suppose so. She lives in Eastvale, I think.' Charlotte paused. 'Why do you want to know? The parties *were* pretty exclusive, but some of the most valued guests brought friends or colleagues, business people they wanted to impress. You could hardly refuse them entry. And there were gatecrashers on occasion, or people who had fallen out of favour trying to sneak back in. I suppose what I'm saying is there's no real written record of everyone who attended them. There was a lot of word of mouth. Connor's parties were very popular, sort of like an exclusive luxury nightclub.'

'I'll bet they were,' said Annie. 'Who manned the door?'

'Roberts. He could be quite diplomatic when required to be.'

'Did you usually attend?'

'Me? Hardly ever. My job was done by the time the parties started. I had staff members working behind the scenes making sure everything went smoothly, and some making sure everyone's drink was topped up, the canapés didn't run out and nobody was stuck alone in a corner. They chatted with guests, worked the room, helped make people feel at home.' She laughed. 'Glorified waitresses, really. I was usually in touch by phone over the evening in case there were any glitches, but there rarely were. Sometimes I'd drop by if there was a special event, like live music I wanted to hear, or a theme night.'

'Theme night?'

'Yes, Connor had themed parties, too, sometimes.'

'Fancy dress?'

'Sort of. Roman times, sixties, twenties flappers, that sort of thing.'

'Fancy dress and period behaviour?'

'Who knows what they got up to? If I did drop by, it would never be for long.' She twisted a ring on her middle finger. 'And certainly not to spy. Why are you asking me all this? What's going on?'

'Who made sure that the cocaine dishes remained full?' Gerry asked.

'So that's it.' Charlotte spread her hands. 'I'd be a liar if I said that I didn't know there were drugs around, just as there were sexual favours being given, and taken, but I can assure you I had nothing to do with either. I've told you. My work was behind the scenes.'

'Boys will be boys,' Annie said.

Charlotte shrugged.

'But were you ever present when drugs were taken?' Gerry asked.

'Surely you can't arrest me for that?'

'I'm sure we could find a charge without resorting to making something up if we wanted to.'

'Connor *was* my employer,' said Charlotte. 'It wasn't my place to criticise his habits. You may judge me wealthy on the basis of this house, but I'm not a rich woman. I needed to work. Still do.'

'You mentioned events organising?' Annie said, in a move to get Charlotte off the defensive.

'That's right. I'm a partner in an events organising company.'

'What kind of events?'

'All sorts. Mostly corporate. Product launches, gala dinners, parties, retirement dos, presentations, AGMs, conventions. You name it. Pretty much anything except weddings. I hate weddings. They're too much of a nightmare, and there are plenty of other companies around to deal with them.'

'How did you get into the business?'

'I suppose I drifted there. It was something I found I had a knack for – finding the right venue, the right band or DJ if either was required, working with a chef on a menu, keeping costs down – whatever was required.'

'Was that your background?'

'Good heavens, no. I was fortunate enough to attend Oxford. I studied Economics and Management at St Hilda's. I suppose you could count that as a bit of a background.'

'Cheltenham Ladies College?'

Charlotte laughed. 'Where on earth did you get that idea? No, nothing like that. Just a Halifax comprehensive. Though I did get a scholarship.'

'So you went into the business straight from university?'

'Not quite. After three years of studying I felt I needed a break. Let my hair down. I went travelling with some like-minded uni friends.'

'Where did you travel?'

'All over. First the Far East. Thailand, Vietnam and Cambodia. Then we spent some time bumming around the Mediterranean.'

'Sounds exotic. Are you married?'

'Widowed. Five years now. Leukaemia.'

'Yet you still live here alone?'

Charlotte played with her ring again and glanced around the room. 'In this huge mansion. I know it's too big for me, but I couldn't bear to leave,' she said. 'I know it would make sense. I could sell this place for a tidy sum, buy a nice little flat in Headingley or somewhere and live off the profit. But it's my home. Gareth and I lived here all our married life. And it's mortgage-free now. I can just about afford the upkeep as long as I keep working.'

'How long were you married?'

'Just ten short years, but I wouldn't change them for anything.'

'How did you come to work for Mr Blaydon?' Gerry asked.

'I helped organise a gala dinner for him when I first got in the business. I'd known him vaguely on and off for a while. He used the company I worked for before frequently for his business events.'

'So you go back a long way?'

'Well, not *that* long,' said Charlotte. 'I'm not that old.'

'Was he a friend of your late husband's?'

'No.' Charlotte paused. 'Truth be told, Gareth disapproved of him, of his business practices.'

'It's true they left a lot to be desired,' said Annie. 'But you gave up event organising to become Blaydon's PA?'

'I needed a break, a change. A challenge, even. It seemed like a good opportunity. After Gareth died I had what you might call a fallow period. I needed to get back to work. Connor offered me a job. There was a fair bit of foreign travel involved, which I enjoy, and the duties weren't too onerous.'

'Where did the foreign travel take you?'

'All over. Sometimes Connor had parties or business meetings at his villa on Corfu. I organised meetings in America sometimes, and a convention once in Cape Town.'

'Sounds like fun,' Annie said.

'Yes. I enjoyed it.'

'Did you ever meet someone called Leka Gashi in your travels?'

'That animal? Towards the end, Connor was mixing with some seriously undesirable people. He said they were important to his property development plans, but if you ask me, they were just using him.'

'For what?'

'Contacts, mostly. He'd built up a lot of contacts within the community and the establishment over the years.'

'What about money laundering?' Gerry asked.

'I don't know anything about that.'

'I understand that he invited people from all walks of life to his parties,' Annie said. 'At least the higher walks. Judges, senior police officers, politicians, clergy, actors, footballers, the odd rock star or two.'

'Connor collected people. And he liked to be among the movers and shakers, the stars and entrepreneurs. He liked to be seen with them. Photographed.'

'And Gashi?'

'He wanted to appear respectable. I would have said it was impossible for a man like him, but he thought that with Connor's contacts and prestige, some of it would rub off on him. Like the others, he probably thought that knowing Connor would make him appear respectable.'

'But instead some of Gashi's criminality rubbed off on Connor?'

'I don't know about that. I wasn't his business manager. He had other people to deal with all that stuff. I never saw him do anything illegal. I just didn't like Gashi. He was a crude pig of a man.'

'Was he sexually aggressive?'

'Not towards me, except with his eyes. But I would imagine so, yes. He was a man used to getting what he wanted, no matter what.'

'As we understand it, they were old friends. Blaydon had known Gashi for years. Did you know that?'

Charlotte blinked and gave a brief shake of her head. Her hair danced over her shoulders.

Gerry glanced at Annie and raised an eyebrow. 'What about Petar Tadić?' she asked.

'Another of Connor's gangster friends. Fortunately, I didn't have much to do with him.'

'We think Tadić supplied the girls. What did you know about the sexual favours?' Annie asked.

'Nothing. That was purely Connor's domain. As I said, I did the food, sometimes the entertainment, the ambience, but the drugs and women were nothing to do with me.'

'You didn't help Tadić supply girls for him?'

'God, no. What do you think I am?'

'You must have known what was going on. Couples disappearing into bedrooms, girls hanging around naked by the pool.'

'I know there were always plenty of pretty girls about, models and so on, but beyond that I didn't inquire. And I was rarely present. It wasn't my business. I just assumed they were WAGs, as I believe they're called. Many of Connor's guests had beautiful models or actresses as girlfriends, and some of the wealthy and powerful men had young attractive wives. And the last time I heard, sex wasn't illegal.'

'Depends on how old the people involved are,' Annie said.

'And how willing,' Gerry added.

'Are you saying the girls were underage?'

'Some of them look that way,' said Gerry. 'Didn't you notice? Didn't you think so at the time?'

'Like I said, I wasn't there often. And when I was, I hardly paid them any attention. They were just decoration. I had other things to think about.'

'Of course,' said Annie. 'Like making sure everyone's glass was full.'

Charlotte stood up. 'I've had enough of this. I think you should go now.'

'I must say,' Annie went on, 'this seems rather naive of you, assuming they were wives and girlfriends. You don't strike me as a particularly naive woman. Didn't you feel uncomfortable, being involved with all those orgies? It wasn't what you signed up for, was it?'

'I told you, I wasn't around for any orgies. Maybe I was burying my head in the sand, not wanting to know why the women were there, or where they came from. But things changed, slowly, subtly. I was starting to feel uncomfortable with Connor's new friends and ways. When I first started three years ago, things were far more civilised, before Gashi and Tadić appeared on the scene. In fact, I left at the end of April, before . . . before Connor died. I had the opportunity to return to my old line of work in partnership with a friend.'

'Mrs Westlake,' said Annie, 'Connor Blaydon was murdered. He didn't just die. Someone helped him on his way. Let's call a spade a spade.'

'Gashi.'

'Why do you say that?'

'He seems like the sort of man who would do . . . that.'

'Kill someone?'

'Yes.'

'Did you ever hear him talk about killing people?'

'Good Lord, no. He wouldn't talk like that in front of me. But I'll bet you he was involved. Either him or one of his little gofers.'

'Can you help us prove it?'

'No. I told you, I was involved in getting back into events planning. I didn't like the company Connor was keeping, the way things were going. There seemed no more . . . moral centre, for want of a better term. Things were spiralling into chaos.'

'Fair enough,' said Annie. 'Please sit down again. We've got a few more questions.'

Charlotte sat down slowly but remained on the edge of her seat, as if she were going to get up and leave the room at any moment.

Gerry consulted her notebook. 'There was a party at Mr Blaydon's house on 13 April, this year,' she said. 'Were you present?'

'It's highly unlikely. As I said, I rarely attended. Let me consult my diary.'

'Would you do that, please? And while you're at it, perhaps you could also let us know where you were on 22 May.'

Charlotte left the room for a couple of minutes and returned with a large desk diary. 'No,' she said, holding it open for them to see. 'I thought so. I was out of the country the week of 13 April.'

'Where were you?'

'Costa Rica.'

'Costa Rica,' said Annie. 'Very nice. Why were you there?'

'Connor sent me. I was organising an international business conference.'

'Was that normal?'

'Perfectly. I told you my job involved a certain amount of travel. Connor was a partner in a new hotel complex development there, and he wanted to bring the investors together with the ideas men and the architects. They all needed to be wined and dined.'

'Naturally,' said Annie. 'Would you have any idea at all who might have been at that party?'

'I'm afraid not.'

'Who might know?'

'Someone who *was* there, I imagine. Maybe Gashi?'

'He was there?'

'Sometimes.'

'Ever heard of someone called Phil Keane? Might have been a friend of Blaydon and Tadić.'

'It doesn't ring any bells.'

'Hugh Foley?' Annie said, remembering what Banks had told her about Keane's relationship with the murdered Faye Butler.

'No. Sorry.'

'And the 22 May?'

'Nothing specific,' said Charlotte. 'Though I think we had a book award dinner to organise in Bradford. I remember it was towards the end of last month.'

'Would anyone be able to corroborate that?'

Charlotte gave her a puzzled glance. 'Corroborate? Why?'

'Would anyone?'

'Maybe. I don't know. I'd have been back and forth, setting things up. Someone might have seen me.'

Annie took the enhanced photo of the girl from the SD out of her briefcase and passed it to Charlotte. 'Do you recognise her?'

Charlotte examined the photo through narrowed eyes and passed it back. 'No, I'm afraid I don't. Though I'm not sure I'd recognise my best friend from that. She looks rather the worse for wear.'

'We think the girl was drunk and possibly drugged,' Annie said. 'And though the images are hard to distinguish, the video clearly shows that she was raped.'

'Raped!' Charlotte repeated. 'I don't know what to say. What video is this?'

'It appears that Blaydon's right-hand man Neville Roberts left a small collection of X-rated movies behind.'

'From the parties?'

'Mini spy-cams in the bedrooms.'

'My God. I had no idea that Connor filmed his guests without their permission.'

'Not Blaydon,' Annie said. 'Neville Roberts. Do you know anything about him?'

'Not much. He was a bit of a dark horse, clearly. I hardly ever talked to him. He was around often, yes, but he was a rather taciturn person, quite surly, and our worlds rarely crossed. He was more of a manservant, really, a sort of butler. Connor liked the luxury. But Roberts had nothing to do with Connor's business dealings.' She tapped the photograph. 'I have to say I've never seen anyone in that state at Connor's house. Not while I've been there.'

'But you're so rarely there,' Gerry reminded her.

'Yes. Even so. I always thought that whatever went on, they still remained fairly wholesome and civilised.'

'A sort of Playboy Mansion thing?'

'If you like. Not that I've ever been to a Playboy mansion.'

'You're doing it again. Pardon me, but isn't that a little naive? Especially as you mentioned things spiralling into chaos.'

'Perhaps. As I said, I *was* fast becoming disillusioned. Even so, I'm honestly shocked by that picture. This is appalling.'

'Hardly surprising,' said Annie. 'As I said, she'd just been raped. We have the whole thing on a MiniSD card.'

'No,' Charlotte whispered, hand at her throat. 'I still don't believe it. Did Connor do this?'

'Why do you say that?'

'I don't know . . . I . . . you said it was one of his parties, you're asking me about it . . . I don't know . . . I just . . .'

'Unfortunately,' Gerry said, 'this is the closest we can get to a likeness of the victim. As you say, it's not very good. And there are no usable facial images of the man involved. Was this an ordinary party or a themed one?'

'Ordinary, I think. At least I don't remember any mention of a theme.'

'You're sure you don't recognise her?'

'I'd tell you if I did.'

'She didn't work for you behind the scenes or anything?'

'I honestly can't tell from that photo.'

'We'd really like to find out who this girl is,' Annie said, 'and it goes without saying that we'd like to catch the man who raped her. If you remember anything, however insignificant it seems to you, please let us know.' She passed Charlotte a card. 'And we'd appreciate a list of names. Any guests you might remember, especially badly behaved ones, and the names and addresses of your employees who attended that party.'

'Of course.' Charlotte stood up again and touched her hair.

She showed them out and they saw her standing at the bay window watching as they got in the car. 'What do you think?' Gerry asked.

'For all her shock and outrage,' said Annie, 'I don't think she was telling us everything she knew.'

'I got the impression that she was holding back, too. Maybe I should have a look into her background?'

'And there was something else,' Annie said.

Gerry headed for the ring road. 'What?'

'She never even offered us a bloody cup of tea.'

'So you're absolutely sure no one from the NCA or Immigration Enforcement is following Zelda, or making enquiries about her past?'

'I told you, Banksy,' said Burgess. 'I'd know. And they're not. Danvers and Debs aren't convinced that Hawkins wasn't bent, but they don't think Zelda had anything to do with his death. They just want to know why she was poking around asking questions about him. What you've just told me about the Phil Keane problem should settle that line of inquiry for them. She was clearly doing it to help you.'

'Have they been talking to immigration about her?'

'Not their style.'

'So I can tell Ray there's nothing to worry about?'

'Yes. At least nothing that I know of.'

'OK. Thanks.'

'No problemo. See you later.'

At least he didn't say 'alligator', Banks thought as he hung up. Burgess's Americanisms were a bit hard to take sometimes, especially when they were archaic, too.

So that was that. First Banks had told Burgess the details of his talk with Zelda, then Burgess had told him how he was certain she wasn't being targeted. He would find time to pop by and see Ray and Zelda together tomorrow morning and give them the good news. If Zelda was suffering from paranoia about the immigration process, nothing he said would cure that completely, but at least it would set Ray at ease and put him in the right state of mind to be there for her.

It was almost eight o'clock. After the phone call, Banks got in his car and picked up a Chinese takeaway in Helmthorpe, and before doing anything else, he tucked into his spring rolls, chicken fried rice and garlic shrimps in the kitchen, drenching them with lashings of soy sauce and washing it all down with simple tap water.

It was another mild evening. After dinner, Banks took George MacDonald Fraser's *Flashman at the Charge* outside, along with a glass of Côtes du Rhône Villages, and sat in his lounge chair facing Tetchley Fell to read for a while.

At first, it was enough just to sip his wine and feel himself unwind as he gazed on the fellside with its criss-cross patterns of drystone walls and enjoyed the gentle breeze on his skin. The breath of wind took the edge off the heat and carried the sweet, dry smell of fresh-mown grass with it, along with a hint of wild garlic and mint. The green fields on the gentle lower slopes slowly gave way to sere grass higher up, where he had walked with Zelda, and finally to outcrops of grey limestone at the top like Henry Moore sculptures shining with an unexpected golden hue in the evening sunlight. Occasionally a sheep bleated way up on the hill, and the swifts made their graceful loops and spirals in the sky. There seemed to be fewer of them this year, he had noticed.

Often when Banks watched the aerial ballet, he thought of Bob Dylan's line about a bird never being free from the chains of the sky. He had also been recently discussing some of Dylan Thomas's poetry with his informal tutor, Linda Palmer, over Sunday lunches up at Low Moor Inn. As far as he was concerned, the jury was still out on the boozy, bardic Welshman, but he had loved the music of 'Fern Hill', whatever the words meant, and the line 'I sang in my chains like the sea'

had stuck with him. It was similar in meaning to the other
Dylan's observation, he thought.

But it didn't do to overanalyse too much. He had learned
that from Linda. Poetry wasn't something to be translated or
decoded into a 'message', the way it had been taught at school.
True, some poems were overburdened with learning and literary allusion, and they needed some level of exegesis, but most
poems meant what they said and said what they meant in the
best way, often the only way, possible.

It had certainly been an interesting day. First the walk with
Zelda, then Ray's angry visit. He knew that Zelda had gone
away annoyed at him for pressing her on matters she would
rather have kept to herself, no matter how hard he had tried
to be understanding. The thing was, he still wasn't certain
that she had told him all she knew. She was holding back
about something, but he didn't know what it could be. She
had told him only things she thought he already knew, or
might suspect. Yes, she had come clean about seeing Keane
with Hawkins and asking questions about her late boss, and
she had told him about finding Faye Butler, and how that had
led to a dead end. But had it? For some reason, he thought,
there was more. And he couldn't forget that Faye Butler had
ended up dead – tortured and murdered – not so long after
Zelda's visit to her.

Ray's concerns also worried him. It was natural enough that
Ray would see possible immigration and residence problems
as the main source of Zelda's anxiety and depression, but
Banks wasn't convinced. Yes, she was worried about being
deported back to Moldova, but he didn't believe that was all
that was worrying her. He remembered the times during their
walk when she had looked over her shoulder to make sure
they weren't being followed. Who else did she think was after
her? Her old abductors and abusers? But why? Surely they

had lost track of her by now. It was also unlikely that Tadić and his like would even remember Zelda, let alone recognise her after all these years. She was the super-recogniser, not him. But until she was willing to talk even more openly, he realised that he wasn't going to find out anything else. And he was still no closer to Phil Keane than he had been when Zelda had first mentioned seeing the photo of him with Tadić, before last Christmas.

Banks opened his book and slipped back into Harry Flashman's version of the disastrous Charge of the Light Brigade as he sipped some more wine. Colonial Britannia at her best. And so the evening passed, quietly and pleasantly as the sun made its way down in the western sky, below the hills, painting an abstract design first of grey and pink behind the slow-moving strata of long thin clouds, then of crimson, orange and purple under the darker, heavier ones. In the distance, a car's rear lights followed the winding road over Tetchley Pass into the next dale.

Banks sat on, sipping his wine and enjoying the nature show, until the evening's chill made him shiver and there was no longer enough light left to read by. Then he took his wine and moved back inside. He checked his phone to see if he had missed any messages. He hadn't.

When the evenings stretched out as they did in summer, he rarely watched television or movies, unless it was raining. He didn't even listen to much music. Sometimes he played the guitar Brian had bought him, wondering when he would get the fingering of even the basic three chords exactly right. And that reminded him: it was only two days until the Blue Lamps' farewell concert at the Sage. Tracy and Mark would be going with him, along with Ray and Zelda. It promised to be a fine evening. Maybe they would all manage to get together with Brian for a drink or two over the river afterwards.

He wondered how Tracy and Mark were getting on in Tenerife, where they had gone for their honeymoon. He was glad they had decided against a destination wedding, unlike so many other young couples these days. It was selfish in the extreme, he thought, going off to Cyprus or Malta to get married when half your family either couldn't afford to attend, or were too old and ill to travel. Healthy and independent as they were, Banks's parents wouldn't have been willing or able to travel so far for their granddaughter's wedding.

Tonight Banks felt restless for some reason, and he couldn't settle down with the guitar. He was sick to death of playing 'Bobby Shafto' but seemed unable to move beyond it. He searched through YouTube for interesting music and ended up watching a few Grateful Dead concert clips.

Halfway through a fine 'Scarlet Begonias', Banks's mobile played its blues riff. He was in half a mind not to answer, but habit kicked in and he put the TV on pause and picked it up. It was going on for eleven o'clock, and he always felt a tremor of apprehension when the phone rang so late. Had something happened to Tracy? Or Brian?

He recognised the number as Ray Cabbot's. Puzzled, he answered, but couldn't make out what Ray was saying at first. He asked him to repeat it, and this time it came through loud and clear: 'She's gone,' Ray said. 'It's Zelda. She's gone.'

7

Lit by Banks's headlights, the B-road to Lyndgarth unfurled like a ribbon over the moorland, passing by fast-flowing becks and grassy hillocks, until the lights of the village came into view, nestled in a hollow and scattered around the lopsided village green. It stood at the junction of Swainsdale and Lyndsdale, where the river Lynd joined the Swain. Just a couple of miles to the north, the valley sides rose steeply on either side to form two curved limestone scars. It never got completely dark at that time of year, and a three-quarter moon made the scars stand out like bands of light floating above the darkness of the valley.

Banks drove along the high street, beside the green, past the chapel, two of the village's three pubs and the Spar general store, then turned left and carried on west for another mile or so until he pulled up at the short turn-off for Ray Cabbot's cottage. All the lights were on. Ray must have heard the car coming, or seen its lights, as he was standing in the doorway smoking and waiting.

When they went inside to the living room, Ray stubbed out his cigarette and poured himself a generous measure of single malt. He offered the bottle, but Banks declined. Ray's hands were shaking as he lifted the glass to his mouth.

'I don't know what to do,' he said. 'I should never have left her.'

'Calm down and tell me what happened,' said Banks.

'I don't *know* what happened. All I know is she's gone.'

'There's no note or anything?'

'No.'

'What time did you get back from Leeds?'

'Around half ten. The lecture finished at nine so I headed straight back after a few questions. I was worried about Zelda. I told you we'd parted on bad terms. She was upset, angry. I wanted to . . . I mean . . .' He put his glass down and hung his head in his hands. 'Oh, Christ, Alan, what am I to do?'

Banks touched his shoulder. 'Try to stay calm, Ray. Did she take anything with her? A suitcase, clothing?'

'I don't know. I haven't checked. But her car's still here, round back.'

'She can't have got far then. Are you sure she isn't at a friend's house in the village? Or in the pub?'

'She wouldn't do that. I mean, she doesn't really have any close friends in the village. People are still a bit frosty. We do go to the pub. Mick Slater, the landlord, is a decent guy. But I don't think she'd go there by herself, especially not at night. You don't understand, Alan. When I said she was *gone*, I didn't mean gone as in she'd left of her own free will. I meant she's gone as in she's been *taken*.'

'How do you know?'

Ray jerked his head towards the back of the house. 'Her studio. It's a mess. Like . . . I don't know.' He put his hand to his chest.

'OK?' Banks asked.

'Fine. I just get a bit breathless sometimes, a bit of tightness in the chest, especially when I'm upset.'

'You should go see a doctor.'

'Bah. Waste of time.'

Banks brought him a glass of water from the kitchen, touched his shoulder and said, 'Stay here. Take it easy.'

Then Banks walked out back and across the stretch of grass to the large garden shed that served as Zelda's studio. The door was wide open and the lights on. Inside, there was enough room for her to set up an easel to paint, or tools to sculpt, and a workbench where she crafted jewellery, but not much more.

In the far corner, undamaged, stood a stack of canvases and sketches, mostly imitations of famous artists – Magritte, Modigliani, Hockney, Dali. They were good copies, though mostly unfinished. Zelda was a skilled imitator, but she wasn't a forger. She had never tried to pass any of them off as originals. On the other hand, if you wanted a competent version of *A Bigger Splash* or a Modigliani nude to hang on your wall, she could knock one off for you, for a price.

Banks saw what Ray meant about the mess. There had clearly been some sort of struggle near the door. A wine glass lay shattered on the floor, its contents splattered all over the threadbare carpet. The easel had been knocked over, paints spilled, a work in progress ruined, and Banks saw what he thought to be a smear of blood on the workbench, though he supposed it could be paint or red wine. There was a smell of turpentine and oil. On her workbench, Zelda had a small vice and set of tiny engraving tools for her delicate jewellery work. He leaned forward and examined the vice closely. There was no blood on it, and it didn't appear as if it had been used to crush her fingers or toes. That was something to be grateful for. Banks left the workshed as it was and went back to the main house.

'See what I mean?' Ray said. 'Someone took her against her will.' He was smoking another roll-up, taking short, nervous drags.

'Are you sure you didn't have a fight and throw stuff around and she walked out?'

'Of course not. Don't be so bloody silly. You saw the state of her studio. You surely can't believe *I* did that? Or Zelda herself? I told you we had an argument earlier, but not a stand-up, drag-down fight. I've never once been violent towards her.'

'It looks like there was some sort of struggle,' Banks said. 'Have you checked the rest of the house to see if she's hiding anywhere? Or hurt.'

'First thing I did. She's not here.'

'Let's check her clothes,' said Banks. 'You can tell me if anything's missing.'

Ray stubbed out the cigarette. They went upstairs and Ray led him into a small bedroom. 'This is hers,' he said.

'You mean you . . .?'

'We have separate bedrooms,' Ray said.

The room was neat and tidy and showed no traces of a struggle whatsoever. The walls were painted in pastel greens and yellows, hung with random sketches and paintings, and the duvet was burgundy. Banks and Ray searched through the wardrobe and drawers. When they had finished, Ray said, 'No. As far as I can tell, everything's where it should be. But I don't . . . you know . . . I didn't keep an inventory. I'm not saying there isn't a T-shirt or a pair of knickers missing. But she didn't have a lot of clothes. It seems normal to me.'

'What about the surrounding countryside? Have you been out searching for her?'

'No. I haven't had a chance yet. I phoned you pretty much straight away, soon as I'd seen the studio and checked the house.'

'We'd better have a look,' said Banks. 'She might be out there, not far away. She may have run off, or simply gone for a walk. She might be hurt. Trapped.'

'I never thought of that,' said Ray, jumping at the idea that Zelda might be nearby after all.

'Got a torch?'

They went downstairs and Ray fetched two torches from the utility room under the staircase. 'They're not much cop, I'm afraid, but it's all I've got.'

'That all right,' said Banks. 'The moon's pretty bright. We might not even need them.'

To the east of the cottage, a grassy slope ran down to the edge of Lyndgarth village, about half a mile away. It was a wide-open space and hardly a likely spot for concealment. As far as Banks could see, it was uninhabited. On the other side, however, the cottage stood on the edge of moorland which stretched for miles to the west. It was rough terrain, covered in heather and gorse, with a number of dangerous bogs, several wooded areas and deep gullies. The natural light was almost enough to see by, but they carried their torches in case they came to a gully or pothole. About a mile to the south-west stood the dark ruins of Devraulx Abbey, suitably Gothic and ghostly in the moonlight.

As they walked, they called out Zelda's name, but got only silence or the cry of a frightened bird in return. After a while, it became clear that they needed their torches to illuminate the tangle of roots under their feet, which slowed their progress.

After almost an hour's wandering with no success, they returned to Ray's cottage and flopped down on the living-room chairs. Ray rolled another cigarette and lit up again. 'What if she's further away, bleeding, or she broke her leg or something? Shouldn't we go out again? Further, this time.'

'I don't think it's very productive to start thinking along those lines, Ray. She's not bleeding to death. There was no great amount of blood in her studio, if it's even blood. And if she is out there hurt, it's a mild night, and she'll have no trouble lying low until morning. You know how quickly it gets light here in summer. By then I'll have a search party organised.'

'I can't help thinking something terrible's happened to her. Maybe she's unconscious. Or dead?'

'She'll be fine, Ray. Zelda's a lot more resourceful and resilient than you imagine. Think what she's endured over the years. And think about this: if someone wanted to kill her, or hurt her, they could easily have done it here and just left her body in the studio. Don't you think that's what they would have done?'

'Probably. But what's happening to her? Do you think someone might be hurting her?'

Banks knew that the worst thing about dealing with missing persons was imagining the terrible things they might be suffering, such as torture – right down to fingernails being pulled, teeth extracted, electrodes attached to private parts, limbs smashed, bloody beatings and, especially when women were involved, rape. There was no way of stopping such images for an empathetic person, which Ray clearly was. Banks felt empathy, too, but he had learned to control it over the years. Such imaginings could cloud his judgement and the procedures that had to be followed in these cases. The thing to concentrate on was finding the missing person alive and not to be distracted by what he or she might be suffering in the meantime. It was hard, but he had learned to do it most of the time. The fears only came back in the dark hours, three or four in the morning, when he lay awake and terrible images crowded his mind. Ray was already at that stage.

'There's no evidence that anyone harmed her in the studio,' Banks said, 'and I assume if it was information they wanted, they could have got it out of her there.'

'But who could have done this? Might immigration have taken her?'

'Well, for a start,' Banks said, 'they haven't yet stooped to abducting people from their homes by force. Even they wouldn't go that far.' Though even as he said it, he wondered. Certainly if someone put up resistance, immigration officers might use the same sort of force as the police would to make an arrest in similar circumstances. He still very much doubted that was what had happened.

'Do you think she might have been kidnapped?'

'Maybe. The thing is, we don't know. All we know is that she's gone and that it looks as if someone took her against her will.'

'I've got money. I can pay the ransom. Up to a point. I can sell more paintings.'

'Let's not get ahead of ourselves, Ray.'

Ray stood up and started pacing. 'But we have to do *something*. We can't just sit here.'

'I need to call it in,' said Banks. 'Get a team set up. Lines of inquiry. Time can be crucial in these cases, and we've already wasted too much.' He didn't want to tell Ray that most murders occur soon after a person goes missing. On the other hand, it had made sense to check the house and the surrounding countryside thoroughly before gearing up for a full missing person investigation. 'Did you touch anything in the studio?' he asked.

Ray shook his head. Banks hadn't either. He had deliberately kept his hands in his pockets.

'Did you leave it exactly as you found it?'

'Yes. The door was open, the lights on.'

Banks reached in his pocket for his mobile. Nobody would appreciate such a call in the early hours, but it had to be done. When he connected with the comms room he asked for the duty officer and explained in clear terms what had happened, stating that, in his opinion, Zelda had been forcibly abducted by persons unknown and that AC Gervaise should be informed at once. All patrol officers should keep their eyes open for a woman matching Zelda's description, which he gave them, with a little help from Ray. He also asked that they organise a search team for the immediate moors as soon as it was daylight, and have AC Gervaise alert the CSIs to come and search the victim's premises. 'And tell them to be careful driving in,' he added. 'There might be tyre tracks and Lord knows what else out there. Fingerprints and trace evidence in the studio.'

Ray sat pale and shaking as Banks talked on. When he'd finished, Banks put his phone away and made some notes about timing. 'You need to know they'll be a lot harder on you than I've been,' he said. 'The first suspect in a missing persons case is always the one who reports it, along with the missing person herself.'

'But you know I'd never do anything like that,' pleaded Ray. 'Isn't it obvious? I love Zelda. I could never harm her.'

'Doesn't matter what I think. And to an objective inter-viewer, it won't be obvious. People kill for love as often as they do for profit or hatred. You need to tell them absolutely everything you think will help us find Zelda. And I mean everything. Don't gloss over the row you had because think-ing about it makes you feel bad, or you think it'll make them suspect you more. Tell them. They'll also want to know her habits, haunts, friends and so on. Any problems or worries, too. Whether you thought she was having an affair. I know we think she was abducted from her studio after a struggle, and that's what it looks like, but she may have run off and gone to hide somewhere, or to be with someone. Maybe she wrecked the studio herself in a fit of rage, or she decided to disappear and the mess is a red herring or a cover-up.'

'She wouldn't do that,' Ray said. 'And there's nobody else. I'd know.'

'The point is that we *don't know* what happened. All we have to go on is guesswork. Just tell them what you know about the work she did and the people who abused and enslaved her. Her fears about Immigration Enforcement, her relationship with Annie. I know you say she didn't tell you much about her past, and it's possible I can fill in a few blanks myself, but tell them everything you *do* know. It may all be connected.'

Ray swallowed. 'What now?' he asked.

'I don't suppose you want to go to sleep?'

'No way. I need to stay awake. Someone might call. A ransom demand or something. Or maybe Zelda herself. Annie. My God, I should call Annie.'

Banks stood up. 'I'll do that,' he said. 'I need to talk to her. The officers should be here soon. I'll head to the station and start organising things from there.'

'No,' said Ray, reaching out and grabbing his elbow. 'Don't go. Stay here with me, Alan. Please. I'm at my wits' end and I can't be alone. I want you to head the investigation. I need to know you're on this a hundred per cent.'

Banks disengaged his arm gently. 'All right,' he said. 'I'll do my best. I don't think my being a friend will disqualify me from trying to find Zelda, and it may even give me an advantage in any search, but there's always a possibility my bosses might think I'm too close to things. I'll stay here for now and talk to the team when they arrive. There's one condition.'

'Anything.'

'Seeing as I won't be driving home for a while, you can clear some space on your sofa and pour me a large glass of that fine Highland Park right now.'

After he finished the whisky, sleep didn't seem to be an immediate possibility, so Banks left Ray and went to check out the studio again. This time he took a pair of latex gloves from the crime scene kit in the boot of his car so as not to disturb any evidence that the attackers might have left there.

First, he picked up Zelda's leather satchel-style shoulder bag, the one she always carried, from the chair. Its contents were as one would expect: mobile phone, keys, purse and cigarettes – but in addition she also carried a small digital camera, a black Moleskine notebook, a Kindle and a little white case of AirPods. There were a few other inconsequential odds and ends – paper tissues, tampons, a combination penknife/corkscrew, hairbrush, lipstick, a couple of rollerball pens and a charger for the iPhone.

Zelda had a desk in the far corner of the studio, which seemed untouched by the struggle, and on it sat her MacBook along with a small flat-top printer. Banks knew better than to touch the computer, even with his protective gloves on. The CSIs would rush it to tech support for a thorough check. It was easy to lose data inadvertently if you didn't know what you were doing, and Banks would have been the first to admit that he didn't. He wasn't tech-illiterate or a Luddite by any means, but the inner workings of the CPUs and vagaries of internal architecture and configurations of computers were way beyond his grasp.

He glanced over at the titles on the bookshelf above the desk. As he would have expected with Zelda, there were a lot of literary classics – Dostoevsky, Kafka, Dumas, Flaubert, Dickens, Hardy – along with an odd selection of children's books, mostly by Enid Blyton, Jacqueline Wilson and Roald Dahl, and a few Modesty Blaise novels by Peter O'Donnell. There were also, he discovered on further investigation, a half row of non-fiction books concerned with the stories of women trafficked and raped by terrorist groups such as ISIS and Boko Haram, especially Yazidi and Rohingyan women, including *The War on Women* by Sue Lloyd-Roberts, Dunya Mikhail's *The Beekeeper of Sinjar* and Nadia Murad's *The Last Girl*.

One of the desk drawers was filled with printer paper and spare cartridges, another with a selection of pens and pencils, rulers and other stationery items. But this drawer also contained some more personal items – photos of her and Ray in happier days, a few sentimental souvenirs from trips they had made together. There was a newspaper clipping about the discovery of Faye Butler's body, which made sense now that Banks knew Zelda had met Faye. There were also some official papers, including her French passport. It still had a few years left on it, and when he examined the stamps he noticed the most recent was from Chişinău, dated the previous Friday. He knew that was where she had grown up, and where she had first been abducted from, and he wondered what she had been doing back there so recently.

When he had finished, Banks stood at the centre of the room and opened the notebook. It wasn't a diary or a journal, but more of a catch-all. There were fragmentary shopping lists, titles of books she wanted to read, quotations from books she had been reading and memos to herself, as well as poems and story ideas, passages of self-analysis, descriptions of dreams and fantasies. There were also several lengthy descriptions of landscapes: an unnamed stretch of the Croatian coastline, the moorland around Windlee Farm, a view of London from somewhere on the South Bank near Blackfriars Bridge, a London hotel called the Belgrade.

There were flashes of memory, too, mostly bad – a vicious beating in Ljubljana, a john who threatened her with a knife in Pristina, a failed suicide attempt in Minsk. It made for harrowing reading. In addition, several pieces read very much like fantasies of revenge against people who had harmed her: a pimp in Paris called Darius, Goran Tadić and someone called Vasile Lupescu. These sections might also be notes towards a story, or stories, she intended to write someday. Zelda was an artistic type and a keen reader; perhaps she had ambitions towards fiction and this was a record of her imaginings.

Banks hoped the notebook might offer some clues to Zelda's whereabouts, and he would study it further for that very reason. But it also put him in a difficult position. At the moment, he was the only one in the possession of these private musings; if he didn't include the notebook with the rest of Zelda's possessions, he would be guilty of withholding evidence. But evidence of what? he reasoned. Fantasising about a murder isn't the same as committing one. Jotting down notes for a mystery story isn't a crime.

Besides, he couldn't, in all conscience, create more problems for Zelda when she was probably living in terror of her life. He would ask her about the notebook when he found her.

Without further thought, Banks slipped the notebook in the inside pocket of his jacket and went back to the main house.

Dawn broke early over Lyndgarth Moor, and by the time the sun was up, a semicircle of officers moved slowly west from the isolated cottage. Seen from afar, they could have been grouse-beating but for the police uniforms most of them were wearing.

Back in the house, Banks and Ray Cabbot sat drinking strong coffee with a fresh-faced AC Gervaise, who had only just arrived smelling of soap and shampoo. Banks had had a fitful night on the sofa and wondered if he looked as bad he felt, while Ray, he imagined, hadn't slept at all. His clothes were wrinkled, his eyes blurry and red. Two detectives from the Northallerton HQ at Alverton Court – DS Flyte and DC Bharati – had appeared with the search team and CSIs, and they had already questioned Ray. No wonder the poor bloke was exhausted, Banks thought.

No one was yet any nearer to finding Zelda or to working out what had happened to her. She hadn't been seen by any of the night patrols, and though her description had gone out nation-wide, the general thinking was that she couldn't be that far away. No one would want to risk a long journey with a kidnapped woman and all the possible encounters with police cars and CCTV cameras that might occur. Whoever took her had probably planned it all out in advance and had a place already prepared somewhere in the Dales. Perhaps a deserted farmhouse or ruined barn, Airbnb, or a remote cottage rental. It wasn't as if there was any scarcity of isolated spots and abandoned buildings out there. It depended on what her abductors planned to do with her, of course. And when they planned to do it.

The CSIs agreed there had been a struggle in the studio but found no immediate evidence of harm being done to Zelda. The suspect bloodstain turned out to be paint. They were still working out there, collecting trace evidence, fingerprints and anything else that seemed relevant. The search team had first gone through the house and grounds, even though Ray assured them he had already done so. They were just doing their jobs, Banks told him, and it paid to be thorough, but Ray complained anyway. He must have smoked a whole pouch of Drum, and the front room stank of smoke.

One positive outcome was that the CSIs were able to determine the direction in which a car had travelled by the pattern of fresh tyre tracks – and it had turned on to the moorland road, an unfenced track, heading westward, deeper and deeper into the wild heathland dotted with tiny hamlets and remote farms. West wasn't the best way out of the area if the abductors wanted to link up with any of the major motorways. They would have about a two-hour drive over rough moorland terrain to get anywhere, and they probably wouldn't want to be so exposed for that long. They could have no idea when the hue and cry over Zelda's disappearance would go up.

'So what's next?' Ray asked.

Gervaise glanced at Banks. 'You're SIO, Alan,' she said. 'What do you think?'

'We'll see if the early search teams turn up anything,' Banks said, 'then we'll start a door-to-door in the village and out in the dale, asking if anybody saw or heard anything unusual. We'll also talk to Zelda's friends and try to find out about anyone who might wish her harm. We don't know what actual time she was taken yet, do we?'

'You know I was over at your place late yesterday afternoon,' Ray said. 'About half five, six. Then I drove to Leeds, gave my talk and got back here by about half past ten.' He glanced at Gervaise. 'Soon as I realised something was seriously wrong I phoned Alan and he was here in, what, twenty minutes?'

'If that,' Banks said. 'And it was about a quarter to eleven when Ray phoned.'

'So any time between about five o'clock and ten-thirty,' said Gervaise.

Ray nodded.

'Tell me, why did you call Superintendent Banks rather than the police station?'

'The other blokes asked me that, too. I would have thought it was a no-brainer. I know him. He lives nearby. He's a mate. And he's a detective. Made sense to me.'

'What about your daughter?'

'Annie? Dunno. I didn't think of her at first.'

'Why not? Just because she lives further away?'

'Not really.'

'Because she's a woman?'

'No. Because she's my daughter.'

'You might as well know,' Banks said, 'that Annie and Zelda don't get along too well.'

'Oh?' said Gervaise, glancing at Ray. 'And why's that?'

'None of your—'

Banks cut Ray off. 'Plenty of reasons,' he said. 'You know families. They just got off on the wrong foot, that's all. It's hardly relevant. You don't think Annie had anything to do with this, do you?'

'It pays to be thorough and not discount anything,' Gervaise said. Then she smiled. 'But no, I don't think DI Cabbot is a suspect. Though I do think she's too close to the case to work it in an objective manner. She's a relative.'

'Zelda and I aren't married,' Ray said.

'A mere technicality,' said Gervaise. 'I'm going to keep her on the Blaydon rape case for the time being. DC Masterson, too. You can have DS Flyte and DC Bharati, Alan. Let's see how this goes today before we have another meeting and decide whether to raise the investigation to another level and bring in more troops.'

'I think it's pretty obvious something's happened to Zelda, don't you?' said Ray. 'Why wait? What do you lot need to get you started, a dead body?'

'Ray,' said Banks. 'Everything that can be done is being done. When we see where we're going, we'll know whether we have to allocate extra resources. What we hope is that we'll have Zelda back safe and sound long before we need to make that decision.'

Ray rolled another cigarette and gave him a look that said, 'Bullshit.'

8

'How's Ray really doing?' Annie asked over a late lunch in the Queen's Arms. 'All he told me was that he was coping and not to come over because the house was full of cops already.'

They were sitting outside, in the shade of a large umbrella, Banks munching on fish and chips and Annie picking away at a quinoa salad. The landlord Cyril stopped short of vegan sausage rolls and plant-based burgers, but this was his one recent gesture towards the rise of healthier eating. Annie was drinking fizzy water and Banks was trying one of the no-alcohol beers, another gesture to modern times. He was surprised how good it tasted.

'Not so well,' said Banks. 'He's smoking like a chimney and hitting the bottle pretty hard. But it's true the CSIs are going to be at his house for a while longer. You know what they're like. I just dropped him off at my place and left him there with a bit of Pink Floyd in the background to calm his nerves.'

'No ransom demands or anything?'

'No. Nothing. He's got his mobile with him, just in case. Besides, Flyte and Bharati are still at the house, and they're trained to deal with situations like this.'

'I should go and see him.'

'Maybe. Give him a little while to decompress first. I wish Winsome wasn't still on maternity leave. I don't know Flyte or Bharati well. They seem OK, but . . . let's just say I could do with DS Jackman.'

'I know what you mean. I paid Winsome a visit yesterday.'

'How's she doing?'

'She's in excellent spirits. And the baby is a real sweetheart.'

'I'll bet she just can't wait to come back to work, can she?'

'Dream on.' Annie paused. 'You know Zelda and I have our problems, but this is terrible. I hope nothing awful's happened to her.'

'Whatever it is, it's not likely to be good.'

'What do you think it's all about?'

Banks paused for a moment and heard a snatch of 'Be My Baby' coming from inside. Phil Spector's 'Wall of Sound'. It reminded him of better times, listening to music on the front step on a Sunday afternoon with his school friends. How good the old Dansette had sounded then. And how exciting the music had been, heard for the first time. Now Spector was in jail for murder and Ed Sheeran was topping the charts. 'Either it's a set-up and she's done a bunk,' said Banks, 'or someone's taken her.'

'Why would she fake her own abduction?'

If Zelda *had* killed Goran Tadić and felt that his gang had found out about it, that might be one good reason, Banks thought, but he couldn't tell Annie that. Besides, he still wasn't convinced by her writings that she had done anything of the kind. More than anything else, she seemed to have been questioning her ability to commit such an act, something even Banks himself had wondered about from time to time. He had killed plenty of people in his fantasies. 'I don't know,' he said. 'Last time we talked she told me a few things I didn't know, about seeing Keane with her boss, and finding his ex-girlfriend, Faye Butler. Remember, I told you he was going by the name of Hugh Foley? But I still got the impression that she was holding back. That there was something important she *couldn't* tell me, or wouldn't. And she seemed anxious, on edge. I didn't think our conversation was strained, but Ray said she was pissed off when she got home, and they had a row. Maybe I hit a nerve. I think she may be in big trouble. If she did do a runner, it was probably because she felt things were closing in on her and she needed to escape. She might also have been worried about Ray, about him getting dragged into whatever it was. He's a bit of an innocent, your father, in a lot of ways.'

'Always was. In his own world. What things might Zelda need to escape from?'

'I think it's something to do with what she wouldn't tell me. Someone was after her. She was always looking over her shoulder.' He laughed. 'You know what they say: just because you're paranoid, it doesn't mean there isn't somebody following you.'

'Who?'

'That I don't know. I have my suspicions. It was probably someone from her past. Tadić, maybe. But I've no idea *why*. She's either crossed someone, or she knows something they're afraid she'll tell. The only good news is that they *took* her alive. They didn't leave her in her studio beaten or dead, and they didn't appear to have tortured her. That means there's a good chance that she might still be alive. I'm hoping the door-to-door and forensics on the studio will give us some sort of a lead. The only trouble is that forensics can sometimes take a long time, and time is one thing we don't have. All we know right now is that there was a struggle and they drove off to the west, on that unfenced moorland road. That's an awful lot of area to cover.'

'Did they take anything?'

'Not that we can tell. Her computer was still in the studio, and her shoulder bag with her phone, purse and so on. Passport, too, in a drawer.'

'Odds are if she did a bunk she'd have taken her passport and money,' said Annie. 'She wouldn't get far without them.'

'What I thought,' said Banks.

'So they've probably not taken her out of the country.'

'Depends who we're dealing with,' said Banks. 'No doubt her old traffickers know safe routes out, as well as in. And if Keane, or Foley, is in with them, he could probably fix up a fake passport quickly enough.'

'Any forensics yet?'

'Not much. One of the CSIs found six cigarette ends in a hollow within good viewing distance of Ray and Zelda's cottage. They're not Marlboro Gold, which was Zelda's brand, or Ray's roll-ups, so whoever took her might have been staking the place out for a while. They're being analysed.'

'Have you considered that if Keane is with them, he might also be up here, and you might be in danger. What if he wants to finish what he started?'

'No, I hadn't thought of that,' said Banks. 'Thanks for reminding me.'

Annie slapped his arm. 'I'm just saying you should be careful, Alan, that's all. And remember, he's not alone this time.'

'Thanks.'

'Think nothing of it,' said Annie. 'Just because I'm not officially allowed near the case, it doesn't mean I can't help you if you need me.'

'Of course not,' said Banks. 'I know that and I appreciate it. Just watch yourself, that's all. AC Gervaise is bound to have her eye on you. And as you know, with Zelda missing and probably in danger, not to mention Ray on my back, I'm going to have to live and breathe this case, but keep me informed on the rape investigation, too. Anything new?'

The music jumped forward a few years to Tim Hardin's 'Hang on to a Dream'. Another tortured soul and heroin casualty.

'We still haven't identified the victim,' Annie said. 'According to Charlotte Westlake, there were no guest lists for the parties, so we're still stuck with finding out who was there on the night in question.'

'Do you think this Charlotte Westlake was involved?'

'I don't think she's telling us everything. Though she could hardly be the rapist – that was a man – and I doubt that she facilitated it. She said she was in Costa Rica at the time of the party, and it's true. We checked. She says she doesn't recognise the girl in the photo, but that's not surprising, given its poor quality.'

'Could she be lying?'

'I think she could. There was something a bit suspicious about her reaction to the whole mention of the rape and the minicams.'

'What do you know about her?'

'She used to be plain old Christine Pollard from the local comprehensive in Halifax – though I doubt she was ever plain. Then she got into Oxford. Apparently, she was the one in her year to make it. She drifted into events planning, met Gareth Westlake at a function she helped organise for his construction company. That was when she became Charlotte Westlake. Charlotte was her middle name. I guess it sounded a bit posher now she'd gone up in the world and mixed with a different set. Gareth died of leukaemia five years ago, as she told us. No children. Then three years ago she bumped into Blaydon at an opening party for a new shopping development he was involved with – the one before the Elmet, out Selby way. She'd known him vaguely from before, apparently, and he needed a PA. She took the job and the rest is history.'

'No connections with Gashi or Tadić?'

'Not that Gerry could find. Not before going to work for Blaydon, at any rate. Not that we expected any.'

'No form?'

'None. Again, we didn't expect any.'

'So what next?'

'Gerry's arranged to talk to her ex-secretary this afternoon. Tamara Collins. She took care of the actual party invitations by text or email. She works for that solicitor's firm on Market Street now. You know the one, just a few doors down from the Costa Coffee.'

'I know who you mean,' said Banks. 'Proctor, Maddox and Reaney. I used to walk past there every morning on my way to work, back when Sandra and I were together.'

'Apparently there were a lot of word-of-mouth invitations, too,' Annie said. 'If we can just track down some of the invitees and show them the girl's picture, someone might remember seeing her and know who she is, or who was with her that night.'

'I doubt anyone will talk.'

'But they can't all have been involved, can they? It was a big party. You've seen Blaydon's mansion, how many rooms there are, with the swimming pool and all. Not all the guests were rapists. It was very late at night. There must be quite a few who don't know what happened and would be as appalled by the news as Charlotte Westlake said she was. Probably most of them. Maybe they saw the victim around the pool or some-where, noticed who she was talking to or hanging out with. Maybe someone was bothering her. Maybe she said some-thing to someone.'

'It's worth a try,' said Banks. 'Good luck.'

Ray Cabbot sat in Banks's back garden, where they had talked just the previous evening, which seemed a lifetime ago now, and rolled another cigarette. How his whole world had fallen to pieces in such a short time. Shifted and crumbled. He was oblivious to the sunshine, the birds and the beautiful view.

Even the muted strains of David Gilmour's 'Shine On You Crazy Diamond' coming through the open windows of the conservatory failed to move him or console him in any way. Ever since Banks had left him alone at Newhope Cottage, he had been fighting the urge to attack the collection of single malt whiskies, but had resisted so far. He didn't know how much longer he could hold out. Only oblivion could take away the pain of losing Zelda and save him from the terrible images that filled his mind.

Faceless men ripped off her clothes and pawed at her; they stuck knives in her until the blood flowed; they beat her face until it was misshapen and unrecognisable. His beautiful, vulnerable Zelda lay dying with no one to help her, no one to hold her as her last breath ebbed. But it wasn't just the pain and the violence, it was what she must be feeling that also tore at his heart. The loneliness, the fear, the despair. After all she had been through, had she found herself a captive again in the hands of people who lacked any semblance of empathy? Was she going to die alone and in agony?

Ray had never felt so impotent, so useless, in his life. And their last words to one another had been angry ones. He would never forget the sound of the studio door slamming. Zelda was so rarely angry. Why hadn't he gone after her? Surely, she would have let him in if he had knocked? Then he could have apologised and comforted her and taken her to Leeds with him and none of this would have happened. She had listened to his lectures before and said she enjoyed them. They could have gone for dinner afterwards, perhaps booked in at the Dakota and made a night of it. Instead he was exiled to Banks's garden while heavy-handed coppers went through his home and belongings.

He could just imagine their reactions to some of his work: 'Hey, have a look at this one, Joe. Got a right set of knockers on her, she has.' 'I'll bet that's his missus.' But what could he do? For better or for worse, they were the only people he could rely on to find Zelda. And Alan. Where was Alan? Organising things, he had said. Yet it all seemed so disorganised. He couldn't see what sort of plan they were following, how they hoped to get anywhere closer to finding Zelda by going through his things. They would be in her drawers, too, fingering her underwear, her personal stuff. Making crude comments, holding things up for everyone to see.

Ray stood up and walked over to the back fence. He felt caged. Maybe he should go for a walk up Tetchley Fell? But the mere sight of it made him feel out of breath. He was in no fit shape to go hiking. He stubbed out his cigarette, went inside and stared longingly at the bottles of Macallans and Highland Park. He knew Banks wouldn't mind if he helped himself to a tipple. The thing was, he felt like shit already, having drunk too much the previous night instead of sleeping. And he needed a clear head in case Zelda called.

But his head wouldn't clear. Maybe a little drink would help. He took out his mobile for the umpteenth time and checked for missed calls. Nothing. The music finished, and he couldn't be bothered putting anything else on. Images of Zelda terrified and bloody filled his mind again. He sat back down and put his head in his hands. He wished he were painting. Usually everything else went from his mind when he took a brush in his hand. But perhaps even that wouldn't work this time, even if he was allowed back in his studio. This was too serious to permit easy escape, if only for a second.

He rolled another cigarette, pictured the bottles on the shelf inside. Then he heard a car pulling up out front and jumped up. They'd found her. Surely that's what it was. Alan was hurrying to give him the good news. He left his roll-up burning in the ashtray and dashed through to the front of the house with visions of Zelda running into his arms.

Costa was usually busy after work, but Gerry and Tamara Collins managed to find a table for two in the back. After Gerry had brought the lattes, they settled down to talk amid the hubbub of conversation and the hoarse gurgling of the espresso machine. Tamara was probably about Gerry's age, late twenties, and pretty in a sharp-featured, no-nonsense sort of way. Her clothes were conservative – white blouse, navy skirt and jacket – as one would expect from a legal secretary.

Gerry took her notebook out. 'How do you like your new job?' she asked.

'I'm very glad to have it.'

'It's a bit different from working for Mr Blaydon, I should imagine?'

Her expression darkened. 'Yes.'

'How long did you work for him?'

'Three years. But I was working for Mrs Westlake.'

'Technically, I know, but Blaydon employed both of you. Was he a good employer?'

'The pay was OK, the hours not bad.'

'And the boss?'

'To be honest, I didn't see very much of him. I worked at his office in Leeds. Mrs Westlake was his personal assistant. She didn't have anything to do with the property developments or the estate business, but she had an office there. Mind you, she wasn't there all the time. Well, it makes sense, doesn't it? If she was supposed to assist him, she probably had to be out and about a lot. And Mr Blaydon himself was in and out, here and there. We didn't see him very often. He travelled quite a lot. I think he had a yacht or something. It wasn't as if we were all together in one big room. And he wasn't a grabber, if that's what you mean.'

'He never behaved inappropriately?'

'Oh, Lordy me, no.'

'Why did you leave?'

'I had this job in my sights for a while. It's closer to home and the pay's much better. The work's more interesting, too. The opportunity finally came up about a month ago.'

'Did you ever get invited to one of Mr Blaydon's parties?'

Tamara laughed. 'Me? Lord, no! Why would he invite me? I don't think he even knew I existed. The parties were just to impress important people – friends, influencers, business colleagues and so on.'

'I understand he liked to have a few pretty women around, too.'

Tamara blushed. 'Well, I certainly wasn't one of them.'

'Where did he get them from?'

'How would I know? I just worked in the office. Basic secretarial duties for Mrs Westlake.'

'Where do you think?'

Tamara held her coffee cup in both hands. 'I heard things, like you do.'

'What things?'

'Just the usual. Office gossip. You know, that he hired models to be nice to his guests.'

'Models or escorts?'

'I wouldn't know about that.'

'What about drugs?'

'Again, I heard rumours. I can't say they interested me very much.'

Gerry leaned forward. 'Tamara, we think – in fact, we *know* – that Mr Blaydon used a lot of girls from Eastern Europe, probably supplied by sex traffickers. His parties were also well known for their cocaine use. Did you ever meet a friend of his called Leka Gashi?'

Tamara shook her head. 'I'm not saying he was never in the office. People came and went. But I was never introduced to anyone by that name.'

'Petar Tadić?'

'No.'

'We also know that Mr Blaydon used, or allowed to be used, a number of his properties as pop-up brothels. Did you know that?'

'Pop-up brothels! God forbid. Of course not. Like I said, I had nothing to do with renting out properties or anything like that. I worked for Mrs Westlake organising travel, accommodation, dinners, meetings, events and that sort of thing. That was all.'

'I understand you sent out the party invitations.'

'Well, I sent out texts and emails sometimes, yes. Made phone calls.'

'Were you working on 13 April this year?'

'I suppose so.'

'Do you remember sending out invitations to a party for that date?'

'They would have been sent out about two weeks earlier. That would make it the end of March, or thereabouts. I can't remember the exact date. I mean, it was a pretty menial task, to be honest, and it usually didn't take very long. I just got it done and out of the way as soon as possible. Sometimes it was fun seeing a name I recognised, like a pop star or footballer, but that's all. It was pretty boring otherwise.'

'I can understand that,' said Gerry. 'Do you remember any names from that specific party?'

'I'm sorry, I can't,' said Tamara. 'Maybe that means there weren't any I recognised. Nobody really famous.'

'Would you try and write down any names you do remember?'

'Yes, of course.'

'For any other parties that you can think of, too.'

'All right.'

Gerry fished out the digital image of the rape victim and passed it to Tamara. 'Do you recognise this girl?'

Tamara held the photo and studied it from different angles. 'Do you know, I . . . She looks very upset and dishevelled here, very different, but maybe . . .'

'Maybe what?'

Tamara handed the photo back. 'I think maybe I saw her in the office once.'

Gerry felt her pulse quicken. 'When was that?'

'Before 13 April, that much I know. February? March?'

'What was she doing?'

'She wanted to see Mrs Westlake.'

'Can you remember what it was about? It might be important.'

'No. But Mrs Westlake interviewed people for jobs and wrote cheques or made some payments in cash. Sometimes people dropped by to pick up their payment. Not everyone likes electronic bank transfers.'

'And this girl came for cash or a cheque?'

'I'm just saying that she might have done. Or maybe she was after a job. She didn't tell me. I mean, there was nothing unusual about her. I do remember she was very pretty. Quite tall, long-legged, short reddish hair, maybe hennaed.' Tamara dabbed at a latte moustache. 'Mrs Westlake put the personnel together for the events Mr Blaydon held, including the serving and kitchen staff and people to coordinate them on site. She didn't trust most outside caterers. Not just for the parties, but business events, too, gala dinners, retirement parties, employee of the month awards and so on. She liked to use her own core team. I don't know for certain why this girl came to the office, but that would be my first guess. For a job.'

'So there would be records in Blaydon's business files? Bank details, name, address?'

'There should be. It was all above board. But accounts handled all that.'

'Are you sure she came to the office to see Mrs Westlake?'

'Yes. That's why I remember her. She came up to my desk and asked if Mrs Westlake was in, and if she could see her. Said she had an appointment but she was a bit early. She waited in the reception area for a while, glancing at a magazine. I do remember she seemed nervous. You know, not really concentrating on what she was reading, just flipping the pages, looking at the pictures. Putting it down and picking up another. Then when the time came I showed her into the office myself.'

Gerry thought it odd that Tamara had recognised the girl from the photo when Charlotte Westlake, who must have had far more dealings with her, hadn't. Was Charlotte lying? They would have to re-interview her. 'I don't suppose you remember her name, do you?' she asked.

Tamara thought for a moment and said, 'Do you know, as a matter of fact I do. I asked her, you know, so I could tell Mrs Westlake who was here to see her. Announce her, like.'

'And?'

'Her name was Marnie. I'm afraid I can't remember her second name, but I remember her first name struck me as odd. It's not often you come across someone called Marnie.'

'No,' said Gerry, scribbling away in her notebook. 'No, it isn't.'

'It's from an old film, isn't it?'

'Yes,' said Gerry, who had seen just about every 'old' film there was with her parents when she was growing up, and had a surprisingly good recollection of most of them. 'Alfred Hitchcock. Tippi Hedren and Sean Connery. It's about sexual violence. And Marnie was a sexually repressed kleptomaniac.'

DC Dev Bharati was a keen young detective from County HQ, handsome, slim and casually dressed, and he was clearly excited to be involved in such a high-profile case. He was a bit too deferential for Banks's liking, but that probably wouldn't last. Still, it made a change from the easy familiarity of Annie, Gerry and Winsome, with whom he was more used to working.

'I thought you'd want to know right away, sir,' Bharati said as he drove Banks into Lyndgarth. 'DS Flyte is still with him.'

They pulled up outside the Black Bull in the high street. Bharati had to duck as he walked through the doors. The beams inside were also low, and he had to watch where he walked. DS Samuel Flyte was sitting at a rickety table with the pub's landlord Mick Slater, a grizzled old denizen of the public house trade. Banks had met him before on a number of occasions and found him gruff but sound enough.

Flyte was a few years older than Bharati, fat but not obese. He reminded Banks of his old oppo, DS Jim Hatchley, now long retired and by all accounts practically taking up residence at Eastvale Golf Club. Hatchley had resembled a rugby prop forward gone to seed, but Banks guessed there was more muscle than fat in Flyte's bulk. He was also bald, with a shiny head, a small moustache, a red face and a slow, countryman's manner of moving, along with the habit of appearing to think for a moment before answering any questions. He stood up when Banks entered and shook hands. He was wearing a tight-fitting navy suit, already a little shiny around the elbows.

There were plenty of people in the pub, and Banks had no doubt most of them were talking about what had happened on the edge of the village. He recognised a couple of reporters from the local papers, but the London press hadn't turned up yet. As soon as they got wind of what had happened, they'd be up the M1 quickly enough, and Zelda's dirty laundry would be spread all over the front pages of the national media. Another good reason for hanging on to the notebook.

Banks sat down with Mick Slater, Flyte and Bharati. Slater offered drinks, but they all refused. The two detectives did so because Banks was present, he assumed, and Banks declined because he didn't want any alcohol and rarely drank tea or coffee in the afternoon.

'Let's get straight to it,' he said. 'I know you've probably told DS Flyte already, but I'd like you to tell me exactly what happened. Start with when.'

'It was three or four days ago,' said Slater. 'Just before the weekend.'

'What time of day?'

'About now.'

Banks saw DC Bharati make a note of the time. 'And what were the man's actual words?'

'He asked if I knew of a young woman living in these parts. Said he was an old friend and he hadn't seen her for some years, but he'd heard she was living in Lyndgarth. A place called Windlee Farm. He didn't have a full address and his satnav was going wonky. Well, they do that a lot around these parts. Then he described her. Her appearance, the slight accent. It sounded to me as if he was talking about Mrs Cabbot.'

It sounded the same way to Banks, though it was strange hearing Zelda described as Mrs Cabbot, especially as she and Ray weren't even married. 'So you got the impression that he didn't know exactly where she lived?'

'Right. It's easy enough if you have a street address in a small village like this, but Windlee Farm isn't exactly in the village, as you know. It's over half a mile away from any other houses here. I don't even know what the address is, myself, or even if there is one. I think it's on Lyndsdale Road, but that could be wrong. The road changes its name every hundred yards, it seems. And I don't think there's a number. Must be a postal code, of course, but I'd be hard pushed to tell you that, either. It's just known as the Old Farm around these parts. Anyone who wants it knows that. And knows where it is.'

'It's like my place,' said Banks. 'Newhope Cottage. In Gratly. No street address. No street. What did he look like?'

'Medium height, stocky, fortyish maybe, cropped black hair, five o'clock shadow – the kind you get with those special razors – thick lips, fleshy nose and beady eyes. Moved like the sort of bloke who probably thinks he's God's gift to women, if you catch my drift. Flash clothes, too, just a bit too gaudy, if you ask me, and jewellery. You know, gold chain, big rings, that sort of bling. He looked like a bit of a thug, to be honest. And he had an accent.'

'What sort of accent?'

'European. Not French or Italian. Maybe Bulgarian or Polish or something like that. Could've been Russian. Who knows? Bit of a harsh edge to it. Guttural. Just the sort we voted to get rid of.'

'What did you tell him?'

'Nothing. Like I said, I didn't like the look of him, and I don't like to give out that kind of information about my customers on spec. You never know who you're telling, do you? Could be planning on burgling the place. Or raping her or something. I don't know Ray and his missus very well, but they come in here for a drink or two now and then, and they always seemed nice enough to me. This bloke looked like trouble, and Mrs Cabbot, well, she's an attractive woman, out there on her own sometimes . . . you know. Like I said, you never know what someone has in mind.'

'That was good thinking,' said Banks. 'You did the right thing.'

'Seems as if he found her, anyway, doesn't it? Maybe I should have reported it straight away. At least told Ray and Zelda, given them a chance.'

'Not your fault.' He must have asked someone else, Banks thought, or driven around until he saw the name on the front of the cottage. Then when he'd found it, he staked out the place from the hollow over the weekend before making his move, probably after seeing Ray leave in the late afternoon. There would be an accomplice somewhere, too. Maybe someone had seen him out on the moorland? You tended to get quite a few ramblers out there on weekends.

'Did you see his car?'

'No.'

'I did,' came a voice from the left.

Banks turned. 'And you are?'

'Kit. Kit Riley.'

'Kit's a regular,' Mick Slater said.

Banks looked more closely. Kit was an elderly man, a bit dishevelled in a grubby, striped rugby shirt, baggy brown cord trousers and a leather gilet, despite the weather. His white hair stuck out at all angles, and he clearly hadn't shaved in a week. He had the weather-beaten complexion of a lifelong farmer.

'You saw the car?' Banks said.

'Aye. I were just leaving, like, and he pushed past me, rude as can be. *Foreigners.* Sooner we're shut of 'em, the better.'

'But you did see his car?'

'Oh, aye.' Kit paused and glanced down at his glass, which was almost empty.

Banks sighed. Everyone had watched too much television these days, it seemed, and expected something in return for whatever information they gave the police.

Banks nodded to Mick Slater. 'Give him what he wants.'

'Ooh, ta very much. I'll have a whisky, please, Micky, my boy. A double.'

Slater poured the drink. When Banks reached for his wallet, the landlord shook his head, as if to indicate he'd bear the expense. 'No, it's only fair,' said Banks, passing some money over. Slater shrugged and got the change from the till.

'Right then, Kit,' said Banks, after Riley had taken his first sip and smacked his lips. 'What kind of car was it?'

Riley sipped some more whisky theatrically before saying, 'It were a Ford Fiesta.'

'You're sure?' Banks asked, heart sinking.

'I know my cars,' said Riley. 'I tell you, it were a Ford Fiesta.'

Only the most popular car in the country, with about 100,000 registrations last year alone. 'What colour was it?'

'Dark green. Or blue. Hard to tell.'

'You didn't get the number, by any chance?'

'Stopped writing down car numbers when I was twelve,' Riley replied.

Banks felt a memory rise up from deep in his mind. Sitting on the secondary modern school wall by the main road junction with his best friends, Steve and Paul, writing down the makes and numbers of cars that went by. He must have been about ten or eleven. Why on earth had he thought to do something as pointless as that? Probably because his friends did. But it wasn't even as serious a pastime as train-spotting, standing at the end of a windy platform in the rain jotting down train names and numbers, then going home and neatly crossing them off in your book with pencil and ruler. There was no book of car numbers, as far as he knew, only pictures and descriptions of models in the *Observer's Book of Cars*.

It was a pity that Kit Riley had given up the practice so early. Inquiries about a dark Ford Fiesta wouldn't get very far. It was clear that whoever was looking for Zelda had made no effort to hide the fact. He had gone into the pub on the village high street, obviously rather exotic in his bling, and described Zelda to the landlord. So he clearly wasn't worried about his description being circulated. Why? Did he think the police were too stupid to trace him? Was he so confident and arrogant that he could afford to do what he wanted right under their noses? Banks had known plenty of criminals who were, who would think nothing of walking into their local, shooting someone they had a grudge against and walking out again. And how did the man know what Zelda looked like unless he knew her? He must have seen her somewhere, or at least seen a photograph of her.

'Is that all?' he asked Kit.

'Aye. Oh, there's one more thing.' Kit glanced down at his empty glass.

Banks ignored the gesture. 'Go on. Tell,' he said.

Riley seemed disappointed, but he knew when he'd gone too far. 'There were another bloke with him. Waiting in the car, like. I didn't get a good look at him, but it wasn't someone I'd care to meet in a dark ginnel, I can tell you that much.'

9

Ray looked terrible, Annie thought, when he answered the door to Banks's cottage. And it was hard not to feel hurt at the expression of disappointment that crept over his features when he saw her. She wouldn't deny that there were 'issues' between her and Zelda, but that didn't mean she wished her any harm. Whatever Annie thought of Ray's choice of partner, he clearly loved Zelda, and it was good for him to have someone to share his life with. If only she weren't so damned young and attractive. It was hard to trust anyone as beautiful as her, and Annie lived in fear that she would run off with some young stud and break Ray's heart. Literally.

'Annie,' he said. 'I thought . . . Is there any news?'

'Sorry.'

For a few moments they just stood there staring at one another, then they hugged, long and hard, Ray sobbing on Annie's shoulder. A little embarrassed, they moved apart and Annie followed Ray through the front room and down the hall, watching his elbows move as he rubbed his eyes with the backs of his hands, then through Banks's kitchen and conservatory. 'I was sitting out back,' he said.

'Mind if I join you?'

'I'm not very good company right now, but you're quite welcome.'

Annie smiled. 'Oh, Dad, I didn't expect you to be good company. After all, it's not often you are.' She hardly ever called him 'Dad' or 'Father', but he didn't react when she did this time. Nor did he react to her little tease.

'My house is swarming with coppers,' he said.

'Don't worry. I'm sure they'll be respectful.'

They sat down. 'Want a drink?' Ray asked.

'No, thanks. I'm not stopping long. Alan told me you were here, and I wanted to see how you're doing.'

Ray spread his arms, then started rolling a cigarette. 'Well,' he said, 'as you can see.'

'We'll find her,' Annie said.

'I think I might have one. A drink, that is.' He left his unlit cigarette on the table and disappeared inside, emerging a few seconds later with a tumbler of whisky.

Annie felt like telling him to take it easy with the booze, but she held her tongue. It would only antagonise him. And maybe a drop or two of whisky wasn't such a bad idea for him at the moment. 'I know you think I don't like Zelda,' she said, 'and I know we got off on the wrong foot, but just put it down to me being silly, my silly feelings. And being overprotective of you. You know I want you to be happy, and if she makes you happy—'

'She does,' Ray said. 'You have no idea. Since your mother . . .'

'That's a long time ago,' Annie said.

'I haven't forgotten her, love, you know that. I never could. Zelda's not a replacement, she's . . . I don't know . . . a new start for me. Something I thought was way behind me. And beyond. You can't always be prepared for when things like that happen.'

'I wouldn't know,' Annie said.

'I'm telling you. It's true.' Tears welled up in his red eyes again. 'I don't know what I'll do if anything happens to her.'

'Oh, Dad.' Annie reached out and touched his arm. 'There is *some* news,' she said. 'And another reason I'm here. I just talked to Alan on the phone, and he told me Mick Slater from the Black Bull said there was a bloke in the pub asking after Zelda the other day, or at least someone who resembled her very closely. Said he didn't tell him anything. Didn't like the look of him.'

Ray picked up the cigarette, rolled it around between his fingers for a while, then put it in his mouth and lit it. 'They think that's the man who took her?'

'We don't know,' Annie said. 'But we'll definitely be checking into it.'

'Any idea who he is?'

'No.' Annie paused. 'But Alan said it might be a good idea, if you're up to it, if maybe you could go up there and help with a sketch. Mr Slater can give a pretty good description for you to work with. Only if you feel up to it. I'll drive you.'

Ray stood up so fast he knocked his tumbler over on the table and whisky flowed over the sides. 'Do I feel up to it? You bet I do. Come on, what are we waiting for?'

'No, the nose isn't quite right. A bit broader. And there's a sort of bump.' Mick Slater touched his own nose. 'Right here, about halfway up. As if it was broken or something. And the lips were a bit thicker.'

Ray got to work with the rubber then put pencil to paper again.

'That's it,' said Mick. 'Now the eyebrows. A bit thicker, too. Not bushy or anything, but not quite so thin. Dark and heavy, and nearly meeting in the middle. A heavier brow. Hairline back a bit. That's it. That's him.'

They were in a small office behind the bar, and there was just enough room for Ray and Mick inside, while Banks leaned against the door jamb gazing on from the sidelines. It was always fascinating to watch a master at work. Ray was a

serious artist, not a police sketch artist, but he had helped
Banks out in that capacity before, and he was good at it. It had
seemed only natural to ask Annie to try and get him to help
sketch a description of the stranger, with Slater's help. So far,
things seemed to be going well.

Banks turned and glanced around the pub. He had accepted
Slater's offer of a pint of shandy when Ray arrived and was glad
that he had. It was getting hot in there, and the sweetness of the
lemonade and the bitterness of the beer made a perfect antidote
to the heat of the day. The Black Bull was an odd sort of place:
dark and dingy on the inside, with an uneven flagstone floor,
scratched tables and rickety chairs, but a great summer draw
outside with its tables looking out on the village green and a
beer garden out back. Unlike the Relton Arms, it had a small
playground area and a bouncy castle for the kiddies. Banks
could imagine the interior on a dark winter's night, the locals
sitting silently around a blazing fire, dogs dreaming at their feet,
while the wind howled and the rain battered at the windows
outside. Lockdowns would be common there, and the local
bobby would probably be on the inside of them.

Finally, Ray put down the finishing touches and passed the
sketch to Banks.

'It's as good as I can get,' said Slater. 'I'm not that great at
detail.'

'It's fine,' said Banks, then glanced at Ray. 'Thanks. Look, I
have a pretty good idea of who this might be. I'll show it to a
couple of colleagues who will know for certain and get back to
you.'

'Is it bad?'

'I'll check it out, Ray. If I'm right, it'll help us with the
search.'

'Why won't you tell me now? What don't you want me to
know?'

Banks turned to Slater. 'Thanks for your time and trouble, Mr Slater,' he said. 'And thanks for not giving this stranger any information. I'd appreciate it if you'd keep quiet about this until I've had the chance to check a few things out.'

Slater nodded, and they returned to the bar with their drinks.

'Why won't you tell me what you think?' Ray persisted. 'Who is it? Why would he want to take Zelda?'

'Because I'm not sure yet,' Banks said.

'But if you're right, is it bad news?'

Banks took a long pull on his shandy and said, 'Yes, Ray. You want me to tell you. All right. If it's who I think it is, it's bad news.'

'It's Petar Tadić, all right,' said Burgess, just seconds after Banks had emailed him Ray's sketch. 'Where did you get it?'

Banks told him about Mick Slater and Ray collaborating.

'Brazen bastard, isn't he?' said Burgess. 'If you need any help on this, we've got trained experts here we can send up. Negotiators and the like.'

'Thanks, I might take you up on that if we don't find her soon,' Banks said. 'But right now there's nothing to negotiate. I'd appreciate it if you could find out whether Tadić is back in London, though. And if you find him, bring him in for questioning.'

'We can try. We have a pretty good idea of some of his haunts, but they keep changing. I'll see what I can do.'

'By the way, talking about haunts, have you ever heard of the Hotel Belgrade?'

There was a brief pause before Burgess answered. 'It used to be one of their hangouts, the Tadićs and their crew. Why?'

'No reason. It's just something that came up.' Banks could hardly tell Burgess that the hotel was mentioned in Zelda's notebook. 'Used to be?'

'Yes. It seems they've moved out en masse. We're not sure where yet.'

'When was this?'

'Less than a month ago.'

'One witness from the village says there was another man waiting in the car for Petar. What about the brother, Goran? Anything on him?'

'Goran hasn't been seen lately,' said Burgess. 'He must be lying low. Probably on holiday in Split or somewhere. These people are always on the move. That's how they keep a few steps ahead of us.'

'Thanks. Have you got an up-to-date photo of Petar? That might work better than a quick sketch.'

'I'll check.'

'Great. If you find one, can you send it directly to Adrian Moss?' Banks gave him Moss's fax, phone and email. 'In the meantime, I'll have Adrian get the sketch out to the news media, as well as on Facebook, Twitter and so on. Adrian's already blasted them with Zelda's disappearance, so they'll all have their tongues hanging out for more. And we'll get copies to patrol cars, beat officers, PCSOs, the lot.' They said their goodbyes and Banks hung up.

Adrian Moss was their media liaison officer, and though he was a bit of a trendy prat, with his wet-look hair and shirt hanging out, Banks had to admit he was very good at his job. If anyone could saturate the media with Zelda's disappearance and give the press a good story, Moss could. The photo of Zelda that Ray had given them wouldn't do any harm, either. Most men who saw it would certainly be motivated to find her, and quite a few women, too.

Moss's only problem was that he didn't appreciate his own talent for blowing smoke and always seemed to want to give away far more than Banks was comfortable with. He would have his work cut out when the national media horde arrived the following day. Which reminded Banks that Ray would need to be protected from them. The CSIs had finished for the day at Ray's house, and he had gone straight home from the Black Bull, so Banks had Newhope to himself. He was willing to take Ray in again tomorrow, if necessary, when the CSIs would no doubt turn up again.

On his way home, Banks had made a detour to the station. Moss had already got one of the TV crews set up in the press room, so Banks had recorded a brief impromptu appeal on television for any sightings of Zelda. Now he sat outside his cottage in the mild evening warmth, a glass of wine on the table in front of him.

Why had Tadić abducted Zelda? And why now? Banks wouldn't have been surprised if Tadić didn't even remember what he had done to her thirteen years ago. So why was she now suddenly so valuable, or so dangerous, to him?

Banks flipped through the Moleskine notebook again. The last entry concerned a visit to Chişinău at the end of the previous week to see someone called Vasile Lupescu, another demon from her past. There were several lengthy descriptions of the Moldovan countryside, complete with its wineries and peasants in traditional dress, along with old memories of Chişinău. On her flight home, she had written about their conversation, how Lupescu had at first denied setting her up for her abductors, then admitted it and finally insisted that he had been forced into it by threats against his family. It was a tense and dramatic scene, and it confirmed Banks's suspicions that the notebook was most likely a record of feelings and inquiries about her past, perhaps noted down for use in a story or memoir of some kind. Zelda clearly felt very strongly about the people responsible for ruining her life – and quite rightly so – and this notebook must be one of her ways of expressing all that, including fantasies about what she would like to do to some of them.

But it *could* get her into trouble. The disjointed meanderings might mean nothing to most people, but some police officers took everything quite literally, made no allowance for wishful thinking and fantasy. It could get Banks into trouble, too. He was beginning to think that taking it might have been the first step on a slippery slope to career suicide. At the very least it was misappropriating evidence. What on earth did he think he was doing? Protecting Zelda? From what? Whatever his rationale, Banks knew he should have left it where it was, let it become an exhibit in whatever followed. But it was too late for that now. There was no way he could explain hanging on to it to his superiors, and he knew as well as anyone that what might seem like a minor transgression could quickly blow up into a full IOPC investigation, meaning at least temporary suspension, and possibly being fired.

The Hotel Belgrade, Burgess had said, used to be a hangout for Tadić and his cronies until recently. How had Zelda found out about it? From Faye Butler? And had she gone there searching for Keane, only to find Goran Tadić instead? How would she have reacted to that? By fantasising about killing him? What had happened at the Hotel Belgrade? In their talk at the Relton Arms yesterday, Zelda hadn't mentioned anything about finding the Tadićs in London.

Just in case, Banks phoned the hotel, identified himself and asked if a woman matching Zelda's description had checked in recently. The answer was no. Had someone of that description ever stayed at the hotel? They couldn't possibly remember something like that. Guests came and went, many attractive women. Had she been seen there around a month ago? There was no way of knowing that. CCTV? Overwritten by now. Besides, there had been personnel changes, too, and changes in management. It was a fast turnover business. Tadić? No, they had never heard of anyone by that name.

Frustrated by the lack of response, Banks considered arranging for a team to search the place, but he had no real evidence for ordering such an action. And what would they find? As Burgess had said, the Hotel Belgrade *used to be* the Tadićs' hangout, but they had moved on, and no one there admitted to having heard of them. In any case, they would be unlikely to be keeping Zelda there.

Blue tits and goldfinches flitted around his shrubbery, ate at the feeder and splashed in the birdbath, until a local cat jumped over the wall, arched its back and mewed at Banks, then loped on. Only a robin, intent on searching the grass for worms at the bottom of the garden, was unflustered and didn't fly off. The other birds returned, and bees sucked on fuchsia that hung from branches like teardrops of blood.

Banks yawned. It had been a long day, and he hadn't had much sleep the previous night at Ray's. There wasn't anything more he could do tonight, and if he was going to be of any use in the search for Zelda tomorrow, he was going to have to be on the ball. So instead of pouring another glass of wine, he picked up Ray's overflowing ashtray from the table and went back inside, where he dumped its contents into the waste bin and went to bed, taking his mobile with him. Some Brian Eno ambient music might see him off to sleep early tonight.

Zelda woke up with a dry mouth and a terrible headache. When she found the nerve to open her eyes, she thought at first that she was in complete darkness. As her sight adjusted slowly in what little light there was around the boarded-up window, she realised she was in a room, lying on a floor that felt like bare boards. When she tried to move, she found that she was chained by her right ankle to a heavy old iron radiator fixed to the wall. She tried to jerk free a number of times but quickly realised that she couldn't. Then she shouted out, but her voice merely echoed in the empty room.

As her eyes adapted further, she came to see that the room she was in was more like an office than anything else. All the furniture had been removed, desk and filing cabinets, and she couldn't make out the colour of the walls. They seemed to be partially covered in that material with holes in it. She had seen it before in offices. The ceiling seemed high, and there was only the one window. Her hands were tied together with plastic handcuffs that only tightened if she tried to escape from them.

So what had happened? Zelda tried to piece it all together. Why was it all so vague? She and Raymond had argued and she had shut herself in her studio drinking wine and working on a painting. Angry brushstrokes. Red slashes. Why was she angry? Alan, that was why. He had pushed her into telling him certain things that she hadn't wanted him to know. Maybe enough for him to find his way to the truth. And Raymond had hardly been sympathetic. Raymond. What happened to him? He had gone out, of course. The Leeds Art Gallery lecture he had been so nervous about. But would they leave someone to wait for him and hurt him when he got back?

As far as she could tell, she seemed OK in herself, apart from the dry mouth and headache. They had injected her with some sort of anaesthetic, she remembered; that was what was making her feel this way. Nausea, too, perhaps because the room was so hot and stuffy. But there was no pain in any of her limbs, and everything felt intact. She hadn't been raped or sexually interfered with in any way. She would know.

She hadn't heard their car. All she knew was that suddenly the studio door burst open and there stood two men. One of them was Petar Tadić, of that she was certain – she would recognise his stocky body, his near non-existent neck and his beady eyes anywhere, even after all the years – but she didn't recognise the other one. As far as she could tell, Tadić didn't recognise her.

Had they found out what she had done to Goran and tracked her down? That could be the only explanation. It was as she had feared; they had resources, contacts and methods that the police lacked. Something might have led them to poor innocent Faye Butler, and under torture Faye might have given them enough clues to lead to Zelda. They wouldn't have reported Goran's death to the authorities, but would most likely have got rid of the body themselves, perhaps in several pieces. She had thrown her glass at them and struggled when they grabbed her, but the needle went in and its effect was quick. She remembered nothing more, not even how much time had passed, how long she had been out.

Now here she was, shackled in her prison. What was their plan? What were they going to do to her? If they wanted her dead – an eye for an eye – then surely they would have killed her by now. Or did they intend to kill her slowly? Starvation, perhaps? Just leave her here, chained to the radiator, until she died.

She hadn't eaten since her lunch with Banks, and she was starving already. How long ago that seemed. How petty her irritation with him. She wished he would walk through the door right now. She could do with a Willie Garvin to rescue her. What would Modesty Blaise do? Try to escape, obviously. But how? She looked around her in the darkness, but it was hopeless.

Zelda tugged at the chain again; it was still securely fastened to the radiator. And the iron chain was padlocked tightly around her foot. A heavy, strong lock, by the feel of it. She pulled at it, but it did no good. Though her hands were cuffed in front of her, rather than behind, they still weren't much use. The cuffs were tight and hurt whenever she tried to reach out. She wasn't going to escape trussed up like this. Somehow, she had to get free of her chains. But how?

As she was thinking of possibilities, she heard footsteps coming closer down the hall outside her door.

10

Banks was in his office early the following morning, having made his way past the crews of two TV vans parked in the market square and a knot of reporters on the front steps of Eastvale Regional HQ.

While Stephen Hough played some late Brahms piano music in the background, Banks pored over Ordnance Survey maps, but he was distracted by mulling over whether he should cancel his outing to see the Blue Lamps' farewell concert at the Sage that evening. Mark and Tracy could easily get there by themselves. Though he had arranged to have a meal with them beforehand over the river in Newcastle, they would surely understand that he had a crisis on his hands. He also had tickets for Ray and Zelda, but they would have to go unused unless he could find someone in the station who wanted them.

But if he stayed at the office or at home, what would he do but worry? He could take his mobile to the concert with him, set on vibrate, even in the hall; he wouldn't be far away, and he could respond immediately to any breaks in the case. It wasn't as if he was expected to be out crawling over the moors with a magnifying glass and a deerstalker looking for clues himself. But could he even pay attention to his family and the music if he went? That wasn't the issue, he realised. He mustn't let his son down just because leaving the investigation for an evening made him feel as if he were playing truant. This wasn't about him; it was about Brian. Wherever Banks's mind was, at least his physical presence should be there in the Sage concert hall while his son played one of his last gigs with the band he'd been with for years.

Eno's *Reflection* had done the trick the previous night, and Banks had slept well. First, he called Ray to find out how he was doing. Ray was hungover and depressed and told him the 'bloody forensics blokes' had just turned up again to make his day even worse. Banks told him that the media would probably arrive in Lyndgarth soon, and he could go and hide out at Newhope Cottage if he wanted. But Ray said he was going to lock himself in his studio and try to immerse himself in work and music. It was the only way he thought he had any chance of surviving this whole business. He had just taken delivery of a rare vinyl copy of Jan Dukes de Grey's 1969 debut album *Sorcerers* and that should get him through the morning. Even Banks didn't have that one, only *Mice and Rats in the Loft* and *Strange Terrain*.

Next, Banks phoned Adrian Moss and asked him to organise a press conference for later that morning. Zelda had been missing for a day and two nights now, and they were no closer to finding her, so the more publicity the better. Surely someone had seen something?

His last call was to the Croatian authorities asking them for help in locating Tadić. It appeared they knew all about Petar and Goran and said they would be only too willing to help if either was foolish enough to return to Croatia any time soon. But they had no idea where the brothers were.

AC Gervaise had talked to Assistant Chief Constable Ron McLaughlin and the chief constable himself, and Zelda's disappearance was now an official Category-A investigation, with a budget to match. They would need it, too, with the extra men drafted in, then the Swaledale Mountain Rescue

Team, based at Catterick Garrison. Banks had heard that it cost around a couple of thousand just to get the SAR helicopter up the air. Still, with its heat-seeking capabilities, it could help isolate a living human figure in a vast landscape.

Despite their name, the search team didn't restrict themselves to Swaledale, but also carried out operations in Wensleydale and Swainsdale. They had worked on the Claudia Lawrence search back in March 2009, when Claudia, a chef at the University of York, had disappeared. Sadly, Claudia still hasn't been found, though various theories of her murder have been brought forward, including the possibility that she was a victim of the serial killer Christopher Halliwell. The search team had also helped out in recent flood relief efforts, including the collapse of Tadcaster Bridge.

Frustration began to set in quickly, as it so often did with missing persons cases. Things just weren't happening fast enough. Every moment Zelda was missing Banks felt the tension in him rack up a notch. It was partly the impotence, of course, and the not knowing, but also the fear of what might be happening to her and, as time went on, the fear that she might already be dead.

Banks shuffled the papers on his desk. There was a lab report informing him that the cigarette ends found in the hollow near the cottage were Ronhill, a popular Croatian brand, and that they would yield DNA if required. Again, it was all pretty brazen, or careless, on Tadić's part. DNA tests were expensive, but flushed with his newly approved budget, Banks ordered one.

Radio 3 was playing Weinberg's 'Kaddish' Symphony, No. 21. It was close to the end when a melancholy keening female voice entered. The strange melody was so moving that Banks stopped what he was doing for a few moments and just listened. He didn't know the composer's work well but had read about him recently in *Gramophone* and liked what he was hearing. Amazing to know there were at least twenty more symphonies out there waiting to be heard. Weinberg had also written quite a lot of music for viola, one of Banks's favourite instruments, up there with the oboe. He had known a very beautiful violist years ago, and had almost had an affair with her. Almost.

When the symphony finished, the announcer mentioned that the wordless singing was performed by the conductor of the City of Birmingham Symphony Orchestra herself: Mirga Gražinytė-Tyla. Even more impressive. Banks only wished he could learn to pronounce her name.

As his thoughts began to drift, he was struck with an idea he thought might produce some positive results. Zelda, Banks was almost a hundred per cent certain, was being kept somewhere in the area. But where? It seemed unlikely they would keep her in a village or small town, as newcomers would draw too much attention in such places – especially newcomers like Tadić and Zelda – where everyone knew everyone else's business. But given that Blaydon owned dozens of vacant properties all over Yorkshire, and that Tadić had been connected with Blaydon, wouldn't these be logical places to search, along with recent holiday cottage lets, Airbnbs, converted barns and so forth?

The problem with this line of thinking was that Blaydon was dead. But that didn't have to be a game-stopper. Tadić had used Blaydon's properties before as pop-up brothels, so he probably had a good idea of what was available out there. In the same way, Leka Gashi had used them for his county lines operations. The connection might seem obvious, and something to be avoided by a cautious criminal, but as Banks had already seen, Tadić was far from cautious: he was brazen and arrogant. Perhaps he might also be careless or stupid enough to use one of Blaydon's empty properties to keep Zelda.

Banks phoned through to the squad room and talked to Gerry, who assured him that their files on the Blaydon murder investigation contained comprehensive lists of all the properties on his books. Ever since he had become more interested in speculation and property development – projects like the Elmet Centre – rather than mere ownership, Blaydon had let many of the places he already owned go to seed, or had simply rented them out and forgotten about them. Now he was dead, his daughter would inherit them, along with everything else, but she had already indicated that she had no interest in her late father's businesses and would rather just sell the whole kit and caboodle and go live in St Kitts and Nevis.

Banks asked Gerry if she could make time to come up with a list of vacant, isolated Blaydon properties within a radius of, say, twenty miles of Windlee Farm, and she said she would.

'So Charlotte Westlake is lying about not knowing the girl?'

'So it would appear,' said Gerry. She was sitting at her desk in the squad room of Eastvale Regional HQ the day after talking with Tamara Collins. 'The interesting question is why.'

'We both felt there was something she wasn't telling us,' Annie said. 'And this is probably it. She's more involved than we thought.'

'It's not much, though, is it? Mistaken identity. Poor photograph. Easy to explain away. Maybe she genuinely didn't recognise this Marnie from the photo, especially if she didn't know her well?'

'It's a connection. That's what's important. And it tells us she's a liar. You specifically asked her if it might have been someone who worked for her at the parties, and she had every chance to come up with a possibility or two. Remember, she didn't study the photo closely. She just rejected it out of hand. Fair enough, it's not a great photo, but if you'd hired the person depicted in it, there's a reasonable chance you might recognise her from it, don't you think?'

'I suppose so.'

'Why should we trust anything she tells us? For all we know she might be in cahoots with Tadić on supplying the girls. Maybe she's a madam with a ready-made stable.'

Gerry smiled. 'Hang on a minute . . . It *is* still possible that Charlotte was telling the truth and she didn't recognise Marnie from the picture.'

'I know. I know,' said Annie. 'Maybe I'm exaggerating, making too much of it. But we have to consider that Charlotte Westlake *might* be lying, out of loyalty to Blaydon, or to cover up some involvement of her own. In exactly what, I don't know. Remember she said she knew him vaguely before she went to work for him. Maybe he's the rapist, and Marnie told Charlotte about it, cried on her shoulder? What would Charlotte do about that? At the very least she ought to be able to supply us with the victim's last name now we can tell her the first one, which is a hell of a lot more than we have right now.'

'True enough,' Gerry agreed. 'But are you also thinking Charlotte might have had something to do with Blaydon's murder because of what he did to Marnie?'

'Or Marnie herself,' she said. 'But I can't see either of them going that far. And gutting him . . .? No. Charlotte's already told us she was finding Blaydon's behaviour harder and harder to take. That's why she left.'

'If she's telling us the truth about that.'

'Fair enough. But Marnie was just another employee. And what about Gashi? Maybe *he* was the rapist? Maybe he killed Blaydon because he thought he had something on him, or he found out about Roberts filming it? Don't forget, we've always leaned towards the theory that the Albanians killed Blaydon. We just lacked any evidence. Maybe this is it? At least it gives us a clearer motive. Perhaps we should go and have another word with Charlotte, push her a bit harder.'

'We could have the local force pick her up and bring her in,' Gerry suggested. 'Use an interview room. Give her the full treatment. Be more intimidating.'

Annie thought for a moment. 'Good idea. We've got Tamara's statement that Charlotte met with the girl in her office. That gives us something to confront her with, more ammunition.'

'Sounds like a plan,' Gerry said, sliding off the desk. 'I'd better get back to work on Blaydon's empty properties for the super first, see if we can find a suitable property Tadić could be using to keep Zelda prisoner.'

'It's as good an idea as any.'

The door opened and the bright light of a heavy-duty work lamp flooded in. Zelda blinked at the onslaught. When her eyes adjusted, she noticed Petar Tadić standing there with a scruffy, thuggish man she didn't know. She retreated to her corner and pulled up her knees. She could tell from the way Tadić looked at her that he still had no idea who she was, that they had met before, that he had raped her. The light elongated and distorted their shadows on the walls, so they resembled deformed creatures from a horror film. Freaks. Dracula in his cape. Nosferatu.

'Sit up straight against that wall by the radiator,' Tadić said.

Zelda didn't move.

Tadić stepped forward and kicked her on the hip. She cried out.

'Against the wall.'

Zelda shuffled herself into position.

Tadić turned the light full on her, and his sidekick took a digital camera from his pocket and squatted in front of her.

'Hold your head up. Don't smile for the camera,' Tadić said and grinned.

That was easy to do. The sidekick took several photos of her head and shoulders. 'Done, boss,' he said.

'Give the camera to Foley. He'll know what to do.'

He picked up the light and they left without another word. Zelda breathed a sigh of relief as she was once again consigned to darkness.

The interview room wasn't especially designed to scare the shit out of anyone questioned there, nor was it created to inspire a sense of calm and well-being. The walls were either institutional green or dishwater grey, depending on the light, which came in through a tiny high window covered by a grille. The furniture consisted of a metal table bolted to the floor, along with two hard-backed chairs on each side. Against one wall stood another table laden with tape-recording equipment, and high in one corner, the CCTV camera looked down on the proceedings and recorded every twitch and tic. The room's starkness was symbolic of its purpose: to get down to the bare bones.

The day Charlotte Westlake was led inside, the walls were decidedly pale grey in contrast to the bright sunshine outside, and to Charlotte's yellow blouse and green skirt. There was no air-conditioning, and the heat rose steadily throughout the interview. At the end, everyone was sweating, not only Charlotte Westlake.

When she was brought in, she first leaned, palms down, on the table and addressed Annie and Gerry: 'I want it on record that I very much resent this intrusion into my life for no apparent reason.'

'Sit down, Mrs Westlake,' said Annie. 'The sooner we get started, the sooner we'll be finished.'

Charlotte sat slowly, the anger still etched into the hard lines of her face. She wore her hair pulled back, fastened in a loose bun at the nape of her neck, and the tightness of her hairline accentuated her high cheekbones and narrow jaw. Her sapphire eyes were blazing with rage. 'Should I be sending for my solicitor?'

'Up to you,' said Annie. 'As far as we're concerned, this is what we call an "intelligence interview" and you're here simply to answer a few questions about a crime. You haven't been arrested or charged with anything.'

'I know you lot,' she said. 'You're sneaky. You'll get me to admit things.'

'Admit to what things?'

'You know what I mean. You're at it already.'

Annie leaned forward and tapped her pen on the table. 'This could be very simple,' she said. 'You answer a few questions, tell the truth, and it's all over. Call your solicitor and, well, things can get very long and drawn-out from that point. We could fix you up with a duty solicitor, but somehow I don't think that's what you want. You complained to the officers who brought you here that you have tickets for Opera North tonight. If you simply let us do our jobs, there's no reason why you shouldn't be there to enjoy the show. Believe me, we're not trying to trap you into admitting anything criminal. This entire conversation is being recorded for your sake as well as ours, and you haven't been cautioned. We can go through all the motions if you want, and perhaps we can charge you with wasting police time, or impeding an investigation, but believe me, it'll be far more binding on you should anything more serious come of our little chat. And it'll take time. So what's it to be?'

'I'm not being held on any charges?'

'No.'

'So I'm free to go?'

'Yes.'

She stood up. 'Then what's to stop me?'

'Nothing,' said Annie. 'Go ahead, if you like. All you need to know is that we think you have information we would like to have in our possession, too, and we don't give up that easily. You either lied to us or you were mistaken the last time we talked to you. This is your chance to put things right. Maybe your last chance. So walk, if you wish. We can't stop you. But we're not going away.' She paused. 'And you would be obstructing us in our investigation.'

Annie held eye contact with Charlotte for what felt like a long time before the latter slowly subsided back into her chair and said, 'Fine. Let's get on with it, then, get it over with. What do you want to know?'

Gerry, who had been sitting quietly taking notes of anything that might not be obvious from a sound or video recording, slid over the photograph of Marnie. 'Last time we talked to you,' she said, 'you told us you didn't know this girl.'

Charlotte glanced at the photo, then quickly turned away. 'That's right,' she said, her voice hesitant and shaky.

'Her name is Marnie. Does that help at all?'

'Marnie . . . I . . . I . . .'

Annie took over and tried to set her at ease. 'Easy to be mistaken. We admit it's not a very good image. But take another look. Go on. Take your time.'

Charlotte studied the picture, then said, 'Well, it *could* be her . . . I suppose. She *does* seem sort of familiar on closer inspection.'

'So you *do* know a Marnie?'

'I . . . er . . . yes.'

'Is this her?'

'It could be. Who told you that?'

'It doesn't matter. The point is that we found out. What's her surname?'

'Sedgwick. Marnie Sedgwick. If that's who she is. Is this the one . . .? I mean, God, I'm so sorry about what happened to her.'

'How old is she?'

'Old enough. Nineteen.'

'Old enough for what?' Gerry asked.

'To do the job I employed her for, of course, which might have included serving alcohol at some events.'

'Did it?'

'No. She turned out to be better suited to behind-the-scenes work.'

Annie picked up the questioning again. 'How did you become acquainted with her?'

'If it is the person I'm thinking of, then she's an employee. An occasional employee, I should say.'

'Gig economy?'

'Has to be, in my business. I can't guarantee her full-time or even part-time employment. It's on an event-by-event basis. I used her as and when she was available and when I needed someone.'

'For Blaydon's parties?'

'Yes. And his other events – sales conventions, retirement parties and so on. The usual sort of events most businesses have to cope with.'

'Did you first meet her when she applied for a job?'

'Yes. I don't advertise. At least, only by word of mouth. It would be one of the other girls who suggested her.'

'Which one?'

'I have no idea. As I said, I don't know her well. All I know is she came to me looking for a job, I interviewed her, and she seemed satisfactory, worth taking a chance on.'

'Perhaps you can furnish us with a list of all your employ-ees, however casual they may be? I do believe we asked you for this last time we talked. We haven't got it yet.'

'I know . . . It's just . . . I don't know. What about privacy?'

'Theirs or yours?' said Gerry. 'We're not interested in tax avoidance, if that's what you're worried about. We don't care how many jobs they're doing on the side, or whether they're claiming benefits at the same time. Nor do we care whether your business is registered in Jersey or the Isle of Man. Not our department.'

Charlotte gave her a sour smile. 'Yes, of course.'

'So Marnie's one of your regular helpers now?' said Annie.

'Yes. She was.'

'Is she not still with you?'

'No. That was when I was working for Connor.'

'And now?'

'I'm afraid I have no idea where she is.'

'You let her go?'

'She could have come with me, but she chose not to.'

'Where did she go?'

'I have no idea. She didn't confide in me.'

'Any idea why she left?'

'I assumed she'd found something else. Something better paying, better hours, or steadier work, perhaps.'

'Did she say what?'

'No.'

'How was she as an employee?'

'She was a bit reticent, shy, when it came to the hostess work, and she made it clear that she didn't like doing it. That's why she didn't work out on the service end. She'd worked as a waitress in a family restaurant, but this was different. There was a lot of alcohol involved, and the men . . . Well, I'm sure you know what I mean. Her attitude might have made her seem stand-offish. But she was good at the practical aspects of the job, the backroom stuff. She was no slouch. And she was reliable. Always turned up on time. You'd be surprised how rare that is these days.'

'Just not so good at chatting up the men at front of house?'

'That wasn't part of her job. And it's a strictly hands-off policy with my serving girls. Connor knew that. It's not as if there weren't enough of the other kind of women around recently. Marnie's an attractive girl, it's true, but she isn't the type to display her cleavage and a bit of thigh. She's a very serious girl, a thinker rather than a talker. She's also good at being invisible when she needed to be. I liked that about her. And mostly she was stuck in the kitchen. You have no idea how much cleaning up, restocking and ongoing maintenance there is to be done at events like those parties. They don't run as smoothly without a lot of skilled help, you know.'

'Maybe all of Blaydon's guests didn't know about your hands-off policy,' Gerry cut in. 'She certainly wasn't invisible to one particular person on the night this image was captured. Sometimes people want what they can't have, more than what's on offer. Perhaps someone thought she was too stuck-up and wanted to bring her down a notch or two?'

'I wasn't there. I told you. I'm sorry about what happened. It's terrible. You can't believe how sorry. Maybe if I'd been there . . .? But it wasn't my fault. I was in Costa Rica.'

'Yes, we know,' Annie said. 'But the point remains that you *do* know Marnie Sedgwick. You employed her to work at that party on 13 April, as you had done before, even though you weren't present yourself.'

'Yes, but I don't see how you could possibly hold me responsible for anything that occurred at that party.'

'Who said anything about holding you responsible? We're after information, that's all, not to apportion blame. Do you *feel* responsible?'

'No. I'm just upset. You're twisting my words. I knew this was the sort of thing you'd do.'

'Why did you lie to us about knowing Marnie?'

'I didn't lie. I just wasn't sure. It's a bad photo. Maybe I didn't look closely enough. I don't know. I just didn't want to get involved.'

'Involved in what? Did you already know what had happened to Marnie? Did you lie about that, too?'

'Know? About the rape? Good Lord, no. But when the police come calling, you don't think it's about your TV licence being overdue, do you?'

'Is it?'

Charlotte just stared at Annie.

'Joke,' Annie said.

'Does it surprise you, what happened to Marnie at the party?' Gerry asked.

'Of course it does. It appalls me. I organised *parties* for Connor, not orgies. The guests were thoroughly vetted. I know they could get a bit wild sometimes, but every one of them was a trusted—'

'Oh, come off it!' said Annie. 'He invited people he wanted to be seen with, people he wanted to impress and people who might do him some good in business, make him more money. Do you really believe he wouldn't bend over backwards to give one of them what he wanted if it was important to him? They were no more vetted for their morality than the American president. For crying out loud, you had Petar Tadić supplying trafficked girls, and Leka Gashi brought bowls of cocaine. So who saw Marnie Sedgwick and thought she was part of the package, too?'

Charlotte sat forward and placed her palms flat on the table again. 'I've told you, I don't know. I wasn't there. I didn't even know there'd been an incident until you came along.'

'Are you sure about that?' Gerry asked.

Charlotte glanced sideways at her. 'Yes.'

'Blaydon never told you?'

'I don't even know if *he* knew. And if he did, he didn't tell me. Why would he? Isn't it the kind of thing you cover up? He's hardly likely to tell me that something so terrible happened in his house to one of my staff, at an event I organised, even if he didn't do it. People were always slipping off to bedrooms, as I told you. I was getting tired of it, the atmosphere was becoming poisonous.'

'But you said you only rarely attended the parties,' said Annie.

'One hears things. And I popped in from time to time. Some of these things are hard to miss, even on brief acquaintance. I'm not that bloody naive.'

'You also told us that you thought these girls were wives and girlfriends, not professionals brought in for the purposes of sex.'

'That was certainly true in the earlier days.'

'When did it start to change?'

'Around the end of last year.'

'Any ideas why then?'

'Connor got involved in a major new development. A shopping centre and housing estate.'

'The Elmet Centre?'

'Yes. And that's when he brought in Tadić and Gashi, along with a whole host of new business colleagues and hangers-on. That's when his behaviour started to worry me, and the parties started to change in character.'

'So you're not too surprised that something like this might happen? The rape,' Annie said persistently.

'Perhaps not. Seeing as you put it like that. But I'm still shocked.'

'Well, surely it would fall on someone to keep the girl quiet, slip her an extra bob or two, tell her it was an unfortunate incident best put behind her? Who better than you?'

'Well, I didn't. I knew nothing about it.'

'Perhaps she came crying to you, and you comforted her? She told you Blaydon had raped her. One of *your* girls. You saw red. Maybe you killed him?'

'That's ridiculous.'

'Is it? Where were you on the afternoon of 22 May?'

Charlotte seemed knocked sideways by the question. 'Is this a trick question? I've already told you. I'm not sure. We were working on a book award dinner in Bradford, but I was back and forth. Where were you?'

'We're asking you.'

'Bet you don't remember where *you* were.'

'We may ask you to come up with a bit more detail at some point. Something solid we can check.'

Charlotte said nothing.

'Where does Marnie Sedgwick live?' Gerry asked. 'We'd like to talk to her, get her side of the story. Maybe find out why she didn't report the rape.'

'Lots of women don't report rapes because of the way they get treated by the authorities.'

'What way?'

'As if *they're* the guilty ones.'

'OK. Point taken,' said Annie. 'But we'd still like to hear it from her.'

'I don't know her address.'

'Come on, Charlotte. Don't be coy with us now we're

getting along so well. She was on your books. An employee. You must have an address and phone number for her.'

'No. I mean it. I did know. I mean, yes, I had an address for her before, along with her other details, but I heard she'd moved on after that party. Left the area. I don't know where, honestly. And I don't know why, though I suppose I can guess now.'

'Where are your old employment records?'

'With Connor's stuff, I should imagine. I assume you've got it somewhere.'

'You could save us a lot of time. I'm sure you probably kept a note of it in case you wanted her to work for you again.'

'I could probably dig it up,' Charlotte said.

Annie clapped her hands together. 'Good. Now we're getting somewhere. Soon as you get home, please. Along with that list of employees. Didn't you ever wonder why Marnie moved on after the party?'

'Not especially. Girls come and go.'

'Like buses, there'll be another one along in a minute?'

'If you must put it so crudely. I'm a businesswoman. Marnie was one of my employees. That's all there was to it. Now can I go?'

Annie leaned back in her chair. 'You know,' she said, 'it took us a while to get this much out of you, and I'm still not convinced you're telling us the whole story, or the whole truth. But we'll leave it at that for the time being. You probably do remember a lot more than you've admitted to, including names. In which case, if I were you, I'd be very careful from now on.'

'Oh, why's that?'

'Marnie Sedgwick was raped at a party held by Connor Clive Blaydon. A party you organised, no doubt attended by a number of famous faces and up-and-coming Jack-the-Lads that Blaydon had some reason to want to impress. Now, if Blaydon himself didn't rape Marnie, the actual rapist probably has a great deal to lose if he's caught. We don't know who he is. Not long after this party, Blaydon and his so-called butler Neville Roberts were murdered in a particularly nasty manner. I'd worry about that, for a start. We were thinking that maybe it was Gashi's gang, or even Tadić's – after all, they're both international gangsters with about as much respect for human life as Godzilla – but what if it wasn't them? What if it was something to do with what happened to Marnie Sedgwick? Revenge? Self-protection? What if her rapist killed Blaydon? If you do know something you're not telling us, that could put you in a rather dangerous position, couldn't it?'

Charlotte had paled. 'Are you telling me that my life is in danger?'

'We're just warning you to be careful, that's all,' said Gerry. 'Seeing as you employed Marnie and supplied her for the party, another possibility is that some people might have got the impression – the wrong impression, of course – that she was part of the entertainment, and that what happened to her was partly your fault, that you should share some of the blame with the rapist and with Blaydon himself. Maybe Marnie told her father, or her boyfriend, what happened? Maybe one of them killed Blaydon? People jump to conclusions sometimes and act before they think. That's what makes our job so difficult.'

'So what are you suggesting? That you give me police protection?'

'Love to,' said Annie, 'but we're stretched to the limit right now. Still waiting for those twenty thousand new coppers we've been promised.'

'So what *are* you saying?'

'OK, here's the deal,' Annie said. 'You go away and have a good think. A good long think. And you see if you can remember what you haven't told us, then come back and put that right. Especially if you've heard rumours of anyone Marnie may have hung around with at the party, or anyone who'd been bothering her. Say, perhaps, one of the other girls working that night noticed something. If it was Blaydon who raped Marnie, you can tell us. You don't have to worry about him. He's dead. But if it was someone else, someone still alive . . . well, time becomes an issue.'

'But how can I? I don't know anything.'

'You know some of the characters involved. Names. Maybe some of the same people were at previous parties? Maybe you noticed someone expressing an unusual interest in Marnie when you dropped by? Perhaps this person asked Blaydon for a special favour, and Blaydon had good reason to grant him his wishes. Who was he trying to win over, or impress? Perhaps you stood in the way? Maybe that's why he sent you to Costa Rica, to get you out of the picture, clear the decks so to speak. Have you ever thought of that?'

'No, I haven't,' said Charlotte. 'But thanks for putting the idea in my mind. I can try to think back, if you like, but what about in the meantime? What am I supposed to do?'

'In the meantime,' said Gerry, 'you can send us the information we asked for, then take our advice and be very careful.'

On the second visit, Tadić stood over Zelda. 'You know why you're here?' he asked.

'No,' said Zelda. 'I don't even know where here is.'

Tadić laughed, a hoarse, phlegmy sound. 'That doesn't matter. Do you know who I am?'

Again, Zelda shook her head.

'My name is Petar Tadić. Does that help?'

Again, Zelda said, 'No. I'm hungry and thirsty. Can I have—'

With surprising speed, Tadić gave her a backhander that sent her head sideways into the cast-iron radiator. She could taste blood and her head was ringing, starting to throb with pain. She thought she could feel blood oozing into her hair and over her ear.

'Does that help your memory?'

She was about to say no again, but realised what would happen if she did, so she kept quiet. Tadić was a man who liked the sound of his own voice, she remembered.

'Let me tell you, then,' he said, squatting in front of her. 'You're the bitch who murdered my brother.' He put his face so close to hers that she could smell curry on his breath. It almost made her sick. 'Eh, my beauty? Am I right?' He caressed the side of her face where he had just hit her. 'Am I right?'

'I don't know what you mean,' Zelda said. 'I haven't—'

But before she could say any more, he hit her again, in the same place. Her head reeled, and she tasted burning bile in her throat. Luckily, this time her head didn't crash into the radiator.

'It's no use denying it,' Tadić said. 'I saw you on the hotel CCTV. The sexy red dress. Yes? Oh, I saw you. My men are very good. They talk to Foley's girlfriend, Faye Butler. She tells them plenty before she dies. They find restaurant where you saw her with Foley and Hawkins. They find taxi driver who drove you back to your hotel after you kill Goran. They find out your name and where you live from hotel. But not quite, because you give no street and number, do you? Just house name Windlee Farm and that village. Lyndgarth. But we find it. And now we have you. What do you think of that? Good detective work, yes?'

Zelda vomited down the front of her T-shirt.

Tadić jumped back up so fast he almost fell over, but he couldn't escape getting a few flecks on his polished leather Italian shoes.

His partner lurched towards Zelda, but Tadić held him back. 'No,' he said. Then he took a handkerchief from his pocket, cleaned off his shoes and tossed it in a corner.

'Kill her now, boss,' the man said. 'Let *me* kill her.'

'No. That is too easy.' Tadić towered over Zelda. 'Why did you kill him?' he asked. 'Why did you kill Goran?'

Zelda tried to control her breathing, raised her head and looked him in the eye. 'You and your brother abducted me outside an orphanage in Chişinău many years ago.'

'I don't remember you. Or Chişinău. Is that why you killed my brother?'

'Yes,' Zelda spat.

Tadić kicked her again, this time in the stomach. She doubled up in pain. They stood looking down on her as she struggled to hold back more vomit. When she could trust herself to speak again, she asked, 'What are you going to do to me?' Her voice felt thick. She probed a broken tooth with her tongue, tasted blood and vomit.

Tadić grinned. 'Do? I could sell you to the Albanians. They know what to do with a *kurva* like you. But no. Like killing you, it is also too easy. No. I have a friend who tell me about special house in Dhaka. Do you know where that is? Bangladesh. Long way. Sick old men who go there like young girls or boys best, but a white woman like you will be novelty. For a while. Do not worry. You will not survive for long. If the diseases don't rot your pretty little *pička*, the drinking water will poison you. But it will be a slow death. Long and slow and painful. You will have much time to remember what you did to Goran.'

Zelda felt panic rush through her. She jerked and tugged at her chains again and tried to drag her hands apart so much the plasticuffs bit into her skin.

Tadić and his friend just stood there laughing. 'You can scream as loud as you like,' Tadić said. 'There is no one to hear you.'

When the strength went out of Zelda's struggle, she was aware of the light disappearing and the door closing. She lay in the darkness alone again, her face and her teeth aching, head throbbing, and the thought came to her that she would not be able to bear the future they were planning for her, however short it was likely to be. Not only that, but she *couldn't* let it happen. And the only way she knew of stopping it was to kill herself before they got her to Dhaka.

II

According to Charlotte Westlake's records, Marnie Sedgwick had lived in York on a cul-de-sac terrace of tall, narrow Victorian brick semis. It wasn't far from the city centre, and most of the houses were divided into flats and bedsits. Though it was some distance from the university, it looked like student housing, and Annie wondered if Marnie had been a student, working part-time for Charlotte.

They walked up the steps and Annie rang the bell with the empty nameplate beside it. They had phoned ahead and the landlord said he would meet them there. They heard someone coming down the stairs and Duncan McCrae, the landlord, opened the door for them.

'Right on time,' he said, rubbing his hands together.

'We don't like to disappoint,' said Annie, stepping forward. 'Shall we go up?'

'There's nothing to see, like I told you on the phone,' said McCrae, 'but be my guest.' He led the way to the first floor, at the back, where Marnie's tiny bedsit overlooked an alley full of wheelie bins and the backyards of the houses opposite. Beyond them lay train tracks. McCrae hovered in the doorway as if he was worried they'd steal the silverware. Only there wasn't any silverware. There wasn't anything except an empty three-shelf homemade bookcase built of bricks and boards.

'Exactly when did she leave?' Annie asked.

'End of April.'

That worked out at a couple of weeks after the rape, Annie reckoned. 'Did she take all her stuff with her?'

'There wasn't much to take. That's the thing. She just left one day and left the mess to me. As far as I could tell, she probably didn't take more than a suitcase with her. Clothes and some personal stuff. She left the rest. A few books. Some cutlery, dishware, pots and pans. Household things. That's about all. Here one day, gone the next. But her rent was up to date.'

Annie managed to hold her tongue before saying how happy she was to hear that. 'What about a forwarding address?'

McCrae just shook his head.

'Previous address?'

'No.'

'You didn't ask for her details?'

McCrae shifted from foot to foot. 'Well . . . er . . . no.'

'What happened to her things?'

'Bin bag in the cellar. I thought I'd keep it a little while, you know, in case she called back for it.'

'We'll look at it when we're done here,' Annie said as she started wandering about the small room. She peeled back a moth-eaten curtain and saw the hot plate with two shelves above it, both bare. There was nothing else in the room.

'Where did she sleep?' Gerry asked.

'Mattress on the floor, under the window there, and a ratty old sleeping bag,' said McCrae. 'I threw them both out.'

Annie sniffed the air. It was stale and foisty, as one would expect in a room shut up so long in warm weather. She tried to open the window but couldn't budge it.

'Bloody painters,' said McCrae. 'Only painted it shut, didn't they?'

'What was Marnie like?' Gerry asked.

'Like? Well, just ordinary really. Quiet. She never said much. Seemed a serious sort of girl. Used to have posters on the walls – save the planet, that sort of thing. Always polite, though. A smile and a hello. Well brought up. You could tell. I never had much to do with her, really, so there's not a lot I can tell you beyond that.'

'What happened to the posters?' Annie could see the bare patches where they used to be.

'I took them down, dumped them.'

'Did you notice any changes in her behaviour or demeanour?'

'Eh? Come again.'

'Anything different about her around the time she left?'

'I didn't talk to her much the last few weeks she was here. I don't live here, of course, so I wouldn't know. But I don't think she went out much. I mean, if I was around fixing something, I didn't see her coming or going. Like I said, she left at the end of the month.'

'Did you *see* her at all?'

'Once or twice.'

'How did she seem on those occasions, the last two or three weeks?'

McCrae seemed stumped by the question. 'Tired, mostly,' he said. 'Her eyes, you know. Puffy. With bags under. As if she hadn't been getting enough sleep.'

'Or crying?' said Annie.

'Aye, maybe that, too.'

That made sense, Annie thought, given what Marnie had been through. Why had she not sought help? What had been going on in her mind? 'Was she a student?' she asked.

'Miss Sedgwick? No, I don't think so. You'd have to ask the others, though.'

'How did she get around?'

'She had a car. A Fiat, I think.'

'So Marnie was wealthy?'

'No, I'd hardly say that. You wouldn't, either, if you saw the car. But she had a paying job. Two, actually.'

'What jobs?'

'A cafe in town. Waitress. One of those chains. Ask. Zizzi. Pizza Express. Something like that.'

'You can't remember which one?'

'I think it was Pizza Express, but I can't be certain. She gave me a slice once. Pizza, that is. She brought some home from work with her and I happened to be in the hall. I think the box was Pizza Express but I wouldn't swear to it.'

'And the other?'

'Catering of some sort, or helping caterers. That one was occasional. Just when she was needed, like.'

'Did she have any close friends among the other tenants?'

'I did see her chatting with that Chinese lass from 3b once or twice. They seemed quite close.'

'OK. I think we've seen enough here,' said Annie. 'Can we go and see the stuff she left behind her now?'

'Follow me,' said McCrae. He led them down to the ground floor, where he fumbled for a key in his pockets and opened a door to the cellar. It was more of a basement, really, Annie thought, having imagined a grim and sooty old coal cellar, and she was surprised McCrae hadn't done it up a bit, given it a lick of paint and rented it out as a basement apartment. Instead, it was full of junk.

McCrae took them over to a black bin bag in a corner. 'This is it,' he said.

Gerry went back to the car to get the proper bags to store the stuff as evidence. There wasn't much, as McCrae had said. Books, mostly philosophy and psychology as far as Annie could tell; two plates, cups, glasses, knives and forks; and a pan and kettle she would have heated on the hot plate. That was it. No personal items – notebooks, diaries, lists of addresses, letters, nothing like that.

'What about post since she left?'

McCrae walked over to a battered chest of drawers, opened the top one and took out a bundle of envelopes fastened with a rubber band. 'I keep the mail of any tenants who leave for a while, if they don't arrange a forwarding address, just in case there's something important. You'd be surprised. Over the years I've had cheques, passports, you name it. These are just junk mail.'

Gerry took the bundle. They might hold some clue as to where Marnie had gone. 'Thanks,' she said. 'We'll take these, too.'

After they had carried out Marnie's stuff and stored it in the boot of the car, they tried the door to 3b, occupied by a student called Mitsuko Ogawa, who was definitely not Chinese, as even Annie's rudimentary grasp of foreign languages told her. But there was no one home. She scribbled a little note, added her mobile number and said they'd be back later, then she grinned at Gerry. 'If you ask me, it's lunchtime. Fancy a pizza?'

Zelda still couldn't tell whether it was night or day. At one time, she thought she could hear traffic beyond the boarded-up windows, or an airplane fly over, but even then she thought she might be imagining things. One thing she wasn't imagining was that nobody was coming to rescue her. No Willie Garvin. No doubt the police were trying to find her, but they clearly had no more idea where she was being kept than she did. And there was no way she could see of getting a message out.

She spent a lot of time trying to figure out ways of killing herself before they could take her to that brothel in Dhaka.

She tried to wrap the leg chain around her neck to strangle herself, but it wasn't long enough, so she only managed to strain a muscle in her thigh. She tried holding her breath, and swallowing her tongue, but found she could do neither. She always gasped for breath on the verge of passing out and never got as far as putting her fingers in her mouth to push the rolled ball of tongue down her throat. She couldn't face trying to bash her brains out against the radiator.

She was a coward, she had to admit. If she were to die, she wanted it to be as easy and painless as possible. Pills, preferably. There was no way she could stand Dhaka, so she had to do it somehow. Maybe there would be more opportunities along the way? Maybe she could even catch somebody's attention and get free – at an airport, for example, or on a flight. It would be a long journey; they would have to escort her through at least one airport, if not more. She was certain that even Tadić didn't have a private jet. Or did they plan on travelling overland, smugglers' routes? No doubt that was why she was being kept here so long, so that they could work out the routes and phoney visas. She had already figured out that the photographs they had taken when she first arrived were for a fake passport, no doubt to be supplied by Keane, the man she thought had killed Hawkins and who had once tried to kill Alan Banks.

Alan. Raymond. She thought of them often; sometimes she thought she would burst with grief when she pictured Raymond alone and desolate at Windlee Farm. He would be a complete mess. That would be one way to die, she supposed. Grief. And what was Alan doing? He would do whatever he could to find her, of that she was sure. But it was hopeless.

Despite the fear and the will to suicide, Zelda was hungry again. As long as her body survived, it would demand sustenance, just as it needed movement and air. She could stand up, but she couldn't move far in her leg iron. She marked time every now and then, just to keep her circulation going.

After that second visit, Tadić's sneering sidekick had returned to deliver a chamber pot and throw a plastic bottle of water and a Big Mac at her. She had seen the way he looked at her, and knew that only fear of Tadić stopped him having his way. That and the vomit on her T-shirt, perhaps.

The Big Mac was cold, but she had gobbled it down. The water she tried to make last. The chamber pot was a blessing, as she imagined the only alternative – short of squatting on the floor – would be for one of them to accompany her to the toilet whenever she needed to go. A chance to wash and change would be nice, though. Surely, they would want to clean her up before they travelled? A bath, perhaps? Fresh clothes. But what was the point of any of it if she was going to die anyway, either before she got to Dhaka, with any luck, or soon after she arrived there, if the worst happened?

Sometimes she thought that she couldn't take her own life because she still had dreams of escape, hope of being rescued. It was true, these things *could* happen, though they grew less likely hour by hour. If she didn't eat, then perhaps she would get ill and die of malnutrition, rather than by her own weak hand. But she thought that would take much longer than they planned keeping her here.

Also, in some of her darkest moments, she had a strange feeling of elation out of nowhere. It was like a smell – not of the sea, but of the seaside – and a vague image of being a little girl walking with her hand in her father's at Odessa flashed through her mind. A sense of safety and warmth. But it was also neither a smell nor an image; it was an inchoate memory of total happiness she had perhaps never experienced. How could you have a memory of something you had never felt? But that was what it felt like.

In the embrace of that perfect happiness, she had not a care, not a worry, not a thought, but the sheer pleasure of being. No fear of what was to come or regret for what was past. It was pure and simple happiness, the ghost of childhood's essence.

But it was rare and fleeting. Most of the time she felt a deep and paralysing sense of fear and dread, edging into despair, that no amount of reason or epiphany could dispel.

Driving in York was an absolute nightmare, Gerry thought as she steered her way along narrow streets lined with parked cars, braked sharply for pedestrians and missed a turning that forced her to make a long detour. But parking was even worse. Finally, in frustration, she pulled into the forecourt of York Explore Library and Archive and threw herself on the mercy of the woman in charge, who told her she could leave the car there until they were finished.

'Next time we'll take the bloody Poppleton Park & Ride,' Annie said as they crossed the road and walked the short distance down to Pizza Express. The city was bursting at the seams with tourists and locals out enjoying the fine weather, and this area around the bridge was always crowded. It led ultimately up past St Mary's and the library to the Minster, which stood at the top dominating everything, a magnificent Gothic construction, its main tower obscured by scaffolding.

Pizza Express was in an old building with a high ceiling on Museum Street near the bridge and opposite the Museum Gardens. The large dining area reminded Annie of a banquet hall in some ancient stately home. They flashed their warrant cards, and Annie asked the girl who showed people to their tables if she might talk to the manager. The girl disappeared through a door to the back and came out moments later with a tanned young man in a suit and tie. He didn't look old enough to be a manager, Annie thought, but what did she know about the hospitality industry? He introduced himself as Mark Baldini.

She showed him the photograph. 'Do you remember a woman called Marnie Sedgwick? Does she still work here?'

'Marnie. Yes, I remember her,' he said. 'She left around the beginning of May.'

'Do you remember the circumstances of her leaving?'

'It was so sad,' Baldini said. 'Marnie was a good worker. She'd been here about a year, but towards the middle of April she changed. She wasn't concentrating, seemed to be dragging her feet. She wasn't attentive, she mixed up orders, delivered things to the wrong tables.'

'What did you do?'

'I liked her. And as I said, she was a good worker, so I took her aside into the office and had a word with her.'

'How did she react?'

'She didn't react much at all. She agreed she wasn't doing a great job, said she wasn't sleeping well, that she couldn't concentrate. I asked her if she was ill or if there was anything wrong, anything I could help with, and she shrugged and said no. I asked if she thought she could attain her previous high standard of work again, and she said she'd try.'

'Did she?'

'Nothing changed. I hated to do it, but I knew in the end I'd have to give her notice. I was going to tell her she could come back when she was better, like, and I'd do my best to make sure she got her job back, but she couldn't go on as she was.'

'How did she respond?'

'I never got to tell her. The next day she got an order wrong, and the customer was very snappy with her. He was one of those pushy, loud-mouthed blokes. You know the sort. Always right, always angry. He shouted at her, called her a stupid cunt, and Marnie dumped the pizza on his lap and ran out in tears. That was the last I saw of her. I made sure we paid her what we owed her, into her bank account, like, a standing order, and that was it. What was it? What was her problem? Do you know?'

'That's what we're trying to find out, Mr Baldini,' said Annie. 'Was she close to any of her colleagues here? Anyone who's still here?'

'Yes,' said Baldini. 'Mitsuko. In fact, it was Marnie brought her to us, got her the job. I think they shared a flat or lived in the same house or something.'

'Mitsuko Ogawa?' said Annie.

'Yes. Lovely girl. Terrific waitress.'

'Is she here now?'

Baldini glanced around. 'She should be.' Finally, he pointed to a table in the far corner where a petite young woman was serving pizza and salad. 'That's Mitsuko.'

'Can you do us a favour?' Annie asked.

'Depends what it is.'

'We're going to have some lunch here, so could you give Ms Ogawa an early tea break or whatever and ask her to join us at our table? We won't keep her for long.'

'Of course. Take as long as you like. We're not too busy right now.'

It was mid-afternoon, and the place still seemed fairly full to Annie, though she and Gerry had no difficulty getting a table for four. Busyness in a place like this was all relative, she supposed.

When their waitress came by, Annie ordered a margherita pizza and side salad, and Gerry picked a Diavola. Both ordered Diet Cokes to accompany their meals. They had barely got their order in before a young woman joined them at the table. She introduced herself as Mitsuko Ogawa and sat down. Annie guessed that Mitsuko was around Marnie's age.

She was small, with shoulder-length black hair drawn tight from her forehead and fastened at the back. Her eyes shone with concern as she sat down and smoothed her dress over her knees.

'Mr Baldini said you wanted to talk to me about Marnie,' she said, with a slight Geordie accent. 'Do you know where she is? What's happened to her?'

'I'm afraid we don't know where she is,' said Gerry. 'That's one problem we were hoping you might help us with. I understand the two of you were close?'

'I thought so,' Mitsuko said.

'What do you mean?'

'Something changed. I don't know what it was, but she just wasn't the same after. Did Mr Baldini tell you what happened here?'

'Yes. He said her work went downhill and she left in tears.'

'That's about right.'

'Do you have any idea why? What was wrong with her? He said he thought she might be ill.' They had a very good idea of what was wrong with Marnie, but they couldn't tell Mitsuko; they were hoping she might be able to tell them more than they knew already.

'She wasn't eating properly,' said Mitsuko. 'Or sleeping very well. But I don't think there was any illness as such. Just a sort of malaise, you know, weariness, depression. She lost interest in everything. But I don't know why. We used to be friends. When she first moved into the house a year ago, we spent a lot of time together, you know, just talking, listening to music. We'd go out to the pub, the cinema, concerts. Marnie likes art-house movies – Bergman and Kurosawa, that sort of thing. And she likes goth rock. You know, old weird stuff like Joy Division, Nick Cave, Sisters of Mercy. All that dark stuff. My taste is a bit more mainstream and upbeat. Action thrillers and Marvel. And I prefer music you can dance to. But we liked each other.'

'So you'd say you are close friends?'

'Yes,' said Mitsuko. 'Yes, I would. I've been beside myself since she left. Has something happened to her? *Please* tell me if it has. I've been worried sick.'

'Not that we know of,' said Annie. 'We're just trying to find her. What's she like?'

'Marnie? I suppose she struck me as fairly complicated, really, serious, sensitive, deep-thinking, but she can also be pretty happy-go-lucky a lot of the time. She's great fun. We had some laughs. She loves life, but that doesn't mean she doesn't see the problems in the world. She's especially serious about climate change. That Greta is a real hero of hers. Or should I say heroine? She's generous, thoughtful, interested in people. I got the impression she was maybe a bit secretive. Like, you'd spend an evening with her and realise you'd told her your deepest darkest secrets but you hadn't learned much about her in return. Enigmatic, I guess. But I suppose we all are, to some extent.'

'Did she tell you about her life?' Annie asked.

'Not much,' said Mitsuko. 'Bits and pieces over the time we knew each other, I suppose. But that's how it happens, isn't it? I mean, you don't usually sit down and tell your new friends your whole life story at once. You find out about people slowly, over time. Bits and pieces come out when something reminds you of a particular incident or sparks a memory. That's what it was like. She comes from down south somewhere, but I don't remember where, if she ever even told me. It was near the sea, I think. I know she missed the sea. But she could be annoyingly vague on details. She'd just moved up here when we first met a year or so back. Wanted a change of scene. I could relate to that.'

'Did you make such a change?'

Mitsuko smiled. 'Yep. All the way from Sunderland. My dad came over here to work for Nissan when they opened the plant in 1986. He and my mother liked England so much that they stayed. I was born here.'

'Why did Marnie move to York? Was she a student here?'

'No, she wasn't at uni. And I don't know why she moved – except for that change of scene I mentioned.'

'I see. Are you sure you can't remember where she came from? We're really keen to find her, and anything to speed that up would help us a lot.'

'I'm sorry. She talked about her father quite a lot, what a great guy he was, how kind and gentle. Hang on, though. She did say something once about it being Hardy country. Her dad liked Hardy. We did him at school. That's Wessex, isn't it?'

Annie had no idea. She shot Gerry a glance.

'That's right,' Gerry said. 'Well, Wessex isn't a real place, but Hardy based it mostly on Dorset. Plenty of sea around there.'

Annie rolled her eyes at Mitsuko. 'The benefits of a public-school education.'

'We never did Hardy at school,' Gerry protested. 'Far too risqué. I read him off my own bat one summer holiday when I was at uni. *Tess of the d'Urbervilles*. You should try it.'

'Life's too short,' said Annie. 'I'll stick with Martina Cole and Marian Keyes.' She turned back to Mitsuko. 'What did Marnie have to say about her childhood?'

'She said she had been happy growing up. I got the impression it was a pretty ordinary childhood. You know. Caring parents, and all. Like mine, really. Did well at the local comp. She was all set for uni, and she said she'd done her first year at Nottingham, studying History, I think. But she soon realised she simply couldn't afford to finish it, that she'd end up so much in debt she'd never get it paid off. I mean, History might be fun, but it's hardly a passport to a high-paying job, is it? Not that I think that's what uni should be about or anything. Her folks were great, she said, but they didn't have a lot of money, and she wasn't going to even ask them to help her out. So she dropped out.'

'And came here to work at Pizza Express?'

'Yes. That's about it. I suppose you could say both of us are trying to figure out what to do with our lives, where to go next. I mean, this job isn't meant to be permanent for either of us.'

'And you?'

'I'm at uni,' Mitsuko said. 'English Literature. Also pretty useless for the job market.'

'Did Marnie ever tell you anything about the other job she had?'

'You mean the posh parties?'

'Yes.'

'Well, I think she only worked a few, but she said she got paid as much for one of them as she did in a week working here, so that was a big incentive to do more. She didn't care much about all the celebs and so on, but I think she kind of liked the job in a way. She said most of the time she was in the kitchen, or driving back and forth from base. It was like some sort of industrial kitchen on *MasterChef*, she told me. She did talk about a footballer she met – she knows I'm a big Sunderland fan – and what an egotistical jerk he was. And a guitarist from a band I liked who didn't have anything much to say to anyone. Little vignettes like that. There were a lot of boring old politicians and businessmen there, too, but she didn't have a lot of contact with them. She worked behind the scenes.'

'Can you give us their names?' Gerry asked. 'The footballer and guitarist. We may have heard of them.'

Mitsuko looked puzzled but said, 'Sure,' and told them. Gerry had heard of the footballer but not the guitarist. Annie knew of neither.

'What about the man who threw the parties,' Annie asked. 'The man whose house it was? Connor Clive Blaydon?'

'Was that his name? She never said. Just that she was working for an old friend of her boss.'

'Did Marnie say exactly what she did there?'

'A bit of everything. Dogsbody, she said. Loading and unloading the dishwasher, arranging trays of canapés, opening wine bottles and tins of caviar. She'd lend a hand with just about anything if they got busy or someone didn't turn up.'

'What about meeting the guests, serving drinks and so on?'

'She got to serve drinks occasionally, but she didn't like it much. Mostly they had a bunch of scantily dressed women to do that.' Mitsuko lowered her voice. 'She did say there was stuff going on, you know. Escorts and that sort of thing.'

'Did she mention anyone in particular, anyone who had shown interest in her?'

'I don't think so.'

'What about unasked-for attention?'

'Uh-oh. Well, that's always a given, isn't it, for someone like Marnie? Even here. She isn't exactly beautiful, but she's definitely striking. And sexy, I suppose. In that innocent sort of way, you know, without realising it, or at least without emphasising it or playing it up at all. She just *is*, you know.'

'Natural?'

'Very.'

'Anything serious? At the parties.'

'She got offers, you know. A thousand quid if you spend the night with me. That sort of thing. Some old wrinkly who liked young girls. Maybe the occasional pat on the bum.'

'How did she react?'

'Shrugged it off, mostly, like you do.'

'Did she mention any names?'

'Apart from the footballer and guitarist? Not really. Not that I remember.'

'The name of anyone who propositioned her?'

'No. I don't know if she even knew their names. I mean, I'm not saying it happened a lot, just that she thought it was a bit of a laugh, that's all.' Mitsuko paused and frowned, as much as her tight forehead would let her. 'Is this going somewhere? Why are you so interested in the parties? Did something happen to Marnie there?'

'I don't know,' said Annie. 'Did something?'

'It wasn't long after her last party gig that she . . . you know . . . Did something bad happen to her there?'

'Did she talk to you about that particular party?'

'No. That's when she . . . she went strange. We never got to talk about it. Oh, my God. That's what this is about, isn't it? Something happened to her. Is she hurt? Is she dead?'

'Nothing like that.' Gerry rushed to reassure her. 'We're just trying to find her, that's all.'

'But something happened, didn't it? Please tell me. Was it drugs?'

'I'm sorry, Mitsuko,' Annie said. 'We can't give you any information. Right now it's confidential. You mentioned escorts. Did she talk to you about the things that went on at these parties? Sexual things, or other stuff.'

'She said there were drugs. Mostly cocaine. But she never took any. She wouldn't do that. And she thought some of the women with impossibly big boobs were hookers. They would sometimes disappear with a guest for a while. Apparently, the place had a lot of bedrooms. Sometimes people got lost, she said, and wandered into the kitchen and got embarrassed. And once she saw some naked girls swimming in the pool.'

'Sounds pretty exciting,' Gerry said.

'Marnie didn't think so,' said Mitsuko. 'She just thought it was sad. Or funny. But it paid well.'

'Did she ever mention Charlotte Westlake?'

'Her boss?'

'Yes.'

'Once or twice, just in passing, like.'

'Did she say how she first heard of Charlotte?'

'No. She didn't tell me. And I never thought to ask. It was just a job, you know, like this. I did . . . never mind.'

'What were you going to say?' Annie prompted her.

'Nothing. It was just an impression, but from the way she talked, I sort of felt she'd known this Westlake woman from before.'

'From before? When?'

'I don't know. But don't you just get feelings like that sometimes, from the way someone talks about someone? I don't know, body language, a facial expression. It was just a passing fancy.'

'Did Marnie drink much?'

'She liked a drink – white wine was her favourite – but she didn't overdo it, no. I've only seen her drunk about once or twice in all the time I've known her.'

'How did it affect her?'

'First she'd get very funny, silly, then she'd fall asleep.'

'You mentioned drugs. Did Marnie take any? You said she didn't touch coke; what about others?'

Mitsuko looked away.

'You can tell us,' said Annie. 'We're interested in finding her, not arresting her for smoking a spliff or whatever.'

'Ecstasy a couple of times, at parties. And maybe the occasional smoke. But that's as far as it went. Never the hard stuff. Like I said, she wouldn't have taken any of that stuff at those parties she was working.'

'Did she have a boyfriend?'

'She went out a few times with Rick, one of the guys from the pub we hung out in. The Star and Garter. He's nice enough. Fancies himself a poet, and Marnie was a sucker for artistic types. All that goth darkness and stuff. But I don't think it was serious.'

Gerry made a note and Annie asked, 'Is Rick still around?'

'Sure. Should be. But I don't think he'll be able to tell you anything. They split up around the same time she started getting strange.' Mitsuko paused. 'I'm still really worried about her, you know. That she might do ... you know ... might harm herself. She was soooo depressed when she left.'

'Do you know if she saw a doctor?'

'I suggested it, but she just shook her head.'

'Did she give you any idea at all of what might be going on, what caused her state of mind?'

'No,' said Mitsuko. 'And in the end, I just learned to stop bothering her. She'd get mad, tell me to shut up and leave her alone. I couldn't get through to her. And it hurt, you know.'

'I can imagine it did,' Annie said. 'Do you know where she went?'

'No. She just took off after that incident at work. I was working here that day, too, and Mr Baldini said I should go after her and make sure she was all right. He's very nice. So I did, but when I got back to the house, she was packing a few things in a suitcase. I asked her where she was going, and she said she was just going away for a few days to be by herself. I asked her what was wrong, but she told me it was nothing, not to worry. And that was it. I was dismissed. She drove off and she never came back. I left emails and messages on her mobile but got no response. I've been worried about her ever since. It's been over six weeks now and not a word. When you find her, please let me know. I won't try to see her or anything if she doesn't want. I just need to know that she's all right. Will you tell me?'

'Yes,' said Annie. 'Do you have a recent photograph you could share with us? The one we have is very poor quality.'

'Sure. I think.' Mitsuko pulled out her mobile from her back pocket and searched through her photo library. 'We went for a cheap city break to Rome last October,' she said. 'It was amazing. We saw the Sistine Chapel, the Colosseum, the Pantheon, everything. Here.' She turned the phone so they could see a clear picture of Marnie with a Roman ruin in the background. 'That was taken in the Forum.'

'Thanks,' said Annie. 'Can you email it to me?'

'I can AirDrop it,' Mitsuko said.

In a few moments Annie was asked if she was willing to accept the photo. She clicked yes, and there it was. She held out the phone and Gerry bent forward to see it too. It was the first time they had seen what the person they were after looked like. The image from the SD card did her no justice at all. Marnie was a lot more attractive than Annie had been able to tell from the video capture. And no doubt the fact that she was enjoying a weekend break in Rome, and hadn't just been assaulted, helped a great deal. Her big dark eyes stared directly into the camera, her complexion was pale and flawless and her short hair definitely hennaed. She wore a simple white T-shirt, no make-up or heavy jewellery, and had no tattoos on her arms or neck, but there was something of the goth in her appearance, both challenging and defiant. It was perhaps more of an attitude than a style, Annie decided, something in her stance and the seriousness of her expression.

Their pizzas arrived. Mitsuko asked if there was anything else, and they said they didn't think so. Not for the moment. She said she would be around the restaurant if they thought of anything, and went back to work.

As they tucked into their lunch, Annie thought about Marnie and remembered her own experience. After she had been raped, she had wandered around in a depressed haze of guilt and shame, wondering how she could ever have let such a thing happen to her. But it was her anger that ultimately saved her. She never let go of the fact that it *wasn't her fault*; it was the fault of the bastards who raped her. And clinging to that idea was probably what saved her from Marnie's fate, whatever it was. Annie had clawed her way out; Marnie seemed to have gone under.

She completely understood why Marnie hadn't been able to tell her best friend what happened. She had never shared what happened to her with a living soul until she told Banks in a moment of weakness on their first case together. It was a long time ago now, but the pain and shame would never completely go away; they were deep down, rooted in her very being. But that didn't mean she couldn't live a normal life, couldn't function properly. She did. She wanted to find Marnie and tell her that she could do it, too, even if at first she wouldn't believe it.

As soon as she got back to the station from York, Gerry got on her computer. A search through the databases revealed that a Marjorie Sedgwick lived in a place called Wool, in Dorset. According to Gerry's information, that came under the Purbeck North policing area. She made a note of the address, then phoned the Purbeck police.

A youthful-sounding PCSO answered her call, saying he knew the Sedgwick family by name and that they did, indeed, live in Wool, though he was very careful to point out that he didn't know them because of any criminal activity, suspected or real. When Gerry pressed her case and asked why he knew the name, he grew evasive and muttered something about a tragedy. Even though he had verified who Gerry was by calling back the Eastvale number she had given him, he still seemed reluctant to say more.

'If you can't or don't want to talk to me,' said Gerry, 'can you please put someone on who will?'

There was silence, then the sound of the handset being set down on a hard surface. Gerry tried to picture the location. Many of these police stations were much like the ones in rural Yorkshire, nothing more than the local copper's living room with a filing cabinet and a few wanted posters on the walls. She imagined a thatched roof cottage with a blue POLICE sign over its door and opening hours noted down the side.

'Sergeant Trevelyan here,' came a new voice at the other end. 'Who am I speaking to?' Gerry thought Trevelyan was a Cornish name. Still, Cornwall wasn't that far from Dorset. His accent didn't give anything away; it was pure RP.

'My name is Geraldine Masterson,' she said. 'I'm a DC at Eastvale Regional Police HQ in Eastvale, North Yorkshire. I'm making enquiries about a local girl called Marnie Sedgwick, and the database has led me to a Marjorie Sedgwick in Wool, Dorset. Your PCSO seemed to recognise Marnie's name.'

'Not many who wouldn't around these parts,' said Trevelyan.

'Oh, why is that?'

'Not the best of reasons, I'm afraid. Poor Marnie Sedgwick only went and killed herself, didn't she? The tragedy's still fresh in everyone's mind.'

Gerry felt her skin prickle. 'Killed herself?'

'Aye. Jumped off Durdle Door.'

'When did this happen?'

There was another pause, then Trevelyan said, 'May. Seventeenth May.'

About a month after the rape, Gerry realised, and five days before Blaydon's murder. She made a note on her desk pad.

'Can I send you a photo of her, then we can be certain we're talking about the same person?'

'Go ahead. Text it to my mobile.' He gave her the number. A few seconds after she had sent the image, she heard a ding and Trevelyan came back. 'Aye,' he said. 'That's poor Marnie, all right.'

Christ. Gerry felt a chill flutter in her chest. 'You said she jumped off Durdle Door?'

'It's a limestone arch in the sea near Lulworth Cove. The water's worn a hole in it over the years, so it's like an open door in the rock. The beach there is a popular tourist spot.'

'I've seen pictures,' said Gerry. 'Would you mind if my colleague and I come down to see you? We'd like to talk to the family, too, if possible.'

'It's all right by me,' said Trevelyan. 'Hell of a long way to come, if you ask me, though, and I won't have any more to tell you than I have right now.'

'Will you arrange for us to see this Durdle Door and to speak with Mr and Mrs Sedgwick?'

'Easy enough. I'll certainly ask them. You understand they might not wish to dredge it all up again. It's still raw.'

'We can be very gentle. Please try, Sergeant. It's important.'

'I'll do my best. See you soon then?'

'We'll talk to you soon.'

Banks hadn't heard the Blue Lamps live for quite a while, but they were every bit as good as he remembered, their bluesy feel, rhythmic complexity and subtle use of harmonies as strong and as familiar as ever. To Banks's ears, it was CSNY meet the Allman Brothers, but with an unmistakable edge of more recent pop styles in the mix.

It was a nostalgic evening, and they played songs from their earliest albums mixed in with more recent work, along with a few covers they had revisited now and then over the years. At one point, Brian announced, 'I feel like I've been listening to this song since I was in my cradle. This is for my old man. He's here somewhere tonight. Love you, Dad!' The crowd cheered and the band launched into a bluesy 'Visions of Johanna', with Brian taking the lead vocal and a soaring lyrical guitar solo. Emotion fizzed in Banks's chest and almost made it to his eyes. As with most of Dylan's mid-sixties songs, he didn't understand a word of it, but it sure had a powerful effect on him.

The Sage was full, and the fans both enthusiastic and saddened by the occasion. Some waved banners saying 'PLEASE DON'T TURN OFF THE LAMPS!' but everything was good-natured, including the band members, and no one felt cheated when the show ended after the fifth encore.

Banks kept checking his mobile during the performance, but nothing new came in. When the show ended, surprised by how the music had allowed him to put Zelda out of his mind for a short while at least, he nipped outside to phone Annie, who had been in charge during his absence, and told her about a derelict hunting lodge he had remembered on the fells above Swainshead. It turned out that the place had already been searched and found to be empty. As had the Blaydon properties they had searched so far. The only news was that Burgess had come up with a good photograph of Petar Tadić, and Adrian Moss had pasted it all over the media.

Cursing their lack of success and his own inability to come up with any better ideas, Banks made his way to the backstage area, where Tracy and Mark were already waiting for him with Brian and the rest of the band. The dressing room was crowded with lucky fans, hangers-on and a few journalists. After all, the demise of the band was a major event. There were two more dates left on the 'farewell' tour before the absolute final performance, back in London again, but this one was close enough to home ground to make the news.

Banks managed a few brief words with Brian, who regretted being unable to come and spend the night at Newhope Cottage because the tight schedule called for an early start to Edinburgh the following morning. It was a pity, as Banks had looked forward to spending some time alone with him, listening to old blues and Bob Dylan and talking about everything under the sun. Banks would have driven him to Edinburgh in the morning under normal circumstances, but he couldn't take the time off, either. After London, Brian said, when the tour was over, he would have some time off before starting a trainee sound-recording job he had set up at a studio down there, so he would come up for a few days then. Banks was no lover of big noisy parties, no matter what their purpose, so he said his goodbyes to the other band members and made his way towards the exit. Tracy and Mark said they would stay on just a little longer and take a taxi home. They had just got back from Tenerife that day and were feeling tired.

In the afterglow of 'Visions of Johanna', Banks played *Blonde on Blonde* on the way home, arriving in the middle of 'Sad-Eyed Lady of the Lowlands'. He felt lonely when he pulled up outside his dark cottage. Normally, living alone never bothered him much, but spending even a little time with Brian and seeing Tracy so happy with her new husband reminded him of when he had a family, when home was a place of love and comfort, where there would always be someone waiting for him. These days, his life seemed to lack purpose – or at least any purpose other than putting bad guys away. Zelda haunted him, too. Not only what might be happening to her now, but what the future might hold. Not very much, he suspected, and none of it pleasant. They *had* to find her.

The outside light usually came on automatically when he approached the front door, but tonight it didn't. He made a mental note to replace the bulb tomorrow. He used the light from his mobile, managed to get his key in the lock and open the door. He stepped over the threshold, looking forward to a quick nightcap, but before he could shut the door behind him, he sensed a sudden movement, then felt something hard hit the back of his head. He pitched forward into the cottage, and after that, he felt nothing.

12

Banks first became aware of a throbbing pain in his head. When he opened his eyes, he saw he was in semi-darkness. It was a blessing. Bright light would have hurt. He also realised that he was tied up. He wasn't sure how, or how securely, only that when he moved his legs to try to straighten them out, something tightened around his neck like a noose. Trussed was the word that came to mind. Trussed like a Christmas turkey. Hog-tied.

He didn't know how long he had been like that before he heard a door open and someone placed a portable work light down beside him. He shut his eyes, but not quickly enough to prevent the pain of the light exploding inside his head. He couldn't even raise a hand to cover his face.

When he did open his eyes again, he could only see the shadowed and hunched profile of the man who stood before him, but that was enough for Banks to recognise him. He was looking older, his hairline had receded and he carried more weight around the middle, but Banks didn't have to be a super-recogniser to know it was Phil Keane. He also noticed that he was being kept in a cavernous space, an abandoned factory or control centre of some sort, with large rusted wheels, heavy pipes and valves, pumps, storage tanks, hanging wires and broken consoles.

'Well, well,' said Keane. 'We meet again. You cost me a lot, you know. Because of you I had to leave the country, get a new identity, find a new line of work. But perhaps I should thank you. It's proven even more profitable than my previous work.'

'You've got a funny way of showing it,' Banks managed to mumble with a mouth that felt full of treacle. Keane was holding something, and Banks saw it was a large can. The kind you carry petrol in. 'Where's Zelda?' he asked.

'The girl? She's nothing to do with me. Petar's taking care of her. He has a score to settle. He's made plans for her. Fortunately, he's agreed to let me settle my old score, too.'

'If either of you harm her—'

'Oh, stop it,' said Keane, unscrewing the can. 'You don't know how pathetic you sound. We're going to do exactly what we want, and you're not going to be able to stop us. This time I'll get to finish what I started.' He shook the can and Banks heard the petrol slosh inside it. Soon he could smell it, too. 'We're clearing out of here very soon,' Keane said. 'It's time to move on. A good fire is just the thing we need to make sure we leave no traces.'

Keane splashed the petrol on the floor around Banks's feet.

When Tadić came into her room again and set the light down on the floor, he came alone. Zelda sensed some new purpose in his visit other than mere torture or gloating.

'We are leaving soon,' he said. 'Mr Foley has your new passport in the car, along with sufficient funds for the journey. It will be a long and hard one, and perhaps not as comfortable as you would wish.'

'So let me loose to clean myself up a bit. At least give me a fresh T-shirt.' Zelda's top was still crusted with dried vomit from the time Tadić had hit her.

Tadić smiled. 'Yes. Of course. A good idea. All in good time. We have nice new clothes for you in the car. But you are right about the T-shirt. It is disgusting.'

He knelt before her and took a flick-knife from the pocket of his leather jacket. He held it close to her face and flicked the blade open to make sure she saw it glinting in the light. Then he slid it under the material of her top and started cutting until the T-shirt was in shreds on the floor.

So this is it, Zelda thought. This is when he takes his pleasure. Feeling half-naked and exposed was nothing new to her, but it had been so long that she found herself feeling embarrassed and shy. She wanted to protect herself from his gaze and raised her cuffed hands up to cover her breasts as best she could.

Tadić merely laughed. 'Very modest for a *kurva,*' he said, unfastening his belt and unzipping his trousers. The light cast grotesque shadows of him on the wall. He took off his leather jacket and dropped it on the floor, then grabbed her by the hair. 'On your knees.'

Zelda had no choice but to submit. But as she did so, an idea formed. When she was kneeling, and Tadić had his trousers down around his ankles, he put the blade of the knife to her neck, right by the jugular vein and carotid artery. It wouldn't take much to cut them, Zelda thought. Just a slip of the hand, a nervous tic even, and she would be free. Could she do it? She hadn't been able to swallow her tongue or hold her breath, but perhaps she could accept death this way. She closed her eyes, felt the cold steel on her skin, felt his hand press against the back of her neck, pulling her forward.

'Open your mouth.'

Zelda opened her mouth and felt him enter her. She almost gagged, but managed to stop herself. Instead, she offered a silent prayer to the God she didn't believe in and bit down as hard as she could.

*　　*　　*

In that moment, Banks was certain he was going to die. Then he heard sounds from somewhere deep in the building, upstairs, perhaps. Someone shouting, a banging noise, a chain scraping along a floor.

Keane smiled. 'Sounds as if Petar is having his fun. I must say, he's a bit of an animal when it comes to the fairer sex. I can't say I approve. Me, I'd rather wine and dine and seduce a woman than simply take her. Like I did with Annie. How is she, by the way?'

'Bastard.'

'Doesn't matter,' Keane said, splashing more petrol over the floor between himself and Banks, who was still feeling too woozy to resist. Even if he hadn't been trussed up, he wouldn't have been able to offer much opposition.

'Tell me about Faye Butler,' he said. 'Why did you kill her?'

'Don't think this is going to be one of those long drawn-out confessions you get in movies when the hero is about to die,' Keane said. 'And don't think you're going to keep me talking until the cavalry comes. Nobody's coming. Faye was collateral damage, that's all. I didn't kill her. Maybe Petar got a little overeager to find out what she told your lady friend up there about his business. Like I said, he's an animal with women.'

'Did you kill Hawkins?'

'He was taking Goran and Petar's money and giving them crap in exchange. They lost a whole shipment of fresh girls because of him. You don't pull those kind of tricks on the Tadićs and live. They let me prove myself.'

'Bully for you. What happened to Goran?'

Keane paused. 'You don't know? You really don't know? Well, well. I'll tell you that, at least. Goran's dead. The girl killed him. Knife. Made a right mess. Petar and the others disposed of his body to prevent a police investigation. Then they carried out their own. Why do you think all this is happening?'

'Petar's revenge?' Banks said. 'But *you* don't have to do this. You don't have to be a part of it. You disappeared before. You can do it again.'

Keane paused. 'You don't understand. I *want* to do this. This is a favour granted me by Petar. And who knows, maybe I'll pay Annie another visit, too, before I leave here for good.'

Banks struggled against his ropes, but it was no use. He only felt them tightening around his throat. Keane stood in front of him holding the petrol can. The rest of the abandoned factory was quiet now.

'Just a little more, I think,' said Keane, and splashed some of the petrol over Banks's trousers and shoes.

Zelda had no idea what it would feel like when the knife cut into her neck. She had seen movies where the blood gushed out, but they conveyed no idea of the sensation. Would it hurt? How long would it take? What would dying feel like? Like going to sleep, she hoped. But surely she would find out very soon. His muscle would twitch and the knife would cut her open. The end.

She felt nothing. No pain. Nothing.

Tadić screamed, dropped the knife and clutched at his genitals with both hands. Stunned to still be alive, it took Zelda a moment to adjust her perspective. She had expected death, but perhaps now she had a chance to achieve freedom instead. He hadn't twitched in a reflex action but had instead dropped the knife and moved his hands to the source of the pain, thereby leaving himself open. But she had to act quickly.

Tadić fell to the floor and his grotesque shadow twisted and turned on the wall. Zelda saw the knife where it had fallen. She stretched her leg as far as she could with the chain still on and reached out her cuffed hands, but it had fallen just outside her grasp. She had no idea how long it would take Tadić to regain control, but she didn't think she had much time. He was in the foetal position on the floor groaning. It was awkward with her hands cuffed, but she managed to remove her belt, hold it in a loop with both hands and hook it over the knife like a lasso. It just reached. Slowly, she pulled the knife towards her.

Tadić's groans were less frequent now, but he was still sliding around on the floor in his own blood. Zelda tossed her belt aside and grasped the knife as best she could with both hands cuffed together. Tadić kicked out, either deliberately or still in agony, and his foot caught her on the shoulder. She almost dropped the knife but instead managed to lunge out with it. She felt it bury itself in his flesh. Now she got to her knees again and plunged the knife in and out of Tadić's chest and stomach until he stopped moving. It was only then that she saw her first cut had severed his femoral artery in his right thigh, and the blood was still gushing out. She slid back towards the radiator and landed against it, breathless, dazed and miraculously still alive.

Tadić lay unmoving in the pooling blood, and Zelda knew enough to be certain he would never move again. With some difficulty she tried to saw through her plasticuffs with the knife. It slipped twice and she cut her palm and thumb, but she got free. She rubbed her hands together to get the circulation going, then crawled towards Tadić's jacket, still lying where he had dropped it on the floor, dragging her leg chain with her. When she got close enough she went through his pockets. Eventually she found his keys, and after several tries found the one that fit the padlock on her leg iron. She was free. Alive and free. She massaged her ankle. But it wasn't over yet, she felt certain. Tadić hadn't been alone; there were others. She put on his leather jacket, wiped the knife on his jeans and crept towards the door, holding the blade before her.

The whole place stank of petrol. Banks felt his head swimming with the fumes, as if his consciousness were water gurgling down a drain. But the pain in his head kept him awake. For a moment, he couldn't remember who it was that stood in front of him, and why. Then it came rushing back. It wasn't a dream. He was in some sort of abandoned factory and Phil Keane was about to start a fire. He imagined the flames slowly creeping over his skin, through to the flesh and down to the bone. Like most people, he had only had mild burns in his life, but they had hurt enough. How long would it take for him to die? How much would it hurt?

'I think that's about enough petrol, don't you?' said Keane. 'Should be a nice little blaze. There's plenty of combustible material in the building. Probably bone dry after the recent weather. And we're far enough away from civilisation that there's not much chance of the fire brigade making it here until there's nothing left.'

As Keane talked, Banks fancied he glimpsed movement in the shadows behind him. It was out of the lamp's range, so he couldn't be sure. Maybe he was just imagining things. Or maybe it was Tadić come to watch the fireworks. But this shadow seemed to be creeping slowly, deliberately, up behind Keane. Surely Tadić wouldn't do that. Another wave of nausea and dizziness swept through him, and he lost track of the shadow, if there was one.

'I just have to make sure Petar and the girl get out first,' Keane said, 'then I'll be back.' He took a red disposable cigarette lighter from his pocket and flicked it so it flamed for a moment. 'Don't go away.'

There was definitely movement behind him. Silent. Slow.

Then suddenly, Keane seemed to jerk to attention. His hands went behind him and he dropped the can, petrol gurgling at his feet and over his shoes. Then he jerked again and dropped to his knees.

The next thing Banks knew, Zelda was stepping around Keane's body and cutting his bonds. Keane moved behind her and she turned around, blocking Banks's view, so that he couldn't be sure whether it was her or Keane who struck it, but the lighter flared briefly and Keane's petrol-soaked clothes went up in flames along with the floor around them. Keane screamed.

'Run!' cried Zelda, helping Banks to his feet and slapping out a tongue of flame that caught his trouser leg. 'Get out! Quick! Run! Run!'

Banks ran.

Running wasn't easy. Banks's head was bursting, and he kept tripping over himself as he made his way through the door and into the night outside, the flames at his heels. It was dark, but there was enough moonlight to see that he had been in an abandoned water treatment plant. The rectangular reservoirs stood before him empty of water and filled only with weeds, ghostly in the moonlight. He ran around the first one and headed for the woods beyond, with no idea of where he was going. He could hear the flames roaring behind him and turned to see how close Zelda was, then stopped in his tracks.

She wasn't there.

The flames were quickly engulfing the building, already eating their way through the roof, but he had to go back. He stood in the doorway and saw there was no way he could go any further inside. Parts of the ceiling were collapsing, the whole floor was blazing and the fire was spreading fast to every last corner. He called out Zelda's name but got only the roar of the flames in return.

He looked towards the spot where he had been tied up and thought he could make out Keane's burning body, but that was all. So what had happened to Zelda? Why hadn't she been right behind him? Should he have waited and made her go first? He hadn't been thinking clearly, couldn't think clearly because his head hurt and his thoughts were muddled. The heat was too much, and he staggered back towards the reservoir. Before he could stop himself, he fell backwards over the edge into the bed of weeds and felt his head jar against the hard bottom. And there, as the fire raged, he lost consciousness again.

13

When Banks opened his eyes, he had no idea who or where he was for the first few seconds. It was a fleeting sensation, but terrifying while it lasted. Then he saw he was in a white room, in a hospital bed with stiff sheets. He must have somehow got a private room because there was nobody else near him; nor was there another bed. He could see through the window that it was daylight, though what time it was he had no idea. Someone had removed his watch. But why was he there? What was wrong with him? How had he got here? Try as he might, he couldn't remember. Had he had a heart attack? A car accident? No, he could feel his heart beating more or less normally, and all his body parts seemed to be in working order except his brain. His head hurt and he felt sick and dizzy. Perhaps he'd had a stroke or cerebral haemorrhage? He could see that he had a line in the back of his hand with a tube leading to a drip of clear fluid on a stand, and there were the usual machines beeping away. Heart rate 80, blood pressure 145/83. That wasn't too bad, was it? Maybe his heart was beating too fast, but then it always had done.

He wished someone would come and explain what was happening. The only thing he knew about hospitals was that if there was nothing wrong with you when you went in, there would be when you came out. He also knew that despite all the criticism the NHS came in for in the media, when it came to an emergency, they couldn't be beat.

Was he an emergency? In intensive care? He was sure he
must have work to do, a case to be getting on with. *A case.*
That rang a bell. He was a detective. He had been on a case.
Was that how he had got injured? He could feel bandages on
his head. Perhaps some scumbag had coshed him. But why?
What was it all about? He couldn't remember.

'Ah, good,' said a voice in the doorway. 'I'm glad to see
you're back in the land of the living again.'

'Who are you?'

'Dr Chowdhury.'

He looked about twelve, Banks thought. Surely they didn't
entrust serious injuries to twelve-year-olds yet? 'Where am I?'
he asked.

'Eastvale General Infirmary.'

'What's wrong with me? Why am I here?'

'You don't remember?'

'No.'

'Can you tell me your name?'

'Alan Banks.'

'Address?'

'Newhope Cottage, Gratly.'

'What line of work are you in?'

'I'm a detective superintendent. A policeman.'

'What day is it?'

'No idea.'

Dr Chowdhury laughed. 'It's Thursday,' he said. 'You had a
very lucky escape. You sustained a nasty blow to the back of
your head – two blows, actually – and that sometimes causes
short-term memory loss, along with other symptoms: dizziness, nausea, headaches. One of the head wounds required a
few stitches, but that's all. Fortunately, there's no skull frac-
ture, or we'd have whizzed you up to Newcastle or down to
Leeds already.'

'I can't remember being hit on the head.'

'That's not unusual. You have a concussion. It should be only a temporary condition. Your memory should come back.'

'How long?'

'Before it comes back? Not long, I shouldn't think. Days rather than weeks. Maybe even hours. But you need rest.'

'How long have I been here?'

'You were brought in at a quarter past two this morning.'

'And now?'

'It's eight o'clock in the morning. You've been under observation regularly during the night. We're always especially careful with concussion patients where loss of consciousness is involved.'

Banks glanced towards the window again and saw his mobile and Bluetooth headphones on his bedside table. 'How did these get here?'

'A young lady brought them not long ago,' said Dr Chowdhury. 'Said her name was Annie. But you should know that mobile phone use is strictly prohibited in here.'

Bless her, thought Banks. 'Don't worry, I won't be using the phone,' he said. 'What happened to me?'

'All I know is that you were brought in by ambulance with a head wound and minor burns to your ankles. There was also some bruising, most likely caused by a fall, and rope marks on your neck, wrists and feet, as if you'd been tied up.'

'Burns? Tied up?'

'Yes, I know it sounds strange. But the burns are nothing serious. We've dressed them. As for the rest, it's superficial.'

'Where was I brought from?'

'I believe it was a disused water treatment plant outside Eastvale.'

'I know that place,' said Banks. 'Not from last night. From before. I've driven past it dozens of times. I always wondered when they were going to knock it down and use the land for something useful.'

'Well, it's gone now,' said the doctor.

'Gone?'

'Fire. Burned to the ground.'

'Why was I there?'

'I have no idea.'

A vague memory of flames came into Banks's mind. It gave him a sudden feeling of nausea. 'Zelda,' he said.

'What was that?' the doctor asked. 'I didn't catch it.'

'Nothing,' said Banks. He wasn't certain of the importance of what he'd said yet, himself, so he could hardly explain it to a stranger. 'Who found me?'

'I suppose it must have been the firefighters. They were the first responders at the scene.'

Banks fell silent. Talking had worn him out already, and he was starting to feel sick and dizzy again.

'Nausea and dizziness aren't unusual in cases like this,' the doctor said, as if aware of what Banks was feeling. 'That, too, should pass soon enough.'

'Not soon enough for me,' said Banks. 'How long do I have to stay here?'

'We'd like to keep you in one more night for observation and to conduct some tests.'

'What tests?'

'Nothing invasive, don't worry. A severe jolt to the brain such as you have experienced can cause any number of problems. For a start, we need to test your reflexes and make sure there's no lasting physical damage. As far as other symptoms are concerned, it's mostly a matter of self-monitoring over time. I'll give you a list of things to watch out for. We'd also like to conduct an MRI scan, but for that we'll have to arrange to take you to the Friarage in Northallerton. We don't have an

MRI machine here. Until then, rest as comfortably as you can. Rest is very important in cases of concussion.'

'Always a pleasure to be here,' said Timmy Kerrigan, lifting the crease of his trousers at the knees as he eased his bulk into the chair and crossed his legs in interview room three. As usual, he was expensively and garishly dressed, this time in a navy bespoke suit over a psychedelic waistcoat, lilac shirt and green bow tie. Short golden curls topped his round head and, along with his peaches and cream complexion, made him appear quite angelic. Annie had decided to talk to Timmy instead of his brother this time, as he was marginally more garrulous and slightly less unpleasant to be around. But Timmy Kerrigan was a long way from being an angel.

Gerry was busy digging up whatever she could on Marnie Sedgwick's background. They had already talked briefly to the ex-boyfriend Rick, who had said he hadn't seen Marnie since the middle of April. She had become very unreliable and moody, he said, and he had decided to end the relationship and move on. He had a new girlfriend now, a drummer in a local rock band, and she confirmed that Rick had been with her almost constantly since early May. He also said he didn't know anything about the parties Marnie had worked, and he had certainly never been to one. There was no reason to disbelieve him as he was so far out of Blaydon's sphere of interest as to be almost non-existent. Unfortunately, they had had no success with the sparse list of guest and employee names Tamara and Charlotte had emailed. People either denied they were present, refused to talk or said they hadn't noticed anything. The footballer and guitarist Mitsuko had mentioned said they hadn't seen anything out of the ordinary and had spent most of the evening by the pool.

Annie was still worried about Banks. The doctor who wouldn't let her see him earlier that day had assured her he would be fine and his injuries weren't serious, but he was no more forthcoming than that. She had visited Banks's cottage as soon as she heard he had been taken to hospital and found his front door open, his mobile and keys lying on the hall carpet. She had picked up the mobile and grabbed Banks's headphones from the conservatory. She knew he would be insufferable in hospital without his music. The keys she would hang on to until he went home. There wasn't much more she could do except call the CSIs to check out the cottage.

For the moment, though, Annie tried to concentrate on Timmy Kerrigan. 'Timmy,' she began, 'first of all, you should know that this is simply an intelligence interview. You're not under arrest and you're not being charged with anything, OK?'

Timmy nodded and his chins wobbled. 'I rather thought so,' he said, glancing around the room, 'seeing as I haven't done anything. But why the dull decor?'

Annie smiled. 'You'd be surprised how it concentrates the mind. No interruptions. Can we start?'

'Whenever you're ready.'

'You were at a party thrown by Connor Clive Blaydon at his home near Harrogate on 13 April this year, right?'

'If you say so. We've been to a few of Connor's parties, Tommy and I. He's a good friend. Was. I can't remember the exact dates.'

'Now, we have evidence that a young woman was raped at that party, and we're trying to find out who did it.'

'Well, don't look at Tommy and me.'

'We know that Tommy has – what shall we say? – other interests, but as for you . . .'

'Whatever you've heard, it's a vicious lie,' Timmy protested.

Annie had heard rumours of his interest in young girls often enough to believe them without further proof, but she realised there was no point in angering him. It was clear from the video, poor as its quality was, that Timmy Kerrigan was entirely the wrong shape and size to have been Marnie's rapist. 'That's as may be,' she said, 'and it's not our concern at the moment, but what I want to know is whether you saw this girl at the party. Your brother said he didn't recognise her, but we only had a very poor photo to show when we talked to him.'

She slid over a print of the photo Mitsuko had AirDropped her. Timmy picked it up and studied it, then nodded. 'Maybe,' he said. 'I think she was there, but she wasn't . . . how shall I say . . . part of the entertainment.'

'She worked for the events organiser in the catering area, mostly back in the kitchen and behind the scenes. But apparently, she brought out drinks once in a while.'

'That must have been when I saw her. A very pretty girl. Gamine, I'd say.'

Annie ground her teeth. 'Yes.'

'I do hope she's all right.'

'As a matter of fact, she isn't,' said Annie. 'Not all right at all. In fact, she jumped off a cliff and died.'

'Oh,' said Kerrigan. 'That's a terrible tragedy.'

Annie almost believed he meant it; it was probably the closest to sincerity that Timmy Kerrigan got. Timmy linked his pink sausage-like fingers on the table. He was wearing a large gold signet ring, Annie noticed, so deeply imbedded in the flesh it looked impossible to take off.

'Do you know the events organiser?'

'Charlie? Yes, of course. Though she hates being called that. Charming lady. In fact, she's organised a couple of private dos for Tommy and I over the last three or four years. Retirement parties and so on. Extracurricular, so to speak. She organised the opening of The Vaults.'

'I thought that when you retired people, they were in no condition to have a party.'

Timmy cocked his head. 'Very droll. Have you considered a career in stand-up?'

'I'll stick with what I'm doing for the moment.'

'The stage's loss.'

'You were at other parties, weren't you? Earlier in the year.'

'I suppose you could say we were regulars.'

'Did you ever notice Charlotte Westlake introduce Marnie to anyone?'

'No. They seemed to know each other, though. I mean, I did see them talking together in the background on a couple of occasions.'

'It's a big house. Where did you hang out?'

'Tommy and I tended to stick by the pool except . . . you know . . . when nature called. I enjoy a swim now and then.'

Annie cringed at the mental image of Timmy in his thong trunks. Once seen, never forgotten. 'I suppose that was where most of the action was?' she said.

'The synchronised swimming and so on? Yes, I suppose it was.'

'I was thinking more of the naked women.'

'Can't say as I noticed.'

'Oh, come on, Timmy. You could hardly fail.'

'One gets used to these things. Besides, what's wrong with swimming as nature intended in the privacy of a friend's home?'

'So you and your brother sat around the pool, smoking cigars, drinking whisky and ogling naked women.'

'That last part is pure invention on your part. I don't ogle, and Tommy . . . well . . .'

'Tommy has no interest in naked women?'

'You could say that.'

'Blaydon was no doubt a very woke host. I'm sure he catered for all tastes and genders.'

Timmy giggled. 'Very good. Yes. Yes, he did that, all right.'

'So you saw Marnie on the evening of 13 April?'

'Yes. I've already told you that.'

'Did you see her with anyone?'

Timmy thought for a moment, or at least Annie assumed that was why his brow furrowed. 'No,' he said. 'That's about it. Except for Connor, of course.'

'Marnie spent time with Connor Blaydon?'

'Well, it *was* his party, after all, wasn't it?'

During the day, Banks slept as well as anyone can sleep in a hospital, but – even though he had the room to himself – there always seemed to be something going on somewhere, and it usually made noise. In addition, the nurse kept waking him up to make sure he could be woken up.

The paracetamol seemed to dull his headache for a while, and whatever they gave him for the nausea worked, too. Just after lunch, as he was trying to relax listening to the Pavel Haas Quartet playing some Shostakovich string quartets, he had more visitors. He didn't recognise the man with AC Gervaise, but they both looked serious.

'This is Superintendent Newry from Police Conduct,' said Gervaise. 'He'd like to talk to you. He has agreed to my being present during this interview, which I am assured is merely a preliminary. In no way are you accused or suspected of anything.'

'So why is he here, if there's been no complaints against me?'

'Standard procedure,' Newry said. 'Given the ... er ... unusual circumstances of your adventures.'

Newry was a small pudgy man in his fifties with thinning hair and a large round head. He looked angry. In fact, he looked as if he were permanently angry: red face, tight mouth, etched sneer. The hospital chair creaked as he sat down. His trousers tightened against the flesh of his thighs.

'Got your memory back yet?' Newry asked.

'No,' said Banks. 'It's still a blank. What's all this about? What's happened?'

'The fire investigation officers were able to enter the scene at the water treatment plant,' said Newry. 'They found two bodies. Now do you remember anything about how that came about?'

'Who are they?' Banks asked.

'We won't know until the post-mortems have been carried out. To be honest, there's not much left for her to work on. They were both very badly burned, and as yet we don't even know if they were male or female. But that's not the point. Do you remember anything?'

'No,' said Banks. *Zelda,* he thought. Please let it not be Zelda. Why did that thought flash through his mind? There was nothing in his memory to justify it, only that he connected what had happened, what he couldn't remember, with Zelda's disappearance, which was the case he had been working on. He remembered that. Had she been there, at the treatment plant? Had she been caught in the fire?

'How I hate these memory-loss cases,' Newry said. 'A person could say anything, or nothing, and we'd have no way of proving it. Any thoughts on the matter?'

'On your suspicions about my memory loss, or on what happened?'

'The latter will do for now.'

'I'm told I was knocked unconscious,' said Banks, 'and when I came around, I was here in hospital. As far as I know, I didn't go to the plant for any particular reason, by choice. Why would I? I must have been taken there. By whom, or why, I have no idea.'

'I understand that,' said Newry. 'And your DI Cabbot has already found evidence of your abduction back at your cottage. Your doctor also mentioned marks that ropes made on your wrists, ankles and throat. It's what the Americans call "hog-tied".'

'Perhaps that's why my throat's sore and my wrists hurt.'

'I should think so. And I'm sure you can understand why we're interested in any information we can get right now.'

'I know what you're after,' said Banks. 'A scapegoat. And it's not going to be me.'

Newry raised his eyebrows and glanced towards AC Gervaise. Banks could see she wasn't happy with what was happening.

'Any more questions?' he asked.

'Any guesses?' Newry went on. 'As to who it might have been? And why you were taken there?'

Banks took a deep breath before answering. 'As you probably know, we are involved in trying to find a woman who was abducted from her farmhouse near Lyndgarth on Monday. Her name is Nelia Melnic, though everyone knows her as Zelda. We think a Croatian sex trafficker called Petar Tadić was behind that abduction, in collusion with a wanted criminal called Philip Keane. We don't know why Zelda was taken, unless it was to settle an old score or to stop her from disclosing something incriminating she knew about Tadić, and I have no idea why they should want me, too, if that's what happened. Unless Keane felt *he* had a score to settle.'

'Was this Zelda being kept at the treatment plant? Is that why you went there?'

'I didn't go there. I was taken there.'

'Right. Could that be why you were taken there, then?'

'How would I know?'

'Was the woman there?'

'I have no memory of what or who was there. I don't even remember being there myself.'

'Your memory for some things seems pretty good to me.'

'Yes, it is. I can even remember my own name. But I don't remember what happened last night. It's called short-term memory loss, or temporary amnesia. At least, I hope it's temporary. Ask Dr Chowdhury. He'll be happy to explain it to you.'

'You have a history with this Keane, I understand?'

'He tried to kill me once, if you call that a "history". Drugged me. Set fire to my cottage with me inside it.'

'Something like that stays with you, I should imagine.'

'Surely the question is whether it stayed with *him*. Enough for him to want to repeat his attempt. And no, I haven't been dreaming of revenge for the last ten years.'

'Do you think Keane was the man who set the fire at the plant?'

'He has a history of arson, so it wouldn't surprise me, but I have no memory of anyone starting a fire. I don't even remember a fire.'

'You have burns on your ankle and legs. How did you escape?'

'I don't know that I did. I mean, I know I must have, because I'm here, but I don't know whether I was inside the building in the first place, or whether it was burning when I was. Or how I got out, if I did. Maybe I was always where the firefighters found me?'

'Surely if you were taken to the plant by someone who had a reason, you must have been inside at some point? And there are the burns.'

'They hardly prove anything. I told you, I don't remember being inside the building. I don't know where I was taken. Or why. I don't even remember *being* taken.'

'Yes. Of course. The memory loss.'

'Take or leave it,' said Banks.

'As a matter of fact,' Newry went on, 'you *were* inside the building. Forensic tests on your clothing show traces of petrol and dirt and grease from the floor.'

'You took my clothes?'

'Naturally. You'll get them back in due course.'

'I'm tired now. The doctor says I need rest. Please fuck off.'

Newry stood up and gestured towards AC Gervaise. 'I imagine we'll be talking again before too long,' he said. 'In the meantime, do get that rest, Superintendent Banks, and perhaps your memory will have come back by the next time we meet.'

'Is that some sort of thinly veiled threat?'

Newry managed to twist his features into what he probably thought was a smile. 'It's nothing of the kind. Good day.'

Gervaise waited until the door closed behind Newry before saying, 'Was that really necessary?'

'What? Arseholes like him give me a headache, and I've already got a big enough one to begin with. If you ask me, he's watched too many episodes of *Line of Duty*.'

'Even so . . . he's only doing his job.'

'He's already after handing out blame before he even knows what happened. Is that his job?'

'Are you sure you don't remember anything?'

Banks stared at her. 'Not you as well? Bloody hell. I don't believe this.'

'All right, all right, Alan. Don't get your knickers in a twist. I'd understand, you know, if you didn't want to tell Newry anything right now, until you're sure.'

Banks sighed. 'It's because I don't know anything, ma'am. Believe me, I wish I did, and when I do, you'll be among the first to know.'

AC Gervaise stood up and patted Banks's arm. 'You must be feeling unwell. You're calling me ma'am. I'll let you get some rest now.'

Banks breathed a sigh of relief once he was in the room alone again. Memory was definitely a funny thing, he thought. Little flashes came back, but he couldn't put them all together into a coherent narrative. At one point when he was talking to Newry, a wave of panic had passed through him, and he heard a voice in his head shouting, 'Run! Run!'

He did remember a fire now, and he also remembered that the voice telling him to run was a woman's voice. And when Newry had told him about the bodies, he had felt a tremor of fear that one of them might be Zelda's. But he couldn't say for certain that it had been her voice, or that he had even been inside the treatment plant, let alone seen her there. Nor did he know where the fire had come from, how it had started.

And when you can't remember something, it's like it never happened, and you can't believe your memory will come back, because you don't know you ever had it to lose in the first place, no matter what the doctor said. It was all too confusing. Even thinking about it made his head hurt again. He kneaded his pillows so they propped him up comfortably and leaned back to listen to the 'Lento' movement of Shostakovich's seventh string quartet.

14

'Wouldn't you just know it,' said Annie on Friday morning. 'We get a rare chance to visit a beauty spot and what happens? It fucking pours down.'

She and Gerry had arrived in Dorset late the previous evening, tired after a long drive, and were enjoying breakfast at the Castle Inn, West Lulworth. Annie, still trying hard to stick to the pescatarian course, if not total vegetarianism, had gone for the kippers, but Gerry was indulging in a rare full English. It was one of the things that annoyed Annie about her – not that she wasn't a veggie, but that she seemed able to eat whatever she wanted and not put on any weight.

Outside, the rain sluiced down the mullioned windows, blurring the view of distant hills. They had set off from Eastvale around lunchtime the previous day, after the Timmy Kerrigan interview, and though the weather had been good, the journey had taken them close to seven hours, including heavy traffic around the M18, a quick sandwich stop near Oxford and getting lost in the winding Dorset lanes. After a brief snack and a couple of glasses of wine at the bar, they had both been ready for bed, and Annie had just managed to stay awake long enough to make a couple of phone calls before drifting off to sleep.

First, she had spoken with AC Gervaise and learned that Banks was spending the night in hospital under observation and that he seemed to be having problems with his memory.

There was nothing she could do to help him right now, not from so far away, though she was glad that she had made time to deliver his mobile and headphones before she and Gerry set off for Dorset. Gervaise had also mentioned that the firefighters had discovered two unidentified charred corpses in the abandoned water treatment plant where Banks had been found. Now Annie was worried that one of them might be Zelda. Ray would fall apart if anything happened to her. She had asked Gervaise to call her again if there were any developments but had heard nothing yet. Last of all, she had called Ray to check up on him and tell him about Banks, without mentioning the burned corpses. Ray had sounded a little drunk, and there was loud music playing in the background: Led Zeppelin, 'Dazed and Confused', one of Ray's old favourites she remembered well.

Sergeant Trevelyan turned up outside the inn at ten o'clock on the dot, as he had promised. Annie and Gerry squeezed into his Land Rover, and what would have been perhaps, on a fine day, a pleasant twenty-minute walk, became a five-minute drive in the pouring rain. Luckily, Trevelyan was well-supplied with umbrellas, and when they arrived at their destination he handed one each to Gerry and Annie.

He was probably in his mid-fifties, Annie thought, maybe a bit old for a local sergeant. Most officers his age would have retired by then. He had a squarish face topped with grey hair worn in much the same style as Boris Johnson. His manner was brusque but friendly enough, Annie thought, especially as they were a couple of interlopers no doubt spoiling the rhythm of his day. She imagined that he was usually in uniform, but today he wore jeans and a light grey windcheater.

Once on the path, Annie felt the power of the wind as well as the rain. She held her umbrella close and kept her eyes on the muddy ground to make sure she didn't trip over any undergrowth or a half-buried stone. All this meant she didn't get to appreciate the beauty of the spot until they arrived at the cliff's edge, because she had been staring at her feet, but once she looked up, she was impressed. She couldn't believe she had never been there before, despite having grown up not too far away in St Ives, Cornwall. And somehow, in the grim weather, with a rough grey sea and white breakers below, it was even more awe-inspiring than she had imagined. They stood on the top of a rugged cliff overlooking a semicircular stretch of beach, deserted at the moment. 'Is this the spot?' Annie asked Trevelyan, raising her voice to make herself heard over the wind and the crashing waves.

Trevelyan pointed to the west. 'See that arch sticking out into the water there,' he said, 'the one with the hole in it?'

Annie saw it. From a distance it resembled a petrified brontosaurus, its long neck bent to drink from the sea. Still, she remembered, this area was supposed to be part of the Jurassic Coast, so why not? 'From there?' she said.

'Aye,' he said. 'She ran out there and jumped right off the end, bounced off the cliff and landed in the sea. It wasn't as rough as it is today, but it still took a while to find her. Too late, of course.'

They stood gazing at the spot, each lost in thought, the wind howling and raging around them. Annie tried to put herself in the mind of the young girl, humiliated and shamed by a rape that was no fault of her own, standing on that edge. What thoughts must have been whirling about in her mind? Was she already determined to jump, or did she suddenly decide to do it on the spot? Spur of the moment. Bad pun, she told herself, but unintentional.

After a few minutes, Trevelyan broke the silence. 'Seen enough?'

Both Annie and Gerry nodded.

'Right. I know a nice little tea shop not too far away that should be opening its doors just about now. Shall we go and have a chat?'

That same morning, as Annie and Gerry were watching the rain in Dorset, an ambulance took Banks over to the Friarage hospital, in Northallerton. He didn't think he needed it – he could have driven himself if someone had brought his car – but the rules were the rules. All his tests had shown good reflexes, and the MRI – noisy and claustrophobic, but otherwise painless – revealed no brain injury, so Banks was discharged.

Dr Chowdhury had already given him a list of symptoms to watch out for – including problems with speaking, walking or balance, numbness, blurred vision, fits or personality changes – and told him not to watch TV or use his iPhone, to lay off the booze, take paracetamol for his headache and to get in touch if his memory didn't return within a few days.

Most of all, he was supposed to avoid stress and get plenty of rest. But how was he supposed to do that, he wondered, with Zelda still missing, two burned bodies in the treatment plant and his memory of events scrambled beyond recognition? Superintendent Newry from IOCC would no doubt be on his case again soon. If you were a policeman, you didn't get to stumble out of a burning building leaving two bodies behind you and not remember a thing without at least a stiff interrogation.

The doctor also suggested that it might be a good idea to get someone to stay with him for the first forty-eight hours to watch out for any danger signs that may be more easily spotted by an outside observer, such as personality changes. As far as Banks was concerned, that was a no-no. He had had enough being woken up at regular intervals during his two nights in hospital. Besides, he didn't know anyone who would do it, or who he wanted to do it. Ray Cabbot probably would, but Banks knew that Ray was in no shape to play babysitter with Zelda gone. And Ray's presence would just make him feel edgy and guilty about not having found her.

It would be too awkward having Annie around, even if she wasn't away in Dorset. They had ended their relationship some years ago, mostly because they worked together, and he was of higher rank, but there were enough sparks remaining to make both wary of too close contact. Talk about stress. Anyone else, like Ken Blackstone in Leeds and Burgess in London, was simply too far away. Family was out of the question, too. He wasn't going to burden Brian with his problems when he only had two or three more gigs to play with the band, or intrude on Tracy's newly-wedded bliss with Mark. He figured he could probably keep an eye on himself.

Getting home was another matter, though, as his car was still in the drive outside Newhope Cottage. He had no qualms about asking a local constable to drop him off.

When he got there, three CSIs were still puttering around the front, and they gave Banks an embarrassing round of applause when he got out of the car. *Wonderful,* he thought, now even his home was a crime scene. He thanked the constable, and she drove off back to Northallerton.

'Found anything yet?' Banks asked Stefan Nowak, the Crime Scene Manager.

'Tyre tracks,' answered Nowak. 'Fingerprints on your door frame. Most of them probably yours. A few drops of blood, also probably yours, but hardly enough to cause anyone great concern. And cigarette ends. Whoever did it must have had a long boring wait. They're similar to the ones we found near Ray Cabbot's cottage a few days ago. Ronhill. Croatian. Go ahead and get some rest. You look terrible. We're done now.

We've got all there is to find. Oh, and maybe you should check your valuables, you know, just to make sure they didn't take anything. There's no evidence they even entered the house, but just to be on the safe side.'

'Thanks, Stefan. I will,' said Banks, trying to think exactly what his valuables might be. 'Though I very much doubt that was what it was about.'

'Seeing as it's not a serious crime scene, and the house wasn't broken into, you can go in. We won't seal the place up with tape.'

'You mean me getting bashed on the head and abducted isn't serious?'

'Well, if you put it that way. John! Bring that crime scene tape over here.'

'Away with you,' said Banks, smiling. 'On your way.'

Nowak walked towards the CSI van, grinned back over his shoulder and waved.

It was strange, Banks felt, that he could understand all the events Stefan was talking about – fingerprints, Croatian cigarettes, blood – but he still couldn't remember a thing about what happened to him two nights ago. Apart from a flickering image of flames and a voice – Zelda's voice? – telling him to run, it was still a blank.

He went into the cottage and saw that nothing appeared to have been disturbed in the front room. His computer was still intact. The entertainment room and kitchen were also untouched. Nothing was missing or out of place. They had come for *him*, not his possessions.

Besides, what other people might call valuables were just things as far as Banks was concerned: electronic equipment, books, CDs, DVDs and so on could all be replaced. Most of them, at any rate. The only true valuables he owned consisted of mementos of his own and his children's growing up: letters, old photographs, certificates, newspaper cuttings, and odds and ends from his grandparents, like a World War One bullet, a fragment of shrapnel and a tarnished cigarette lighter with a dent in it, which his grandfather had said saved him from a German bullet. Banks smiled. Everyone in the family knew that was a tall tale, but they all pretended they believed it for the sake of the old man's pride. After all, he had fought at the Somme and survived.

Thieves often took or destroyed things like this, with sentimental value for only the owner, but in this case, the box in which Banks stored them still nestled securely beside a similar box of his old *Beano* and *Dandy* annuals on top of his wardrobe.

Feeling tired, Banks thought he would go into the conservatory, have a glass of wine and maybe doze for a while. He remembered Dr Chowdhury's strictures against alcohol, but doctors were always saying things like that. One glass wouldn't do any harm. He opened a bottle of Languedoc and put on an old Bill Evans CD, the Half Moon Bay concert, then settled down in his favourite wicker chair, feet up on a low stool. He wasn't supposed to watch TV or work on his computer, or even play games on his iPhone, but he didn't feel like doing any of those things, anyway. Surely a little cool jazz wouldn't do any harm? It was good for the soul, as was the wine. Dr Chowdhury had cleared him for sleep, and the tests showed no serious damage. Which was just as well, as he started drifting off during 'Autumn Leaves'.

'Unfortunately, it's not the right time of day for one of our famous cream teas,' said Trevelyan, 'but if you're still around this afternoon, may I recommend that you sample one here?'

Annie wasn't hungry so soon after breakfast, but she thought they might stick around another night, as they had to go to

Wool to talk to the Sedgwicks later. Tea time would be very late to set off on such a long drive back up north if the weather remained so bad. Was there anything in a cream tea she wasn't supposed to eat? Only calories, she thought. She wondered how Alan and Ray were doing back up in Eastvale. She didn't want to phone and spoil Banks's rest, if that was what he was doing, and she trusted AC Gervaise to call if there were any developments.

The three of them sat at a window table in a twee cafe in West Lulworth watching the passers-by hurry past, heads down, umbrellas up. The inside of the window was slightly steamed up, and along with the splattering of rain, it gave the view an Impressionist effect. And it was too hot in the cafe. Why did everyone have to turn the heating up when it rained? Annie sipped some tea and turned her mind back to the place they had just visited. Lulworth Cove and Durdle Door. Again, her heart weighed heavy at the thought of Marnie standing there, her life in pieces, then falling. No, jumping. And not standing. *Running.*

'It was a lovely day,' Trevelyan said.

Annie thought she might have missed something as she had been so lost in reverie. 'What? When?'

'The day Marnie Sedgwick died.' He gestured towards the window. 'It wasn't like this. The sun was shining, not a cloud in the sky, the water was all blue around the cove from the minerals in the rocks. There were boats out.'

'It was daylight?'

'Mid-afternoon.'

'I meant to ask you this before,' Annie said, 'but can you be absolutely certain that Marnie took her own life? There was no one else around?'

'There were lots of people around for a weekday,' said Trevelyan. 'That's why we can be sure. More eyewitnesses than you could shake a stick at. There was one group of Japanese tourists saw the whole thing. In shock, they were. We had to get an interpreter. They were on some sort of Hardy tour – Thomas, that is, our local celeb. One of his characters goes for a swim in the sea at Lulworth in *Far from the Madding Crowd*, and they all come by the coachload to see the spot. Can't understand it myself, as it never happened, it was all just made up.'

'Terence Stamp,' said Gerry.

Annie looked at her. 'Come again?'

'The one who swam out to sea, faked his suicide. Sergeant Troy, played by Terence Stamp. I've seen the film. Julie Christie as Bathsheba Everdene. There's a more recent version with Carey—'

'OK, Gerry. But remember, we're *not* on a Hardy tour.'

'Sorry, guv. My dad was a movie buff. I can't help it. And I was just thinking, you know, the suicide connection.'

Trevelyan smiled at the exchange. 'It's a good point,' he said to Gerry. 'Though Marnie Sedgwick wasn't faking it. At least twenty people saw her run out on Durdle Door and launch herself off the end. As you saw, the arch bellies out a bit and she hit the rock face as she went down. The pathologist says that was what killed her. A head wound. Fractured skull. After that she dropped in the sea and the waves battered her against the base of the arch until a boat managed to get close enough to haul her out. It was too late by then.'

Both Annie and Gerry silently contemplated Marnie's fate. 'Do you get a lot of people jumping off this Durdle Door?' Annie asked.

'Every summer. It's quite a popular sport among the young folk.'

'But they don't all die.'

'Of course not. We have the occasional serious accident, though, and the air ambulances are out there often enough, but there are spots where you can jump safely and avoid the outfling and the rocks at the bottom. The tides, too, of course.'

'But Marnie didn't do that?'

'No.'

'Would she have known the lie of the land?'

'According to her parents, Lulworth was one of her favourite spots. She loved the whole Jurassic Coast, no matter what the season.'

'Did she leave a note?'

'No. But there again—'

'Many suicides don't,' said Annie. 'We know. But there's no doubt in your mind that it *was* suicide?'

'None at all. Either that or she slipped and fell, but the majority of our witnesses say she definitely ran off the end.'

'*Ran,*' said Annie. 'You've mentioned that a few times and it strikes me as odd. Why was she running?'

'Nobody knows. Maybe she didn't want to give herself a chance to change her mind.'

'Or maybe she was being chased,' said Annie.

Trevelyan flashed her a stern glance. 'We're not the country hicks you might think we are down here, DI Cabbot. While there was hardly a major investigation, we did ask around. Marnie *had* been seen walking with and talking to a man in the car park and on the cliffs earlier. We couldn't get any sort of decent description except he was older, slender, medium height, with a touch of grey and, whoever he was, he was never seen again. The only unusual thing about him was that he was wearing a suit. You don't get a lot of that around here. There was certainly no one chasing her when she ran out on to the Door and jumped off the end.'

'What were they doing? Arguing? Holding hands?'

'Just walking and talking, as far as we know,' said Trevelyan. 'Nobody noticed anything unusual or potentially alarming.'

'Any photos or videos of him?'

'None that we saw.'

'Was there an investigation?'

'Only a cursory one, as I said, for the coroner's court.' Trevelyan took a tablet from his briefcase. 'And there's more. I don't want to upset you, but . . .' He turned the tablet on and went to the menu, then passed it to Annie. 'One of the Japanese tourists was taking videos of Durdle at the time.'

Annie held the tablet so that only she and Gerry could see it and pressed the start button for the video clip Trevelyan had selected. It began with a slow panorama of the sea and cliffs, the wind whistling in the microphone, white gulls swooping over the water's surface. Then there was an audible human gasp and the image jumped chaotically before it caught the end of Durdle Door and a human figure running. She didn't launch herself so much as fall like a rag doll and bounce off the cliff face. Annie felt sick and Gerry looked pale. But they watched it again. There was no indication that she had simply overbalanced or tried to dive into the sea.

'Sorry,' said Trevelyan, 'but that's pretty conclusive, I'd say. There's no sign of anyone chasing her. Naturally, we made sure the video was never shared on social media.'

'What about her stuff? Her mobile and so on?'

'The mobile must have gone with her over the cliff. We never found it. She had nothing else except a few quid and a set of car keys in her jeans pocket. Her car was in the car park. She'd even paid.'

'How long?'

'Two hours. She arrived at 12.27.'

'And was seen with the man when?'

'Around that time in the car park and about fifteen minutes later on the cliffs.'

'After that?'

'She jumped at 12.54, according to the timer on the video.'

'What happened to the man she was talking to?'

'Someone saw him get into a car at about ten to or five to one. They couldn't be certain.'

'What sort of car?'

'A posh one was all we heard. Maybe a Jag or a Beemer. Silver.'

'CCTV? ANPR?'

Trevelyan shook his head. 'It was too late by the time we heard all this. Recordings had been wiped over. To be honest, we didn't scour every possible source. There was no evidence that the man had anything to do with Marnie's suicide.'

'But he might have given her cause,' Gerry said.

'We'd still no reason to suspect him of any crime.'

'Isn't it a bit odd, though,' Gerry went on, 'that Marnie would bother paying for the parking when she was intending to take her own life?'

'People follow habit, as often as not,' said Trevelyan. 'If you're the sort of person who always pays your way, you'll just as likely do that even if you're planning suicide. Still, it's true that we don't *know* she was planning any such thing. It might have been a sudden decision – it might even have had something to do with the man she was talking to – but as far as we were concerned, her death did not involve foul play or suspicious circumstances. Maybe you see it differently.' Trevelyan put the tablet back in his briefcase and paused a moment. 'Now,' he said, 'I think you'd agree that I've been both patient and helpful so far. But you still haven't told me anything about *why* you're interested. Wouldn't this be a good time to tell me?'

'I'm sorry,' said Annie. 'You're right, of course. We have evidence that Marnie Sedgwick was raped at a party in the house of a man called Connor Clive Blaydon back on 13 April of this year.'

'Do you have any idea who did it?'

'No,' said Annie. 'The only evidence so far consists of a poor quality microSD recording from which we managed to enhance a picture of Marnie, but not of the rapist. We only found the recording some time after the event, while our CSIs were searching Blaydon's house. He was murdered in a particularly brutal fashion about a month later.'

'And you think that's connected with what happened to Marnie?'

'We don't think anything. We don't necessarily think Blaydon was the one who raped her. He could have been, but now we know for certain that Marnie didn't kill him. She died five days before he did. But everyone we've talked to has told us about the change in her after the date of the rape. How she became depressed, moody, anxious. Now you tell us – *show* us – that she took her own life about a month later.'

'You thought she might have been killed?'

'There was a possibility that the rapist might have feared his identity being revealed,' Gerry said. 'We had to consider that he might have decided the best course of action was to get rid of Marnie. That's why my ears pricked up when you mentioned she was talking to a man.'

'I'm sorry,' said Trevelyan. 'If I'd known any of what you've just told me before, I'd have made sure we tracked him down. But, as you saw, he wasn't anywhere near her when she went over the edge. Nobody was. And she didn't try to stop herself from falling. It seemed quite deliberate to me.'

'But she may still have been running away from him.'

'I suppose so.'

'It's not your fault,' Annie said. 'There was no way you could have known what had happened to Marnie back up north. Or her parents. She didn't tell anyone, as far as we know. We're still only just putting it together ourselves, and we don't know who raped her. Besides, this makes even more sense. I mean the suicide. Given her state of mind. Everyone says she'd been anxious and depressed ever since it happened.'

Trevelyan seemed lost in thought for a moment, then he said, 'It didn't make a lot of sense to us at first, even though her parents pretty much echoed what you say. But what you've told me just now at least puts it in context. There's more.'

'More?'

'Yes. We didn't want to tell her parents at first. They were upset enough that their daughter had killed herself. But they would have found out one way or another. Post-mortems and coroners' reports are a matter of public record, for a start. Not to mention the possibility of loose tongues.'

'What is it?' Annie asked, though she already had an inkling.

'The post-mortem revealed that Marnie was pregnant when she died.'

Banks awoke with a start when his phone played the blues riff. The Bill Evans CD had long since finished. It was late afternoon and shadows were lengthening across his garden and over the sloping stretch of land between the back of his cottage and the lower pastures of Tetchley Fell.

Banks answered. It was Ray Cabbot. 'Alan, I heard what happened. Annie told me you got hit on the head. Are you OK? Do you want me to come over?'

'No, Ray. I'm fine. It's OK. You're better staying there in case . . . you know, in case Zelda shows up.'

'Right. I don't suppose you've found anything new? She's been gone nearly four days now. I'm going crazy here.'

'Afraid not,' said Banks. 'But I've been out of commission all day and I don't remember anything. Annie would have told you, though, if there was any news. Just hang on.'

'Annie said something about a fire. I've tried calling her, but she's not been answering her phone.'

'No. She and Gerry are in Dorset following up a lead on a rape case. They're probably pretty busy.'

'Dorset? Are you sure Zelda hasn't been hurt? Did you find her?'

'People have mentioned fire to me,' said Banks. 'Unfortunately it's something I don't remember.' But as soon as he said it, he had the strange sensation that it wasn't true, that the state of his memory now was different from when he had drifted off to Bill Evans. That the pieces had rearranged themselves while he slept. He didn't want to risk saying anything to Ray, but he wanted to explore what that difference was. Could it have come back? Nobody really understood how memory worked. Maybe it was the music. Or a dream. He had no idea what triggered it, but he felt that it was all back, what happened two nights ago, and if he could just get some quiet time alone he could access it. 'I'm really knackered, Ray,' he said. 'And the doc says I've got to take it easy, so let's leave this for now, shall we? I can't tell you anything. I'm sure I'll be right as rain tomorrow. Let's get together then, OK?'

'OK,' said Ray. 'Sorry about . . . you know . . . Have a good rest.'

People kept saying that, but Banks was hardly likely to get a good rest until he had remembered what he could. The images were still fragmented, his memory in flux, but there were more of them now, and some were firming up into clear pictures. He found that it didn't take much effort to put them into a linear narrative. Waking with Keane looming over him, the smell of the petrol, a dark figure emerging from the shadows, Keane stiffening, stabbed from behind, spilling petrol, then Zelda stepping forward to cut his bonds. And the flames. It got a bit blurred again after that, with a sudden whoosh of flame and heat and Zelda shouting for him to run. Then he had woken up in the hospital bed.

There were still a few blank spots to fill in. The things Keane had said, for a start. There was something important in that, he remembered, without being able to grasp exactly what it was. He relaxed. It would come, and it was no good trying to force it. Perhaps some more music and another nap would help?

But it wasn't to be. No sooner had he put some solo Thelonious Monk on, than his phone went off again. He was tempted not to answer, as it was a withheld number, but he gave in at the last moment and paused the music. As he had suspected, it was Burgess on the line.

'How's the head?' he asked.

'Word sure gets around. It's fine, thanks.'

'Memory?'

'Still a bit untrustworthy.'

'I'd keep it that way if Newry's on your trail.'

'You know about that?'

'Sure. And him. He's a real bastard. Guilty till proven guilty.'

'Thanks for the warning.'

'That's not why I called you.'

'Oh?'

'No. We found an arm – at least, a recycling plant worker out Croydon way did. Severed just below the shoulder. Wrapped in a black bin liner. It fell out right in front of his forklift.'

'Whose arm?'

'No idea. And no other body parts yet. They're still scouring the area. The bad news is that there's no hand, therefore no prints.'

'Why tell me?'

'Thought you'd be interested. This arm, there's some decomposition, but it's not too badly preserved, and it's got a tat. A bit faded, but still readable with our technology. Looks like someone tried to scrub it off with bleach but didn't quite succeed.'

'Of what?'

'My experts tell me it's the insignia of some Croatian crime gang. "Loyal unto death" or some such codswallop.'

'Croatian?'

'Thought you'd be interested. I'll send up the details. And make sure you get plenty of—'

'I know. Rest. Believe me, I've been trying. Thanks. Talk to you later.'

Banks ended the call. An arm, he thought. Interesting. Then he started the solo Monk again and lay back in his chair.

There was a definite aura of mourning in the Sedgwick household, though the curtains weren't closed and neither Mr nor Mrs Sedgwick was dressed in black. There was a family photo taken in happier days on the mantelpiece, but no shrine to Marnie with candles burning and a vase of flowers. The mourning resided more in the general atmosphere and the numb, mechanical way Mrs Sedgwick – Francine, she asked them to call her – made tea and carried in the tray while her husband – Dennis, please – put out a gateleg table in front of the green velour sofa. It was an unremarkable house on an unremarkable street, and its view consisted almost entirely of other unremarkable houses, with just a glimpse of the rolling green Dorset countryside in a gap between two terraces.

The Sedgwicks looked older than Annie had expected, given that Marnie had been only nineteen when she died, but both seemed fit and trim despite a few wrinkles around the eyes and a touch of grey. Francine wore her hair long with a ragged fringe, and Dennis had his neatly cut with a side parting and a forelock that flopped over his brow. They were both casually dressed in jeans and short-sleeved shirts.

The rain continued to batter against the large arched window in the living room as they settled down to tea and the McVitie's chocolate digestives Francine had laid out on a plate. Annie took one, but Gerry and Dennis didn't.

'We're sorry to bring up memories that might still be painful for you,' Annie said, 'but we need to talk to you about Marnie. Is that short for Marjorie, by the way?'

'It is,' said Francine. 'Her name is Marjorie, but she couldn't pronounce it when she was young. It came out as Marnie, and it just kind of stuck. Especially when she got older and thought Marjorie sounded too old-fashioned.'

'Nothing to do with the movie then?' said Gerry.

Francine frowned. 'What movie?'

'Never mind.'

Annie gave Gerry a sharp glance and went on, 'We were wondering how long Marnie had been home until she . . . you know . . .'

'Committed suicide?' said Dennis. 'I know you're not supposed to say that these days. It's no longer PC, though Lord knows why, but that's what happened. How long was it, dear? Not long.'

'She came down at the beginning of May,' said Francine. 'I can't remember the exact date. The third or fourth, I think. But she was only home for a couple of weeks or so before she died.'

'And during that time how did her behaviour seem?'

'There was something wrong. She wouldn't tell us what it was, and we couldn't guess, but we knew things weren't right with her. She shut herself up in her room a lot, missed meals because she said she wasn't hungry. And mood swings. She had mood swings. We were starting to think we should try to persuade her to see a doctor when . . . it happened.'

'Did Marnie have any eating disorders? Anorexia? Bulimia?'

'No, never. She'd always had a healthy appetite, that's why it seemed so strange.'

'She wasn't drinking or taking drugs as far as you know?'

'No,' said Dennis. 'I'm not saying she might not have experimented while she was at uni or living up north, but not while she was here. I've done a drug awareness course, and I think I would have known the signs.'

'What kind of work do you do?'

'I'm a teacher. Local comprehensive. And Francie here works in human resources at the hospital. I started my summer break early, and Francie is still on medical leave. Her nerves are bad.'

'Sorry to hear it,' Annie mumbled. 'We'll try not to take up too much of your time.'

'There's no point pussyfooting around us,' Dennis said. Even though his wife looked alarmed, he went on, 'We know that Marnie was pregnant when she jumped.'

'Dennis!'

'Sorry, love.' Dennis leaned over and patted his wife's hand. 'But it's the truth.'

'We know,' said Annie.

'What we'd like to know,' Dennis went on, 'is why the police are coming around now, over a month after our Marnie killed herself. And why the North Yorkshire police?'

'Marnie lived in York,' said Gerry. 'That's not technically North Yorkshire – they're very much a nation of their own – but we think Marnie is connected with an incident that took place between Harrogate and Ripon.'

'What sort of incident?' asked Francine.

Gerry glanced at Annie, who gave her a slight nod. 'It was a rape,' Gerry said. 'At a party.'

'I told you,' said Mr Sedgwick to his wife. 'I told you Marnie wasn't the sort of girl to get herself into trouble.'

'But, Dennis,' she said. 'She was *raped*. Our Marnie was raped. Oh, God.' She wielded a handkerchief from beneath her cushions and started to cry.

Annie thought it was true that Dennis Sedgwick had made rape sound preferable to getting pregnant through consensual sex, but she didn't think he had intended it to come out that way. It had been a thoughtless statement, but not a cruel or brutal one. She distracted herself with her tea and a biscuit while the Sedgwicks settled themselves back down again, and said, 'It's more than likely she had no idea what was happening to her. It looks as if someone slipped something in her drink. Rohypnol, something like that.'

'She was drugged?' said Dennis.

'It appears that way.'

'Where was this party?'

'At the home of a man called Connor Clive Blaydon. Have either of you ever heard of him?'

They both shook their heads.

'What was she doing there?' Francine asked.

'She was working,' Gerry said.

'But I thought she worked at Pizza Express?'

'She did,' Gerry explained. 'But she had another job – part-time – working for an events organiser.'

'Doing what?' asked Francine.

'Backroom stuff. Mostly in the kitchen. Helping the caterers. Organising.'

'Then how did she become a victim?'

'We don't know. One of the guests must have had his eye on

her and managed to get her alone. He might have persuaded her to have a drink he had drugged.'

'She was always too trusting,' Dennis said. 'Even when she was a little girl.'

'We can't know for certain,' Annie said, 'because we haven't yet found any witnesses willing to speak to us, or anyone who admits to knowing anything.'

'Why not?' asked Dennis.

'Mr Blaydon, the host, was murdered about a month after the party. The 22nd May, to be precise.'

'And you think these events are connected? Marnie's rape and Blaydon's murder.'

'Not necessarily,' said Annie. 'We're just keeping an open mind. As you can no doubt work out, this was after Marnie's suicide.'

'Well, at least you're not trying to accuse her of murder.'

'No,' said Annie. 'But as I'm sure you understand, with both a rape and a murder occurring so closely together, on the same premises, we can't leave any corner unexamined. This Blaydon was involved with some pretty shady characters, and we think our best bet is that he was killed by a member of the Albanian Mafia.'

'Mafia?' gasped Francine. 'What was our Marnie doing with the Mafia?'

'Nothing,' said Annie. 'She was helping to organise the party, that's all. She had nothing to do with the guests. I doubt she even knew there were such dangerous characters around.'

'Until it was too late,' said Dennis.

'Yes.'

'Who was she working for?'

'A woman called Charlotte Westlake. She was Mr Blaydon's personal assistant, and her background is in events organising.'

'How did Marnie come to be working for her?'

'It seemed she just wanted another job. Needed the money. Mrs Westlake told us that most people who apply to her for jobs do so via word of mouth, so clearly someone who already worked for her, or had worked for her, suggested Marnie try it.'

'Who was this?'

'We don't know. We have a list of present and previous employees, so it's something we can find out if we need to. But it probably doesn't matter. The fact is that she was working at this party at Mr Blaydon's house when someone drugged and raped her. She didn't tell anyone.'

'Then how do you know?'

'There was a recording,' Gerry said. 'A very poor one – the cam wasn't working properly – but we managed to recreate an image of her face. Mrs Westlake's secretary had met her when she came for a job interview and identified her from that image as Marnie.'

'A *camera*?' said Francine. 'My God, are you saying someone *recorded* all this? Are you sure? Couldn't there be some mistake?'

'There could be,' said Annie, 'but we don't think so. As I said, we know that she was working at the house the night the attack occurred. Would you like to see the picture?'

'Is it . . .'

'It's just head and shoulders.'

Mrs Sedgwick nodded and Annie took out the photo and showed it to her. She put it down. 'It could be anyone, couldn't it?'

Her husband picked it up. 'Francine's right,' he said, tossing it back towards Annie. 'This doesn't prove anything.'

'We think it was Marnie,' Annie went on, 'and we think that was why people say she was behaving strangely after that party. Mood swings. Depression. Shutting herself away. She couldn't concentrate on her job at Pizza Express, so she left, then came home. That's when you were briefly reunited.'

'Did she know she was pregnant?' Francine asked, moving the hankie away from her face.

'We don't know,' said Annie. 'We don't even know for certain that the rape caused her pregnancy. If she knew, she never mentioned it to anyone we've talked to. All we can say is that she might have known, might have sensed the change in herself, even after just a month or so, while she was back with you. A missed period, perhaps, cramps, nausea, bloating, mood swings. And she was certainly upset enough by the rape itself for that to affect her behaviour. Do you know if she saw anyone in the two weeks she was down here? Old friends, perhaps?'

'They've all moved away. There's not much for young people to do around here. Most of them leave. Besides, she hardly ever went out.'

'Only the walks,' said Dennis.

'Yes, that's true. She went for long walks sometimes. Disappeared for hours. We were quite worried about her.'

'A witness saw her walking and talking to a man on the cliffs the day she died,' Annie said. 'Do you know who that might have been?'

'The police mentioned that to us, too,' said Dennis. 'We have no idea. Could it be important? Could it be the man who . . . who raped her?'

'There's no evidence that he had anything to do with what happened to her,' Annie said. 'And we don't know who raped her. But it's always good to talk to people who . . .' She paused. 'Well, I don't suppose we'll manage that now. Whoever he is, he'll be long gone. It probably isn't relevant.'

'We always told her not to talk to strangers,' said Dennis.

'It wasn't a stranger,' Francine said. 'That's what they're saying. If she was walking and talking with him, he was probably someone she knew.'

'We don't know,' said Annie. 'Did Marnie have any siblings, brothers or sisters?'

The Sedgwicks looked at one another in silence for a moment, then Francine said, 'No. Marnie was an only child. I . . . you see, we couldn't have children of our own, and . . .'

'Marnie was adopted?' said Annie, giving Gerry a puzzled glance.

'Well, yes. I assumed you knew.'

'Nobody told us.'

'It didn't make her any less our own. We couldn't have loved her more if I'd given birth to her myself.'

'No, of course,' said Annie. 'It's just that we didn't know. It never came up in any of our investigations.'

'There's no reason why it should, is there?' said Dennis.

'I suppose not. You just took us by surprise, that's all. How old was she when you adopted her?'

'Just a baby,' said Francine. 'They had to keep her in a while longer than usual because she was born early. But she was a beautiful tiny perfect baby.' She collapsed into sobs, and her husband embraced her.

Annie sat thinking and Gerry scribbled away in her notebook.

15

Banks felt a lot better the following morning after his first night at home. He was even hungry enough to scorch some toast to eat with his coffee. The headache was almost gone, as was most of the nausea. The dizziness still came and went, but the main thing was that he had got his memory back, or most of it, and had even managed to shuffle it into what seemed like the right chronology. The problem was what to do with it.

The missing fragments had fallen into place. He remembered Keane telling him that Zelda was being kept in the same building, and that she was with Petar Tadić, who was settling a score of some kind. Then Keane went on to tell him about Tadić torturing and killing Faye Butler, and his killing Hawkins, who was double-crossing the Tadićs. And he saved the best for last: Zelda had killed Goran Tadić, just as she had written in her notebook. So it wasn't fantasy. Now Banks really could be charged with aiding and abetting the murder, should it all come out.

Banks thought again of the severed arm Burgess had mentioned. What had Petar Tadić done with his brother's body? Could it be his? It wasn't every day they found severed arms in recycling plants, even in London, nor was it unknown for gang members to chop up dead colleagues and scatter the parts over a large area. No time for ritual or honour when you've got a body to get rid of. So it *could* be Goran's arm. On the other hand, there were other Croatian criminal gang members in the country, so it wouldn't do to jump to conclusions without more evidence.

Banks also now remembered Zelda yelling for him to run as the fire flared up. He had done so instinctively, without looking back, but when he got outside and turned to see her, she wasn't there. He had gone back to the doorway, he remembered, to see if she was still inside and whether he could get to her. The place was an inferno by then, and there was nothing he could do without sacrificing his own life, and his instinct for self-preservation had kicked in. He got the hell out of there. He had staggered away, half choked, then fallen in the weed-filled reservoir, hit his head on the bottom and passed out.

Now he was convinced that he should have waited for Zelda, even though the flames were quickly spreading, or at least made sure she went before him, instead of just running off without thinking. If she had been trapped by a falling beam or something and burned to death, he would never be able to forgive himself. He vaguely remembered brief snatches of consciousness, the firefighters picking him up, paramedics loading him on to a gurney, someone shining a light in his eyes, someone gently shaking him in the night, but most of it was blank until he woke up in the hospital bed.

But now that he had his memory back, he was stuck with a serious dilemma. He still didn't know where Zelda was, or even if she was still alive. Newry had simply said there were two bodies in the burned-out treatment plant. Keane was certainly one of them, but the other could be Zelda's or Petar Tadić's. It was also possible that there was a third body the search team hadn't yet found, and that all three were burned to a crisp in there. Burned human remains sometimes went undetected, or were damaged by firefighting and recovery operations. Fire scene investigators often couldn't tell the human remains from other fire- and water-damaged debris.

If Zelda had survived, though, she had probably run off through a different exit and gone somewhere she thought was safe. But things had changed. Now he knew she was a murderer – at least an *alleged* murderer, according to Keane – and he was a cop. He was supposed to catch murderers and see that they went to trial and, if found guilty, received their due punishment. But this was Zelda. *Nelia Melnic*.

He had read parts of her notebook, but he had brushed them off as fantasy at the time. What if it was true, as Keane had said? What if Zelda had killed Goran Tadić? What was he going to do about it? He had seen her kill Keane with his own eyes. A good argument for self-defence could be made for that killing. But Goran Tadić? Perhaps the same was true, but he knew nothing about the circumstances of what happened. Maybe Keane was lying; it wouldn't be the first time. But he had thought Banks was about to die, so why bother lying to him? To send him to his grave thinking a woman he cared for was a killer? Was Keane *that* cruel? Perhaps. The sensible, logical, moral thing to do was report what he knew to AC Gervaise, or Superintendent Newry, and leave it to others to track down Zelda, and to the jury and judge to decide on her fate.

But he couldn't do that.

So what the hell was he to do?

Annie and Gerry had skipped the cream tea and started out from Wool shortly after they had talked to the Sedgwicks, but not before Gerry had phoned the General Register Office and managed to persuade someone there to track down the birth details of Marjorie Sedgwick. They told her not to expect an answer until the following day as they were short-staffed. Now it was the following morning, and they were both tired. It had been a long journey back and a late night.

'We didn't dig deeply enough into Marnie's background,' Gerry said as she sat on the edge of Annie's desk in the squad room, coffee in hand. 'My mistake. I'm sorry. I should have found out what happened to her before we went to Dorset.'

Annie swivelled in her chair. 'Not to worry too much,' she said. 'We hadn't known her full name for very long. It's still early days, and we've got more to work with now. It probably won't make any difference in the long run. We're not racing against time.'

'I suppose the question we should ask ourselves is whether we still have a case to investigate now that the victim is dead.'

'Good point,' said Annie. 'We'll certainly have to scale down. The budget's bound to be cut. But let's carry on until we hear something from the AC. We can at least argue that we think the rape and Marnie's suicide could be somehow connected with Blaydon's murder.'

'Fair enough,' Gerry said. 'And if Charlotte Westlake was more involved than she's letting on, we may be on to something.' She glanced at her watch. 'We should find out what the registry has to tell us soon enough.'

'Let's not forget,' Annie added, 'there's still a rapist walking free out there.'

'Perhaps not,' said Gerry. 'I've been thinking. You know, maybe you were just being provocative the other day, suggesting that Charlotte Westlake might have killed Blaydon, but let me play devil's advocate here and suggest that Blaydon was the rapist, and Charlotte was keeping quiet either out of fear or some sort of misplaced loyalty. Why have we never seriously considered Blaydon for the rape before?'

'We did discuss it with Alan the other day,' Annie said. 'But we dismissed the idea. And it hasn't been very long since we found the cards.'

'Yes, but why? We never followed up. We never took it *seriously*. Maybe we dismissed it too soon?'

'It was hard to follow up. Blaydon was already dead. And we had no clear image of the rapist from the SD card images.'

'Fair enough,' Gerry argued. 'It's blurry and vague. But the image in the recording is as likely to be him as just about anyone else. Same size, shape and gender, at any rate. OK, maybe you can tell it's not a giant or a hugely overweight person, but other than that . . . You couldn't recognise your own father from it. Think about it.'

'We just never thought of Blaydon as a rapist, did we?' said Annie. 'A crook, yes, a gangster or wannabe gangster, yes, maybe even a killer, but a rapist? Maybe you're right and that was short-sighted of us.'

'We had nothing concrete to link him with Marnie until you told me Timmy Kerrigan saw him talking to her at the party.'

'True,' said Annie, 'but that doesn't necessarily mean anything.'

'I think it does,' Gerry said. 'It's the first time we've had any sort of evidence or witness statement linking Blaydon and Marnie *together*. Sure, she worked at his parties, at least a couple of them, at any rate, and he probably knew of her existence through Charlotte. But until you talked to Timmy Kerrigan, nobody reported having actually *seen* Blaydon and Marnie meeting and talking. Remember how Charlotte told us she was getting worried about how decadent the parties were becoming, how they were crossing boundaries of taste and morality? Perhaps we were seeing Blaydon in free fall, and that was where he landed. Rape. Take the boundaries away and you're left with moral anarchy. What he wanted, he took. And maybe he wanted Marnie.'

'You're suggesting that he drugged Marnie's drink and took her to the bedroom?' said Annie.

'Why not? It would have been easy for him. He was the boss. It was *his* house. He knew the layout. He had access to any room he wanted. All he had to do was get her alone for a while and give her a drugged drink. Apparently, he didn't know about the minicam with the motion detector that Roberts had set up. Think about it. End of the evening. Marnie's been working. She's tired. Her parents said she was always too trusting. Blaydon was an old friend of Charlotte Westlake's. Maybe Charlotte's been protecting him?'

'But she has no reason to do that. He was dead before we ever talked to her. She'd nothing to fear from him. I mean, why protect a dead man?'

Gerry shrugged. 'I'm not saying it's a perfect theory.'

'OK,' said Annie. 'Let's say we run with that for a while and see where it leads us. What happens next? Who killed Blaydon?'

'Well, it wasn't Marnie. She jumped off Durdle Door on 17 May and Blaydon and Roberts were killed on 22 May. The Albanians still look good for it, I'd say. The ballistics, the gutting. It's their style. But who's to say Blaydon wasn't also the rapist and that his murder had nothing to do with the rape? We shouldn't necessarily let one crime distract us from another.'

'So maybe we could go back to my original screwball suggestion,' said Annie. 'That Charlotte Westlake murdered Blaydon. Let's face it, she doesn't have much of an alibi for 22 May. Organising some book award in Bradford? Really?'

'What was her motive?'

'Anger at what he did to Marnie? Female solidarity? After all, Marnie was *her* employee, not one of Tadić's hookers.'

'Still, that's pushing it a bit as a motive, isn't it?'

Annie laughed. 'Like yours, it's hardly a perfect theory. Maybe Roberts was the intended victim and Blaydon was collateral damage? Roberts could have been blackmailing

Charlotte about something, and she uncovered his whole scheme, threatened to tell Blaydon. Maybe Roberts had a recording of her we didn't find? Maybe because she took it when she killed them?'

'Too many maybes,' said Gerry. 'We're going around in circles here. It's making me dizzy.'

'It doesn't mean we should stop searching, though, does it? Even though Marnie and Blaydon are dead. And I think we should definitely have a much closer look at Charlotte Westlake. We've interviewed her twice, and I don't believe she's been completely honest with us on either occasion.'

'I'll get on it.' Gerry's phone rang, and she grabbed the handset. She listened for a while and made some notes, then thanked the caller and put down the handset.

'Come on, then, give,' said Annie. 'You're like the cat that got the cream. What is it?'

'Marnie's father is listed as unknown,' Gerry said, 'but the mother's name is Christine Pollard.'

'No way!' said Annie.

Gerry smiled. 'Way.' They high-fived.

'Have you got an address?'

'The parents in Halifax. That was nineteen years ago, mind you. I'll talk to them if they're still there, then maybe we can haul Mrs Westlake in again. Arrest her this time. Suspicion of murder. The full works: caution, lawyer and all, if that's what she wants.'

Annie rubbed her hands together. 'Oh, goody,' she said. 'I'll oil the rack and sharpen the thumbscrews.'

There were still a few firefighters and CSIs at the old water treatment plant when Banks pulled up at the cordon they had erected around the main building, where all the damage had been concentrated. The control room took up the entire lower floor, and upstairs there had been a number of offices and a staff common room, where the second body had been found. Since then, searchers had looked again for any traces of a third victim, but found none. That was good news.

Banks showed his warrant card to the officer with the clipboard who guarded the scene and walked towards the entrance.

'Better take care,' said one of the fire investigation officers. 'It can still be a bit dodgy in there.'

Banks thanked him, put on the hard hat the officer handed him and went inside. The smell of wet ash and burned rubber was almost overwhelming inside the building. Its acrid, gritty texture caught in his throat. He also thought he could discern an undertone of petrol, which took him right back to the night it happened and set off a surge of panic that fortunately passed quickly. A man turned from collecting samples, pulled his face mask aside and said hello. Banks recognised the lugubrious fire investigation officer Geoff Hamilton. They had worked together on a narrowboat fire set by Phil Keane some years ago.

'Anything new?' Banks asked.

'Nothing startling,' said Hamilton. 'Your CSIs found evidence of a car parked at the side entrance, in the old staff park. The ground's concrete, cracked and weedy, and the tracks are too faint to tell us much, but there were some oil stains and skid marks. It was definitely there. And recently.'

'Anything else?'

'This is where you were tied up,' Hamilton said, pointing to an area not far from the main door. It was still possible to see what had once been ropes, now twisted and charred, on the ground, and chalk marks had been made around the area where Keane's body had fallen. 'You were lucky,' he went on. 'You can see where all the petrol was. Someone obviously cared whether you lived or died.'

'Yes,' said Banks, remembering Zelda's face close to his, her breath pungent with days of bad food, fear and a trace of vomit, the speed with which she worked at his bonds with the knife before the flames whooshed up around them. Then the shouted instruction: 'RUN!' *He should have looked back.*

'Is this our old friend again?' Hamilton asked.

'Doesn't it have his signature?'

'There are similarities. It's multi-seated, different spots connected by streamers. Not entirely as random as it might have seemed. I'll have to get more analyses done, gas chromatology and so on, and compare them with the records.'

'No need to bother, Geoff,' said Banks. 'It was Keane. I was there.'

'So I heard,' said Hamilton. 'Don't let it become a habit.'

'I promise. By the way, you might check with the Met fire investigation service on a fire at a house in the Highgate area a couple of months ago. It presented as a typical chip-pan fire, but . . .'

'Not his style, if this is anything to go by.'

'He may be versatile. I'd say it's worth a closer look, but as he was likely one of the corpses they hauled out of here, maybe there's not much point in pinning a crime on a ghost. But there are a couple of coppers I can think of down there who wouldn't mind knowing. Just one for the record books, maybe, if you've got a spare moment.'

Hamilton grunted. 'Chance would be a fine thing.' Then he put his face mask on again and knelt by a pile of charred rubbish.

Banks went upstairs to the other marked crime scene. There was tape across the doorway and most of the floor had collapsed, so he stood for a few moments and stared at the chain, darkened by fire, attached the solid metal radiator, half disappeared through the burned floor. Was this where Zelda had been kept? Though the fire had only spread up there later, it had done as much damage as it had everywhere else. The walls were charred and the ceiling partially collapsed. The firefighters had been a while turning up, mostly because there had been no working alarm and no one present had been in a position to call them. So how had they been informed? Banks wondered. Who had called them? The building wasn't very far from the A1, though it was hidden from the motorway by a stretch of woodland. The flames would possibly have been visible to a passing motorist once they had reached their apex.

He went back downstairs and found the side door that led to the small staff car park. He could see the CSIs had marked off an area with an oil stain and tyre tracks where someone had accelerated too quickly. Zelda? It made sense. She had cut Banks free then dashed off to save herself. She would have been in a hurry to get away before anybody found her. Maybe hurt and in pain, too. But where was she?

The road out wasn't much more than an unfenced laneway, but after curving a mile or more around the woods and running parallel to the A1 for a while, it came to a roundabout that fed into the main artery. From there, she could have gone anywhere. CCTV and ANPR would be no use because they had no idea what make of car she was driving or what the number was, and the A1 was always busy. It could be the dark Ford Fiesta that Kit Riley had told them about in the Black Bull, but there were thousands of dark Fiestas on the roads. They might be able to find out, given time, but it would probably be too late by then. She would have dumped the car as soon as she could and found some other mode of transport.

Banks went back through the building and stood by the rectangular reservoir. Its bottom was covered in weeds and shrubbery after years of neglect, and that was what had cushioned Banks's fall. If he had hit the hard bottom full on, he might have done himself even more serious damage. At least a broken limb, if not a fractured skull. He gave a shudder as he shouted farewell to Geoff Hamilton and the others and headed back to his car. Just before he got there, he turned and asked one of the investigators, 'It's a bit isolated around here, isn't it? Do you know who called it in?'

The investigator scratched his head. 'I can't say for sure,' he answered, 'but I do remember the boss saying it was a woman's voice.'

A thin drizzle had started when Gerry pulled up that afternoon outside Mrs Pollard's house on the outskirts of Halifax. It was a dark stone semi, millstone grit, probably, halfway up a hill, with a pub at the bottom and a fine view of the Pennines beyond, including a couple of enormous woollen mills with tall chimneys, now mostly converted into craft shops, art galleries, cafes and local theatre venues. Misty rain hung over the valley.

Tracking Mrs Pollard down had been easy enough – she was still at the same address listed by the General Register Office – but Gerry wasn't quite sure how to broach the subject of her visit. She certainly didn't want Mrs Pollard to think she was looking for evidence of her daughter's wrongdoing, yet she could hardly lie and say she was checking a job reference. Should anything she learned from this visit become important in a court case, then a lie like that could easily get it dismissed. The visit would have to appear to be related to Blaydon's murder, which it was in a way, but without even the vaguest of hints that Charlotte Westlake might be responsible for that.

When Gerry introduced herself, Mrs Pollard asked to see her identification, which she studied closely for half a minute before handing it back. 'You can't be too careful these days, love,' she said. 'I had a bloke on the phone the other day telling me my bank account had been hijacked and asking for my details. He even knew the last three transactions I'd made on my Mastercard.'

'It's very sensible of you to be cautious,' said Gerry, following her inside. 'These scammers are getting very clever these days.'

'Now sit yourself down and tell me what it's all about,' said Mrs Pollard – or Lynne, as she asked Gerry to call her. But first, unlike her daughter, she offered tea, which Gerry was happy to accept after her drive.

Lynne Pollard disappeared into the kitchen and fussed for a while, while Gerry took the opportunity to examine the living room. She didn't remember seeing many photographs at Charlotte Westlake's house, just one of Charlotte and a man she assumed to be Gareth, her late husband, but Lynne Pollard more than made up for it. There were framed photographs of Charlotte's graduation, her wedding, Charlotte as a child and as a teenager (Gerry guessed), not to mention Charlotte with Adele and Charlotte with Daniel Craig. How these meetings had come about, Gerry had no idea. She was glad she had discovered that Charlotte was an only child, because any sibling visiting this shrine would go away with an enormous inferiority complex, if that wasn't an oxymoron.

Lynne Pollard came back with a teapot, cups and all the necessaries on a tray and perched at the edge of an armchair upholstered in what resembled a Laura Ashley pattern. She was a short plump woman with a recently permed head of blue-grey hair. Her face was round and relatively unlined, with a smooth pinkish complexion, small nose and a wobbly double-chin. She wore brown slacks, moccasin-style slippers and a loose beige cardigan over a white blouse. Apart from a couple of rings, the only jewellery she wore was a cross on a silver chain around her neck. She wore a little lipstick and a touch of rouge, but no mascara or eyeliner.

'You've got a nice view,' Gerry said.

'On a good day, yes. Cradle of the Industrial Revolution. That's what my husband used to say.'

Gerry happened to have discovered in her researches that Mr Pollard had died not terribly long after Charlotte Westlake's husband, but she thought it only polite to ask after him. 'Is your husband deceased?'

'Yes. Cyril passed on three and a half years back. Heart. Just like that. Went to bed one night, dead by morning. Never smoked in his life, took a one-hour constitutional every day, hardly touched a drop of alcohol except a small dry sherry at Christmas. It just goes to show you, doesn't it?'

Exactly what it went to show her, Gerry had no idea. Maybe that life was fleeting and one should enjoy every moment. Well, she tried to do that already.

Lynne Pollard stirred milk and sugar into the tea. 'So what's all this about? It's not every day I get a visit from a police detective.'

Gerry gestured towards the photographs. 'You must be very proud of your Charlotte,' she said.

'Christine,' Mrs Pollard corrected her. 'She was always Christine at home. And, yes, Cyril and I were terribly proud of her. She got into Oxford, you know. Oxford! The only girl from her school to do it in the year.'

'What about her career?'

'Oh, wonderful. You know she mixed with some of the most important, famous people you can imagine. Politicians, pop stars – there's her with Adele – you name it. If they needed something organising, they asked for Christine. Well, Charlotte, I suppose, as it was her *professional* name.'

'How did you feel when she went to work for Mr Blaydon?'

'Is that what this is about? Connor Blaydon?'

'You knew him?'

'Met him on a couple of occasions. Perfect gentleman. You know, there's been a lot of lies and slanders slung around about him since his death.'

'It was murder, Mrs Pollard, and I'm one of the officers investigating what happened.'

'We all know what happened, love. And it's Lynne. Those foreigners killed him, that's who. Wanted him to be part of their evil crime empire and he wouldn't have it. Turned them down flat.'

'Did Char—Christine tell you this?'

'Yes. She knew him well enough. Why haven't you arrested them yet, that's what I'd like to know?'

'They're on the run,' said Gerry.

'Then you'd better hurry up and catch them before we cut ourselves off from the Continent for good.'

Gerry didn't see any point in telling her that Albania wasn't yet a member of the EU. Not that it mattered much any more. 'Yes,' she said. 'It's Connor Blaydon's murder I came to talk to you about. Christine has been very helpful – as you say, she knew him best – but we wondered if you too could shed any light on his background, maybe fill in a few blanks?'

'I don't see how I can help you, love. He was Christine's friend.'

'Yes, but you met him. You said so.'

'Only on a couple of official occasions.'

'How long had Christine known him?'

'I know she did some events for him early on, when she was first in the business after university. Then she cut back a bit on the events when she married Gareth and it was after he died that she went to work for Mr Blaydon. But you already know that.'

'When did she leave university?'

'When she was twenty-one. 1998 that would have been.'

'And after that?'

'She went off travelling with her friends.'

Gerry remembered Charlotte saying something about going to Thailand and Vietnam, then the Mediterranean. 'For how long?'

'Nearly a year. She'd saved up a lot from her summer jobs, and it was something she'd always wanted to do.'

'So she came home when?'

'July, it would have been. July 1999.'

'And she lived with you here?'

'No. She had friends in Oxford and she stayed with them until she got herself fixed up with a job. Surely she could tell you all this. Her memory's probably a lot better than mine.'

'I don't think there's anything wrong with your memory. Besides, it's useful to get a different perspective. I'm especially interested in the time she spent abroad. Do you know where she was last, say, June that year?'

'1999? They were in Greece then.'

'Whereabouts?'

'I honestly don't remember exactly. Greek names. I've never been very good with those. Tell you what, though, just hang on a minute.'

Gerry heard her go upstairs, then the sound of cupboard doors opening and closing. A minute or so later, Lynne Pollard came back down with a cardboard box and put it on the low coffee table. As far as Gerry could tell, it was full of envelopes and postcards.

'I've kept everything she's ever sent me,' Lynne said. 'Every letter, every card, ever since she went on her first school exchange when she was fourteen.'

Gerry looked at the treasure trove of Charlotte Westlake's past and smiled at Lynne. 'Where shall we begin, then?' she asked.

Banks pulled up in the car park of Eastvale General Infirmary at three o'clock that afternoon and headed straight for the basement. The high-tiled corridor echoed as he walked along towards the autopsy suite and Dr Karen Galway's office.

Dr Galway was sitting at her L-shaped desk, which was piled high with file folders. She was wearing a powder-blue blouse, and her white coat was hanging from a hook behind the door. She had bright green eyes, a rather long nose, thin, tight lips, and a high domed forehead over which hung a fringe of greying hair. A framed print of Rembrandt's 'The Anatomy Lesson of Dr Nicolaes Tulp' hung on the wall opposite her desk. While Banks admired the artist's skill, he could think of any number of Rembrandt paintings he would rather have hanging on *his* wall.

'Catching up with paperwork?' he asked.

The doctor rolled her eyes and spoke with a trace of Dublin accent. 'Like you wouldn't believe.' She swivelled her chair to face him. 'Sit down, please. I wasn't expecting you. I heard you'd caught a nasty bump on the head.'

Banks sat. 'Two. I'd say it's an occupational hazard, but it really isn't. Must be the first time in years.'

'You saw Dr Chowdhury here?'

'Yes.'

'He's very good.'

'He looks about twelve.'

Dr Galway laughed. 'I'll tell him you said that. Actually, he's thirty-three. A graduate of the Faculty of Medicine, Imperial College London. By the way, aren't you supposed to be resting? It's customary for concussion sufferers to rest.'

'It was a couple of days ago. And I'm sitting down, aren't I?'

'You know what I mean.'

'I suppose I should still be resting, but in reality, life gets in the way. Or in this case, criminal investigation.'

'You have short-term memory loss, don't you?'

'What?'

'Very funny.'

'Yes. That's true, but there's nothing wrong with the rest of my memory.'

'I just didn't expect you to be back at work so soon, that's all.'

'We still have a missing person to find as well as a rape and murder to solve. I can't afford the luxury of rest at the moment.'

'In that case, what do you want to know?'

'Have you completed the post-mortems yet?'

'I was in at six o'clock this morning. There wasn't a lot left to work with. I've been as thorough as I know how, but I'd be the first to admit I'm not well experienced with burn victims. As a matter of fact, of all the bodies I have to perform post-mortems on, they disturb me the most. I'm not shirking my duty or making excuses, you understand, just being honest. And if you think you need a second opinion, I wouldn't hesitate to call in an expert in the field I know in Edinburgh. He's worked in various war zones around the world, so he's more than acquainted with the properties of fire. I worked with him briefly in Iraq several years ago, and he handled most of the tough burn cases.'

'I hardly think that will be necessary. What have you found out?'

'The damage was quite advanced in both cases, and the remains are very fragile. Fire causes any number of changes to the human body – blistering, skin splits, exposure and rendering of subcutaneous fat. Then the muscles that overlie the bones retract when they're exposed to extreme heat. That's what causes the so-called pugilistic position often found in burn victims. What I'm saying is that kind of damage makes it almost impossible to identify any pre-fire trauma the victim might have been exposed to.'

'So you can't say if either of them was shot, stabbed or bashed on the head?'

'I didn't say that. The skin, flesh and fat are gone. So badly damaged by fire and by being transported here that they won't tell me what happened. But if the victim had been shot, I would expect to find a bullet – if not the hole it made – and if he was bashed over the head, as you so eloquently put it, I would expect damage to the skull indicating that, unless it exploded from the inside, of course.'

'Of course,' said Banks, feeling momentarily sick. 'Have you?'

'No. Stab wounds are particularly difficult, for example. Because the skin blisters and splits in fire, and the inner organs are consumed, any trace of an original knife wound in flesh would probably be erased. On the other hand, if the knife came into contact with a bone, then there could be evidence of that contact on the bone.'

'A notch?'

'That kind of thing, yes.'

'And is there?'

'On one of the bodies, yes.'

'Which one?'

'The one on the lower level.' Dr Galway twisted in her chair and pointed to a spot on her back. 'Fifth rib, posterior left.'

'Meaning?'

'There's a slight nick on the bone that could be a knife mark. I'll be further analysing and measuring it, of course, and may soon be able to tell you something about the weapon that caused it. But don't get your hopes up too high. It's a tiny nick and there could be other reasons it's there.'

'What would the result of such a wound be?'

'Most likely, depending on the angle and the length of the blade, it would have pierced the lung.'

'Would the killer, assuming there was one, have needed expert knowledge?'

'Not necessarily. He wouldn't have had to be a trained commando. It could have just been a lucky stab. Lucky for the killer, I mean. An expert would have known exactly what he was doing, of course, but that knowledge wasn't essential to the deed.'

It was Keane, Banks knew. Zelda had stabbed him twice in the back. He had witnessed it. 'And the other victim?'

'No sign of knife wounds, but I wouldn't rule it out.'

'Did they both die in the flames?'

'Impossible to say. They were both so badly burned that it wasn't possible to measure smoke inhalation. I'm sorry to be so vague, but it's well-nigh impossible to determine these things from the remains we had left.'

'Can you get DNA?'

'The sixty-four-thousand-dollar question.'

'Can you?'

'It's possible. Bones can be quite durable when all else is burned beyond recognition. The DNA may be degraded or contaminated, but there's a good chance it won't be. These bones are only semi-burned in places, especially the ones found on the upper level, not black or blue-grey, so there's still hope. The teeth, too, could be a possible source. I'm working on it with Dr Jasminder Singh from your forensics lab. There is just one more thing.'

It was probably the answer to the question Banks had been afraid to ask. 'Yes?'

'The pelvic bones were badly burned but still held their shape. Both victims were male.'

16

Banks had hardly been in his office ten minutes before a sharp rap at the door was followed by AC Gervaise and Superintendent Newry.

'What the hell are you doing here?' Newry demanded.

Banks turned down the Thea Gilmore CD he had been listening to. 'My job,' he said.

'I thought I made it clear to you that you were off the case until further notice.'

'You did nothing of the kind.'

'Don't play clever buggers with me, Banks. I already know you've visited the treatment plant, and talked to Dr Galway at the mortuary.'

'I dropped by both. True.'

'And asked her about the fire victims' post-mortems?'

'Also true.'

'I'm within a hair's breadth of suspending you from—'

'Superintendent Newry!' said AC Gervaise. 'A little restraint, please. There have been no complaints against Superintendent Banks. He hasn't been accused of any wrongdoing.'

'Not yet. But what if I accuse him? I've got two victims whose deaths are unaccounted for. There's a chain secured to a radiator in the upstairs staffroom, and it looks as if someone was restrained there. Ropes on the lower floor were most likely used for the same purpose. Your man here was found unconscious outside the building in question without any reasonable explanation.'

'You think I chained someone to the radiator, then tied myself up, stabbed someone and set the place on fire?' Banks said. 'When did I do all that?'

Newry turned to AC Gervaise. 'Detective Superintendent Banks can't account for his whereabouts or his actions during the time the events unfolded in the water treatment plant, and he was found on the premises by the firefighters, with forensic evidence to prove he was at some point *inside* the plant. He claims to have lost his memory—'

'Claims?' said Banks. 'You don't believe me?'

'Let's just say I have my doubts,' Newry snarled. 'I've told you what I think of these memory-loss cases. It's just a bit too bloody convenient, isn't it?'

'Not for me. And don't you think you should leave your prejudices at the door?'

Newry looked at Gervaise. 'Do you permit this kind of insubordination under your command, Chief Super-intendent?'

Gervaise glanced between the two of them. 'Superintendent Newry,' she said. 'With all due respect, I expect any officer under my command to push back when unnecessarily provoked, and when it comes to the truth, I am still inclined to believe someone is innocent until proven guilty. All in all, I prefer to take the word of one of my most trusted detectives over that of a . . . a . . .'

'How about a jumped-up little Hitler?' Banks suggested.

Gervaise shot him a stern glance. 'That's enough from you, Superintendent Banks. That's not helpful. Let's just all calm down and have a rational look at this situation.'

Newry sneered. 'Well, fortunately, *with respect*, ma'am, what happens next doesn't depend on what you think,' he said.

'Then go talk to the chief constable.'

'Believe me, I intend to. I'm not letting go of this.' With a hard, angry look at both Banks and Gervaise, Newry pushed his chair back roughly and stalked out. 'We'll be talking again. Soon.'

'There goes a man in search of a heart attack,' said Banks. 'I hate to think what his blood pressure must be like.'

'Don't be so bloody flippant, Alan. Don't you understand what a predicament you're in? For Christ's sake, Newry wants you suspended. ACC McLaughlin and I are fighting in your corner, but we're running out of steam, and you're not helping by giving ammunition to the opposition, if you'll forgive me a mixed metaphor. I want you to take sick leave. As of now. Lord knows, you're due enough.'

'Gardening leave?'

'It's *sick* leave, Alan. Not suspension. Because you sustained an injury on the job. We'll leave the insurance claims and whatnot for later. This is the best compromise we can come up with right now. Even the chief constable is on side with this. You know as well as I do that an officer can be suspended for months, even years, without resolution, for no reason at all. Newry hardly needs a solid case to scupper what's left of your career. But sick leave . . . Your doctor also agrees it would be advantageous in combatting stress and shock.'

'But what about Zelda? She's still out there. I've got a responsibility to her. And to Ray. And what about the Blaydon—'

'You're not the only detective in the station. Don't you trust your team?'

'Of course I do, it's just—'

'You want to be in the know. You want to be in control. All right, I understand. We'll keep you in the loop.' She paused. 'Is that good enough?'

Banks sighed and gathered his things together. 'It'll have to be, won't it?'

Banks's headache and dizziness returned with a vengeance before he had even managed to pull the Porsche into his driveway. He hurried upstairs to his medicine cabinet, took three extra-strength paracetamol and went to lie down on his bed. The dizziness soon passed, but the headache persisted until the drugs wrapped it in cotton wool and pushed it away to a far, quiet corner of his brain.

It was too early to go to sleep, and he wasn't tired, so he got up and went back downstairs into the small study-cum-sitting room at the front, sat down at his desktop computer, answered a few long-overdue emails and browsed Apple Music for anything new. There wasn't anything he desperately wanted, so he went through to the kitchen, made himself a toasted cheese sandwich and went into the conservatory to eat. Outside his windows, the shadows were lengthening, and clouds blanketed the peak of Tetchley Fell. He could hear sheep bleating high on the hillside.

As he ate, he considered his position. He had to accept the sick leave. Chief Superintendent Gervaise, his area commander, and ACC Ron McLaughlin were going out on a limb for him, and it would be ungrateful to do otherwise, not to mention hammering another nail in the coffin of his career. Whether you were guilty or not, suspensions and IOPC investigations had a nasty way of sticking to your record like shit to a shoe. They guaranteed entry into a Kafkaesque world from which you were bound to emerge – if you emerged at all – a changed and probably broken man. The brass bullied and lied, cliques closed ranks, punishments were decided upon and meted out before judgement was passed, hopefuls queued up at the bottom of the greasy pole leading to your job, federation or superintendents' association reps objected and waved their hands in the air, and things marched irrevocably on towards that fateful gate where all who enter must abandon hope. The streets and shelters were littered with discarded detectives. You would have more hope of success as a refugee begging asylum from Priti Patel than you would as an honest copper dragged deep into the maw of an internal investigation.

So, sick leave. What was he going to do with himself? He wasn't going to sit at home and be sick, that was for certain. How did things stand right now? That was the place to start. Banks finished his sandwich and poured a glass of wine. Then he put on a Jerry Garcia Band concert from Lunt-Fontanne, New York, October 1987, and settled back to relax. The nice balance of versions of old Motown numbers, Hunter/Garcia originals and Dylan classics was just right, laid-back yet uplifting. And Jerry was in great form.

He was almost certain that he had his full memory of the lost night back now. Just to be clear, he ran through the series of events in chronological order several times in his mind until they felt right. He supposed he wouldn't know if anything was missing unless he sensed an absence, but as he didn't, he accepted this version as the truth.

What it meant was that Zelda was out in the wind somewhere. He had deliberately not told anyone yet about the return of his memory in order to give her as much time as possible to get as far away as she could. He knew he shouldn't approve of her vigilantism, that people taking personal revenge for ills done to them was the beginning of a very slippery slope, but he couldn't help himself. He also realised that in giving her time to get far away he was aiding and abetting a murderer escape, but he decided he didn't care.

If Zelda had killed Goran and Petar Tadić, she had had good reason, and she had killed Keane in order to save Banks's life.

She didn't have to do that. She could have crept out of some other exit, the way she had obviously done after she had cut him free and the fire started. But she had risked her own life to save Banks from Keane, just the way Annie and Winsome had done that first time, back in Newhope Cottage. Many more instances like that, he realised, and he'd be getting worried about his masculinity. Wasn't he supposed to be the one doing the saving?

The upshot was that he couldn't throw Zelda to the dogs, no matter what. And if he were honest with himself, he liked her too much to do that. And worried what it would do to Ray.

So should he spend his sick leave trying to find her? He thought perhaps not. Zelda was resourceful, and if she wanted to disappear, she would. No doubt, when he admitted to getting his memory back and told Newry as much of the truth as he could get away with, there would be a police search for her, perhaps involving Europol. How intense and long-lasting it would be, he had no idea. It wasn't only the police. The Tadićs hadn't worked alone; they weren't even the heads of their organisation. There might be other criminal gang members on Zelda's trail, too, and no doubt they would put a price on her head. The last thing Banks wanted to do was lead them to her. Zelda had her contacts; she knew how to disappear. And if she wanted to get in touch with Ray after some time had passed, then she would find a way.

When it came to the Tadićs, Banks realised there was one thing he could do. He remembered Burgess telling him about the arm they'd found with the Croatian gang tattoos, and the faint possibility that it might belong to the missing Goran Tadić. If Jazz Singh could get a DNA sample from the burned body in the upstairs room of the treatment plant, then it might be worth checking it against the arm.

He phoned the lab and found she was still there.

'Jazz, if you compare two DNA samples, can you tell whether the people were brothers?'

'Without going into a lot of complicated detail, yes, probably,' said Jazz. 'Full siblings share around fifty per cent of their DNA. Why?'

'Would you do me a favour and compare a sample from the body in the treatment plant, the upstairs one, with a sample I'll get Detective Superintendent Burgess from the NCA to send you?'

'I can do that, yes.'

'Thanks, Jazz.'

'Is this on the abduction case budget?'

'Yes.' Banks didn't tell her that he was on sick leave and wasn't supposed to be ordering DNA tests.

Next, he phoned Burgess, who agreed to get a sample sent up for comparison. At least that would tell them whether the bodies were brothers, which meant in all likelihood that they were Goran and Petar Tadić.

Banks let his mind drift back to the treatment plant to see if he could remember how Zelda had seemed. He hadn't been able to tell if she was hurt because he hadn't got a good look at her. She had crept up behind Keane from the shadows and stabbed him. After that, with the flames and smoke, it was soon chaos. She had come close enough to him to cut through the ropes that were binding him, close enough for him to smell her breath, and he hadn't noticed anything to indicate that she had been hurt, then she had shouted for him to run. And she had taken off by herself. But she had found time to phone emergency services about the fire, perhaps because she was worried about him. She could be anywhere now. Mostly, Banks hoped she'd had time to get out of the country. She would have a far better chance of disappearing in mainland Europe.

And what about Ray? Maybe there was a way he could let Ray know she was OK without giving too much away about what happened, but he didn't know how. However he did it, it would mean lying to his friend. If Ray knew the truth, he would fret that she would never come back to him, or that she would be caught and put in jail if she did. On the other hand, if he told Ray nothing, he would assume all was lost and sink deeper into depression.

But so much depended, Banks realised, on him keeping his cool. He would have to stop putting Newry off, simply tell him he'd got his memory back, submit to an official interview and give him a version that worked for everyone.

Especially Zelda.

Late that evening, Banks was listening to Jessye Norman singing French songs when he heard a loud knocking at his door. Edgy since the attack, he picked up a knife from the kitchen as he went to answer it, only to find Ray Cabbot standing there, not too steady on his feet. Ray lurched forward and almost fell into Banks's arms – not to mention the blade of the knife – when the door opened. As he helped Ray in, Banks glanced out front and saw his car parked at an awkward angle. The bloody fool had driven over, despite the state he was in. Or probably because of it, Banks speculated.

Once Ray was inside, he seemed to steady himself and followed Banks down the hall and through the kitchen to the conservatory where Banks had been sitting. He walked with the exaggerated gait of a drunk pretending to be sober.

'Got a drink?' he asked.

Banks certainly didn't think he needed one, but he was the last person to be moralistic or judgemental about drinking. Instead, he poured Ray a decent measure of Highland Park and himself a generous glass of Gigondas, his first of the day.

'Whass this music?' Ray asked.

'Debussy songs. Why, don't you like it?'

''S'all right, I suppose. Bit artsy-fartsy.'

Banks used his phone to change the stream. Instead of Duparc's 'L'invitation au voyage' there came Tim Buckley's *Blue Afternoon*. 'That do you?' he said.

'I suppose it'll have to.'

'What is it, Ray?' Banks asked. 'What's wrong?'

Ray took a hefty wallop of scotch. 'You know what it is. It's Zelda. I miss her.' He put his head in his hands. 'Oh, God, Alan, I miss her like I can't say.'

'I'm sorry, Ray. I'm sure she'll be back.' As he tried to reassure Ray, Banks went over his strategy in his mind. He could tell him only so much of the truth if he hoped to do him any good at all.

'You know what happened, don't you?' Ray said. 'You didn't tell me anything on the phone yesterday. You said you felt ill, and I gave you time to recover. But you know now, don't you? And I'm here, begging you. You remember, don't you? Tell me. Is she all right? Where is she?'

'I remember most of it now,' said Banks, 'and I'll tell you what I can.'

Ray handed over his empty glass and Banks went into the kitchen to refill it. His own glass was still over half-full. Back in the conservatory, they sat at right angles to one another by the round glass table. The twilit sky outside was indigo and a dim orange-shade table lamp provided the only other light in the room.

'Well? Is she all right?' Ray prompted him.

'Depends what you mean by "all right",' Banks said. 'I only saw her very briefly, and things were . . . a little hectic.'

'Was she hurt?'

'Not that I could see.'

'How did she look?'

'Fine, Ray. She hadn't been harmed in any way. Just kept there against her will for a few days. She'd had a terrifying experience. No doubt she'd have liked to be able to brush her teeth, change her clothes and have a nice long shower, but other than that . . . whoever it was hadn't hurt her.'

'Thank God for that. Did you talk to her? What did she say?'

'There was hardly time for conversation. The bloody building was on fire. We had to get out of there. But she said to tell you not to worry, that she'd get in touch, and she would be back when she could.'

'She's coming back?'

'I'm sure she'll come when she can. But don't tell anyone.'

'Why can't she come now?'

'I don't know. There are things she has to deal with.'

'What things?'

'She didn't say.'

'When will she be back? Did she say that?'

'She didn't. But her situation here, the people who took her—'

'Where are they? Are they still after her?'

'They're dead,' said Banks. 'In the fire.'

'Thank God for that. So why can't she come home?'

'She will. It's just a matter of time.' Ray reached for his tobacco, looked at Banks and halted. Banks just nodded. 'Go on.' Ray emptied his glass again and Banks went and poured him another refill, a smaller one this time. If he had anything to do with it, Ray wasn't driving anywhere tonight. Tim Buckley was singing 'I Must Have Been Blind'.

Ray lit up. 'I'll go anywhere she wants. You know that. Just tell her that.'

'I'm not in communication with her, Ray,' Banks said. 'I don't know where she is.'

'But she got away? You're sure of it?'

'Yes. She got away.'

'Where might she have gone?'

'I don't know. She might have gone overseas. It was getting a bit too hot for her over here.'

'Those two bastards from the NCA. And she was worried about immigration. But she's got friends there. All over the place. She'll be all right there. How long do you think? I'll go to her wherever she wants. France. Italy. Spain. Greece. Even fucking Moldova, if I have to.'

Banks couldn't help but smile. 'I have no idea. As long as it takes. I'm sure she'll be in touch when she can.'

Ray took a drag on his cigarette and drank some more whisky. 'Then I'll try to carry on as normal,' he said, nodding his head as if in agreement with some inner decision. 'Get on with my work. Right? Just wait for her to come back. It's what she would want.' He tapped his glass. 'And cut back on the drinking a bit.'

'That's the best plan. You've got to stop stressing yourself out. It'll make you ill.'

'What about these people who are after her?'

'They're dead, Ray. I told you. Don't worry about them.'

'Who killed them? Not . . . no?'

'No,' said Banks. 'Not Zelda. We think they went for each other. A falling-out among thieves.'

'You're sure she got away, got out of there?'

'Yes, Ray. Zelda saved my life. I was tied up. She cut me free. That's when she told me to tell you she'd be back. After that, the fire was starting to spread fast, so she pushed me towards the exit. She went out by another door and drove off. Their car must have been parked there. I heard her go. Simple as that. The CSIs found two burned bodies in the place, both male. They can tell by the bones.'

'Are they chasing her?'

'Who?'

'Anyone. The police. The other bad guys. There must have been more than two. She'll be terrified if she's on the run.'

'She's had plenty of time to get far enough away,' said Banks. 'Sure, the police would like to talk to her in connection with the fire, as they've been talking to me. But she didn't start it. Phil Keane did that. And I'll make it clear to anyone who questions me that Zelda and I were victims, that she didn't kill anyone. They'll come to their senses. And I told you, the bad guys are dead. Maybe there are more, but without their leaders, they'll scatter to the four winds. Zelda's safe, Ray. I'm sure of it.'

If Zelda had half the brains Banks credited her with, she would have dumped the car in a long-term airport car park, then taken a train or shuttle to another nearby airport and flown out. She might even have risked the Eurostar. If he were to guess, Paris would be her first choice of destination. It was the last place she had lived for any length of time before coming to England and meeting Ray, and she probably still had friends and contacts there. She would need money, transportation, an escape plan.

Ray stood up and attempted a sloppy embrace, then said, 'I'd better be off now. Thanks, mate.' He held up his tumbler. 'And for the whisky.'

'Off where?'

'Home, of course.'

'You're not driving anywhere, the shape you're in. You can either sleep it off in my spare room or I'll drive you home myself.' Banks still hadn't finished his first glass of wine. 'Or I'll call you a taxi.'

'Whatever,' said Ray. 'Though I think I should be at home, shouldn't I, just in case she comes back? I mean, as you said, she might come home any time. I wouldn't want her to get back to an empty house. But a taxi will take for ever.'

'I suppose you're right,' Banks said, getting up. 'I'll drive you. You can leave your car here. Get a taxi here and pick it up tomorrow.'

As he drove back home after dropping Ray off, Banks thought he would try to find out something about Zelda's life in Paris; maybe knowing more about her time there would help him find her. He didn't want to find her for the police, but for himself, and for Ray. He wanted what he had told his friend this evening to be true. He locked and bolted the front door and went back to his chair in the conservatory, put the Tim Buckley back on where he had paused it, at 'Blue Melody'.

As he sat and thought, he realised that already in his mind he was separating himself from the police, almost as if he were no longer one of them. Planning escape routes for fugitives was hardly something the old Banks would have done. What was happening to him? After all these years, had it come to this? In some ways it was as if a great weight had been lifted off him, but in another it was like dipping a toe into uncharted waters, not knowing where they would lead or what lay beneath their murky depths.

17

It was the first time Banks had been on the other side of the interview table since his training days at Hendon. They had sent a car for him that afternoon, shortly after Ray had been back to pick up his car. Opposite him sat Superintendent Newry and beside Newry a female DI he introduced as Heidi Dunne. As far as Banks could gather, DI Dunne's role was to hand sheets of paper to Newry and to look disapproving, both of which she did very well. The conversation was between Banks and Newry, and even the solicitor sitting next to Banks kept out of it. Reg Courtenay was an old veteran of police affairs, and Banks wanted him there as a precaution. There were no charges against him, nor was he suspended, though this interview was being recorded, he wasn't under caution and was still being treated as a witness only.

'I understand you have regained your memory of the night in question,' Newry began, the sneer of disbelief clear in his tone, as if what he really meant to say was, 'Now you've got your story clear.'

'Bit by bit. It's still a bit blurry in parts, but yes, I remember most of what happened.'

'Perhaps you can help us, then?'

'I'll try.'

'I think you should know before we begin that my main concern, and that of DI Dunne here, who will be forming part of the active investigation team into this matter, is the discovery of two bodies in the burned-out water treatment plant on the eastern outskirts of Eastvale.'

'As I said, I'll help as much as I can.'

'Excellent.' DI Dunne shuffled some papers and Newry said, 'Perhaps you can begin by telling us about the events leading up to your abduction?'

'I was on my way home from a concert at the Sage in Gateshead. My son plays in a band and this was a part of their farewell tour.'

'I know about the Blue Lamps,' said Newry.

'That evening, they had played one of my favourite songs, Bob Dylan's "Visions of Johanna", at my son's instigation, and on my way home I listened to the original album, *Blonde on Blonde.*'

'I don't give a fuck what music you were listening to.'

If he hadn't guessed before, Banks knew at that moment there was no way he and Newry would ever get along. 'It helps if I pick up the threads,' Banks replied. 'If I jump in the story much later, it's far fuzzier in my memory for some reason. And you *did* ask for the events leading up to my abduction.'

Newry grunted. DI Dunne looked disapproving, not to mention disbelieving. 'Carry on,' Newry said.

'Thank you. *Blonde on Blonde.* Terrific album, by the way. You should try it some time. When I turned into my driveway and pulled up in front of my cottage, I noticed that the outside light wasn't working.'

'Someone had removed the bulb,' Newry said. 'There were fingerprints around the socket, but they're not on our files anywhere.'

'Probably Tadić or one of his minions,' Banks said.

'And another possible suspect,' Newry added. 'Minions have been known to murder their bosses from time to time.'

'I should imagine so,' Banks said. 'I used the light on my mobile, opened the door – or got the key in the lock, at least – and that's the last thing I remember before a sharp pain at the back of my head, then waking up in the plant. But even that was very hazy for the first couple of days.'

'Did you have any idea where you were?' Newry asked.

'Not at first, no. I'm no expert on water treatment, so I didn't recognise the purpose of the abandoned machinery, the pumps and pipes and so on. And it was dark. Not completely, but certainly not well-lit enough to recognise where I was. Only later, when I ran outside, did it become clear. But I get ahead of myself.'

'Sorry. Go on.'

'When I came to, I was on my side on a hard floor with my ankles tied together and my legs bent back at the knees. A rope from my ankles was also attached to my neck so that if I tried to—'

'A variation of the hog-tie, I understand.'

'Precisely. My hands were also tied behind me.'

'Were you on the upper level at any time, where the offices are?'

'No. Just down in the operating area.'

'Was anyone else present?'

'Yes. A man I knew as Phil Keane. He'd lately been going under the name of Hugh Foley, and he had been connected with a woman called Faye Butler, found dead in the Thames a few weeks ago.'

DI Dunne leaned over and whispered something in Newry's ear, never taking her eyes off Banks. 'Did you think this Keane was responsible for Faye Butler's death?' Newry asked.

'No. Keane likes fire. I put her death down to Tadić and his crew, the people Keane worked for.'

'I understand that Faye Butler wasn't your case,' Newry went on, 'but why do you think she was killed?'

'I think she was tortured for information, then raped and murdered.'

'What information?'

'Of that I have no idea. Something the Tadićs wanted an answer for, I'm sure.'

'What happened next?'

'Keane started splashing petrol around my feet and on the floor around where I was lying. While he was doing that he admitted to me that he had killed an NCA agent called Trevor Hawkins, who had been Zelda's – Ms Melnic's – boss at the department where she worked. He set fire to his house.'

'How did that come up?'

'What do you mean?'

'Did he just come out with it, out of the blue, so to speak, or was there a context?'

'I asked him. He'd mentioned something about the Tadićs, and I asked him what happened. Zelda had been getting a hard time about her boss's death from the NCA, so I wanted to know.'

'OK. So this Keane tells you he set fire to this man Hawkins's house, working on behalf of the Tadićs. Did he say why they had wanted this done?'

'Only that Hawkins was taking their money and giving them crap in exchange. It's my guess that he'd been tipping them off about possible raids, border checks and so on, but he'd either started to get cold feet, or he'd become greedy and given them dud information.'

'Quite the conversation you had.'

'You asked me. Some of it's conjecture. Besides, all the time he was talking, he was splashing petrol around. It was pretty obvious that it was meant for me, and I could hardly move. I figured my time was up and the best thing to do was keep him talking as long as I could. He knew this, so he said something about it not working, that he wasn't going to confess all just to keep me alive, even if I wasn't going to be around to tell anyone.'

'So what happened next?'

'That's all still a bit of a blur. Something happened. He stiffened. The fire flared up. I thought that was it, but the next thing I knew someone was cutting my ropes and telling me to run.'

'Someone?'

'Nelia Melnic.'

'Ah, the mysterious Zelda. Let me get this straight. She suddenly appeared in the room, incapacitated Keane and cut you free?'

'That's right.'

'How did she incapacitate Keane?'

'I don't know. Knocked him out, I should imagine.'

'But she had a knife.'

'She must have had, to cut me free. As I said, it gets a bit blurry. Maybe she took it from Keane?'

'Who started the fire?'

'I don't know that, either. I couldn't see. Keane, I should think. He was the one with the petrol and the lighter in his hand.'

'But you said this Zelda had knocked him out.'

'He wasn't completely out. Just dazed, I think.'

'Did you ever see Petar Tadić at any time you were in the plant?'

'No.'

'So he didn't suddenly come in and stab Keane and set the place on fire?'

'Not that I know of. If he did, I didn't see him.'

'Only there was forensic evidence of a knife wound on one of Keane's ribs.'

'So I heard. I didn't see a knife at the time. And I'm not sure the evidence of knife wounds on burned bones is conclusive.'

'Is that what Dr Galway told you? But we've already established that this Zelda must have had a knife to cut your bonds. And given the nick on the victim's rear rib, doesn't that seem to indicate that the one is connected to the other?'

'It doesn't necessarily follow. And Keane was hardly the victim, as you put it.'

'As far as I'm concerned he's a victim.'

'It's all a bit hazy, and it happened so fast. Zelda had her back to me. She was struggling with Keane. He'd lurched at her. I was disentangling myself from the last of my bonds that she'd just cut. Then the fire flared up.'

'So she still had the knife in her hand?'

'I don't know what happened to it, I just didn't see it. I had other things on my mind. Like getting the hell out of there. It was chaos. The fire was spreading. Keane was burning by then. Writhing and screaming.'

'By when?'

'By the time I was ready to run.'

'So he was still alive?'

'Yes.'

'The pathologist said it was impossible to check the body for smoke inhalation.'

'He was still alive when the fire started. He must have burned to death in the flames. Or he died of shock. I don't know.'

'Or this Zelda stabbed him.'

'I have no knowledge of any stab wound. But if she did, I'd say it was self-defence.'

'Well, unfortunately, you're not the one to be pronouncing on that.'

'But I was there. I know what I saw.'

'Come on, Superintendent. You can't have it both ways. Either it was chaos, and you don't know what happened, or it wasn't, and you do. Which was it?'

'I don't know. Both maybe. A lot of confusion.'

Newry scowled at DI Dunne, who continued to look disapproving. 'Are you sure you didn't see the woman stab Keane?'

'No, I didn't see anything like that. You keep going on about this knife. Did you find one at the scene?'

'No. She must have taken it with her. Are you sure *she* didn't start the fire?'

'I told you, she was struggling with Keane. I think she was trying to stop him. I couldn't see what he was doing because she was blocking my view.'

'Ah, yes, and the lighter went off mysteriously?'

'You must have found it, or what was left of it.'

'I'm afraid that doesn't tell us a great deal. Is it true that this girl is a friend of yours?'

'A friend of a friend. I know her. Yes.'

'You were searching for her, right?'

'Yes. She'd been abducted from her home three days before.'

'By these men Tadić and Keane?'

'A witness was able to give us a good description of Tadić in the vicinity of Zelda's cottage, but there's no evidence that Keane was involved in her actual abduction. Or mine. Talk to my team about it, or to AC Gervaise, why don't you? They know more than I do.'

'I'm not too sure about that, but I will, don't worry. You tracked this woman, Zelda, to the treatment plant, right?'

'No. You haven't been listening. I told you. I was knocked out and taken there. We had no idea where she was being held. We still had people out searching the moors.'

'Do you like this Zelda?'

'What kind of a question is that?'

DI Dunne gave Banks another disapproving glance. 'Just answer me, please,' Newry said.

'I admire her. Yes. She's had a difficult life.'

'And are you attracted to her? Is your interest in any way sexual?'

For the first time, old Reg Courtenay dragged himself out of his shell of silence and tut-tutted Newry. DI Dunne somehow managed to communicate even more disapproval. Banks said nothing.

'What happened to the girl?' Newry asked.

'I don't know. She must have gone out a different way. I think there was a car out by the side of the building, in what used to be the staff car park. Maybe it was Tadić's or Keane's.' He shrugged. 'I don't know.'

'So she stole a car to make her escape?'

'If you put it like that.'

'I don't know how else I should put it. Did you see this car? Did you know this at the time?'

'No. I'm just speculating. The CSIs found traces of a vehicle recently parked out there. Oil stains. It makes sense. Otherwise, where did she go?'

'That's what we'd all like to know. I was about to ask you the very same question.'

'I wish I knew,' said Banks.

'Why? So you could go and join her?'

Reg Courtenay tut-tutted again.

'Did you see or hear her drive off?' Newry went on.

'Listening for a car was hardly the main thing on my mind. I ran for my life, ended up in the reservoir unconscious again. I might have heard a motor running, but I can't be sure. The fire itself was noisy enough.'

'So the girl cut you free, but you just left her there, in the burning building?'

'It wasn't like that,' said Banks. 'I was still woozy from being hit on the head. She cut my ropes and yelled for me to run. I assumed she'd be running with me, or not far behind. When I realised she wasn't there, I tried to go back in, but I couldn't get any further than the entrance. The fire was raging too hard, and there was plenty of smoke by then.'

'What did you think had happened?'

'That she'd either got out by some other exit or that she was dead. It all happened so quickly. I wasn't thinking very clearly.'

'So you just ran off?'

'Yes. And I fell in the reservoir, where they found me. Hit my head again. If it hadn't been for the bed of weeds, I'd probably be dead. What the hell else was I supposed to do? Go back inside the plant and burn to death?'

Newry waved his hand. 'Sorry. I wasn't meaning to imply anything.'

'Like hell you weren't. The forensic evidence corroborates what I've told you.'

'Up to a point.'

'Is there anything else?'

'Not that I can think of. Not at the moment. DI Dunne?'

DI Dunne pursed her lips and shook her head.

Banks stood up. 'Right then. As I'm still on sick leave, and I'm feeling sicker by the minute, I'll go home now.' He nodded farewell to the others in the room and left.

18

Two days passed uneventfully, and Banks whiled away his time reading, gardening and listening to music – from Mahler's symphonies to Jon Savage's sixties compilation CDs. There were moments when he thought that if this was what not having to work was all about, then it wasn't such a bad thing at all. Other times he felt edgy and restless, longing for some obscure mystery he could sink his teeth into.

The missing persons search for Zelda was effectively over, and now the police wanted to talk to her in connection with the fire at the water treatment plant in which two people had died. Banks trusted that she was far enough away and well enough hidden that they wouldn't find her. Newry believed that she had killed both men, or that Banks had, but Newry wasn't on the investigating team. He was IOPC, and his job was over. The Homicide and Major Crimes team from Durham was tackling the case now. Banks had talked to them and told them what he knew, or as much as he wanted them to know, and it was out of his hands now. He was exonerated. Newry could gripe to his heart's content about the presence of a knife at the scene, a nick on a bone that might possibly indicate a stab wound and the matter of who struck the lighter that started the fire, but it no longer mattered what Newry thought, as what forensic evidence they had supported Banks's story and none of it implicated him. In addition, Banks's injuries, including the memory loss, were verified by Dr Chowdhury and proven to be commensurate with the physical circumstances of his abduction and incarceration.

From the bits and pieces Banks had heard, he got the impression that Zelda wasn't too high on their list of priorities; they seemed to be concentrating more on the Tadić gang's criminal concerns and on Keane's part in them. Gashi, too, was on their radar, his whereabouts unknown, and the disappearance of Goran Tadić was still an issue, albeit a minor one, as he wasn't regarded as much of a loss.

One interesting piece of information, supplied by Jazz Singh at Banks's request, was that a comparison between the DNA from the human arm found at the landfill site near Croydon and that from the body found on the upper floor of the burned-out water treatment plant gave a high indication that the two were siblings. Goran and Petar Tadić, Banks guessed, though there was no absolute proof, as neither was in any DNA database. The corpse's DNA also matched that of the cigarette ends found near Windlee Farm. As they presumably belonged to the man Mick Slater described and Ray Cabbot sketched, the corpse was identified by Superintendent Burgess as Petar Tadić.

But a man can only do so much reading and gardening, and on the second day of his sick leave, Banks made a few phone calls, and on the third, he took an early train from York.

'This is the second time you've had me brought up here,' Charlotte Westlake complained as Gerry tended to the recording equipment in the interview room and Annie settled down in her chair late that afternoon. 'I hope you've got a damn good reason.'

'Be careful, or you might get what you hope for,' said Annie.

'Wait,' said Charlotte. 'As the officer who *arrested* me and brought me here suggested, I requested my solicitor to meet me, so I would be grateful if you would please wait until she arrives. She won't be long.'

Annie and Gerry exchanged glances, then they left a young constable on guard and went down to the canteen for a cup of tea while they waited. Coffee at Costa would have been preferable to weak canteen tea, but they didn't want to leave the station. They had already planned the strategy of the interview, such as it was, the previous evening in the Queen's Arms. Gerry had uncovered more than enough information from her talk with Charlotte's mother and the box of letters and postcards Lynne Pollard had been only too happy to share. The rest had come from the General Register and the various databases available to her online. If she was right about some of the conclusions she had reached, based on scraps of information picked up here and there, Gerry was sure that Charlotte would paint herself into a corner from which the only way out was the truth.

As yet, Annie and Gerry didn't know what that truth was, and the possibilities kept shifting with the information coming in. When all they had was a number of inspired guesses, planning a strategy became that much more difficult. They would have to improvise from time to time. The basis for Charlotte Westlake's arrest – suspicion of murder – was probably a bit far-fetched, Gerry would be the first to admit, but it was a means of bringing her in and throwing her off guard. It would also allow them to keep her in custody for twenty-four hours if necessary.

Charlotte's solicitor, Jessica Bowen, turned up twenty minutes later and after a ten-minute huddle with her client, then they all settled down in the airless room. Gerry got the recording equipment working and made the introductions.

'Are we all sitting comfortably?' asked Annie. When the reply was silence, she said, 'Then I'll begin.'

Jessica Bowen gave her a stern glance for the frivolous *Children's Hour* opening.

'Mrs Westlake,' said Annie, 'was Marnie Sedgwick your daughter?'

Clearly, whatever Charlotte Westlake had been expecting, it wasn't this. She seemed like an animal desperate to escape its cage, squirming in her chair, turning pale, looking towards her solicitor one moment then back to her questioner the next. 'Wha . . .? How do . . .?' Gerry wondered how on earth she thought that they wouldn't discover this information. More burying her head in the sand? Naive or stupid?

'Simple enough question,' said Annie, ignoring the reaction. 'Can you please give me an answer?'

Charlotte took a deep breath and struggled to regain her equilibrium. Her lawyer gave her the nod to continue. 'Technically, I suppose, yes, she is,' she said.

'Technically?'

'I'm her birth mother, but as you clearly know already, I gave her up for adoption. Her true parents are the ones who brought her up.'

'The Sedgwicks?'

'I wasn't aware of who adopted her. It's not standard practice to give the birth mother such information.'

'Did you have any hand whatsoever in her upbringing?'

'None.'

'How old was she when she was adopted?'

'A baby. I never . . . I mean, straight away. As soon as possible. I never even held her.'

'Who was the father?'

'That's irrelevant.'

'Not to us it isn't,' said Annie. Then she turned over a page. 'Very well, we'll leave that for the moment.' She paused and went on in a weary tone. 'Why didn't you save us a lot of trouble and tell us this information right from the start?'

'I don't know. It didn't seem relevant somehow. It was a long time ago. Nineteen years.'

'*Didn't seem relevant?*' Annie repeated. 'That's one of the lamest excuses for lying to us that I've ever come across. Don't you agree, DC Masterson?'

'It's pretty lame,' said Gerry.

'She came back into your life,' Annie said, 'and not long afterwards, she was raped. And you didn't think any of this was relevant?'

'But there's no connection. It's just coincidence. I still don't think any of this is relevant.'

'Try again,' Annie said. '*Irrelevant, coincidence* – these aren't excuses we recognise. And this time, give us the *real* reason why you didn't tell us.'

'I've already told you. Besides, I didn't want to get involved. I knew you'd make too much of it.'

'Better. A little bit,' said Annie. 'But you *are* involved, like it or not. And this lie, or omission, makes you even more so. See, when people lie to us about one thing, we assume they might be lying about other things, too.'

'Why are you doing this to me?' said Charlotte, clasping her hands on the table. 'You're just being nasty. You must know that *I* couldn't have raped poor Marnie.'

'Nobody's suggesting you did.'

'Then why persecute me? Why don't you leave me alone? Any mistakes I've made I've had to live with. You've no right to sit in judgement on me.'

'There's no easy way of putting this,' said Annie, 'but things have taken another turn. I assume you know about Marnie's death?'

'Her . . . what?'

'Her death,' Annie repeated. 'I'm sorry. I thought you might have known.'

'How could I have known? Who was there to tell me?'

This had been a difficult part of their approach to plan. Either Charlotte knew what had happened to Marnie, or she didn't, and there was no easy way of finding out. In the end, they decided it was best to confront her with the truth. Gerry watched closely and believed that Charlotte's reaction was genuine, that she hadn't known.

'It's very important you tell us the truth about this,' Annie said. 'Did you know that Marnie was dead?'

'No.' Charlotte shook her head. 'I'm not even sure I believe you. You're trying to trick me. Tell me that's what you're doing.'

Gerry saw the misery etched in her features and knew she was telling the truth.

'I'm sorry to be the bearer of such bad news,' Annie said.

'What happened? How . . . I mean . . .?'

Annie went on. 'She took her own life just under a month ago, on 17 May. A few days before Connor Clive Blaydon was murdered.'

'A month,' Charlotte repeated. 'All that time. And I never knew. Where? Why? How?'

'Near home. In Dorset. As for why, who knows? I assume it was because she couldn't come to terms with what happened to her and she felt shamed, damaged, broken. Or that she found out she was pregnant.'

'Oh, my God,' said Charlotte. 'Things come full circle.'

'What does that mean?'

Charlotte started to cry and reached for a tissue from the box on the table and wiped her eyes. 'I'm sorry. I can't believe she's dead.'

'Take a minute,' Annie said. 'Can I get you anything?'

Charlotte held her hand up and gulped down some water. 'I'll be all right in a minute. Let's just get this over with.'

'It might take a while,' said Annie. 'We can take a short break if you need to. But if you're OK to carry on, we will.' She glanced at Jessica Bowen, who nodded.

'I'm OK,' said Charlotte. 'I want this all over with and I never want to see you again.'

'That all depends very much on your telling us the truth. You lied to us about your connection with Marnie Sedgwick, and that's why you're here. How did she find you in the first place?'

'The usual way. She applied for her birth certificate when she turned eighteen then tracked me down through one of those online hereditary sites.'

'When was this?'

'January. Just after Christmas.'

'Why did she wait so long?'

'She told me later that she wasn't sure she could go through with it. She'd been very happy with the Sedgwicks, and she didn't want them to feel they'd been inadequate or somehow let her down. It's not unusual for children seeking their birth parents to feel apprehensive, to hesitate.'

'And she came to see you this January?'

'Yes.'

'At the office?'

'No. She got my home address first.'

'How did the meeting go?'

Charlotte shifted in her chair. 'Awkward, as I'm sure you can imagine. But I think she understood finally, how the adoption was best for her, not only me. How I couldn't possibly have been a fit mother. I think she understood.'

'Was she angry?'

'No. She said she had been, at first, but it passed. She was just curious. She didn't want me to take her in or even develop any kind of maternal relationship. As far as Marnie was concerned, the Sedgwicks were her parents. She just wanted to see me in the flesh, so to speak, and for me to know that she existed.'

'Anything else?'

'Later, she came to me at the office. She wanted work. There was no special pleading or anything, she wasn't after any favours. She wasn't even asking for special treatment. She knew what I did and thought she could fit in somewhere. Simple as that. She already had a waitressing job at Pizza Express in York, but she wasn't getting paid very much, and she said she wanted to save to go back to university.'

'But she'd already dropped out of Nottingham.'

'Because she didn't have enough money, and she thought she was wasting her time studying History. She wanted to take on a practical subject like Management Studies or Hospitality.'

'And you encouraged her?'

'I told her I'd done fairly practical subjects at uni, that it was a good idea if she hoped to get a good job. That you can always read history and literature in your spare time, but it's not going to earn you a living unless you teach. I gave her work. It wasn't much, but she was well enough paid for what she did.'

'What about your relationship? Did it thrive?'

'I wouldn't say it thrived, no. There was always a distance. You'd expect that after so many years. As I told you, the Sedgwicks were her parents, no doubt about that. She made it clear and I accepted it. But it didn't degenerate, either. We got on well enough.'

'Why did you give her up for adoption in the first place?'

'The usual reasons. I was too young, too selfish, too irresponsible.'

'What about abortion?'

'I'm from a Catholic family. All right, so my parents were lapsed Catholics, and I've never been religious, but I just felt that abortion wasn't an option at the time.'

'Fair enough,' said Annie.

'I was living a pretty wild life. Free and easy. All the travel, sun and sand and everything. I didn't want to be lumbered with a child to bring up.'

'So what did you do?'

'When I found out I was pregnant?'

'Yes.'

'I went to stay with a friend in Herefordshire, near Hay, where they have the book festival. That was for my . . . what did they used to call it . . . *lying in*? That's what I did. I lay in and waited. The baby was born at the nearest hospital, a small one, and I gave her up for adoption. End of story.'

Annie consulted the notes Gerry had made. 'And after that you put your life back together, got on track, started a career in events planning? Met your husband?'

'Having a child shook me up. I grew up pretty quickly, I'd say, even though I didn't have the responsibility of child-rearing. So, yes, I threw myself into a new career. I happen to be a quick learner. The degree helped, too. Or at least, Oxford did. Connections. I also have some facility with languages. French, Spanish, a little Greek.'

'So what was your reaction when Marnie came to you and told you she'd been raped?'

'She never . . . I mean, I . . .'

'Come on, Charlotte. Don't start lying again. We were doing so well. Who else could she go to? Not her own parents. She wanted to protect them. You were probably more like a big sister to her than anyone else.'

Charlotte turned to Jessica Bowen, who leaned forward and whispered in her ear. Charlotte nodded a couple of times and turned back to Annie. 'All right,' she said. 'Marnie did come to my house when I got back from Costa Rica, and she told me what had happened. She was in a terrible state, emotionally. I . . . I did my best to comfort her. She wouldn't go to the police. I tried to persuade her, honestly, but she didn't want to go through the humiliation, the victim-blaming. She said she thought she could put it behind her. I wasn't too sure about that, but I realised my job, my *only* job, was to give her comfort and support right there and then. Which I did.'

'And now we come to the big question, Charlotte,' said Annie. 'Who did it? Who raped Marnie Sedgwick?'

By five o'clock that afternoon, Banks was sitting in the shade outside La Porte Montmartre, on the corner of the Boulevard Poissonnière and the Boulevard Montmartre, in Paris, with a large glass of excellent red Bordeaux in front of him, watching the world go by. It wouldn't have been true to say that he hadn't a care in the world – he had many – but at moments such as these, the cares receded, and it felt good to be alive.

His last-minute hotel, which went under the uninspiring name of Hôtel 34B, turned out to be a gem. For less than one hundred euros he got a comfortable room, decorated all in white, clean and spacious enough. It didn't have a balcony, but the windows overlooked the street below. The buildings on both sides of Rue Bergère were five storeys high, so it was like looking into a narrow canyon. Cars and motor scooters were parked by the pavements and even though it was only a little side street there was a constant flow of people. He could see three restaurants from his fourth-floor window: *Les Diables au Thym*, *Dr Auguste* and *Bio c'Bon*, an 'organic' salad bar, on the corner with Rue du Faubourg Montmartre, where there were many more restaurants and cafes, along with a *hypermarché.* The hotel was no frills and had no restaurant or bar, but Banks didn't need such luxuries when there were so many places to eat and drink in the neighbourhood. Like the cafe he was in now.

He was waiting for Jean-Claude Meursault, an old friend from the *police judiciaire*. They had first met at an Interpol conference in Lyon fifteen years previously and had stayed in touch ever since. Jean-Claude had retired the previous year, and Banks had attended his farewell party. If anyone knew anything about Zelda's time in Paris, and whether she was there at the moment, it was Jean-Claude.

A *commissaire* at 36 Quai des Orfèvres for many years, Jean-Claude reminded Banks of his hero Maigret, physically as well as in mind and attitude. The Rupert-Davies Maigret, of course. As far as Banks was concerned, Gambon was good, Atkinson was execrable, Bruno Cremer was the French choice, but Rupert Davies *was* Maigret. He was large and burly, and though he didn't smoke a pipe, one would not have seemed out of place in his hand or mouth. He also had that calm, slow manner of the deep thinker about him, though as Banks had once seen when they encountered some trouble in a bar, he could be remarkably quick on his feet.

Banks glanced around at his fellow drinkers: a group of tourists, a couple of old men sitting in silence together, a businessman trying to impress his secretary, an elegant woman sipping white wine and glancing nervously at her watch, perhaps waiting for her lover, two garrulous young Frenchmen sharing jokes. Gauloises smoke drifted over from the next table, reminding Banks of his school exchange with a boy from Lille when he was about fourteen. It was quite a discovery at that age to find out you could order a beer in a bar, then sit and drink it while enjoying a Disque Bleu and no one would think twice about it.

He watched the people passing by. Nobody seemed in much of a hurry. Suddenly, he saw the young Francoise Hardy, tall, willowy, with shiny long chestnut hair, stylishly dressed, carrying four long-stemmed red roses. She noticed him looking at her and flashed him a quizzical smile that for some reason made him feel like a dirty old man. But he wasn't dirty and he didn't feel old. He knew quite well that she wasn't really Francoise Hardy, but Francoise Hardy as she would have been over fifty years ago, when he was an awestruck schoolboy on his first trip abroad in the heady days of *Salut les copains*, Sylvie Vartan, Johnny Hallyday, France Gall and Richard Anthony. And he didn't feel any different now from that young man who had listened to her sing 'Tous les garçons et les filles' as he gazed at her photo on the album cover all those years ago.

He remembered a field outside Lille, surrounded by trees, a stolen kiss with Brigitte while the others immersed themselves in a game of boules. The scent of warm grass, the tang of wine, the softness of her lips yielding shyly. That was it. That was all. That was enough.

'Alain.' The familiar voice brought him back from the past in a rush. It was Jean-Claude. He had always used the French for his name, called him 'Alain'.

Banks stood up and they embraced warmly then sat down. The waiter drifted by and Banks ordered another Bordeaux for himself and whatever Jean-Claude wanted, which was a glass of Chablis.

'I was miles away,' Banks said. 'You know, I just saw a girl who was the spitting image of the young Francoise Hardy.'

Jean-Claude smiled indulgently. 'Always the romantic.'

'Is that such a bad thing?'

'For a policeman, I think it is.'

The drinks arrived and Jean-Claude took a sip. 'Excellent,' he said. 'You know, she was born not far from here. In the ninth, at any rate.'

'Francoise Hardy?'

'Oui.'

Banks's perspective shifted slightly, as if he were viewing the place from a different angle. 'How's retirement?' he asked.

'I'm not sure I know yet. It hasn't been that long, and I've been consulting with my squad on high-profile cases ever since.'

'So you're still working?'

'Basically, yes. But part-time. Less stress.' He tapped his forehead. 'Let the young men do all the running round and my little grey cells do all my work.'

The shadows were creeping across the pavement in front of the Grand Comptoir restaurant over the street, almost reaching the outside tables. Its pale cream facade was still lit in the late afternoon glow. The number of pedestrians passing by started to increase as the Metro disgorged more and more people on their way home from work.

The empty tables soon filled, and the buzz of conversation got louder. Banks and Jean-Claude chatted about old times, opera, football, books, Brexit and the future. Eventually, after the second glass of Chablis, Jean-Claude asked Banks, 'You wanted to talk about something? You were very cryptic on the telephone. Is it something I can help with?'

'Perhaps,' said Banks.

'Then I suggest we finish our drinks and discuss it over dinner. I know just the place.'

Charlotte paused so long that Annie thought she wasn't going to answer. Finally, she cast her eyes down and muttered so softly that Annie had to lean forward to hear her. 'Connor,' she said. 'Connor raped her.'

Annie slapped the table. 'Then why the hell didn't you tell us that from the start? Do you realise how much trouble you've caused; the resources you've wasted?'

'That's not my fault,' Charlotte argued back, her eyes brimming with tears again. 'I didn't tell you because Marnie didn't want anyone to know and Connor's dead, so what the hell does it matter? You couldn't put him in jail. How the hell was I to know there was a video and that you'd end up investigating the rape? I knew it would end like this, with you lot trying to find something to charge *me* with, lock me up and throw away the key. That you'd ruin the life I've worked so hard to build. That's why I didn't tell you the truth to begin with.'

'Oh, spare me,' said Annie. 'You're telling us you lied because you were surprised by the video? That you didn't expect to have to answer any questions? Is that why you also lied about not recognising Marnie from the first picture we showed you, leading us to waste hours of valuable time finding out who she was?'

'Yes.' Charlotte sniffed. 'And now Marnie's dead, too. They're both dead. It doesn't matter. Don't you see? None of it matters any more.'

'Perhaps if you had insisted that Marnie get the kind of help she needed, she would still be alive.'

Charlotte gave her a look of pure hatred. 'How can you?' she said. 'How dare you say that to me? You're a terrible person, a cruel person.' She started to cry again, and the lawyer passed her a tissue.

'Ease up a little, DI Cabbot,' said Jessica Bowen. 'You've just informed Mrs Westlake about the death of her biological daughter. She has reason to be upset.'

'You think I'm being too hard?' Annie said. 'Sorry. It's a sign of the extreme frustration this case has caused me.'

'We're all frustrated,' said Jessica Bowen, 'but let us please try to remain civilised.'

Annie glanced at Gerry, who also seemed dumbstruck by her last comment. Had she really overstepped the mark? Was she cruel? The only thing to do now was to press on to the logical conclusion.

'What was your relationship with Connor Blaydon?' she asked.

Charlotte blew her nose and looked up with reddened eyes. 'What do you mean, *relationship*? He was my boss.'

'Other than that?'

'Are you suggesting there was more to it than that?'

Annie turned over a sheet of paper. 'When Marnie's best friend, Mitsuko Ogawa, told us about her job, she said that you were working for an old friend. We thought it seemed like an odd thing to say at the time, as you'd told us you met Blaydon at a gala event a few years before. You never mentioned a friendship. But you also indicated that you had known one another on and off for some time. Only you were very vague about it.'

'Why should I mention a friendship? There wasn't one. We had a working relationship. I don't know what this Ogawa woman was talking about, but it was likely just a figure of speech.'

'How long *had* you known Blaydon, then?' Annie asked. 'Whether you were friends or not.'

'Like I said, a few years, on and off.'

'How many? Twenty?'

Charlotte turned away. 'I don't know. Maybe.'

Annie referred to the notes Gerry had made again. 'Isn't it true that you had known Connor Clive Blaydon since you were twenty-one, in 1999? You were a rebellious young tear-away gadding around the Greek islands with some wealthy friends you'd met at St Hilda's, cadging lifts and sleeping berths on yachts. Didn't you once cadge a lift on a luxury yacht called the *Nerea*, out of Corfu? And wasn't this owned by one Connor Clive Blaydon?'

Charlotte seemed to freeze. Jessica Bowen glanced from her client to Annie and back. 'DI Cabbot,' she said. 'Exactly where are you going with this?'

'Patience,' said Annie. 'Have patience, and all will be revealed.'

'I'm tired,' said Charlotte. 'And you've upset me.' She implored Jessica Bowen. 'Please, make them stop. It's my right. I'm entitled to a break. I want to go home.'

'Legally, we are entitled to detain you for twenty-four hours without charge,' said Annie. 'But you're right. You do have a right to breaks, meals and so on. Now, we have a destination in mind, and one way or another we're going to get there. If you're tired and need a break, we have a very comfortable cell in the basement. You'll be fed, made comfortable, and we can start again bright and early tomorrow morning.'

'This is a nightmare. I want to go home.'

'I'm afraid that won't be possible.'

'Why not?'

'Because you have to stay in custody until we're satisfied with your answers to our questions,' she said. 'It's the law.'

Charlotte glanced at Jessica Bowen again.

'You'll be all right,' the solicitor said. 'I'll be nearby. You'll be well treated. I promise you.'

But Charlotte didn't look happy in the slightest, least of all when two female officers marched her out of the interview room and down to the custody suite.

'You *know* Nelia Melnic?' Jean-Claude asked, clearly stunned by Banks's revelation of what he wanted to talk about.

'Yes. She goes by the name of Zelda now. She's a friend. Why, do you?'

'No. No. I've never met her. I just know the name. I'm surprised, that's all. I hear she's very beautiful.'

'Yes.' They were having dinner at a restaurant Jean-Claude knew, lost in the maze of backstreets of the 9th Arrondissement. The specialty was seafood, and both were enjoying the house platter along with a bottle of fine white Burgundy, chosen by Jean-Claude. They had been fortunate to get there early enough for a table out front.

'Why are you so surprised?' Banks asked.

Jean-Claude paused, a shrimp midway between his plate and his mouth. 'Because she is famous here, Alain. Perhaps not with the general population, though many will certainly have heard of her, but with the police for certain. She was a legend in the squad room. Did she not tell you?'

'I know something happened here,' Banks said. 'Something serious involving a pimp called Darius. But that's about all I do know.'

Jean-Claude gave him a serious look. 'Most of the story is classified, you understand. I could not possibly tell you all the names and positions of those involved. There was a scandal. Well, a narrowly averted scandal. Very few people know the details.'

'But you're one of them?'

Jean-Claude inclined his head slightly. 'I had some small involvement. To be perfectly honest, though, even I don't know the names of the major players. They were important people, that is all I know. Government people.'

Banks tussled with an extremely recalcitrant langoustine. 'She has a French passport.'

'Mm. You see, *I* didn't know that. Why are you interested?'

Banks told him about Zelda and Ray and the trouble with

the Tadićs, Keane and Hawkins, leaving out the murders and abductions.

Jean-Claude swallowed a mouthful of wine and said, 'So that's what became of her. Perhaps she is the sort of woman trouble follows around?'

'Perhaps,' said Banks. 'The Tadićs are from way back in her past. They abducted her outside her orphanage as she was leaving. But this Darius business is more recent.'

'It was just over three years ago,' said Jean-Claude. 'The month of March. I remember it well.'

'Did you work the case?'

'There was no case. And I told you, even I don't know the full details.'

'But you said you had some involvement. What happened?'

'Darius was a pimp. Or perhaps that does him an injustice. His girls were all beautiful, high-class, très chic and très expensive. With a Darius girl, it was strictly dinner at Maxim's, then back to a suite at the George V, if you know what I mean.'

'No matter what the price,' said Banks, 'the business is the same. I'd say he was a pimp.'

'You would get no real argument from me. We knew of him, of course. He was born in Algeria and came to Paris in his late twenties. A crook from the start. He very quickly made his way up the ladder through a mixture of brutality and business acumen. His rivals seemed to have a habit of disappearing, and he was not averse to hurting the girls when he thought it necessary to keep them in line.'

'A nasty piece of work then?'

'Very nasty.' Jean-Claude paused to finish the remains of his meal, ending with the last oyster, which he washed down with the Burgundy, then went on. 'What nobody knew for quite some time was that he had a little blackmail business on the side. You know, the usual: photos, sometimes film, famous or highly placed victims.'

It sounded very much like what Neville Roberts had been doing back on Banks's home patch. 'But I thought you French were more permissive than us lot about that sort of thing,' he said. 'Don't most Frenchmen have a mistress? Visit prostitutes? I seem to have read only recently about a Frenchman who died while having adulterous sex on a job-related trip, and it was classified as a "workplace accident".'

Jean-Claude laughed. 'So the Frenchman's workplace is his mistress's boudoir? Oh, Alain. What *have* you been reading? Or perhaps it is the films of Vadim, Rohmer or Truffaut that influence you? Yes, we are to a certain extent more liberal than you English as regards domestic arrangements and matters of the boudoir, but remember this was quite recent, and believe it or not, even France has been stricken by a plague of ubermorality in public life since the old days. *#BalanceTonPorc* – what you call #MeToo – has made its presence known here. Just look at the trouble with Roman Polanski, for example. That would never have happened a few years ago. The tide is turning. But if only that were all.'

'There's more?'

'Isn't there always? Dessert?'

Banks patted his stomach. 'I think I've just about got room.'

Jean-Claude caught the waiter's attention and ordered apple tarte tatins and Calvados for both of them. A couple of elegantly dressed French women took the next table. One of them, mid-forties, perhaps, with short, tousled brown hair, a pale oval face and full lips, wearing a cream blazer over a pale blue blouse, was particularly attractive. After they had adjusted their chairs and disposed of their handbags, she turned slightly and gave Banks a quick smile. Then they began speaking in French so fast that Banks couldn't follow at all.

'You were saying there's more?' he prompted Jean-Claude.

'Yes. Darius's clientele, customers, whatever you called them, were very mixed. They included men highly placed in government, ministers, prominent businessmen, even gangsters, Russian oligarchs ... People in possession of closely guarded secrets. Men who, under the right circumstances, might find themselves talking out of turn.'

'I think I know where you're going,' said Banks.

'You are thinking of your Profumo affair, no doubt?'

'Yes.'

'Do you remember what President de Gaulle said about that?'

'No.'

'He said that's what happens when the English try to behave like the French.'

Banks laughed. 'But that was back in the Cold War,' he said. 'Russian spies and all that.'

'Well, it is true that the objectives have changed now that the Cold War is over, but the game remains the same. Darius had some highly placed customers, and some of his most beautiful girls were Russian. Trafficked girls, we suspect. Pillow talk is what it is, and money is always a good incentive for loose tongues. Only this time the matter exchanged involved business dealings, stocks and shares and takeovers, rather than weapons and military or political strategy.'

'And Zelda's part?'

'Your Zelda was one of Darius's favourites. Apparently, she was also very smart and she knew what was going on. And she spoke fluent Russian. Like your *Pretty Woman* film, one client came into her life and fell in love with her, what you would call a cabinet minister, with special responsibilities involving criminal intelligence and the police in general. My boss. Like your Home Secretary. He wanted her to change, wanted them to go away together. He was going to leave his wife and children for her.'

'Emile?' said Banks, remembering Zelda's journal.

'Yes. You know this? You know the full story?'

Banks glanced at the woman at the next table. She was in animated conversation with her friend and was paying not the slightest attention to him and Jean-Claude. 'No,' he said. 'Just a few fragments. Please go on. I promise not to interrupt again.'

'When this . . . Emile . . . had an idea of what was going on, he devised a scheme. If Nelia could somehow get to Darius's cache of blackmail material – especially the audio tapes – and either destroy it or hand it over to him, she would become a heroine of the French people. In secret, of course, as all the best heroes and heroines are.'

'And here's me thinking they were posthumous.'

'Cynic. Well, not in this case.'

'So how did it go wrong?'

'It didn't. Not until the end.' He glanced around to make sure nobody was paying attention. They weren't. 'None of this was for public consumption, but according to Nelia's statement *in camera*, Darius came in while she was removing the documents from his safe. He saw what she was doing and attacked her, tried to kill her. In the struggle, she managed to grab a knife from the table and stabbed him several times. Then, when he was weakened and incapacitated, she slit his throat, just to make sure he was dead.'

'And was he?'

'Oh, yes. According to someone I know who was at the scene shortly after it happened, there was blood all over the place. The girl was calm as anything, like a zombie. In shock, no doubt.'

'So what happened?'

'She disappeared. The rumour was that she had, of course, been pardoned for what happened to Darius and spirited away. Many, many people who would never admit it publicly were secretly more than glad that he was dead and his cache of blackmail material destroyed. Beyond, that, I don't know, except she was never mentioned again. You know more than I do about the aftermath and her later adventures. Emile must have got the French passport for her – he was certainly highly placed enough to do her that favour – and she cleared off, never to darken our shores again. It was to everyone's advantage that the whole affair was hushed up and forgotten. Much went on behind closed doors, you understand. A scandal was narrowly avoided. The documents and tapes were destroyed, of course, a few low-profile arrests were made, and the girl had her freedom ... There was only one extremely tragic consequence.'

'Emile?'

'Yes. Three months later he was killed in a road accident on his way back from a meeting in Strasbourg.'

'Accident?'

Jean-Claude gave a very Gallic shrug. 'So they said. And there was no evidence to the contrary. No witnesses, no forensic indications that he had done anything except fall asleep at the wheel and veer off the road into a convenient tree.'

'Drugs?'

'Toxicology showed nothing in his system except a small amount of alcohol. Not even enough to get him charged with driving under the influence.'

'Darius's partners, no doubt?'

'Yes. Enforcers. But as far as we know they are all working for someone else now, peddling drugs in Marseilles. We keep an eye on them, of course, make sure they don't end up back here, but without their leader, there's not a lot of enthusiasm left in them for Paris.'

'They're not after Zelda?'

'Darius's women all drifted away after his death, some to other pimps, no doubt, and others to an escape from the life, and this Nelia was just one of them. It's unlikely they would still be chasing her after all this time. Loyalty among crooks only goes so far and lasts so long.'

'And Zelda hasn't been seen or heard of here since?'

'No,' said Jean-Claude. 'I will ask around, if you like. Get back to you tomorrow. But I still think the answer will be no.'

'You would know if she had been seen over the past few days?'

'Believe me, if she was here, I will know by tomorrow.'

'Thanks, Jean-Claude.' That didn't mean she hadn't been back in secret, but from what he had heard, Banks now doubted that she would have chosen Paris as the first stop on her escape route. He would have to search further afield, if he was to search at all. He had hoped he might see her here, get a chance to talk and clear some things up, but perhaps it was best to simply let her be, let her live the rest of her life the way she wanted. God knows, she deserved it.

'Tell me, Alain,' Jean-Claude said. 'This Nelia. Zelda. Are you in love with her?'

'I don't know,' said Banks. 'I realise that's an unsatisfactory answer to your question, but I've asked it of myself, too, and the answer is the same. I don't know. Besides, even if I am, it doesn't matter. There could be no future for us, for many reasons.'

Their Calvados and tartes arrived. The woman at the next table took out a compact and checked her face in the mirror as she refreshed her lipstick, catching Banks's eye briefly as she did so. He noticed a wedding ring on her left hand.

'And that, mon ami, is that,' said Jean-Claude. They clinked their Calvados glasses and drank. It was smooth as silk, but burned all the way down. 'And now I have a question for you, Alain.'

'What's that?'

'This Nelia. What is she really like?'

19

The following morning, Charlotte Westlake didn't seem well rested at all. Her eyes were sunken and had bags beneath them. Her cheeks were sallow and even her hair seemed lacklustre.

Annie, on the other hand, was awake and raring to go after a restful night's sleep. Gerry seemed bright-eyed and bushy-tailed, too.

'Good breakfast?' Annie asked Charlotte. She knew that the cells were comfortable enough and the food passable.

She got no answer.

'Service OK?'

'All right, all right,' said Jessica Bowen. 'Enough with the inappropriate humour. Just get on with the interview, if you don't mind. The clock's ticking.'

Annie picked up the threads again. 'Remember, yesterday evening we were talking about your relationship with Connor Blaydon?' she said to Charlotte. 'Would you care to tell us exactly when and how it began?'

'I don't know where you've dug up all this rubbish from, but I don't intend to dignify it with an explanation.'

'How well do you get along with your mother?' Annie asked.

'My mother? What's she got to do with all this?'

'Quite a bit, as it turns out,' said Annie. 'Were you always close?'

'I suppose so. I mean, she is my mother.'

'And I understand that your husband's and father's deaths occurred rather close together.'

'What is this? Are you trying to say I had something to do with my father's death now? My husband's? What is it with you?'

'Dear, dear,' said Annie. 'A night's rest doesn't seem to have made you any more helpful or better tempered, does it?'

'Rest? That's a joke.'

'Where are you going with this, DI Cabbot?' asked Jessica Bowen. 'I'm afraid you're losing me, too.'

'Just this,' Annie went on. 'In DC Masterson's conversations with Mrs Lynne Pollard we discovered—'

'You've been talking to my mother!' Charlotte sat bolt upright and glared at Gerry. 'You went to see my mother! How dare—'

'Mrs Westlake, calm down,' said Gerry. 'I talked to your mother. We had a nice chat. She made us a pot of tea. And a number of interesting points came up.' She opened a file folder on the table and took out two picture postcards. 'Most interesting of all were these postcards she received from you in June 1999. Your mother has kept all the correspondence she ever had with you. Surely it can't surprise you that she kept the postcards you sent her from your world travels? After all, you were doing what she never dared, never really had the chance to do. Travel. She was envious. She saw the world vicariously through your eyes.'

Charlotte regarded her incredulously. 'What are you talking about?'

'It's what she said. Your mother. Lynne.'

'I . . . well, no, I didn't know that . . . but I can't believe you just went there and talked to her behind my back. Surely you can't do that. There must be a law.'

She looked at Jessica Bowen. 'No law, I'm afraid, Charlotte,' Jessica said.

'Is nobody on my side here?'

'As your solicitor says,' said Gerry. 'I didn't need your permission. I was doing my job.'

Charlotte just shook her head slowly.

'These are postcards from you,' Gerry went on. 'I'm sure we could verify the handwriting if we needed to. They're both posted from the island of Corfu, two days apart in mid-June. In the first, you refer to meeting up with a wealthy landowner from Yorkshire called Connor Clive Blaydon, and in the second, you refer to a big farewell party he threw for you and your friends on his yacht, the *Nerea*. Is this true?'

'I did a lot of things I don't remember clearly back then,' said Charlotte. 'At risk of getting arrested for past behaviour, I was either drunk or stoned most of the time.'

'Like Marnie Sedgwick at Blaydon's party,' said Annie. 'Only that wasn't *her* choice.'

Charlotte ignored Annie, but Jessica Bowen gave her a warning glance.

'But is it true, Charlotte?' Gerry repeated. 'Your mother thought it all sounded quite glamorous. Like so much of your life. She's very proud of you and your achievements, you know.'

'I don't need you to tell me that. And if I wrote it on a post-card I suppose it must be true.'

'So you don't deny it?'

Charlotte folded her arms. 'What would be the point?'

'May I see these postcards?' Jessica Bowen asked.

Gerry passed over the cards. The solicitor picked them up, glanced briefly at the photograph of Kavos on one and a view of the Albanian coastline on the other, then turned them over one at a time and read. She passed them to Charlotte, who glanced at them in passing and dropped them on the table. Her body seemed to have tensed up now, Annie noticed. The skin stretched taut over her forehead and cheeks, lips a straight narrow line. She was playing with her ring again.

'Do you admit to writing and sending these?' Gerry asked.

'Yes,' Charlotte hissed. 'So what?'

'These postcards are evidence of your presence on Connor Blaydon's yacht, the *Nerea*, at Kavos, Corfu, on the week of 15 June 1999. What happened during that week, Charlotte?'

'What do you think happened? We partied. Sex, drugs and rock 'n' roll.'

Gerry checked her files. 'You gave birth to Marjorie – or Marnie – on 13 March 2000. If you do the calculations, you'll see that's very close to nine months after 15 June.'

'So?'

'So,' said Gerry. 'Was Connor Blaydon Marnie Sedgwick's father?'

Even Jessica Bowen's jaw dropped at that question.

'How could you even think—?'

'Do the math,' said Annie, 'as the Americans say.'

'It's just a coincidence.'

'There seem to be an awful lot of coincidences in your life,' Annie said. 'But maybe this is stretching it a bit too far. Is it a coincidence if a woman sleeps with a man and nine months later has a baby?'

'You're reading too much into it.'

'Tell me how. Or let me tell you what I think happened. What if you met Connor Blaydon aboard the *Nerea* that June and slept with him? Why not? You've already said you were running wild and fancy-free, sleeping around, and Blaydon already owned the yacht before he bought his first villa on Corfu in 2002. You were twenty-one and he was around forty. Attractive older man, rich and handsome. So you slept with him and you became pregnant. Happens all the time. As you've already explained, an abortion wasn't an option for you, so you returned to England, hid away in the countryside during your pregnancy, gave birth and arranged to have the baby adopted. Marnie Sedgwick. You remained there for a brief period of recovery, then you returned to the normal flow of life with new energy, throwing yourself into building a career. Am I on the right track?'

'Apart from the business about Connor, yes. More or less.'

'Are you sure?'

'Of course.'

'So who was the baby's father?'

'I . . . I don't know.'

'Are you suggesting it could have been one of many?'

'I wasn't exactly celibate, if that's what you mean.'

'But it could have been Blaydon's.'

'You're putting words into my mouth.'

'Yes,' said Jessica Bowen. 'Do stop that, DI Cabbot.'

'A DNA test could prove it one way or the other. Are you willing to risk that, Charlotte?'

Charlotte shook her head.

'What does that mean?' Annie asked. 'Did you sleep with Connor Blaydon on his yacht in June 1999, and did you have a baby in March 2000?'

'Maybe. Yes. Maybe. No. I don't know.' Charlotte put her hands over her ears. 'Can we stop again now, please?' She looked towards Jessica Bowen with a desperate expression.

'Because if you did,' Annie went on, 'and if Blaydon *was* the father of your child, then it means he raped his own daughter, doesn't it? She didn't know who her father was, and he didn't know she was his daughter, but *you* did. And that, Charlotte, I think, gives you a pretty good motive for murder. Is that what you meant when you said things had come full circle?'

'*Murder?* What do you mean, murder?'

'Let's call a halt to this right now,' said Jessica Bowen. 'My client is clearly distraught, and things are taking a turn none of us could have reasonably expected. We'll need some preparation time before we continue.'

Annie sat back in her chair. 'Fine,' she said, dropping her pencil. 'Take as long as you need. I could do with a cuppa myself.'

That morning, Ray woke up from a vivid dream convinced that Zelda would be coming home before dark. He couldn't remember the details, but the feeling of hope and anticipation remained strong in him even through breakfast and a quick perusal of the bills the postman had delivered. Money wasn't a problem. His paintings were selling well and his reputation was gaining in stature day by day. He might not be at Hockney's level, but then few living artists were. Those kinds of millions were beyond him and always would be. Still, he was doing all right; he could pay the bills, and he could support Zelda.

But it had been just a dream. In reality, Alan was coming over tonight when he got back from Paris, Ray hoped with more news about Zelda. He would go out later and buy food, maybe the ingredients for a chickpea curry, along with some beer and wine, and he had already put aside a few LPs for their listening pleasure: Soft Machine's *Third*, Kevin Ayers's *Shooting at the Moon* and Gong's *Camembert Electrique*. They should keep the blues at bay for a while. Anything to chase the demons out, even if only for an hour or two. Perhaps some Edgar Broughton Band? No. The three choices would be enough, then they would move on to something a bit more mellow. Pity Banks didn't enjoy the occasional spliff, though. Ray always felt like a naughty boy smoking dope in front of him. Maybe he would smoke up before Banks arrived this evening, avoid any awkwardness.

After the second coffee, still not inspired to start work, he decided he needed to tidy the place up. First, he dealt with the sink full of dirty dishes, putting as many as he could in the dishwasher and washing the rest by hand. After that, he swept the hardwood floors and vacuumed the carpeted areas. He stripped the bed and put on clean sheets and pillowcases, stuffing the others in the washing machine. He had lived alone down in St Ives long enough to know how to do all these things, as well as cook for himself and anywhere up to ten guests. Hungry at lunchtime, he whipped up a cheese omelette and toast, then drove to the Tesco on the edge of Eastvale and bought what he needed for dinner.

By early afternoon he felt ready for the studio. He was working on a new painting. It started as a portrait of Zelda, but had soon become a sort of composite of all the elements he saw in her. Faces within a face, a collage of possibilities. In some lights, she was a classic Eastern European beauty, from another angle perhaps half Thai or Vietnamese, and from yet another Middle Eastern. Ray was trying to capture all these facets in one small portrait and together, viewed from a distance, they should ideally resolve themselves into a realistic head and shoulders portrait of Zelda against a slightly psychedelic background. He would be the first to admit that there was more than a hint of Love's *Forever Changes* album cover in the work. In fact, he had it propped up on another easel while he worked and had played it many times over the past few days.

After an hour or so, Ray felt tired, so he took a break and rolled a cigarette. His neck and chest ached from the stooped position in which he painted. A quick shot of Macallan and a few stretches soon had him back at the easel again, but now he needed music. He searched through his collection of old vinyl looking for something he hadn't played in a long time and came across *The Thoughts of Emerlist Davjack*, by The Nice. That had some pretty good Keith Emerson organ work on it, he remembered, so he put it on. He remembered seeing The Nice at the Marquee in their brief heyday, Emerson sticking knives between the organ keys to hold the notes down, shaking the thing and all but jumping up and down on it like Jerry Lee Lewis. He smiled at the memory.

There was still a lot of work to do, Ray thought, as he stood back and viewed the painting critically. It lacked a certain clarity in places, and several minor touches stood out just a little too much when viewed from afar, unbalancing the whole effect. He began to wonder whether he could even carry it off. It wouldn't be the first attempt to immortalise Zelda to be abandoned. He moved in closer, chewed on his lower lip and got to work.

Time passed. As usual, Ray paid no attention to it. But he noticed the light dimming, clouds obscuring the sun, and as he hated working in artificial light, knew it was almost time to stop. He also had to get the curry started. Alan wasn't sure exactly when he'd be back, but that was OK; dinner could simmer on low for a long while if necessary, and he could leave out the chickpeas until the last twenty minutes or so.

This time the discomfort in his chest was greater, and when he turned to put down his brush, he suddenly felt as if someone hit him with a piledriver. He sat down. His brow felt clammy with sweat and his stomach was churning. What was wrong with him? Something he'd eaten? The omelette had been fine. He knew the eggs were fresh because he had bought them from the farm down the road just two days ago.

Another blow from the piledriver struck him, this time hard enough to send a pain all down his left arm. He tried to get up, knowing somewhere deep inside that it was time to call an ambulance, but his legs felt too wobbly. His phone was downstairs, where he usually left it when he was painting. He thrust himself to his feet, gripping the chair arm, and stumbled forward. He was having trouble breathing now, and the slightest move made him out of breath. His chest felt as if it were being crushed.

He made it as far as the top of the stairs, where he dropped to his knees. The world was closing down, the pain gripping him tighter. He was aware of The Nice singing 'The Cry of Eugene' as he fell forward on to his face. He grasped at the banister to lift himself up, but he had no strength left. *Oh, God*, he thought. *Oh, God, please don't let it end like this.*

After the short break, both Charlotte Westlake and Jessica Bowen looked as if they had been put through the ringer.

'Are you going to charge my client?' the solicitor asked.

'We're still in the process of gathering evidence,' said Annie. 'She's still under caution. You've been here throughout the interview so far, surely you must realise we have a fair distance to go yet? If necessary, we'll apply for an extension of detention from the Chief Superintendent.' Annie knew that AC Gervaise would authorise such a request.

'I'm not so much interested in the journey as the destination,' said Jessica Bowen. 'My job's a little different from yours, and right now I'm here to safeguard my client's rights and well-being.'

'Well, let's get on with it, then.' Annie opened her file folder. Gerry set the recorders going again.

Charlotte Westlake seemed puzzled and frightened, Annie thought, as well she might, now all her lies were being held up to the light. Annie still wasn't convinced that Charlotte was a murderer, but she was intending to pick and pull at the scab of her tissue of lies until the truth was revealed one way or another.

Annie couldn't see Charlotte Westlake creeping into Blaydon's pool area, shooting him and Roberts, then gutting the naked Blaydon and dumping him in the pool. But she could have done it. The CSIs and pathologist told her that the killer hadn't needed to be especially strong. There was the matter of acquiring the gun, of course, but Baikals are easy enough to pick up, and there were plenty of guests at Blaydon's parties who might have had access and procured one for her – Gashi and Tadić, for starters. But Annie still couldn't quite see Charlotte as a murderer. Surely, she must soon come to understand that if she hadn't killed Blaydon but she knew who did, then she had better give it up before she was charged with murder herself.

There was, however, another ace left in the deck: Leka Gashi.

'OK, Charlotte,' Annie began. 'Do you remember where we'd got to? You had Blaydon's baby – Marnie – he raped her, she told you and you killed him for it. Is any of that wrong?'

'It's all wrong,' said Charlotte. 'You've twisted it all up.'

'Put me right then. Untwist it. Are you saying that Blaydon wasn't Marnie's father?'

'Yes. All right, I slept with him. Once. And I slept with most of his friends. Sometimes more than one in the same day. I was a slut. OK? Let's get that out of the way. But I'm *not* a killer.'

'Why should I believe you now after all the lies you've told?'

Charlotte banged so hard on the table that it rattled. 'Because it's *true*. All right, I lied. I tried to keep things from you. Do you blame me, the way it's turning out, the way you've been treating me?'

'That's entirely your own fault, Charlotte. Lying to the police isn't an advisable route to take.'

They let the silence stretch for a few moments, then Gerry said, 'Did those men you slept with on Blaydon's yacht in Corfu include Leka Gashi? Someone you described as "a crude pig of a man" the first time we talked. Is that accurate?'

'Probably.'

'That you said it, or that you slept with him?'

'Probably both. Back then Leka was a kind of fashionable sexy gangster. Like someone from a Guy Ritchie film. He was exciting to be around. And like Connor, he was young, sexy, devil-may-care. Liked to flash his money around. I was young and impressionable.'

'So you slept with him?' Gerry repeated.

'Yes. Probably.'

'Could *he* have been Marnie's father?'

'Leka?' Charlotte looked away. 'You must be joking.'

'Why not?'

'We took precautions.'

'Doesn't always work. Surely you must know that.'

Charlotte pouted.

'There's no need to sulk,' said Annie. 'Come on, get it off your chest. Tell us what you know.'

Charlotte glanced at Jessica Bowen, who gave her a brief nod. Charlotte seemed to pull herself together, this time taking several deep breaths and relaxing as best she could in her hard chair. To Annie, she seemed like someone who was finally relieved to be unburdening herself. It happened often in interviews, just before the confession.

'It's true I knew them both back then,' Charlotte said. 'Connor and Leka. The summer of 1999. I'd just turned twenty-one and the world was my oyster. Or so I thought. I had friends, money saved – not a fortune, but enough – and there were good times to be had. We spent most of May and the first part of June sailing the Greek islands – Samos,

Santorini, Mykonos, Patmos, Rhodes, Kos – all this before the migrants, before they were the way they are now. And yes, there were lots of parties, sex parties, if you like. And drugs. Mostly cocaine. That's why I was coming to hate working for Connor so much lately. I could see it starting all over again. It was all starting to remind me too much of my misspent youth, the bowls of white powder, the casual sex. I thought I'd put all that behind me.'

'Yes, but you weren't participating this time, were you?'

Charlotte managed a brief smile. 'No. But I was exposed to it. Somehow that seemed enough. And then Marnie came along.'

'Another reminder?'

'If you like. But a breath of fresh air, too. There was such an innocence about Marnie that's hard to describe. She was no ingénue. I don't mean that. She wasn't naive. In many ways she seemed old beyond her years, but she had a special sort of aura. Connor picked up on it immediately.'

'The first time she worked at one of his parties?'

'Yes. Back in March. Nothing happened then, or I would have known, but I could see him when I dropped by, the way he looked at her. And he mentioned her later. I should have known what it meant, done something about it right away, but I didn't. I don't know why. Maybe because I was selfish. Maybe because I didn't read the signs properly. It's easier in hindsight. But I did warn her about Leka and Tadić. To stay away from them. Even before she started working for me. She said she wanted money, and the parties paid good money, but I warned her to just do her job and keep her distance and she'd be fine. The idea of rape never entered my mind. As far as I was concerned, they might be criminals, but none of them was a rapist. And when Connor sent me to Costa Rica, I was just so thrilled to be going somewhere I'd never been before that I never gave a moment's thought as to what might happen while I was away. Or why I was being sent so far away. How could I know? But I didn't kill anyone, honest I didn't. You have to believe me.'

'Go on. What happened next?'

'I'd only been back a couple of days and Marnie came to my house. She was in a terrible state. Like I said, not so much physically – she'd cleaned herself up – but that innocence, that special aura was gone. She was empty, dead inside. She told me what had happened. That Connor had come to see her in the kitchen when most people had left or gone off to their rooms and it was quiet. He persuaded her to have a drink. She soon started to feel dizzy and sleepy and he helped her to a room where he said she could lie down and have a rest. But then he raped her. It was all a blur to her at the time, but she said she remembered the shock afterwards, the inability to move, just lying there as he did it to her. And when he'd finished, he drove her home, dropped her off outside her house.'

'What about her own car?'

'One of his minions must have picked it up the following day and dropped it off. She said Blaydon phoned and told her she got drunk, or she'd taken something, and he was worried, so that was why he drove her home.'

'So what did you do?'

'I tried to bring her out of it, but you were right earlier, she needed the kind of help that only an expert could give her. And I failed. I failed her.' Charlotte started crying silently and Jessica Bowen passed her a tissue. 'Sorry,' Charlotte went on. 'This is all very upsetting. I still can't quite take in the news of Marnie's death.'

'Then what happened?'

'She stayed with me in Adel. We spent some days together, talking, walking in the woods. She seemed to improve a bit.

Then she went back to work, back in York, and after that I
didn't hear from her again. I'd suggested she go home to her
parents and tell them what happened, and she said she would
think about it. I suppose I was trying to pass the problem on.'

'Did you know where her parents lived?'

'No. Why would I?'

'She didn't tell you?'

'I think she was protective of them. All I knew is it was
somewhere down south. I kept thinking she might phone, but
she didn't.'

'And you didn't phone her?'

'No. I had her mobile number, but no, I didn't.'

'Did she ever mention suicide?'

'Good Lord, no.'

'Or pregnancy?'

'No. But how could she, really, if it had only just happened?'

Annie paused. Charlotte had taken a hell of a bruising, from
hearing about the suicide of her daughter to the dredging up
of her own painful memories, but it wasn't over yet. Never
again would she have Charlotte in such a raw, vulnerable state,
readier than ever, perhaps, to tell the whole truth, if only just
to get out of there. 'Charlotte,' she said. 'Tell me the truth now.
Did you kill Connor Clive Blaydon?'

Charlotte looked her straight in the eye and said, 'No. I
didn't.' Then she paused. 'I wanted to, but I didn't have the
guts. Maybe I . . .'

'So who did?' Annie asked. 'Can you help us? Will you tell
us?'

Charlotte nodded. 'Maybe I *am* responsible for what
happened. I don't know. But I invited Leka over to the house
one evening after Marnie had left. I told him I wanted to talk
to him about something important.' She paused, as if for some
brief internal dialogue, shaking her head from side to side as

if in judgement on herself, then hurried on. 'I told him that Marnie was *his* daughter, from all those years ago, that time on Blaydon's yacht. That I'd put her up for adoption but she had tracked me down and come to work for me. Now she wanted to know who her father was, maybe even meet him. I said I wanted to get his permission first, before I arranged anything. I thought he'd be angry and just say no, but he wasn't. He didn't. He knew who I meant. He'd seen her at Connor's. Leka and I had had a bit of fling back then, more than just a one-off, unlike Connor, at any rate. Never since. And he has become a bit of a pig. I meant what I said. But back then he was handsome, gallant, vicious. But never violent towards me. There's not much point even saying this, but he could be gentle. He could be kind.'

'Did he believe you?'

'I think so. He knew I had no reason to lie to him. I made it clear that neither I nor Marnie wanted anything from him, not money, not commitment or anything, and he could just walk away if he wanted. He didn't even need to acknowledge her as his daughter.'

'Didn't he ask for proof or anything?'

'No. As I said, I wasn't asking him for anything. I made it clear she'd had a good family. I told him I just wanted him to know, that's all. He said he *did* want to see her. He quite surprised me. He said I should have told him a long time ago, but it wasn't too late. That he had a wonderful large mansion in the countryside outside of Tirana and all his daughters and granddaughters lived there. Marnie could come with him and join them, be part of his family. She would never want for anything again.'

'What did you say?'

'After I got over the shock, I said I didn't think she'd be interested, that she would be happy where she was again once she . . . Anyway, he wouldn't give up. He wanted to talk to her so he could try to persuade her to go to Albania.'

'What did you tell him?'

Charlotte turned away.

'Charlotte?'

Slowly, she looked up, tears in her eyes. 'I made a mistake,' she said. 'I gave him her mobile number.'

Annie looked at Gerry. 'The man she met on the cliffs,' she said. 'The reason she was running.'

'What?' Charlotte said.

'Nothing. What else did you say?'

Charlotte paused and glanced at Jessica Bowen, who whispered in her ear. Charlotte nodded and went on. 'I told him that she was very upset. I told him what happened at the party. I told him that Blaydon had raped Marnie. Raped his daughter. Leka was already paranoid enough about Connor's loyalty. It didn't take much to push him over the edge. His men had also seen Connor talking to a policeman – Banks – who wasn't on his payroll.'

'And then?'

'A few days later, Connor was dead. I honestly never imagined all this would happen. I thought they might beat him up or something, put him in hospital. He deserved that. And I was angry. I couldn't think of any other way to get back at him. All right, so maybe I was a little bit crazy, too. Marnie absolutely refused to bring the police in. She said she knew what it was like for rape victims. I wasn't strong or brave enough to do anything myself. I thought maybe this would work, if I stirred things up, that maybe Leka or his friends would beat Connor up or something. I never imagined that they'd murder him.'

'And Marnie? Did Gashi tell you that he found her?'

'No. I've no idea whether he ever met her. I never saw Marnie again, and I haven't seen Leka since.'

Annie wondered if what she was hearing was mere naiveté or whether she had been outflanked and outwitted. 'That's what Gashi is, Charlotte,' she said. 'A killer. And we think he might have been to see Marnie in Dorset on the day she died. Maybe he told her he was her father and tried to persuade her to go to Albania with him. We don't know, but she appeared to be running away from him. Witnesses saw a man getting into a posh silver car. Gashi drives a grey Mercedes. It's close enough.'

'He didn't . . .?'

'No, he didn't kill her. She took her own life, Charlotte. She jumped off a cliff.'

'Because of him?'

'I doubt it. Though I'm sure he contributed. If what you told me earlier is correct, I'd guess he was just putting the proposition to her.'

'But he couldn't force her, could he?'

'Maybe. But I don't think so. I think she was upset enough to start with because of the trauma of the rape, and the pregnancy. Gashi only increased her confusion. I imagine that she listened for a while, and when it all got too much for her, her resolve strengthened, and she ran. She didn't want to hear any more. That's why she was running when she reached Durdle Door. Not because he was going to harm her or anything. It was just all too much. She did what she had intended to do anyway.'

Charlotte put her head in her hands.

The Albanians, Annie thought. Dammit, it *was* the Albanians all along, even if not for the reasons she had thought. But she was right. And Charlotte's crime? They called it 'soliciting to murder', and it could carry a life sentence. Gashi certainly wouldn't be helping them, even if they could find him. He was hardly going to admit that Charlotte had more or less asked him to murder Blaydon and that he had done so. And it would be damn near impossible to prove anything; they would have their work cut out convincing the CPS that Charlotte had solicited Blaydon's *murder* merely by telling Gashi about the rape, and that he was the girl's father. Unless . . .

'Is it true?' she asked softly. 'Was Leka Gashi Marnie's father?'

Charlotte stared at her, wide-eyed, and said, 'No.'

'Are you sure?'

Charlotte simply reached for another tissue and nodded.

'Blaydon?'

'No.'

'Then who? Do you know?'

'It was after I got back to Oxford,' she said. 'The middle of July. There was an old boyfriend. His name doesn't matter. We got too carried away to worry about precautions.'

'But Marnie's birthday was 15 March. You say you slept with Blaydon and Gashi in mid-June. That works out at exactly nine months from . . .' Annie put her hand to her mouth. 'Oh, my God,' she said. 'Marnie was a month premature, wasn't she, born after only *eight* months?'

'That's right.'

Annie looked at Gerry. 'We should have known. Francine Sedgwick, Marnie's mother, told us the baby they adopted had been born early, kept in the hospital a little longer than usual.'

'Do what you want with me,' Charlotte said. 'I don't care any more. I've told you the truth and that's all there is to it.'

There was still 'soliciting to murder', which they might have a better chance of proving now that Charlotte admitted she had lied to Gashi about his being Marnie's father, but even then, there were so many extenuating circumstances, the CPS might easily refuse to prosecute. All that remained was 'wasting police time' or 'interfering in a police investigation' or 'obstruction of justice' – lesser charges, but still serious. But it was unlikely that anything much would happen to Charlotte Westlake, Annie thought. And maybe that was all for the best. What would be the point in locking her up in prison? As was so often the case, she would probably be far harder on herself than the law would be on her. After all, she had been indirectly responsible for three deaths: Connor Clive Blaydon, Neville Roberts and Marnie Sedgwick.

Jessica Bowen was busy making notes, and Charlotte was lost in her own grief. Then Jessica glanced up at Annie, questioning.

Annie just shrugged. 'Later,' she said. 'We'll consider all the options. But later.'

They gathered up their papers and left.

20

Banks got back to Newhope Cottage around six-thirty that evening, had a quick shower and changed clothes. He picked up a bottle of Cahors from the rack, then he was ready to set off for Ray's.

After ringing Jean-Claude and finding out that there hadn't been a hint or whisper about Zelda visiting Paris recently, he had spent the morning wandering the bookstalls beside the Seine on the Left Bank, where he had bought a hefty copy of *À la recherche du temps perdu* in the original French. He didn't know why, as he hadn't been able to get very far with it in English, but it had just seemed the thing to do. And it wasn't very expensive. He also bought what he guessed was a reproduction of a sixties poster for Francoise Hardy's debut studio album, *Tous les garçons et les filles*, the picture with the umbrella. She looked just like the woman he had seen on the Rue Montmartre with the four long-stemmed roses.

He had no real news to give Ray, but at least he could try to keep his friend's mind off his worries for a few hours. He sometimes felt a little guilty for contributing to Ray's optimism about Zelda, when he had no definite idea where she was or what she was doing, but then *he* also believed that she might turn up one day, when things had blown over.

He also had a vague idea where she might be, gleaned from the Moleskine notebook, and he thought he could probably track her down if he wanted to. But he would give her time to make the first move, if that was what she wanted to do. She would either return in her own time, or she wouldn't. He had no idea if it was fear of arrest that was keeping her away. The file was still open on the two corpses in the burned-out treatment plant, but given the lack of solid evidence, even that investigation would soon slow to a crawl.

The weather was changing and it was a windy evening when Banks drove over to Lyndgarth listening to Rhiannon Giddens on the car stereo. He pulled up outside Windlee Farm halfway through 'Little Margaret'. All seemed quiet there, except for the wind whistling around the buildings – no sixties rock blaring out of the open windows – but Ray's car was in the drive, and it was unlikely he had gone anywhere without it. Banks walked up to the front door and rang the bell. Nothing. He knocked hard. Still nothing. Next, he walked around the property to see if Ray was in one of the outbuildings, Zelda's studio, or even sitting on the edge of the moor contemplating sketching, as he often did. But he wasn't there, either.

He went back and tried the front door. It creaked open. Ray never was much of a one for security, he remembered, and without Zelda's recent paranoia to drive him, he had reverted to old habits. However, Banks was certain that even Ray would have locked up if he had gone out. There was no smell of food cooking, which was also odd. Banks decided that Ray was either in a deep, alcohol-induced sleep or he was so lost in his work he wasn't paying attention to anything else. He put the wine bottle down and prowled around the downstairs rooms, kitchen, den, living room. Where was Ray? Banks suddenly felt a chill of fear run up his spine. Had they come back? Whoever was left of the gang that had taken Zelda. Had they come back to take revenge on Ray for her escape? But there were no signs of any disruption. At least, not downstairs.

Banks called out Ray's name but got only silence in return. There were no lights on and the downstairs was in shadow. Banks opened the cellar door, flicked on the light switch and went down. Nothing there. Next, he headed for the staircase. As soon as he got to the bottom, he froze. He could see a shape there, a bulk, right at the top, and there was a hand hanging over the first step.

He took the stairs two at a time and knelt by Ray's motionless body, laid two fingers on the carotid artery in his neck. No pulse. The skin was cold, and when he turned on the light he could see discoloration already beginning to affect the flesh. Banks fell back against the wall and slid down, knees together, and held his head in his hands. It couldn't be. Ray dead? Just like that.

But there was no mistake. Banks glanced over the body but could see no signs of physical violence. That didn't mean anything, of course; even a fatal knife wound might not be visible to the naked eye. The only thing to do was not to disturb the scene further and to call in the police. They would need a doctor and a mortuary van, but there was no sense in asking for an ambulance. Ray was beyond ambulances.

Following his copper's instinct, Banks checked out all the other rooms upstairs. Nobody. Ray's studio door was open and soft gold evening light flooded through the large skylight and back windows, illuminating the canvas that stood on its easel. It was Zelda, Banks could see. When he walked closer he saw all sorts of details and realised that it was a sort of optical illusion – one large image incorporating many smaller ones, also of Zelda, or so it appeared. It seemed somehow unfinished, and it would always remain that way now. On his way out he noticed *Forever Changes* on another easel and the cover of The Nice's *The Thoughts of Emerlist Davjack* leaning against the turntable.

With a heavy heart, Banks stepped carefully over Ray's body, made his way back downstairs on shaky legs, then went outside for some fresh air and punched in the familiar numbers on his mobile.

Neither Banks nor Annie had any interest in attending Dr Galway's post-mortem examination. Annie had gone down to the mortuary with Banks to identify the body, and then she had gone home, said she wanted to be by herself for a while. Gerry, too, was devastated. She and Ray had started out on the wrong track, Banks knew, because Ray had teased her mercilessly about her being a nubile pre-Raphaelite beauty and said how he wanted her to pose for him in the nude. But after she had almost died taking down a murder suspect, he had presented her with a beautiful head and shoulders sketch of her that he had drawn from memory. She had it framed and hung it in the pride of place on the wall of her small flat. Since then, they had been the best of friends, and she had given as good as she got in the teasing department.

When it was all over, Banks was the one who walked down that tiled corridor to the doctor's office alone and found himself again sitting under 'The Anatomy Lesson of Dr Nicolaes Tulp' while he listened to Dr Galway's interpretations of the post-mortem results.

'I can state categorically,' she said, 'that there are absolutely no signs of foul play. Your friend died a sad but most natural death.'

'Heart?' Banks said. He had already heard from the CSIs that there was no evidence of a break-in or of any struggle at Windlee Farm, and his own brief examination had told him there was nothing missing, so robbery was not likely to be the motive. The people responsible for Zelda's abduction and his own near demise were all dead – Phil Keane, Petar and Goran

Tadić. Leka Gashi, the Albanian whom Annie had discovered was responsible for the Connor Clive Blaydon and Neville Roberts murders was still on the loose somewhere, but he had no connection with Ray or Zelda.

'Myocardial infarction. A massive heart attack. It would have been quick. He would hardly have known what hit him. A few moments of pain, perhaps, then . . .'

'"The anaesthetic from which none come round."'

She frowned. 'Quite. Well, I suppose you could put it like that, if you happened to be of a poetic turn of mind. What I'm trying to say is that he wouldn't have suffered greatly.'

'Thank you. But would he have known what was happening? It looked as if he was trying to get downstairs to his phone.'

'He would certainly have known something was happening. But not for long.' She paused. 'His arteries were in a bad way. The blood supply to the heart was cut off. The damage was so extensive that he must have had at least some chest pain and shortness of breath over the past few months to warn him that something was seriously wrong.'

Banks knew that Ray would simply ignore something like that, not think it worth mentioning. 'I do remember once or twice he complained of chest pains,' he said. 'Not that I don't have plenty of aches and pains myself.'

'It's probably just your age. We often don't recognise symptoms.'

'And when we do, it often turns out that they're not symptoms at all but simply a result of sitting in the wrong position for too long. Or indigestion, heartburn.'

'There is that. But if you're worried about anything, maybe you should see your doctor and have a full physical?'

'Maybe. It's been a while. But I'm not worried. So a heart attack, then?'

'Yes.'

A heart attack. Pure and simple. Banks was glad it was a natural death. If Ray had been murdered, it would create a whole new set of problems, some for which he might even bear a modicum of blame. 'And the cause?'

'Hard to say exactly.'

'I know he didn't get much exercise.'

'That was quite obvious. He also drank and smoked too much and ate far too much fatty food,' Dr Galway added, with a pointed look in Banks's direction.

'I don't smoke,' Banks said, and she just smiled.

'I'm sorry about your friend, Superintendent Banks,' said Dr Galway. 'Sincerely sorry. But he was in his late seventies and he didn't take very good care of himself. Annie Cabbot's his daughter, isn't she?'

'Yes.'

'How is she doing?'

'About as well as you'd expect, which is not very well.'

'They were close?'

'I'd say so,' said Banks. 'Her mother died when she was very young, and he pretty much brought her up single-handedly. He just moved up here from Cornwall a year or so back.'

'With that young woman who disappeared, is that right?' Dr Galway asked.

'Nelia Melnic. Right.'

'He was upset about her?'

'Very.'

'That kind of stress won't have helped his condition much.'

'Can people really die of a broken heart?'

Dr Galway snorted. 'Only if you take a very poetic view of death, as you seem to do. Stress is a factor, yes, as can be depression, worry, anxiety and any number of mental conditions we don't fully understand yet. All those things put a strain on the heart and its function, but it wouldn't be entirely accurate to say that it breaks. A heart attack involves a kind of paroxysm rather than a snap. The human body is a complex mechanism, interdependent in so many ways. All I can give you is the doctor's viewpoint – the pathologist's, at that. I deal with the dead.'

'You really are very rational, aren't you, doctor?'

'Why, thank you. I try to be. That's the nicest thing you've ever said to me.'

Banks smiled and stood up, leaned over to shake her hand. 'Thanks for doing this so promptly,' he said.

'You'll be able to put his daughter's mind to rest?'

'I'll do my best. It won't be easy, but I'll try.'

'If she ... I mean, if you think she's becoming seriously upset ... there is help.'

'I know,' said Banks. 'And I'll make sure that Annie knows, too.'

'Well, then, I'll be seeing you.'

'Not too soon, I hope,' said Banks, and left. The Unicorn over the road from Eastvale General would be open now, and Banks could do with a pint. Or a double whisky.

On the day of Ray Cabbot's funeral, Banks drove to Harkside to pick up Annie, and for a while he thought she wouldn't come. She sat in her chair, still wearing her dressing gown, hair an unruly mass, unmoving, not speaking, her eyes puffy and red from crying, face tear-stained.

Banks sat with her in silence for a while, holding her hand. When he squeezed gently, he felt no return of pressure. What could he do? He couldn't force her to go. He spoke to her softly, telling her she should get ready. She looked at him, uncomprehending, then all of a sudden seemed to snap out of it.

'I must get ready,' she said. 'Dad's waiting.'

Banks helped her up and told her he would wait downstairs while she got dressed and ready, and not to worry, there was plenty of time.

It didn't take her long. In a few minutes Annie had managed to throw on a dark skirt, top and jacket suitable for a funeral, brush her hair and apply a little make-up to cover the ravages of her grief. She remained quiet as she got in the car and Banks drove to the funeral home in Eastvale. He refrained from playing any music. Annie might think it insensitive, even a requiem, and he honestly couldn't think of anything to play for the occasion.

Ray had left a will, as it turned out, and it stipulated that he wanted his ashes scattered in the sea below St Ives. He had also left a substantial amount of his estate to Zelda and the rest – more than adequate, along with the house – to Annie. He hadn't made any arrangements for his unsold paintings, but Banks imagined his agent would help Annie handle all that. He had left his collection of close to 2,000 vinyl LPs and Marantz turntable to Banks.

When Banks had revisited Windlee Farm a couple of days after Ray's death to make sure everything was turned off and locked up, at Annie's request, he had found a postcard among that day's post. It showed a reproduction of da Vinci's *Annunciation*, and on the back, next to Ray's address, a heart. Banks didn't think he needed to check the handwriting to know that the postcard was from Zelda. The postmark read Belgrade, but Banks didn't think that was where she was. She must have got someone to post it for her. He hadn't told Annie about it.

There was quite a crowd for Ray's funeral, and the small chapel was bursting at the seams. The arts crowd had come up from London, and most of the people who still lived at the artists' commune in St Ives, where Ray had lived for many years, turned up, along with some who had lived there only briefly and left years ago. They all remembered Ray's generosity and encouragement for young artists.

A vicar who had never even met Ray delivered a few platitudes and a prayer, and then the tears streamed down Annie's face as she sat through Banks's short eulogy, which Annie had said there was no way she could do without breaking down, and a reading by Gerry of Christina Rossetti's 'When I am dead, my dearest', which Banks had last heard at the funeral of his first love, Emily Hargreaves. Ray would have hated it, but funerals are about the living. As the service ended with The Beach Boys' 'I Just Wasn't Made for These Times', which Ray had once told Banks was what he wanted to be played at his funeral, there was hardly a dry eye in the chapel.

The funeral tea was held at Windlee Farm, and catered by the Black Bull's Mick Slater. It was nothing special, just sausage rolls, vol-au-vents, scotch eggs and slices of pork pie followed by Black Forest gateau, but it was enough. Slater had also brought a couple of kegs of beer, which most of Ray's friends seemed to prefer to tea. Banks chatted with some of Ray's old artist friends and also fell into conversation with a young woman who said she was a friend of Zelda's from her London days, and she had read about the funeral in the paper. She had come in the hopes that Zelda would be there and was disappointed when Banks told her they didn't know where she was.

Finally, the last guests drove off. It was still light outside, and Banks poured himself another glass of wine and went outside to enjoy the mild evening air and the open views of the moorland. Curlews flew high in the distance, and a lark ascended, singing. Banks thought of the Vaughan Williams music. Annie wandered out a few minutes later and joined him, linking her arm in his. The vast expanse of the moors at the back of the cottage spread out for miles under a thickening cover of dark clouds still in the distance. But there would be rain before long.

'So she didn't come after all,' said Annie.

'She probably doesn't know Ray is dead,' Banks said.

Annie removed her arm from his. 'There you go, making excuses for her again. I suppose you know it's all her fault. If he hadn't got involved with her, none of this would have happened.'

'Annie, Ray was ill. His arteries were blocked. He drank too much. He smoked too much. He ate too much red meat. He never went to the doctor's.'

Annie waved her hand dismissively. 'I know all that. You're a one to talk. But she's the one who brought it all on, the straw that broke the camel's back. You know what terrible shape he's been in since she disappeared.'

'It was hardly her fault she was abducted,' Banks said.

'I mean after. After the fire. When she saved you and ran away.'

'She was scared.'

'So was Ray. And she was supposed to love him. She didn't even bother to come to his funeral. Did you see that picture he was painting?'

'Yes,' said Banks.

'I hate it. You take it.'

Banks knew there was no point in arguing, and the last thing he wanted to do was upset Annie any further, which defending Zelda would most certainly do. It was one of those moments where he would have loved to light up a cigarette, but he made do with the wine.

Annie would get over it in time. Right now she was grieving and looking for someone to blame, and there was just enough truth in what she said to make that someone Zelda. There *were* certain aspects of Zelda's life that made her dangerous company. After all, if she hadn't become an important part of Ray's life, it would have saved him a lot of grief. But what about the love? What about the joy she gave him? The happiness they shared? Annie didn't see that. Banks had seen Ray and Zelda together and heard each speak separately about the other, and there was no doubt in his mind that they loved one another utterly, completely. Perhaps that kind of love can kill you eventually. He watched the distant birds swooping and weaving under the massing rain clouds. He couldn't make out what they were – lapwings, curlews, swifts – but that didn't matter. It was glorious just to witness the aerial ballet.

'We'd better go in,' he said. 'It's going to rain.'

Annie said nothing at first, then she tightened her lips and stalked off ahead of him towards the door. It was going to be a long haul.

21

Croatia was basking in late afternoon sunshine when Banks left his rental car at the bottom of the hill and started walking up the dirt path.

He hadn't got very far when a muscular young man with no neck appeared in front of him, cradling a Kalashnikov AK-47 in his arms. The man said something guttural in what Banks assumed to be Croatian, and Banks said he didn't understand, that he was English, his name was Alan Banks, and he would like to see Nelia Melnic. The man gave him a suspicious glance, pointed to the ground and said, 'You stay here,' then made his way up the hill. In case Banks had any fancy ideas about disobeying the command, another man, looking exactly the same as the first one, appeared, also cradling an AK-47. Banks considered asking him whether the weapon was legal but decided against it.

The first man came back, examined the package Banks was carrying and twitched his head in the direction of the summit. Banks followed him. They arrived at a high stone wall topped with broken glass set in concrete. The man opened the spiked wrought-iron gates and gestured Banks through. He was out of breath and paused for a moment to rest. In front of him stood a petite woman in her early sixties with short silver hair and pale blue eyes that had seen far more than anyone ought. Her wiry body looked strong, as if she had done much manual labour. She held out her hand in greeting and walked forward. Banks shook it. Her grip was firm and her hand calloused.

'Please forgive me if I ask for some identification,' she said.

Banks noticed that his guide with the Kalashnikov was lingering by the gate. Only when he had shown his warrant card and the woman nodded did he disappear.

'One can't be too careful,' she said.

'Is Nelia here?'

'She is.'

'You must be Mati.'

The woman raised an eyebrow. 'And you must be a very good detective.'

'I have my sources,' Banks said.

The woman started walking over the final gentle slope of grass past the side of the house. Banks walked in step beside her. 'Will you tell me why you want to see her?' she asked.

Banks paused for a moment. 'Her partner, Ray Cabbot. I'm afraid he died.'

Mati stopped in her tracks. 'Raymond? Dead?'

'I'm afraid so, yes.'

'When did this happen?'

'A few weeks ago. It took me a while to find you.'

'That's good. I mean that it took the great detective a long time. We depend on being a needle in a haystack. But this news. It is very bad for Nelia. She is not strong.'

'It's not something I've been looking forward to,' said Banks. 'But she should know.'

Mati started walking again. 'Yes. Of course she must know. Please, sit over there and wait.' She pointed to a white table with matching chairs on the edge of a promontory overlooking the Adriatic. 'Forgive me if I do not invite you into the main house, but some of the girls . . . they are not yet ready to see a man again. I have to keep my sons away, too, and they are the gentlest people you could ever hope to meet.'

Banks flashed on the neckless pair cradling their Kalashnikovs. Gentle wasn't the first word that had come to his mind, but he believed her.

Banks sat down at the table and faced the sea. The water ranged from pale green to deep blue and all shades in between. Small crafts and fishing boats bobbed between the islands, and far out to sea he could see the white bulk of a cruise liner. A light refreshing salt breeze blew up from the water. There was a bottle of Plavac on the table, already open, along with two glasses, and Banks saw no reason not to pour himself one.

'Pour one for me, too, please, Alan.'

The voice from behind startled him. He hadn't heard her approach. Instead of pouring, he stood up and faced Zelda again, at last.

She wore a simple, shapeless grey shift and her face was bare of make-up. Her hair was cut very short – not professionally, by the looks of it – and there was a strange pale luminosity about her skin and her eyes he had never noticed before. In an odd way, she reminded him of those old posters of Jean Seberg playing Joan of Arc. She was certainly a long way from the Zelda of Ray's unfinished portrait. Was this one face of her that Ray had never seen? She was still beautiful, Banks thought, but now her beauty was of a different kind altogether.

They sat, and Banks poured the wine. 'So,' he said, raising his glass. 'Here you are.'

'Here I am. How did you find me?'

'It's my job. Don't you remember what a great detective I am?'

Zelda managed a smile. 'Of course.'

'There were clues. Your past. Your books – the stories of abused women. The time you mentioned visiting an old friend in Croatia who ran a hostel for girls who had escaped sexual slavery. And this.' Banks handed her the Moleskine notebook.

'You read it?'

'Yes.'

Zelda flushed and set it down on the table.

'Keep it,' Banks said.

Zelda slipped the notebook in a pocket in her shift. 'So now you know all my secrets.'

'Hardly.'

Zelda hung her head. 'At least you know the very worst.'

Banks leaned forward and took her hand. She seemed surprised but didn't snatch it back. 'Zelda,' he said. 'I'm sorry to be the one to have to tell you this, but it's Ray. I'm afraid—'

'He's dead?'

'Yes. How did you know?'

'I didn't know. But I had a strange dream. What happened?'

'His heart. It happened quickly. There was nothing to be done.'

'The stubborn old fool,' she said. 'He would never go to the doctor. I told him many times. Those pains in his chest. The short breath. The coughing. He ...' But the tears pouring down her face got in the way of talking, and soon her whole body was wracked with sobs. Banks let her cry. He had come forearmed and handed her a clean white handkerchief.

After a while, the sobbing ebbed away and she seemed to compose herself. She gulped down some wine. 'What's that package you brought?' she asked.

Banks handed her the tube. She opened it and unrolled Ray's last painting, the portrait of her. 'Annie wanted you to have it,' he said.

'Thank you.' Zelda studied the picture and put it aside, a strange sad smile on her face. 'How is she?'

'Surviving. It's hard.'

'Yes. I imagine so.' Zelda paused. 'I *was* going to go back, you know,' she said. 'One way or another. I didn't know when. But I was going to go back.'

Banks squeezed her hand. 'I know you were. It's one of those things beyond our control, Zelda. There was nothing to be done. Ray was Ray. He lived his life the way he wanted, and none of us would have changed him for anything. He was lucky to know you in these last few years. Lucky to know such happiness at the end. He knew that.'

Zelda regarded him with her damp eyes. '*I* was lucky to know *him*,' she said. 'You might think we had a strange relationship, that he was too old for me, but it worked. For both of us. We didn't ... you know ... I'm no use that way. But Raymond understood.'

'I don't judge you, Zelda, or your relationship. You know better than that.'

She gently disengaged her hand from his and patted his wrist to assure him it wasn't an angry gesture. 'I should do,' she said. 'And I'm Nelia now.' Then they both took a long sip of wine. It seemed to go straight to Banks's head, which was either something to do with its extraordinary strength, or the sun and sea. 'But you read the notebook,' she went on. 'You know about Darius and Goran. And later Petar and your enemy Keane. That's four people I've killed, Alan. I'm cursed. Bad to know.'

'I preferred to believe the notebook was a work of the imagination. Wishful thinking.'

Nelia gave him a sad smile. 'You're not that much of a fool. It was true. All of it. I killed them.'

'I went to Paris,' Banks said. 'A friend there told me about what happened with Darius.'

Nelia gave her head a slight shake. 'It was bad. I was stealing his blackmail material. Emile had asked me to. Promised me a

French passport. He was going to join me later wherever I went. Darius came in and caught me. He started beating me. There was a knife on the bar, one of those little ones you use to cut limes and lemons for drinks. I stabbed him, but it didn't penetrate very far, and he still kept coming, so I cut his throat. They almost had a scandal, made a quick cover-up, rushed me out of the country fast with a French passport. I think some of them wanted to kill me, but that didn't happen. I like to think Emile spoke up for me. He was true to his word. Later the Sûreté got me an interview for the job with the NCA. So they could keep an eye on me, I suppose. And Darius's musclemen killed Emile. That's what happened in Paris.'

'And London?'

'Goran Tadić? I drugged him in a hotel room and stabbed him to death. I assume his brother and colleagues got rid of the body. I never heard anything more about it until they abducted me from the cottage. They tracked me down through the Hotel Belgrade CCTV and taxi drivers. They also tortured Faye Butler, Keane's ex-girlfriend, until she told them what she knew. Then they killed her. But even when he took me, Petar Tadić didn't know who I was. He didn't remember that he had raped me when I was seventeen. I reminded him before I killed him. I don't know what you want me to say, but you won't get any apologies out of me. I have no regrets. Do what you wish, but I'm glad I killed them, all of them, and I'm glad they're dead. Raymond was worth more than all of them put together.'

'I can't say I disagree,' said Banks.

'And you a policeman.'

'Tell me, what happened at the treatment plant.'

'They kept me chained to the radiator upstairs, in a bare room. It looked like a disused office. It was always dark until they came to see me with their light.'

'How did you escape?'

'It doesn't matter. Petar Tadić made a mistake, and I took advantage. Then I took his keys after I killed him. I came down and saw Keane splashing petrol over you. You know the rest. I crept up on him and stabbed him and cut you free. Then I turned to fight him for the lighter, but he lit it. Pouff. It was so strange. This man, with the last movement in his life, he struck a cigarette lighter and started a big fire.'

'And afterwards?'

'There was a car parked outside the side entrance. Keane's car. The keys were still in the ignition. Tadić had told me that he had come back with my new passport and some money for the journey. They were taking me to a brothel in Dhaka. A terrible place. They told me I would die there slowly of disease and beatings. After I made sure you ran for the main exit, I went out of the side and drove away. I found the passport and money in the glove compartment. I drove to Newcastle and left the car at the airport, then I flew from there to Amsterdam. The passport was in the name of Frieda Mannheim, so I didn't expect any trouble, or run into any. That man Keane was a good forger. After that ... I came here. It was easy to disappear, to lie low. Until now.'

'But why didn't you leave with me, the same way?'

'I think you know the answer to that. I had just killed two men, and you're a policeman.'

'Surely you know me better than that, Nelia? And it was self-defence.'

'Perhaps.' Nelia smiled. 'But I was hardly thinking any more clearly than you were.'

She stood up and walked to the edge of the promontory, carrying her wine. She made such a slight and vulnerable figure against the vast expanse of the darkening sea beyond that Banks found it hard to believe she had wreaked such havoc among the men who had stolen her youth. He knocked back the last of his wine and stood up. 'Raymond left you something else in his will,' he said.

'I don't want anything.'

Banks gestured to the house. 'It might help. With all your work here.'

Nelia nodded, her back to him.

'I'll see to it,' Banks said. 'I'll go now.'

Nelia turned to face him. 'Must you go so soon?' she said. 'It's not dark yet.'

'It's a long drive to Zagreb.'

'Are you going to arrest me?'

Banks looked at her for a long time, then shook his head. 'No,' he said. 'I've had enough of all that. More than enough.'

Then he turned away and walked back down the hill to his car.

ACKNOWLEDGEMENTS

There are many people to thank for helping me get this book ready for publication, starting with my wife Sheila Halladay, who read the first draft and sent me back to the manuscript with many helpful suggestions. At Hodder & Stoughton, I would especially like to thank my editor Carolyn Mays, her assistant Sorcha Rose and copy-editor Sharona. At McClelland & Stewart in Canada, thanks to Kelly Joseph and Jared Bland, and at William Morrow in the U.S.A., Emily Krump and Julia Elliott. It is also important to recognize the efforts of those whose work is yet to be done, especially publicists and sales reps, who will have a far more difficult task this time, for obvious reasons. Thank you in advance.

Also thanks to my agents Dominick Abel, David Grossman and Rosie and Jessica Buckman. I would also like to thank those overseas publishers, editors and translators who have stuck with me over the years. They know who they are. There are many others who contribute, including cover artists, book designers, proof-readers, booksellers and librarians, and I would like to thank all those people. Finally, thanks to my readers, without whom all our efforts would be pointless.

© Pal Hansen

PETER ROBINSON grew up in the United Kingdom, and now divides his time between Toronto, Ontario, and Richmond, Yorkshire. *Not Dark Yet* is the twenty-seventh book in the best-selling Inspector Banks series. He has also written two collections of short stories, and three stand-alone novels, including the #1 bestseller *Before the Poison*, winner of the Arthur Ellis Award, the Golden Crowbar Award, and the Dilys Award given by the Independent Mystery Booksellers Association. Robinson's critically acclaimed crime novels have won numerous awards in Britain, the United States, Canada, and Europe, and are published in translation all over the world. Several Inspector Banks novels have been adapted for television by ITV and have appeared on PBS.

For more information about Peter Robinson and the Inspector Banks series, please visit www.inspectorbanks.com